CHANGELING'S DAGGER

A CASTOR'S GROVE YOUNG ADULT
PARANORMAL ROMANCE

A.J. RENWICK

1

KENYA

Kenya Davidson's lime green sneakers pounded across the pavement as she turned south on 76th Street. Heart racing, she twisted to peer over her shoulder as she ran. There was no one there. So why couldn't she shake the sensation that she was being followed?

Wow, I don't know. Maybe because I'm paranoid this morning?

Her parents' fears were becoming contagious. Despite living in a safe area, so far to the north of the city her mother claimed it should be classified as a suburb, both Courtney and Reuben Davidson were petrified of something bad happening to their only daughter. It wasn't just imaginary muggers and hypothetical thieves that concerned them. What if Kenya tripped over the uneven sidewalk and hurt herself right before a big race?

But I know every inch of these streets. I'll be fine.

Plus, Kenya was an adult now. She'd turned eighteen two weeks ago. It was her decision if she wanted to stretch her muscles. And this morning, it was a necessity.

She'd woken up with her heart already pounding, her limbs already trembling. The qualifiers were today. She couldn't lie in bed waiting. She needed to move, to prepare, to run.

While her parents were still in bed, she'd donned her sneakers, repositioned her curls so that they were safely atop her head, and slipped out the door. She'd be back before they had a chance to miss her.

Near the corner of Underwood Avenue, Kenya swore she heard footsteps a few paces behind. Her breath caught. Without breaking stride, she turned her head. Was that a shadow disappearing between two of the houses?

The toe of Kenya's shoe caught on a pebble, and she stumbled forward before catching herself.

Oh, well done! I can fall, twist my ankle, and get mugged.

Then she could listen to her parents say *I told you so* for the rest of her life.

And maybe they were right. Running in the dim light, alone, hours before a race wasn't calming Kenya the way she'd hoped.

But she refused to give in to the fear. Instead of slowing and speed-walking home, she took a deep breath and turned around.

See?

The sidewalk was empty—no footsteps, no shadow, no vicious mugger. She'd imagined it all. The most dangerous thing on the street was the pebble.

Kenya kicked it toward the road, feeling satisfied as it disappeared down a grate and into the sewers.

You're welcome, Castor's Grove. 76ᵗʰ Street is safe now.

"Excuse me," a female voice shouted from across the street, waving a map. It was a woman about her mother's age, with a round face and rosy pink cheeks. She wore pair of tortoise shell glasses, a bucket hat, and overalls.

A tourist.

Rare, but not unheard of, in this area of the city. Certainly not a reason to be afraid.

Kenya breathed a sigh of relief. She didn't know what was wrong with her this morning. She wasn't normally so quick to panic.

"Would you be able to help me?" the tourist asked, unfolding her map as she crossed the street. As she drew closer, her height became more obvious. Despite the hunch in her back—as though she'd spent years of ducking under doorways—the woman was close to six feet.

"Always happy to help." Kenya smiled and closed the space between them.

Too late, she noticed the glint of silver flash behind the woman's map.

The tourist, who probably wasn't a tourist at all, grabbed the front of Kenya's white shirt and plunged a blade into her chest.

Kenya screamed.

Not because it hurt, but because it seemed like the correct thing to do when a stranger stabbed you in the middle of the sidewalk.

The woman shoved her map into Kenya's mouth, trying to silence her.

The air around the blade burst into a blaze of energy. Red and blue flames licked at Kenya's skin. Heat spread through her veins and washed across the backs of her eyes. The houses, the street, and the woman vanished, Kenya's vision consumed by the fire.

"Counterclockwise thrice," the woman's voice echoed through the flames. She began to twist the blade.

Kenya's muscles burned, contracting and pulsing in a way she'd never known possible. The map fell from between her teeth. She gasped for air and breathed in only fire. It filled her mouth, burning into her throat and chest, transforming her from the inside out as her body began shrinking, rippling and morphing into an unfamiliar form.

With a third and final twist, the woman pulled the blade free.

The flames vanished, and Kenya's vision returned as she dropped to the sidewalk.

She landed on four furry orange paws. Something strange was attached to the bottom of her back. Kenya turned her head and saw it: a long, fluffy tail. She swished it, and it moved at her command.

What the actual hell?

Kenya had no idea who this strange woman was or what bizarre abilities her knife had, but she knew one thing with shocking certainty.

I've just been transformed into a cat.

2

KENYA

"Don't be afraid," the woman said.

"How could I not be terrified?" Kenya asked, spinning her head. Instead of her voice, she heard a high-pitched yowl.

This wasn't real. Kenya must've been dreaming.

The woman crouched onto her knees, bringing her face closer. Her storm-colored eyes still seemed a mile away. The blade that she'd just stabbed Kenya with balanced on her knees. "This is going to seem very confusing, but I promise, I'm going to guide you through it."

Thanks, but no thanks. I am going to wake up.

Kenya lifted what should've been her right hand but was instead an orange paw. She slapped it onto her left. Five claws extended, sinking into the skin.

She yowled.

"Kenya Davidson, your life is about to—"

Before the woman could finish, a dark figure sprung from between two of the houses.

Kenya leaped back, the rest of her claws extending on instinct. The fur rose along her spine, and her tail froze.

This is real?

Before her, the dark figure came into view—a man dressed in black; his face hidden by a hockey mask. Only his hands, large and olive-toned, were visible.

Whatever was going on, he must've been the villain. Only someone with sinister intentions would bother to wear a black turtleneck in the middle of summer.

Which made Kenya's stabber... the hero?

That didn't sound right.

The woman faced down the masked man. Her ears had sprung loose from beneath her bucket hat. They stuck out from her head, large and pointed like a creature from a folktale.

I have got to get out of here.

What was the best direction to run?

Left toward her home.

As Kenya turned, she glimpsed her stabber pulling something new from the pocket of her overalls. It was a small pink cube, as though someone had made strawberry flavored chicken stock. The woman dropped it.

The air filled with powder and the scent of flowers. A heartbeat later, a hand wrapped around Kenya's neck.

"No, put me down!" she mewled, paws flailing through the air the blur of pink, vision obscured. She didn't know who'd grabbed her until they escaped the powder, and the woman's pointed ears came into view.

Footsteps pounded behind them. The masked man was in pursuit.

Kenya's brain rattled in her skull as they raced in the wrong direction, slipping through narrow side roads. The signs blurred. She lost any sense of where they were.

The woman turned through a twisting alley, only to find the path blocked by a gray stone wall.

"Drumbeat!" she loosed the word as though it were a curse and spun around. The masked man blocked her retreat.

The woman was trapped, which meant Kenya was too.

Oh no. This is bad.

Whatever was happening, Kenya was not part of it. She needed out of this alley. Now.

The woman's grip slackened as she retreated to the wall. Her focus was on the masked man, not the girl-turned-cat wriggling in her arms.

Good.

Kenya took advantage of her neck's new flexibility, twisting her head and sinking her teeth into her stabber's skin.

"Ahh!" With a scream, the woman flung Kenya away—straight toward the masked man.

This was not the plan!

At least, it hadn't been Kenya's. Her stabber used the opportunity to jump.

While the woman cleared the wall, Kenya landed like a furry grenade on top the masked man's head. Her claws scrambled for a grip, scratching at his short black curls.

He grabbed her tail, trying to yank her away, but the pain made Kenya's claws sink deeper into his scalp. As he pulled, her back left foot raked over the strap of his mask.

The fabric ripped.

Kenya was flung once more across the alley. She twisted in mid-air, watching as the mask fell to the ground.

Beneath was a square jaw, a pair of pale pink lips, and deep brown eyes. Kenya knew that face.

The masked man was Camilo Lopez, her family's landscaper.

3
KENYA

A swirl of blue and red flames spread from the center of Kenya's chest as she stared at the man before her.

Now that the mask was off, it seemed so obvious. The track pants were tight over his thighs; the black turtleneck threatened to pop off. Camilo's muscles were impossible to hide.

Kenya ought to have recognized him from those alone. She'd glanced at him enough times from her window while he was working.

Yet, despite their frequent proximity, Kenya had hardly spoken to him. The few times she'd tried, he'd mostly ignored her. Which was probably for the best. Training kept her too busy to worry about boys.

At least, that's what she liked to tell herself.

Heat filled Kenya's limbs. Her body trembled, stretching into human form, orange fur sinking into dark skin.

Kenya found herself, ass up, hands and feet pressed to the floor, accidentally in downward dog.

She was a human once again.

"What the hell just happened?" she asked.

Camilo didn't answer. Instead, he ran.

Seriously?

Kenya gaped at the entrance to the alleyway.

First the woman ditched her, now Camilo. Did neither of them think she deserved an explanation?

Kenya pushed herself up, surprised by how difficult it was to breathe. Her heart raced and her muscles burned as though she'd just run a marathon. She rubbed the back of her neck. It was still sore from where Camilo had grabbed her.

While she was a cat, and he'd been hiding behind a hocky mask like some killer from an old slasher movie.

Who the hell is Camilo?

There was no way he was *just* a landscaper.

What did he know about the dagger that had transformed Kenya? Was it a secret government experiment that reconfigured atoms? Why did the woman test it on her?

She'd been about to explain before Camilo scared her off. He owed Kenya answers.

Camilo had turned east, back in the direction of her home. He'd become a black blur in the distance. If she ran fast, perhaps she could catch him.

Kenya raced down the street, pushing her body as hard as she could, barely aware of the aching in her limbs. She was too focused on the agony growing within her head. It felt like an oncoming migraine.

Forcing their way through the pain, were the questions.

Does that blade turn everyone into an orange cat? Why not a dog?

Kenya had always been more of a dog person, and transforming into a German Shepherd or a Rottweiler would've been much more impressive.

And how did my clothes transform with me?

Camilo turned a few feet ahead.

Kenya's headache was getting worse, but she forced herself to continue, chasing his shadow. She stumbled over the sidewalk and around the building.

Camilo had vanished.

Spots danced before Kenya's vision. She collapsed onto her knees on someone's lawn. She was practicing for the Olympics. She could outrun all the boys in her school. How had Camilo eluded her so easily?

The transformation must have taken a toll.

Kenya stared at a drop of dew, clinging to a blade of grass. She focused on her breathing, closing her eyes as she waited for the headache to pass.

A honk interrupted her.

Kenya opened her eyes to see a white jeep pulling onto the curb. Her father opened the passenger door and jumped out.

"Kenya!" Reuben Davidson ran across the street, dressed in a pair of jeans and a white shirt with his daughter's face printed on it. He pulled her into his arms and began inspecting her. "Are you okay? Mrs. Pierce called and said she saw you racing around her block and that you looked disoriented. Have you got a fever?" He pressed his hand to his daughter's forehead, then noticed the red streaks on her palms. He turned back to the car where his wife was climbing out from the driver's seat. "Courtney, she fell!"

"Jesus, of course she did." Kenya's mother muttered a curse as she climbed out of the car. A bright yellow sundress popped against her skin, but clashed with the pair of blue sneakers beneath. There was no sign of her usual matching accessories, and the kinks in her hair suggested that she'd rushed out of the house without taking the time to flat iron it.

Courtney pressed her fingers against her eyebrows and shook her head as she approached her daughter. "What have we told you about running on your own? What if you'd hit your head and passed out?"

Kenya wanted to argue, but a sudden thought stopped her.

What if she had? What if everything that just happened — the woman with the knife, her transformation into a cat, Camilo dressed in black— had been a hallucination caused by a traumatic head injury?

It made more sense than a blade that recombined DNA.

"And today of all days to decide not to listen?" Courtney continued. "Look at yourself! You can't qualify in this state. You're exhausted. I don't even see the point in driving you to the track."

The threat crashed Kenya back into reality.

"No, I'm ready," she said, putting a hand to her chest and forcing her breath to slow.

There was a list of sanctioned USATF events at Mercury Stadium. Kenya was signed up to run the 400-meter race. Her fastest record to date was 51.32 seconds. If she could finish in that time, it would be enough to qualify to compete at the Olympic Trials. She could start training from now.

"Get in the car then," her mother said, already walking back toward the jeep. "We should've left five minutes ago. I don't know why you didn't answer your phone."

"It never rang," Kenya explained, hurrying behind. She climbed into the backseat of the car and pulled her phone out of the pocket of her running shorts. It was dead.

From the passenger seat, her father glanced behind him

to see the blank screen. "I reminded you to charge it last night."

"I did," Kenya objected, tapping the power button. The screen lit up for a second then faded. "I don't know what happened."

But a dead phone was low on Kenya's list of bizarre events for the morning.

Her mother snorted and started the car, while her father turned and patted her knee.

"It's probably just nerves," he reassured her. "You'll be great, my miracle baby. Just loosen up. Relax. Take some deep breaths."

I'm not a baby, Dad.

Kenya didn't bother arguing though. Her father was right about everything else. She needed to focus on the race.

With a sigh, Kenya leaned back against the door and spread her legs onto the seat so she could massage the knots in her calves. Her eyes drifted to the window whenever they passed anyone dressed in black.

"Mrs. Pierce didn't mention anything about seeing Camilo this morning as well, did she?" Kenya asked.

Her mother slammed her foot on the brake as they reached a stop sign. "Camilo Lopez? The gardener?" She turned to look at her daughter. "Are you really thinking about boys right now?"

"I thought I saw him when I was running. That's all," Kenya objected.

"Oh please. Like I haven't heard you and Lily talking about him." Her mother scoffed and pressed the gas. "Honestly, Kenya, I don't know where your head is at right now. But when your time is back to 53 seconds, and you don't qualify for the Olympics, you're going to have no one to blame but yourself. Because we've done everything to help you get there."

"Hey, she's going to the Olympics," Kenya's father objected before she could. "My girl's got a gift. She's not going to squander it. She knows what's important." He grinned at her in the rearview mirror and gave her a thumbs up.

"I do," Kenya agreed, forcing her gaze away from the window and down to her calves where her thumbs were working on a knot. Her entire life, she'd dreamed of running at the Olympics. And her parents had made it their mission to help her achieve that. They'd paid for additional training, woken up to exercise with her every morning at five, consulted nutritionists, learned to cook the exact meals she wanted, and been present at every race she'd ever run.

Kenya wouldn't let herself or them down.

She didn't have time to care about mysterious blades, or impossible transformations, or attractive gardeners.

Qualifying was all that mattered.

4

CAMILO

Camilo Lopez ran in circles, like a madman chasing his tail, searching desperately for the keeper's scent. He couldn't have lost her. If he had—

I'll have doomed us both.

Sweat coated Camilo's skin. His heart burned in his chest. He managed to sustain his superhuman speed for almost thirty minutes before his body betrayed him.

Camilo fell to his knees on a green lawn. His stomach heaved, and the protein bars he'd shoveled in his mouth that morning spewed onto the grass. He stayed there, coughing and hacking until there was nothing left within him, not even spit.

The scent made his stomach turn. But he stayed there. He couldn't bring himself to stand.

The dagger was right there. I almost had it.

And then Kenya had ruined everything by leaping onto his head.

Camilo's fingers curled into fists, digging into the dirt. Every time he exhaled, more of the hope that had kept him sane over the past year escaped, rising from him like smoke from a dying fire.

He closed his eyes and his lips, trying to cling to it.

———

It had been early last fall when Julia first called him into her office to tell him the good news.

She'd been at her desk, left half of her face hidden behind a curtain of blond hair. Her right eye stared at the many monitors that filled her wall, displaying the rooms in The Morgana Center. In the top left screen, Diego Lopez slept in his permanent prison.

The sight of his father made Camilo's chest tighten. There was almost no sign left of the man who'd played make-believe with him in the park, making lightsaber noises as they battled with sticks until Diego allowed his son to vanquish him, repeating the famous line: *Camilo, yo soy tu padre.*

But that was the way the curse worked, eating at the minds of the innocents it afflicted and morphing them into deadly beasts.

It was Camilo's fate. Unless—

"I believe I've found a cure."

At first, Camilo hadn't understood. If they'd found a way to undo the curse, why hadn't they given it to his father? He'd assumed that Julia was talking about a scientific solution, some new medication or procedure.

But she hadn't been.

"Have you heard of a changeling?" Julia asked him.

Camilo shook his head.

"They're magical beasts, disguised as human infants to trick us into raising them. A witch casts a curse to lock away their true nature, but at eighteen, the child's keeper returns to break the spell with a changeling's dagger."

A dagger that could break curses.

It was then that the small embers of hope, stomped near extinction after fourteen years with no progress, began to burn again inside Camilo.

"Where do I find one of these keepers?" he'd asked.

"We've been unable to determine that," Julia had answered, leaning forward and opening a drawer in her desk. But she'd gone on to pull a newspaper from her drawer and toss it onto the desk, open to the page she'd wanted Camilo to see. "But I think I've identified a changeling."

That was the first time that Camilo had seen Kenya Davidson. A picture of her—curls pulled into a poof at the top of her head, white teeth gleaming in a massive grin—had been printed beneath the headline: *Seventeen-year-old breaks high school track records.*

Two days later, Camilo had taken up a new job, providing lawn care to the Davidsons and their neighbors, integrating himself into the community so that he would be in position on Kenya's eighteenth birthday when her keeper arrived.

A year of patience.

And Camilo had ruined it all with a single rash decision.

———

"Hey there, son," an elderly man shouted through his window at Camilo, still trembling on his lawn. "You okay? Should I call an ambulance?"

"No." Camilo wiped his mouth with the back of his hand and pushed himself onto his feet. Medical assistance was out of the question for someone like him. And he had somewhere to be.

Julia was expecting him at the stadium. She wanted a full report on Kenya's movements.

If he didn't show up, there'd be repercussions. His boss had ways of making her displeasure known.

She won't be happy if she learns what I did either.

The elderly man let out a startled yelp as he got a better look at Camilo. Perhaps he hadn't realized that the boy he was offering to assist was an olive-skinned Latino.

Or maybe it was the all-black outfit, vomit, and trembling that had the man rethinking his earlier concern.

Camilo didn't care. His thoughts were elsewhere as he stumbled off the lawn.

Julia's directions had been clear. *Watch. Learn. Report.*

From her perspective, Camilo would be at fault for making a play for the dagger before she'd ordered. It would be even worse if she learned he'd blown his cover.

Over the years, Julia had grown increasingly paranoid about the magical community learning about The Morgana Center. By extension, that included Camilo.

She'll command me to quit.

No doubt with vague reassurances that they could find another changeling. But when?

Camilo didn't want his father to lose another fourteen years.

The keeper will come back to Kenya. I can steal the dagger when she does.

Camilo would just have to lie to Julia while he figured out how.

5
CAMILO

Camilo adjusted his collar as he approached the Romanesque monstrosity that was Mercury Stadium. The fabric of his white t-shirt clung to his chest. He'd ditched his black turtleneck and track pants in his truck. It was parked four blocks south. The opposite direction to where the Davidsons were likely to go.

After this morning, Camilo didn't want to risk giving Kenya any more clues that he was—he didn't like the word stalking—*closely following* her.

The mask was only off for a second. It was possible that she hadn't recognized him.

Camilo joined a queue waiting to enter Mercury Stadium. It was longer than he would have expected for a track and field event, stretching almost to the ostentatious, white marble statues of winged gods that guarded the open gates.

Like most of the architects in Castor's Grove, the stadium's designer had been more concerned with artistic expression than functionality. The massive, white-washed oval with its columns and giant statues stood out amidst the surrounding red-brick storefronts. Visitors would be forgiven for mistaking the building for a historic site or feeling disappointed when they entered and found, not chariot races and gladiator battles, but the city's largest track. It featured a football field in its center, sand pits at one end, and high-jump pads stationed permanently at the other.

The queue carried Camilo up a pathway lined with marble busts. At the top of the stairs, he purchased a ticket and walked toward the archway where two security guards guided the spectators through a metal detector.

Camilo emptied the pockets of his jeans, placed his phone and wallet into a little basket, and walked through the machine. There was no beep, but one of the guards looked up from beneath his thick eyebrows. Judging from his complexion, he might have been a Latino himself, yet his eyes narrowed as though he were searching for something wrong.

"Food on my face, sir?" Camilo asked, hiding his concern behind a cool façade.

The guard frowned, shook his head, and waved him on.

Camilo hurried in before the man changed his mind.

It's the curse.

The magic clung to Camilo. It sent off warning bells in perceptive individuals.

I won't have to worry about that soon.

He tried to believe his own reassurance. The dagger was still within reach. Camilo just needed to figure out what he was going to tell Julia.

The lower level of Mercury Stadium was full of concession stands. Bored high-school students with summer jobs passed popcorn, hamburgers, and fizzy drinks over the counters. A pair of girls posed in their white and blue uniforms, taking photos instead of serving pizza.

Camilo spotted an old man hawking hot dogs. *Perfect.* He ducked his head, keeping close to the wall on the unlikely chance that Kenya was inside.

The vendor gave him his two hot dogs and attempted to upsell him on a cup of coffee, but Camilo could think of nothing worse. He gave the man another five for a bottle of soda instead.

"Hi there!" An overly cheerful voice made Camilo turn.

It was a girl, still in high school if he had to guess. She had light skin and a long black braid that fell over one of her shoulders. From within the long bell sleeves of her yellow top, Camilo glimpsed a pen in her fingers. A notebook was visible in her other hand.

Oh no. She's not one of Kenya's friends, is she?

Camilo hadn't paid much attention to any of them. He could only recall the one with long brown hair and gangly limbs who hung around the most. She had a flower name—Rose or Petunia or something.

"My name's Yasmin Gul," the girl introduced herself with a smile so large and fake that Camilo worried it might cause her cheeks to crack. "I'm with the Grover's Gazette. Do you mind sharing what brought you to Mercury Stadium today, Mister...?"

Camilo froze. If his name wound up in an article that wouldn't just alert Kenya to his presence, it would infuriate Julia.

"Kirk," he grabbed at the first name he could think of. "Cap"—*You can't say Captain Kirk. That's not at all believable.*—"Capulet."

Camilo wanted to slap himself. He'd gone from *Star Trek* to *Shakespeare*. Not much of an improvement when it came to faking a name. He'd need to lie a lot better if he wanted to deceive Julia.

"I'm just a track-and-field enthusiast," he said quickly, hoping that the girl wouldn't dwell on his name. He tried to slip past her toward the stairs, balancing his paper plate of hotdogs and soft drink.

"Really?" Yasmin followed, pen poised on her notebook. "Do you think there might be a bigger story here? Corruption or—?"

"I'm so sorry, sir!" A tall, thin man with a baseball cap rushed over. "My intern's just a little overeager."

He grabbed Yasmin's wrist and pulled her out of Camilo's way. "Look, either let me do the talking of just follow the script. You were assigned to sports not—"

Camilo didn't stick around to hear the rest of the interaction. He had his own boss to find. He searched for the staircase that would lead him to section *M* of the stands.

When Julia suggested meeting in the stadium, she'd acted like she was doing Camilo a favor by not having him come to the Morgana Center. More likely, she wanted a chance to see Kenya in person.

The thought made Camilo uncomfortable.

He didn't like magic any more than his boss, but two weeks of active surveillance had given him a good picture of what the eighteen-year-old was like. Maybe not human, but not cruel or dangerous either.

Except when she digs her claws into your skull.

Camilo ran his hand along the back of his head. He could feel the scars, starting to itch as the skin puckered. It was only now beginning to knit itself back together.

They should have healed by now.

Wasn't that one of the benefits of his curse?

Camilo was rundown. He'd been so anxious about

missing the keeper's arrival that he'd been forgetting to sleep.

I wasn't at my best when I went for the dagger. Next time, I have to be prepared.

He shoveled the hotdog in his mouth as he climbed the stairs to section *M*.

Mercury Stadium had no ceiling. A circular extension of the roof protected the stands, but the field was open to the elements. Athletes stretched in the center of the sunlit grass.

Camilo picked out Kenya easily. It was the lime green shoes.

At least she makes herself easy to stalk.

Camilo scanned section *M*. He spotted Julia in a blue plastic seat near the center.

Blonde hair obscured the left half of her face, hiding it in shadow. She leaned forward, letting her shades fall onto the tip of her slightly upturned nose, and her right eye became visible. It stared at Camilo, a pale, lonely blue. She tapped a large gold watch on her wrist with a thin finger, pointed to the field, and raised her eyebrow. Her lips pulled into an unimpressed frown.

Camilo didn't need words to understand what Julia was criticizing him for.

Kenya was here almost an hour ago. She was expecting me to arrive just afterward.

Camilo was going to need a compelling excuse to explain why that hadn't happened.

6

CAMILO

Julia folded her arms and leaned back against the plastic blue seat, appraising Camilo over her sunglasses. He sat a few chairs away, inventing a story about a lawn emergency.

"... her grandson took a pair of scissors to her hedge. She called in a panic asking me to come at once. Figured I'd best keep Mrs. Evans happy. Her yard has the best view of the Davidsons' house."

Camilo swallowed, fighting the desire to adjust his collar under Julia's cold gaze.

Is she buying any of this?

Julia's eye flicked from Camilo to something behind him. Climbing the stairs toward them was a short man with wild brown hair and massive round glasses. He held three bags of popcorn in his arms.

Camilo's jaw clenched. It was Tate Barron, a graduate student at the university who'd somehow been promoted to head of genetic and virological research at The Morgana Center. He'd maintained his position as Julia's favorite for almost two years.

"I didn't know there was a dress code planned!" Tate said in a deep voice that had no business coming from a man with the body of a pasty white child.

He was referring to their outfits. While both Julia and Camilo had opted for jeans and white t-shirts—the same attire as half of the onlookers—Tate was in a red Hawaiian shirt, which looked like it had once belonged to a sixty-year-old retiree.

Julia claimed Tate was a genius. If that was true, he was the dumbest one Camilo had ever met.

Tate turned two rows too late and had to climb down over the blue plastic chairs to reach them. Half the popcorn tumbled from his arms onto the floor. A particularly buttery piece fell onto Camilo's sleeve and left a yellow smudge when he tried to brush it off.

If Julia didn't want to meet with me alone, couldn't she have brought Holly instead?

At least his boss had left behind the gun.

About five years ago, around the time Camilo had started high school, security at The Morgana Center had increased. More cameras were installed, and carrying tranquilizer guns became the norm for the scientists. They all contained the glowing white liquid that had once been used to subdue Diego.

They're waiting for me to go mad too.

Camilo doubted that Julia had cast aside that fear. Mercury Stadium just didn't allow weapons.

"Got enough for everyone," Tate announced, shaking his popcorn. Despite there being several available seats, he chose the one right beside Camilo. "Oh, you've already had some hot dogs. Well, take it anyway. I know you've got an appetite."

He pushed one of the bags onto Camilo's lap.

"You're too sweet, Tate," Julia said, her tone patronizing as she accepted the popcorn from him. Her hair fell to the side, and for a moment, the black eye patch beneath her shades was visible. A thin white scar peeked out from beneath.

Julia's right eye caught Camilo staring.

He turned away, trying to ignore the guilt creeping into his stomach. His hand almost knocked over the popcorn that had been forced onto him. He wished it had.

Scowling, Camilo made a point of moving the bag onto the floor and pushing it away with his foot. Tate watched the rejection of his supposed gift, eyes magnified by his glasses.

Julia repositioned her shades and swept the curtain of hair back over the left half of her face. "Camilo's just given me a curious story, Tate. What do you see when you examine him?"

Camilo's muscles tensed. *Guess she didn't believe me.*

But genius or not, Tate couldn't disprove Camilo's story. And Julia was unlikely to ask Mrs. Evans herself.

I just need to stick to what I said.

Tate scanned Camilo with bulging eyes and a twitching smile. Most of The Morgana Center's scientists treated their job with cool, clinical indifference. Tate's overeager enthusiasm was significantly more off putting.

"Red rims around his eyes," the scientist observed. "Probably due to lack of sleep. Damp shirt. Sweat from physical exertion most likely. Dirt under his nails, so possibly gardening."

Julia's one visible eyebrow rose in surprise.

Camilo held back a smile. Had he been annoyed to see Tate? He took it back. The scientist's observations and inaccurate assumptions might just convince Julia.

"But more likely," Tate continued, "he's been in a fight."

The hint of a smile vanished from Camilo's face. His short-lived appreciation for Tate left with it.

He caught Julia's eye. There was a cruel twist to her lips.

"Isn't that interesting," she said.

"There are scars on the back of his head," Tate said, voice cheerful. "They ought to have healed by now. Unless it was some sort of new demon..."

From the corner of his eye, Camilo saw Tate's butter-covered fingers reaching toward him. He turned and pushed the scientist's hands away before they could touch his hair.

Tate's teeth gritted, and his eyes winced as he pulled his arms back.

The familiar sense of guilt stirred in Camilo's stomach, and a lump rose in his throat.

Dammit.

The scientist was a nuisance, but Camilo hadn't intended to hurt him. How was it, after fourteen years, he still hadn't mastered his strength?

"I trust that if a demon attacked, you wouldn't hide that from The Center," Julia said. Her voice was clipped, cold. She kept her head straight, pointed toward the field. Behind her tinted lens, it was impossible to know where her eye was looking.

"Of course not," Camilo muttered, folding his hands onto his lap. "I respect The Center's mission."

It was his father who'd first envisioned the potential of using science to combat magic. While he had failed to find a cure to his own affliction in time, Julia, his former partner, continued Diego's work on his behalf.

Though her methodology had shifted over the past five years.

Two additional levels had been tunneled beneath The Morgana Center since Diego's transformation. Instead of laboratories, they featured padded cells and a *testing* room, which Camilo had been forbidden to enter.

That suited him fine. His youth had been spent undergoing numerous trials—blood transfusions, steroid injections, tablets that he threw up minutes later. The Morgana Center had wanted every baby tooth, every nail clipping, every strand of hair he shed. At some point, they must have gotten enough of his DNA.

But the real reason for The Morgana Center's sudden disinterest was their new test subjects.

Julia explained it in simple terms. Demons and other dangerous beasts couldn't be allowed to roam the streets of Castor's Grove. What choice was there but to hold them prisoner, same as Diego?

In theory, Camilo understood. But whenever he heard the demons shrieking in their cells, the decision didn't seem as obvious. And where was The Morgana Center finding these creatures to capture?

The more questions Camilo asked, the more he was punished. Julia had exiled him from the research facility, revoking his access card and growing annoyed whenever he asked to visit. He had no concept of what The Morgana Center was doing. Until last year, when they'd found Kenya.

"Was it her?" Julia's voice, high and cold, sliced through Camilo's thoughts. She was standing as close to the edge as she could get without plummeting into the lower rows, staring over the sea of blue plastic seats toward the field.

He didn't need to see her eye to know that it was fixed on Kenya.

The muscles in Camilo's neck grew tense and stiff. Julia was approaching the truth. If he wasn't careful, she'd piece together that his cover was blown. Then Camilo's chance at the dagger would be gone. He'd spend the rest of his days mowing lawns until the curse finally stole his mind.

But whatever lie he told, it had to be believable. Even if that meant coming dangerously close to the truth.

"It was her keeper," Camilo said. "She came this morning."

"So you attacked?" Julia's head snapped toward him. Her voice was ice. "You swore you could handle it when I gave you the assignment. But you failed. I told you to watch and report back. Instead, you let your own emotions take control, and now you've damned yourself and your father."

Camilo's body tightened with every word, like his muscles were trying to curl into his chest. "I didn't attack," he lied. "She heard me. She's an elf."

"That's even more pathetic." Julia's lips were a thin cruel line.

"Please, I can still get the dagger without being captured," Camilo rose from his seat, body trembling. His voice was unsteady, but he didn't dare shout. Losing his temper could be catastrophic. "The keeper will return. I'll be prepared for when she does."

"You will be," Julia agreed, voice flat as she turned back toward the field. "Because I'm going to prepare you. There's a gift for you in my car. A weapon, of sorts."

She has a plan.

Camilo sighed, his pulse returning to normal as he sank back into his seat. Maybe he'd lost the element of surprise, but he didn't need to panic. Julia had a plan to get the dagger. He closed his eyes and took another breath. "Thank you."

"It's not a reward," Julia said. "Under regular circumstances, I wouldn't hesitate to call this off. We can't risk anyone discovering you. But we're under a time crunch now to obtain the dagger.'

"Why?" Camilo's chest tightened. "Has my father gotten worse?"

"Impossible to say," Tate spoke from beside him with a mouth full of popcorn. "Diego's interaction with the patho—"

Julia held up a finger, signaling her employee to fall silent. "Let me worry about your father, Camilo. I'm the one trying to complete his life's work. If you want to help, you follow orders."

"But—"

Julia held up a finger. It was enough to silence Camilo. "The Center needs the dagger. We can discuss why later." She returned to her seat, crossing her legs and leaning back. Her lonely blue eye stared at the field. "Right now, I want to watch the changeling run."

7
KENYA

Kenya held her ankle, pressing it against her lower back and leaning forward to stretch her hamstring. Coordinators shouted to one another, arranging a group of women on the track. There was only one race left before her own, and she was still struggling to get into the right headspace.

Fast to begin. Recoup energy. Final push at the end.

She closed her eyes and tried to practice her breathing technique.

"Oh my God!"

Kenya stumbled out of her stretch, eyes flying open at the sound of the excited gasp only a few inches from her ear.

The squeal had come from Lily. Kenya's best friend currently looked like a cartoon character. Her long hair was tied in two buns on either side of her head, adorned with sky blue ribbons to match her shorts. She had her hands pressed to her cheeks, and her mouth open in an overdramatic gasp.

"Is that who I think it is?" she asked, staring into the

stands.

Lily was competing in the 5000m later, but she claimed to have only signed up so that she could keep Kenya company. What spectator would have her so excited?

The starting pistol fired, and the next group of competitors took off. Kenya turned to watch for a second before a pair of hands grabbed her cheeks and forced her head to turn toward the top of the stands.

"Look!" Lily insisted.

"Camilo." His name slipped from Kenya's lips. Her heart froze. Memories of her morning run returned.

What is he doing here?

He was near the back, dressed in jeans and a t-shirt—not the morning's all black ensemble—talking to some blonde. Kenya would never have spotted him. She doubted Lily would have either if he hadn't stood up.

"Do you think he came to watch you run?" Lily suggested, nudging Kenya with her elbow as they watched Camilo slide back into his seat. "Maybe you're not the only one with a crush."

"Stop," Kenya snapped. There was an anxious edge to her voice. "I don't like Camilo."

She'd commented on his attractiveness a few times. But she didn't like him. She didn't even know him.

Kenya's heart pounded in her chest. She recalled the hockey mask slipping from Camilo's face.

"Relax, I'm only kidding." Lily gave her a weird look, before stretching her arms into the air. "I know future Olympians don't have time for boys."

"Exactly." *Even if they may have witnessed you transform into a cat.*

"I'm so glad I don't have your talent." Lily leaned forward and grabbed her toes. "I don't think I could commit to a life of just school, work, and training with my parents."

"I do other stuff."

"Like what?"

Kenya didn't have a chance to answer. One of the organizers, dressed in white shorts and an official t-shirt with a USATF logo in the corner stepped into the center of the field, calling for the women competing in the 400m.

"That's me." Kenya's heart pounded in her chest as she turned toward the track.

Lily shouted behind her. "Good luck!"

Given her current head space, Kenya would need it. She took a few deep breaths, trying to clear her thoughts as she crouched behind her line.

This was no time to think about Camilo, or tourists with daggers, or orange cats. All that mattered was the race.

Because it was about to determine the rest of Kenya's life.

———

At the sound of the pistol, Kenya shot off.

She was on the inside of the track. Seven women started in front of her in the outer lanes. By the first fifty meters, that had narrowed down to three.

Kenya kept her pace a fraction of a second longer than she should have.

She needed to save some energy. No one could sprint a full 400m, but she needed to maintain her lead.

Kenya breathed in for three strides, exhaled on the fourth. By the 200m mark, she was in the lead.

But it wasn't enough. She wasn't racing to win. She was there to qualify.

Kenya stared at the finish line ahead. Her muscles burned, still sore from that morning.

No, don't think about this morning.

Images of dancing flames popped into her head.

The ache in her limbs worsened. Heat overwhelmed her legs, like when the dagger had twisted in her chest. Licks of fire coiled around her feet.

Kenya kept running, and the stadium became a blur of concrete bleachers, grassy center, and uniformed organizers.

She heard her parents shout as she crossed the finish line.

It took another 50m before Kenya managed to stop. She collapsed onto the ground, knees and palms pressing into the grass. Her temples throbbed, and her chest heaved. Blue and red flames sank back into her skin.

Can everyone see that or am I hallucinating?

There was shouting on the field, loud whoops from the bleachers. In the first row of seats, her father jumped up and down, pointing to the image of Kenya's face on his shirt.

Courtney tapped on her phone screen. She looked frustrated, but when she caught her daughter's eye, a smile spread across her face. She raised her thumb.

Is that a reassurance not to worry even though my feet were just on fire or—?

Kenya took a few deep breaths, letting her headache subside before she pushed herself to her feet. Her legs trembled.

The other runners had completed the race by now too, though they'd controlled their finishes better than Kenya. Where she'd found herself back in the center of the grassy oval, her competitors were catching their breath on the outside of the track.

"Damn girl!" Lily shouted. She grinned as she jogged toward Kenya. "That was insane!"

"Was I on fire?" Kenya asked, her breath coming short and shallow.

"Are you joking?" Lily grabbed Kenya's shoulders and bent forward so that their foreheads touched. "Yes! I counted forty-seven seconds."

"No, I mean—wait, what?" There was no way that was right. That would be less than the world record.

But even if Lily was off by two or even three seconds, it didn't matter. Kenya had done it.

She would get her chance to be chosen for the Olympics.

"Excuse me, Ms. Davidson?" A short woman in white track pants and an official t-shirt walked up to Kenya. She adjusted the cord of her short-brimmed straw-hat, tightening it under her chin. There was a serious expression on her face.

"Yes?" Kenya stepped away from Lily, suddenly nervous. Had this woman seen the fire come from her feet?

"I'm going to need you to come with me." The official pulled a red lanyard from under her collar and showed Kenya the card at the end. "You've been selected for mandatory drug testing."

8

CAMILO

A smile tugged at the corner of Julia's lips as they watched the official escort Kenya off the field.

The last half of the race, wisps of magic had sprouted beneath Kenya's feet and propelled her forward. She'd moved faster than Camilo had ever seen a human run. But of course, Kenya Davidson wasn't human.

Technically, there was no way for the officials watching the race to know. They couldn't see the magic and, judging from the shouting on the field, both stopwatches had failed to catch her time. And yet—

"Human intuition prevails again," Julia said. "Most of us may have forgotten about magic, but we have a deep-rooted instinct that allows us to identify and eliminate threats."

Camilo crossed his arms. It was one thing when Julia spoke that way of witches or demons, but he'd experienced that *human intuition* himself. It couldn't exactly distinguish harmless from dangerous when it came to magic.

Though perhaps I am a threat.

But Kenya? She was barely an adult. Her parents were

running through the bleachers, trying to follow her out of the stadium.

"They'll think she cheated," Camilo said. There was a twinge of sympathy in his voice that he hoped Julia wouldn't notice. Why should any of them care if Kenya's dream of becoming an Olympian was dead?

"She did cheat." Julia's voice was stern. "Magic is cheating."

I doubt she meant to use it.

But that was no excuse.

Camilo's shoulders tightened. He fought the urge to flick his eyes toward his boss' hidden eye. Instead, he stared at the small crumbs of bread on his paper plate.

Julia stood, evidently ready to leave now that Kenya had been escorted off the premise. "What is our changeling exactly that she runs so fast? A vampire?"

"Just a shifter." Camilo crumpled the plate and shoved it into his pocket. "Transforms into a house cat."

Beside him, Tate coughed, kernels of popcorn caught in his throat. He pounded a fist against his chest then gave them both a weak smile. "I for one would love to test just how powerful the human instinct for the supernatural is."

Camilo fought the urge to roll his eyes. Apparently, Julia's genius was unaware that the conversation had moved on.

"If we conducted a blind study with an image of Kenya and nine regular humans, what are the statistical chances that subjects would be able to identify her as the odd one out?"

"Less than ten percent," Camilo answered without thinking.

"Certainly not." Julia brushed a hand over her hair, ensuring the left half of her face remained hidden. "It would be closer to eighty. Our instincts are strong, or we would have been wiped out."

Julia was mistaken.

If most people's instincts were that strong, it's the supernatural that would've been destroyed.

A dragon could fly over the stadium right now, and most of the spectators would have no idea. They'd never look up. Even if they watched Kenya transform in the middle of the field, their brains would recompute what their eyes had shown them. They'd convince themselves that the girl had never existed; they'd seen the cat run across the field.

It was a state of ignorance Camilo envied. *I'd rather not know if a dragon flew overhead either.*

Especially since Julia might've tasked him with defeating it.

"Of course, you're probably right," Camilo said, finishing the last of his drink. Even if he spoke from experience, he knew better than to argue with his boss.

Camilo hadn't studied chemistry or genetics or evolutionary biology. Firsthand experience with magic didn't count. His opinions were worthless as far as The Morgana Center was concerned.

———

Camilo tapped his sneaker against the concrete floor, counting to three hundred.

Julia and Tate had left the bleachers shortly after Kenya vanished. Camilo had been ordered to wait another five minutes. The timing might be too suspicious if someone noticed. They might guess he was stalking her.

Camilo doubted anyone in the stadium was paying

attention to him. Julia just enjoyed finding creative ways to show her displeasure, so he was being treated like a child.

But if a time-out was the worst repercussion Camilo faced, he'd consider it a small price.

He counted three-hundred seconds, feeling his stomach growl despite the hotdogs. His eyes flicked to the bag of popcorn that he'd rejected from Tate, still on the floor.

Camilo grabbed it and poured some of the kernels in his mouth as he trotted down the steps. It was nice. Salty.

Time served, Camilo stood. He took the popcorn with him. He could throw it away before he reached the parking lot.

"Come on, that has to be a story!" A girl's voice, high and whiny rose above the rest of the crowd from a few feet below as Camilo descended the stairs. He looked down to see Yasmin shaking her notebook at her boss in the baseball cap. "They escorted her off the field. Obviously, she did something illegal."

"That's not—" her boss groaned. "How did you even get assigned to sports? That's all standard procedure for a drug test."

The information only excited Yasmin more. "So maybe she's *doping*?" She whispered the word as though afraid she might get in trouble just for saying it. "I recorded her on my phone, and it was forty-seven seconds. That's like really fast. Right?"

"Oh sure." Her boss took the baseball cap off his head and buried his face. His shoulders shook, whether with laughter or tears Camilo couldn't tell. "She just set a world record, and the officials all missed it."

That sounded more than likely to Camilo. He ran past before Yasmin noticed him and tried to ask *Kirk Capulet* any more questions.

Camilo slipped down the stairs and through the commercial interior. With less customers, most of the hired teens were openly goofing off. A few shouted and waved at one another across the floor. Most scrolled their phones.

Must be nice to be so carefree.

Camilo was nineteen, not much older than the employees he was judging. But he'd been on his own for three years. He needed the income he earned caring for people's lawns.

And he needed the dagger even more.

Parking for the stadium was on the opposite side of the street. Camilo walked down the bust-lined path toward the gates.

"Psst!" Someone hissed.

Camilo stopped and turned. The sound had come from behind the statue of the woman. A plaque near her base identified her as the goddess Victoria. Her knee was as high as Camilo's head, and she had massive white wings, at least fifteen feet tall. The tips of their feathers reached almost to the ground.

Underneath the left one, Camilo could make out a pair of red shoes.

Tate peeped out from behind the wing and waved him over.

Camilo sighed as he approached. If Tate was trying to be sneaky, the Hawaiian shirt was ruining it. The scientist popped like a beacon against the white marble. And what was up with the bag that he was clutching to his chest?

The weapon.

"Julia couldn't be bothered to deliver it herself?" Camilo asked, staring at the black pouch. Whatever weapon was within was much smaller than he'd expected.

"I offered to come. Told her it would attract less attention if someone spotted you talking to another guy your own age."

Camilo snorted. He doubted his boss had needed much convincing. Forcing him to take orders from Tate was yet another punishment.

"Truth is, I needed to talk to you," the scientist whispered, coming out from behind the angel's wing so that they were closer. His eyes landed on the now empty bag of popcorn. "So you did get hungry."

"I just didn't want to leave it for the workers to have to clean." Camilo crumpled the bag into a ball with his fist, regretting not hiding it in his pocket earlier. "Why do you want to talk?"

"Because those scratches are from a cat's claws."

Camilo tried to think of a response. Only his grandmother's favorite curse came to mind.

Hostia!

"Are you working with Kenya to get the dagger?"

"Of course not." Camilo lowered his voice. "She's a Castor. She's one of them."

"Sure, but given your affliction, you could—"

"Kenya has no idea what I'm doing, Tate. The scratches are from her, but she didn't see me. I was wearing a mask."

"Too bad. Julia was thinking, she could be useful."

"Julia *wants* me to work with Kenya?"

"Begrudgingly," Tate admitted. "She doesn't want you to tell her anything about The Morgana Center or yourself, obviously. But Julia's original plan doesn't work without the element of surprise. Sounds like the keeper will be on the lookout for you. She won't expect an assault from her changeling."

Camilo's brow lowered. That was all true, but it didn't

matter. "I've barely spoken to Kenya. She's not going to help me."

Especially if she's realized that I've been following her.

Tate's nose twitched. He pulled a notepad from his pocket and began flipping through. Camilo thought he glanced his own name on one of the pages.

"No, there's a high probability she would." Tate pointed to the notepad. "According to our intel, Kenya is a hetero-sexual, eighteen-year-old girl with no boyfriend. You are incredibly muscular, conventionally handsome. Could be taller—"

"I'm five ten," Camilo objected.

"Exactly. But you have that Latino charm to make up for it."

Camilo's jaw clenched. What sort of stereotypical brush was Tate painting him with?

"Do I look charming to you?" Camilo asked through gritted teeth.

"I'm talking about how Kenya would perceive you. Studies have shown that trust and attraction are linked. There's a good chance that you could convince her to steal the dagger for you. It's not like you haven't got a genuine need for it. She might think it's romantic, like *Beauty and the Beast.*"

Camilo crossed his arms. It was difficult to keep his voice from lowering into a growl. "So I sell her a sob story and hope that she pities me enough to want to save me?"

Even if Camilo didn't hate that idea, it wouldn't work. In his experience, girls knowing about his curse didn't make them see him as fairytale prince.

"I thought Julia didn't want me to tell Kenya the truth."

"She doesn't," Tate said, holding up his hand as a sign

of peace. "I just thought that if she already knew then... But obviously, listen to Julia."

"I will." But Camilo wasn't entirely sold on his boss' plan either. "Kenya's only just gotten her magic. How could she overpower her keeper?"

Tate's eyes widened behind his glasses, giving him the appearance of an overenthusiastic owl.

"With these," he said, unzipping the pouch that was in his hand.

A metal so black that it seemed to absorb the light hummed in the darkness within.

9
KENYA

The testing lab was across the street from Mercury Stadium. Kenya had walked over with the official and her parents, who'd insisted on coming too. It wasn't necessary. The drug test was a simple procedure. Kenya just had to let them take a blood sample and sign some papers.

She could've handled it herself.

Until she spotted Camilo through the window of the reception area.

Kenya signed her name at the bottom of the form and passed it to her mother. "Can you fill out the rest for me? I suddenly don't feel well. I need some air."

Before either of her parents could question her, she jumped up and rushed out the door.

Camilo leaned against the brick building, one hand in the pocket of his jeans. The denim was tight over his thighs, hinting at the muscles beneath. The white t-shirt stretched across his chest. His hand gripped the strap of a circular black bag that was slung across his shoulders.

Kenya's heart pounded as he turned toward her.

I can't let him disappear again.

Without thinking, Kenya raced toward him. She was expecting him to run, or at least step back. He didn't.

The result was that she barreled into Camilo. Her nose collided with his shoulders, and her palms pressed against his shirt. It was like hitting a brick wall.

There's no way I can stop him if he tries to run again.

But maybe she could ensure that he had to take her with him. Kenya clutched Camilo's shirt, twisting the fabric around her fingers and trying not to notice the way it lifted from his stomach.

"Are you following me?" she demanded.

Camilo stared straight at her. "Would you be very upset if I was?"

Kenya's mouth opened and closed for a few seconds. What the hell kind of answer was that?

"We need to talk," she finally managed to respond. "What happened this morning? Who was that woman with the dagger?"

"Not here." Camilo grabbed her hand, detaching it from his shirt with ease. He pulled her down a narrow gap between the lab and its neighboring brick building. The path split into two dead-end alleyways with large trash bins, hidden from the street's view. They took up most of the space.

Camilo didn't seem to care. He squeezed between two, pulling Kenya behind him.

"We should be good here," he said, releasing her hand and straightening. His nose wrinkled for a moment as he looked at the bins.

Kenya sniffed. She couldn't smell anything besides a

light woodsy musk that made her think of hiking through the woods in summer. Given their current location between a crumbling brick wall and two black trash bins, it was surprisingly nice.

What is it?

The obvious answer occurred to her a moment later when she turned to face Camilo.

Oh God. It's his cologne.

Kenya had never been this close to Camilo before. There was less than an inch between them. One deep breath and her body would brush against his muscles.

Stupid thing to worry about right now.

Trying to focus her thoughts, Kenya cast her gaze upward to Camilo's face. Her eyes landed on his lips. She'd never realized how pretty they were before, pink, plump.

Kissable.

Kenya wanted to slap herself. Why had her brain chosen now to remember that she found Camilo attractive? He'd just dragged her down an alleyway. She ought to be afraid.

But it wasn't me he went after this morning.

Kenya pushed her curls down, trying to flatten the rising frizz. She focused on a spot of green moss on one of the bricks behind Camilo's head. "You were going to tell me what happened."

From the corner of her eye, she could see him studying her. He leaned closer. His breath tickled her ear as he whispered. "Your magic was unlocked."

Kenya snorted.

Camilo stepped backward, startled by the response. There were suddenly a few more inches between them.

Had he been standing so close on purpose before?

He's making fun of me.

"I'm not five, Camilo. Tell me the truth."

"You turned into a cat." Camilo crossed his arms. "What else do you think it could be?"

A hallucination? An advanced intermolecular shape-shifting device? Anything else would make more sense.

"There's no such thing as magic," Kenya said, copying Camilo's stance and staring back at him with the same frustrated expression.

He snorted. "Maybe if you live with your head buried in the sand. Castor's Grove is the capital city of the magical world. You've never noticed anything weird?"

"No," Kenya said, but her confidence lessened a second later. Perhaps there were a few things about Castor's Grove that weren't exactly normal. There was a castle in the center of downtown, strange buildings that no one ever entered, and hundreds of tales about creatures living in the surrounding forests.

Her face must have betrayed her uncertainty because the hint of a smile played on Camilo's lips.

"Exactly. You're what they call a changeling— a magical orphan who needed a home. So your keeper slipped you into the crib of an unsuspecting family."

Kenya stopped listening at the word *orphan*. She held up a hand. "Yeah, I'm not adopted. I look just like my parents. Dad's eyes. Mum's smile. Aunt Moira's ears." She pointed to each part in turn.

"That's how changelings work." There was a hint of exasperation in Camilo's voice. He pushed himself off from the wall, closing the space between them as he explained. "The spell they place around you dulls your magic and makes sure you're molded into what people assume you'll be. You're Reuben and Courtney's kid, you'll look like them.

Your name is Kenya, you'll be a runner. Talented athletes want to be Olympians, that'll be your dream."

"Stop." Kenya said, crossing her arms tighter and glaring at him. "This isn't funny."

Camilo kept going. "Your parents adore you. So do your friends. No one on the street looks at you twice because you're exactly what they all want you to be. Until you're done growing and your keeper returns with the dagger and"— he pretended to stab her, twisting the imaginary blade into her chest—"cuts through the spell, so your true nature is revealed."

Somehow, while he was speaking, Camilo had forced Kenya backward, pressing her against the wall. He was almost on top of her, staring at her with unreadable brown eyes.

"You, Kenya Davidson are a shifter."

Kenya stared at his lips as they formed the word.

No, if he's trying to distract me with his looks again, it's not going to work.

"Beep." Kenya made a fake buzzer noise. "You called me a changeling the first time. I get it if you're undercover or something and can't tell me the truth. But at least keep your made-up names straight." She rested her hands on Camilo's chest and tried to push him away.

Instead, he raised his arms, resting his palms against the wall and trapping her there. "You're both. Your keeper will explain it too when she comes back, but I uh..." He glanced down at his feet, suddenly self-conscious. The next words seemed difficult for him to say. "I'd like your help. I need the dagger because...."

Kenya's eyebrows rose, waiting for whatever ridiculous explanation Camilo was going to come up with next.

"Because I do."

Kenya snorted. That had to win for all-time most pathetic lie. "Absolutely not. But good luck with your thievery."

She ducked under his arm before he could stop her and squeezed through the bins.

"Wait!" Camilo was slower to follow, struggling to maneuver his muscles through the narrow space. "You won't be able to compete in the Olympics now you're a Castor. Without the changeling spell, your blood isn't going to be human anymore. It's going to be flagged every time they test it."

Kenya stopped near the corner of the alley. She ought to just leave it, but she was feeling irrationally irritated by Camilo's inability to keep his own lie straight. "Castor is the third thing you've called me," she said, spinning to face him. "And why do you care about my blood test?"

"Because I can help you," he said, scrambling forward. "I'm friends with a lot of scientists. If you get me the dagger, I'll help you fake your test results."

Kenya's muscles tightened. Was he threatening her?

"I don't need fake results," she said, body trembling in fury. This was not at all how she'd expected her conversation with Camilo to go. "I don't use drugs."

Kenya turned the corner, moving back toward the street, and froze. Standing before her was a girl in a long-sleeve yellow shirt, with a black braid over her shoulder. She had a notebook and pen in her hand.

The moment their eyes met, the girl reached into her pocket.

Crap. Who's she?

"Are you not understanding?" Camilo continued arguing as he followed. "You're not human. Any drug test

—" He cut himself off as he turned the corner and saw the girl. "Yasmin?"

"I knew there was a story here," she said, a smile spreading across her face.

Before Kenya could register what was happening, the girl pulled out her phone and snapped a picture.

10

CAMILO

C amilo adjusted the collar of his red polo shirt as he stepped into the rustic blue interior of Talk Latte. Soft acoustic music played from the speakers in the corners of the coffee bar, and chalk signs with puns hung from the walls, complimenting customers. He clung to the strap of the black bag, feeling out of place.

This was the last place Camilo wanted to be.

It was Monday morning, creeping toward nine. Almost forty-eight hours since Kenya had rejected his proposal to team up.

Evidently, he wasn't as attractive as Tate thought.

Or I should've played pathetic and begged.

The thought made Camilo's stomach turn. Or maybe that was just the smell.

Holly had insisted the coffee shop be the location for their meeting this morning, even when Camilo had pushed back. He had no idea why. Perhaps she was punishing him for some unknown offense. Holly was Julia's daughter after all.

Under regular circumstances, Camilo liked to think he

wouldn't have agreed to the pointless demand. But he might've been overestimating his ability to tell her no.

Camilo scanned the café, searching for Holly.

He found her in the corner near the back, a round-faced blonde with a high ponytail and pink lips. The ruffled sleeves of a peach-colored sundress fell over her shoulders, and her chin rested on her palm. She scowled at a copy of the Grover's Gazette on the table.

Camilo cupped his hand to his mouth, exhaled, and sniffed— a quick check to ensure that his breath was good. It was almost impossible to tell. The air was heavy with the scent of coffee. He tried not to inhale through his nose as he slid into the seat.

He smiled, oddly nervous.

When was the last time we hung out, just the two of us?

Camilo couldn't remember. Between her bio-chemistry degree and interning at The Morgana Center, Holly had been elusive the past two years.

"Thanks for agreeing to meet," Camilo said, and he meant it. The sight of her, even scowling, had momentarily made him forget his objections to the location and time— Camilo was going to be mowing lawns in the hottest part of the day as a result. Maybe she had a right to be demanding. After all, he was the one who'd insisted they speak in person.

Camilo needed a favor. Holly was the only one at The Morgana Center who he trusted to help him.

"Surprised you made it." Holly didn't look up. "Thought you'd be too busy with your changeling."

My changeling?

Camilo narrowed his eyes. "Your mom told you her plan."

"Yes, and it was short-sighted." Holly folded the newspaper with a scowl. "As I could've told her if she'd asked me instead of Tate. I don't know what her fascination with him is. He's so weird."

Camilo nodded. On that, they definitely agreed.

"And it's not like he's the only young scientist with ideas," Holly continued, looking less furious now that Camilo was agreeing with her.

He knew the correct response to that. "Of course not. You're brilliant too."

"Exactly!" Holly said, waving the folded newspaper as she spoke. "I don't know why my mother doesn't see that. And now, because she didn't take my input, she's come up with a plan that puts all of us at risk. I mean, working with a Castor? What if Kenya discovers the truth about The Morgana Center and comes after us. She's a serious threat."

Camilo snorted. Was that what Holly was worried about? "Kenya's not dangerous."

That was the wrong thing to say. Camilo knew it as soon as Holly's scowl returned, creating angry lines in her otherwise smooth forehead.

"I suppose you think that because the changeling's enamored with you now, everything's under control. But what if you lose control, and she sees what you really are? She's not going to be interested in you then, is she?"

Holly's voice was cruel and cold as she stared at Camilo.

It reminded him too much of Julia.

He looked at Holly's pale blue eyes. Two of them. A vision danced before Camilo: a claw, lashing forward and slicing Holly's left eye, blood boiling to the surface and painting the entire lens in a vicious red.

The image made Camilo's neck tense. His throat threatened to close. He lowered his gaze and struggled to breathe.

His voice was soft when he managed to speak. "You

don't need to worry about any of that because Kenya didn't agree to help me."

"Oh." Holly's mouth pursed into a circle. She didn't look as pleased by the statement as he would've expected. "That explains why you've still got those." She waved the menu toward the round black bag over Camilo's shoulder.

Within was Julia's gift. A pair of handcuffs. Not exactly the weapon Camilo had been expecting.

The shackles were forged from a strange black metal, so cold it burned. Camilo had spent the weekend practicing with them. He'd need to be able to ignore the feeling of wrongness that crept up his fingers whenever he touched them if he had any hope of binding the keeper.

According to Tate, the handcuffs blocked magic. Once they were on the elf, stealing the dagger would be an easy task. It was just a matter of finding a way to catch her that didn't involve Kenya.

Where did Julia get them?

The Morgana Center's research focused on areas within biochemistry. Camilo was no scientist, but he didn't think forging metal fell under that domain.

There was no sense asking. Holly wouldn't answer. She was as close-lipped as her mother about such matters. Plus, Camilo had more pressing concerns.

"Tate said the handcuffs didn't work on my father. Is that true?"

"He's too far gone, I think," Holly admitted, her voice soft and compassionate, more like the girl Camilo remembered and less like her mother.

"So he's gotten worse." It was exactly like Camilo feared. "I need to see him, Holly."

"I figured that's what you wanted to ask. But I need something too," she said. "Let's order first. We can discuss things over coffee like civilized people. They have a Brazilian dark roast that looks amazing." Holly stood up, twirling the ends of her peach sundress, and smiling at him.

Camilo followed her toward the bar where a barista with a thin mustache and dyed purple hair was grinding a set of beans. He held up a finger when he saw them arrive at the register.

The scent from the beans made Camilo's stomach turn. There were so many smells—bourbon, chocolate, hazelnut, fruits—and even more rose from the surrounding jars. It was too much.

"I need some air." Camilo could feel the disappointment in Holly's eyes as he headed toward the door.

———

Outside, he leaned against the sliver of wall that hadn't been converted into a massive glass window. There were faint scents on the wind: car exhaust, dust, the pines from the park across the street. None of them bothered Camilo like the coffee.

Perhaps they would one day, when his curse took full effect. An enhanced sense of smell was more of a burden than people knew.

Did my father have the foresight to make his cage odorless?

He must have. Diego Lopez had been a genius.

Perhaps that was why a witch had cursed him.

Diego had originally founded The Morgana Center in an effort to cure his affliction. He'd recruited Julia to be his partner. They'd studied in the same program at Castor's Grove University, and she had both money and connections.

The two made a good team. Diego was the visionary,

Julia the businesswoman. While he focused on his research, expanding The Center's mission to help not just himself but anyone negatively affected by magic, she procured funds, walking a careful line with what information she was able to divulge to investors.

They'd designed the cage together as a precaution. It was a metal box, attached to the rest of the laboratory by a series of rods and a single bridge. Within, Diego was sealed behind a wall of tempered glass, thicker than a horse. He'd wanted them to be able to keep studying him. How else would they find a cure?

Holly was pouting when she joined Camilo on the sidewalk. There was a to-go cup in each of her hands. She held one out for him to take. "Would be nice to have a normal date someday."

"This is a date?" Camilo raised his eyebrows. He reached for the cup, and their fingers brushed.

Holly pulled her hand back, recoiling from his touch.

Camilo didn't blame her. Most people would react the same if they knew what he was.

"This isn't a date," Holly said, wrapping both palms around her own cup. "But we'll go on one someday. When your curse is lifted. That's still the plan, isn't it?"

She was referring to the promise they'd made to one another when he was twelve and she was thirteen. Camilo's curse had been growing stronger and more out of control. He was petrified of losing himself and had gone to Julia's house, planning to beg her to lock him away too.

Holly had seen him first. She'd met him just beyond the wall that marked her family's property. And Camilo had broken down.

That might have been the last time she hugged me without flinching.

They'd both made a vow after that. Camilo swore to find a cure for his condition. Holly promised that, once he did, they would be together.

Nothing had happened that would cause either to rescind their words. At least not that Camilo knew.

"Of course that's still the plan." He smiled, and Holly's expression softened.

"Good. Walk with me around the park? That's at least normal. We can discuss terms then."

Camilo chuckled. He assumed she was joking. "Terms for future dates?"

"For the favor you're asking me."

They crossed the sidewalk, stepped through a gold-painted gate, and entered Founder's Park. Benches and trees lined the circular trail. In the center was a large fountain. Three of the city's founders had been carved into the stone. Camilo had missed too many history classes to recall their names.

Holly remained silent, sipping her coffee as though she needed more information.

Can't she just take my word that I need to see my father and help me? Why do there need to be terms?

Camilo pressed his lips together, trying to hide his annoyance. Perhaps Holly didn't understand the importance of his request.

"There's something your mother isn't telling me." Instead of looking at Holly, Camilo watched a pair of sisters chase one another around the fountain. Their parents shouted at them from one of the benches. "The handcuffs don't work on my dad. And suddenly she's desperate for the dagger. I'd feel a lot better if I could just talk to my father—"

"You can't. Sound doesn't travel through the glass."

Holly stopped walking and gave him a sharp look. "Unless you know the code?"

Camilo stopped too. Only two people had ever known which buttons to press on the strange keypad that unlocked the glass door: Holly's mother and his father. One wouldn't say; the other couldn't.

But Diego had left a clue. At least, Camilo assumed that was what the poem was. He'd found it scribbled in the back of his father's copy of *Dune*. The glass door's strange keypad—which at first glance resembled an oversized scientific calculator with additional symbols—was sketched on the blank page beside it.

The science fiction novel and its clue had shown up three years ago in a box of his father's old things. There had been notebooks with it, full of theories that Camilo didn't understand. His abuela had prayed a decade of the rosary over the papers, then sent them to The Morgana Center. She'd hoped the secret to saving her son would be in there, though it hadn't been enough to make her stay. No one bothered to flip through the well-worn copy of *Dune* to see if it contained anything of use. Camilo found the poem by accident. He hadn't considered that it might be a mistake to share it with Holly. She hadn't been working at The Morgana Center then.

"How did the riddle go?" Holly asked.

"I don't remember." That was a lie. Camilo had it memorized.

I deal in numbers
And half absolutes
Nothing's enclosed
If you flip the truth.
Theirs ends with them

His starts with mine
Do deviations recess
Or follow the line?

It was gibberish to Camilo. He'd never solved it, and he didn't want Holly to either. He wouldn't put it past her to enter the cage alone to try to study his father up close. She was always desperate for ways to prove herself to her mother.

Camilo took the first sip of his coffee. The bitterness turned his stomach. He wanted to spit it onto the grass, but he forced himself to swallow.

"Good, isn't it," Holly said. She wasn't watching his expression, or he'd have assumed she was being sarcastic. Her eyes were on a swallow, perched on a branch above her head. "Have you ever heard of the Western Woodlands?"

That's a change of topic.

Camilo shrugged. He didn't think he had. "Probably just another name for the western edge of Castor's Forest. Why do you ask?"

"Just thinking about the dagger."

Camilo froze as a couple strolled past them, arm in arm. Holly continued to sip her coffee. There was something she was hiding from him too.

She caught his eye and smiled. "I'll sneak you in to see your dad. But I want something as well. You need to follow my mom's plan. I admit I was a bit jealous before. Seeing you with her in the Grover's Gazette threw me for a loop, but...."

Camilo frowned. He and Julia were in the paper?

"...the only way to get the dagger is to work with Kenya. But we need to fix my mother's oversight. The changeling isn't human. She could be a threat to The Morgana Center in the future." Holly stared at him, blue eyes unblinking as though daring Camilo to argue.

He'd learned his lesson last time.

"Seems like a conundrum," Camilo said, shifting the cup in his hand. There was a nervous twitch in his calf. He almost took another sip of coffee without thinking.

"It is," Holly agreed. "Which is why we have to neutralize her."

11

KENYA

Kenya sat on the edge of her bed, eyes squeezed shut.

Attempt number fifteen.

She clenched her muscles, imagined them shrinking and shifting, tried to summon the heat that had burned within her when the dagger twisted in her chest.

Nothing.

When Kenya opened her eyes, she was still a human. Her legs dangled over the edge of the bed, barely covered by the blue shorts she slept in. The soft fabric of her old t-shirt brushed against her skin, and the elastic on her silk bonnet slid up her forehead.

Kenya pulled the night cap off. Another movement pulled the lime green scrunchie from her pineapple curls, letting them poof out around her shoulders. She tossed both bonnet and hair tie toward her drawers. The first landed on top of a container of curling cream, the next bounced off a stuffed Wookie and onto a copy of *The Fifth Season*.

So much for magic powers.

Kenya collapsed onto her bed and stared up at the ceiling.

Fifteen times she'd tried to transform into a cat. Fifteen times she'd failed. Proof that Camilo had been lying.

It didn't surprise Kenya. She was a human, not a cat or any of the strange names he'd called her.

But how do I explain the fire around my feet at the race?

Her phone flashed and buzzed from the side table beside the bed. Kenya rolled onto her stomach, crawled up, and grabbed it.

Lily was texting her. Four messages all in succession. Three were shocked faces, but the last one was a question: *have you seen the Gazette?????*

Of course not. Who reads the newspaper? Kenya pressed a pillow under her chin and propped herself up on her elbows as she typed.

Lily responded immediately with another excited face. A few seconds later, she sent a picture.

Kenya opened it, and her eyes grew wide.

There was a photo of her and Camilo coming out of the alley together.

Why would they put that in the paper?

Kenya sat up and zoomed in on the image so that she could read the article itself. It was a write-up on Saturday's races in the top left corner of the sports section. Most was the usual, a mention of a couple of particularly impressive times and congratulations to the great athletes of Castor's Grove.

Then, in the last paragraph, the tone changed.

A standout among the runners seemed to be Kenya David-son. Her time was recorded at 48 seconds, just shy of the world record. After finishing her race, Ms. Davidson was singled out for drug testing, the results of which have come back invalid leading to speculation among many—

Kenya stopped reading. She looked back at the image of her and Camilo and saw the caption beneath: *Kenya Davidson comes from an alley with an unknown man.*

These bastards are trying to imply that he's a drug dealer.

She grabbed her pillow and screamed into it.

Her phone continued to buzz with messages from Lily.

So, obviously you're not doing drugs. But tell the truth... are you hooking up with your family's lawn guy?

If only it were something that simple.

Kenya thought back to her bizarre conversation with Camilo. He'd said her results would come back invalid *or worse.*

Was this just a coincidence?

Or maybe the paper had made the whole thing up. Kenya hadn't been notified of her test results yet. How could they have known?

She flung her phone onto the bed, muffled the still incoming texts with a pillow, and rushed toward the stairs. Kenya needed to talk to her parents. Her mother was a lawyer. If anyone could handle this, it would be Courtney Davidson. Maybe they could sue the paper for slander or libel or defamation or... something.

Kenya's parents were in the kitchen. She could hear their voices as she ran down the steps.

"Inconclusive, not positive, Courtney," her father's tone was angrier than normal. "I don't know how the news-paper found out, or what they're trying to insinuate, but that means there's a problem with the machines, not our daughter."

Kenya stopped at the final stair, holding onto the banister. Did that mean the results had come through? Why had they been given to her parents?

Because I signed the form and left it with them.

They must have added their personal information and contact details.

"We can't be naïve, Reuben," Courtney snapped. She sounded tired. "Have you ever seen her run that fast? She was just at 51 seconds. How could she have gotten her time down by that much that fast?"

"My daughter would never cheat."

Exactly!

Kenya wanted to run into the kitchen and hug her father. She couldn't believe this was even a debate.

"Then how do you explain the picture?" Courtney's voice was soft, almost apologetic. "I know you like that boy, but what would they have been whispering about in an alleyway right after she was tested? You can't tell me that's not concerning."

Kenya's breath caught. She waited for her dad to defend her. There could be any number of innocent reasons that she might've been talking to Camilo.

Reuben didn't respond.

An uncomfortable silence descended on the Davidsons' house.

Kenya's chest grew tight. She stepped off the stairs and felt the white carpet that decorated most of the bottom floor soft between her toes. The kitchen was only a few steps to her left.

But the desire to talk to her parents was gone.

I'm their child. They're supposed to know me better than that.

Something else that Camilo had said turned in Kenya's

mind. He'd claimed she was an orphan. What reason would he have had to lie about that?

But that would mean that Courtney and Reuben Davidson weren't—

Kenya cut off that thought fast, her chest so tight it hurt to breathe.

I can't have them thinking the worst of me.

She needed an excuse for why she'd been with Camilo, something believable.

The image of Lily's last message, still unanswered, popped into Kenya's mind: *Are you dating your family's lawn guy?*

There's no way that would work.

But it was the best excuse she could think of, certainly better than trying to convince her parents that she'd transformed into a cat and Camilo was chasing the magic dagger that had caused it.

Kenya took a deep breath, a lie starting to form in her mind. She wasn't going to be able to pull this off on her own.

It was Monday morning. Camilo would be finishing up at Mrs. Evans' house.

Kenya raced toward the door.

The sound of her footsteps alerted Doc to her presence. The golden doodle barked and came running from the kitchen.

"Crap," her mother muttered. "Kenya, is that you?"

Her father stuck his head out. "Don't run off. We need to talk."

Kenya ignored them both. She patted Doc's head, opened the door, and ran outside.

The road felt hot beneath her feet. She gritted her teeth, wishing she'd stopped to put on shoes, but Camilo might be leaving soon. There was no sign of him in Mrs. Evan's yard, but his silver truck was still parked in the drive.

Kenya hurried toward the property, across the street and two doors down.

Mrs. Evan's house was identical to the rest in the neighborhood: gray panels, blue roof, white door. However, the property itself was larger, giving the widow an extra few feet of garden. It wasn't enough to warrant twice weekly lawn care, but she'd taken a shining to Camilo.

Kenya spotted him around the side of the house. He was crouched by a garden bed under a window, a small shovel in his hand as he planted a row of pink flowers. Although the sun was already high, it appeared that he'd only just started. His outfit was unusual too— a red polo shirt despite the heat, the same black pouch, and white shorts that had already collected a number of grass and dirt stains. He'd rolled them up, showing off the large muscles of his thighs.

Don't stare. If he notices, it'll make what you're about to ask even weirder.

Camilo looked up as Kenya approached, eyes traveling slowly from her bare feet to the loose curls around her head.

"Cute outfit," he said, the corner of his mouth twitching in a smile. "Big Trekkie?"

Kenya wrapped her arms around her chest as she stopped before him. She'd forgotten that she was still in her pajamas. The over-sized t-shirt featured an illustration of the USS Voyager from *Star Trek*.

As if this whole situation wasn't awkward enough.

"I came to tell you that I'm going to help you," she said.

Camilo sprang from the lawn with surprising speed. His amused smirk had been replaced with a slack-jawed grin of genuine relief. "You're going to work with me to get the dagger?"

"Yes, and you'll help me get into the Olympics," Kenya reminded him since it seemed like she might need help with that aspect of things after all. "But there's one more favor you need to do as well."

"Deal." Camilo didn't hesitate. He stuck his hand out for Kenya to shake.

"Perfect." She'd been afraid that she was going to have to fumble through an explanation and embarrass herself by asking him to be her fake boyfriend. This way, they could skip to the part where her parents thought she was on steroids. "Come with me!"

Kenya grabbed Camilo's hand and pulled him toward her house.

He raised his eyebrows, but he didn't resist. "Should I ask?"

Too late now. You already agreed.

"It'll be easier if you just follow my lead when we get there." A nervous laugh escaped Kenya. "Sorry if it seems weird."

When they reached her house, Kenya flung the door open and dragged Camilo inside.

Her parents were in the living room already, standing by the door. Their posture made it clear that they'd been in the middle of an argument, but they fell silent as their daughter walked in, dressed in her pajamas and pulling their landscaper behind her.

Only Doc seemed excited. He wagged his tail, ran up to Camilo, and immediately began attempting to lick his face.

"Mom, Dad." Kenya grabbed Doc's collar, trying to settle him. She didn't need the goldendoodle to start humping someone and make this whole thing weirder. "You know Camilo."

Her parents exchanged a look. They raised their hands in silent, uncomfortable waves.

Off to a great start.

"Hey Mr. and Mrs. Davidson." Camilo smiled at them. He turned his head and leaned over to whisper in Kenya's ear. "What are you doing? You didn't tell them what happened, did you? Because I swear—"

She elbowed him in the ribs, trying to get him to stay quiet. It hurt her more than it did him, but she was pretty sure Camilo got the message. He'd already agreed to go along with her plan. It wasn't her fault he hadn't checked what it was first.

Kenya wrapped Camilo's arm around her waist and leaned her head on his shoulder. She forced a big, happy smile and swept her left arm to the side.

"Surprise!" Kenya announced. "We're dating!"

12

CAMILO

Camilo stood in the center of the Davidsons' living room, afraid to touch anything. Apart from the kitchen, he'd never been inside the family's house. It was whiter than he'd expected, from the carpet to the walls to the coffee tables and couches. The accents were all in gold.

Upon Kenya's unexpected announcement, her parents had excused themselves to the kitchen under the guise of fetching drinks. But the house was far from soundproof. Their voices floated into the living room.

"The guy who mows our lawn?" Courtney hissed.

"He's a nice boy."

"Then why's he taking her down back alleys?"

Camilo tried to ignore the snippets of conversation. Parental disapproval was nothing new. It wasn't like Julia had ever been fond of his friendship with Holly.

She has good reason though.

"I'm sorry about them," Kenya said, leaning against the couch. "Sometimes I think they forget I'm not still twelve." She kept her arms crossed over her t-shirt, pulling it up enough to reveal a pair of blue cotton shorts beneath. They barely covered her ass, leaving her legs exposed. Running had toned and shaped them with smooth, dark curves.

All his months keeping an eye on Kenya, he'd made a point not to notice her in that way. She was in high school, and more importantly not human.

She's graduated now.

And Camilo was only a year older.

Holly would be furious if she could hear his thoughts.

Camilo made a concentrated effort to keep his eyes focused on the goldendoodle who was licking his hand. Attractive or not, he wasn't interested in Kenya. She was just a means to obtain the dagger.

"And you think having a boyfriend will remind your parents you're an adult?" Camilo guessed, keeping his voice low. "You could've found a real one."

Kenya frowned. "Did you not see the paper this morning?"

"Uh... no?" But Holly had been scowling at a copy of the Grover's Gazette. "Am I in it?"

"Both of us are. Remember the picture that girl, Yasmin, took? They're using that to insinuate that you're selling me drugs."

"Oh please." Normally Camilo wrote off people's suspicions of him as a side-effect of his curse. But that wasn't the kind of leap that magic caused people to make. "No one decent is going to believe that."

"Well, my parents did."

"Oh." Camilo wasn't sure what else to say. That couldn't have been nice for Kenya.

At least Holly's earlier jealousy made sense. She'd seen a photo of him with Kenya in an alley and let her imagination run wild. Camilo was sort of pleased to know that it had bothered her.

A stab of guilt quickly popped that feeling. Was that also why Holly had convinced herself that Kenya was a threat?

Camilo's stomach turned as he glanced at the girl before him, scratching her dog's head with a forced smile. Holly wanted to *neutralize* Kenya. But what exactly did that entail?

Holly hadn't made her request clear, only promised to tell him more soon, and dangled a visit with his father before him like it was a biscuit. Camilo didn't get it.

If she had just asked him for a favor, he would've done it. There was no need for all the games, the trades, the deals. And Holly was hiding something.

"Have you ever heard of the Western Woodlands?" Camilo asked.

Kenya stopped rubbing Doc. Her lips pursed as she thought. "Is that the western part of Castor's Woods?"

That's what I said too, but I don't think it's right.

Doc rubbed his head against Camilo's leg. The golden-doodle's tail was wagging furiously, and he tilted his head back, attempting to speak. The effect was a curious mixture of bark, howl, and grumble.

"He really likes you," Kenya said with a smile. "He doesn't talk to just anyone." She stretched one of her legs, using her toes to scratch the goldendoodle's back.

Camilo's eyes traveled up her calf for a second before he caught himself. He refocused on the panting golden mop of fur before him. Dogs tended to like him. "Well, don't tell him, but I'm more of a cat person."

He realized how that sounded the moment he said it.

Luckily, Kenya didn't. Her head was turned in the direction of the kitchen, a distant look in her eyes. "Once my parents are okay with us dating, it'll give us an excuse to spend time together."

Does she remember that she's not twelve? Kenya spoke like she needed their permission.

"And you can explain all about this *magic*"— she said the word with a hint of sarcasm, like she still thought Camilo might be lying— "dagger, and exactly how you expect me to help you steal it."

Handcuffs, practice, and a lot of luck.

Camilo's hand went to the bag at his side. He wondered if to show them to Kenya now.

How do I explain it to her parents if they see me showing their daughter a pair of handcuffs in the middle of their living room?

Camilo pinched his shirt, pulling the fabric from his chest. He could handle disapproval, but trying to convince the Davidsons that his intentions were innocent would be a new level of embarrassing.

It was too soon to give Kenya the weapon anyway. They couldn't afford to make a mistake. She needed to master her powers before trying to steal the dagger.

Camilo would have to train her.

He was thinking about the best way to do so when Kenya's parents returned, hands full of lemonade.

"Welcome to the family, Cam," Reuben said, clapping him on the shoulder as he passed him a glass. "We're thrilled to have you."

"Yes. Just delighted," Courtney agreed, not quite as convincingly behind her husband. She studied Camilo as she sipped her drink, eyes zeroing in on the stains on his pants, the mud on his shoes, and the soil under his nails.

It was nothing compared to the looks Julia gave him,

the ones she thought he didn't notice. Camilo would much rather be judged for some specks of dirt. He could wash those off.

Curses weren't something you could clean.

"Thanks so much, Mr. and Mrs. Davidson." Camilo gave them his most charming smile. He pulled Kenya toward him and wrapped his arm around her, catching her off guard.

Good. She'd thrown him into this fake relationship without warning. This could be payback.

"I'm so relieved to have your approval because I'm just crazy about your daughter." Camilo may have been laying it on too thick, but Reuben seemed pleased to hear it. "And I'd really love to take her on our first official date tomorrow. There's something I'm just dying for Kenya to see."

13
KENYA

The Spook was not Kenya's idea for a great first date. The old cinema was in a crumbling brick building. A wooden sign above had been adorned with painted rats, monster masks, and cobwebs that looked a bit too realistic. It specialized in replaying classic horror movies.

"Did you tell Camilo how easily you scream at jump scares?" Kenya's dad asked, glancing at her as The Spook came into view.

They were in his jeep, driving down Sylvanwood Avenue. The cinema was only about five miles west of their house. Kenya could have taken a bus, but her father had insisted.

"Yeah, he knows," Kenya lied, tapping her fingers against her purse as she stared at the rat on the sign. It appeared to have blood dripping from its teeth. Gross.

The truth was that, outside of magical daggers, she and Camilo had discussed very little. Kenya didn't even know why he'd suggested meeting at The Spook.

"He must be hoping you'll get nervous and cling to him," Reuben teased, poking his daughter.

Kenya's nose wrinkled as she looked at her father. She had no interest in discussing something like that with him. Even if his assumption was completely wrong.

Unless Camilo actually does—

Nope!

Kenya would not let her thoughts start going in that direction. Not again. She'd already panicked while getting dressed, changing from a low fitting red shirt to a sensible white cardigan then back again before settling on a regular gray tank top. Which was ridiculous. Camilo did not care what she wore or how she styled her hair. The only reason she couldn't just show up in her pajamas and bonnet was because her parents might find that odd.

"You know, your mother is a bit apprehensive about you dating," Reuben said, waiting until he was turning into the parking lot to bring up the issue. "She's worried you'll lose focus. But your running's actually improved since you started seeing him, so once you keep up your training, I think he could be an asset to team Davidson at the Olympics." He said the last few words in the voice of an announcer, and then began to cheer.

Kenya smiled. Her dad was a goofball, but he had no idea how right he was.

If Camilo was telling the truth, he was more than an asset to "Team Davidson". He was their only hope.

Reuben stopped in front of the cinema's entrance. It was a wooden door that had been painted black and splattered with red to mimic blood.

So romantic.

Camilo leaned against the bricks beside the door,

checking through his phone. He wore jeans and a black t-shirt. Over his shoulder was the same pouch that had been affixed to his side since the day of her race.

Kenya grabbed her green hoodie from the back seat and climbed out the car. Her father didn't drive off.

Does he think he needs to watch to make sure I get in safely?

Kenya wanted to bury her face in the hoodie.

Camilo looked up and smiled. "There you are. I missed you."

What?

Before Kenya quite understood, Camilo grabbed her hand and pulled her toward him.

Their faces hovered less than an inch apart. She could see the different shades of brown in his eyes, dark around the edges, then lighter toward the pupil, almost the color of honey. He smelled like the woods again.

Camilo leaned in. His lips coming closer to hers.

Kenya's heart pounded in her chest.

Is he going to—?

She raised her hand and blocked his lips. They felt soft against her palm.

"What are you doing?" she hissed.

"Trying to sell that we're in a relationship," Camilo muttered, seeming surprised by her response. "Your dad is watching."

"Exactly."

Kenya waved to her father to leave, then grabbed Camilo's hand and pulled him into The Spook. A lanky man sat behind a curtained ticket booth in the narrow corridor within.

"You can't kiss me in front of my dad." She couldn't believe she even needed to explain something so simple to her *pretend* boyfriend. "I mean, do you normally make out with girls in front of your parents?"

Camilo stared at her, his lips pressed together, brow furrowed. There was a strange, distant look in his eyes.

"What'll it be?" the ticket attendant asked.

"Sorry." Camilo cleared his throat. His brow relaxed as he paid, but the tightness remained at the corners of his mouth.

Kenya had offended him. Maybe he had the sort of parents who were relaxed about him kissing girls in front of them.

"I mean, all families are different," Kenya said, taking the ticket that the man offered her and hurrying behind Camilo.

He didn't slow for her, moving straight toward the concession stand. There was no line.

Camilo ordered three hot dogs, only looking at Kenya when the boy behind the counter asked what she wanted.

She pursed her lips, scanning the menu. "Another hot dog. Sprite. Oh, and a pack of Starbursts. I can pay."

Kenya pulled a fifty from her purse and began to pass it to the man behind the counter.

Camilo stopped her. "I'm not broke."

"I'm aware." Kenya put the fifty back in her purse, eyeing him in confusion as he paid yet again. "You do the lawns of like everyone in my neighborhood. I assume they give you money."

He walked toward the end of the counter without a response. Their food was being piled onto a tray.

Camilo ripped into the packets of condiments that were in a container to one side. He squeezed lines of ketchup onto all four hot dogs.

Kenya pursed her lips. She liked ketchup. But it was

pretty bold of him not to ask. "I've obviously upset you," she said. "Can you just tell me how?"

"You don't need to worry about my emotional state, Kenya. We're not friends. This is a business arrangement. Mutually beneficial for us both."

He squeezed mustard onto all the hot dogs next.

Kenya grabbed hers before he could add mayonnaise. If this was how Camilo acted as a *business* partner, she was going to make sure they became friends just out of spite.

"Okay, fellow associate," she said. "Do you want to tell me why we're watching a scary movie at a cinema together then?"

A smile tugged on the corner of Camilo's lips. He shook his head.

What a professional response.

Kenya's jaw tightened. "Want to tell me what's in your purse then?" She pointed at the black pouch.

"Handcuffs."

Kenya laughed. Camilo didn't.

Is he serious?

"And why do you have"—she lowered her voice—"*handcuffs?*"

Camilo grinned and leaned closer, whispering the answer in her ear. "Because once you can get them from me, I'll know you're ready to steal the dagger."

———

The small theatre was empty when they entered. Camilo led them up the short flight of steps to the row of red seats at the back. He held the tray with all their food balanced in his hands.

The pouch with the handcuffs swung behind him as he walked. Kenya's eyes followed it.

Why wasn't he guarding it from her? He'd issued a challenge. Did he think she'd forgotten? Or was he trying to make it easy for her?

She reached toward the pouch's zipper.

Camilo stopped in the middle of the aisle. His hand moved faster than should have been possible, and his fingers curled around her wrist. Somehow, he didn't spill any of the food.

"I didn't mean for you to try stealing it today," he said, sounding amused. "You need to have control of your powers first." Camilo dropped her arm and took a seat in the middle of the back row. He placed the tray on the seat beside him.

Kenya sat next to it, arms crossed. "How exactly is transforming into a cat going to help me steal anything out a purse?" She tried to keep the bitterness out of her voice. It was only her first attempt. There would be other opportunities to beat Camilo at his own stupid game.

"Haven't you ever heard of a cat burglar?" Camilo grinned before taking a bite of one of his hot dogs.

Kenya stared at him as he chewed, trying to figure out if he was joking. He must have been.

"There's also your super speed," Camilo said, licking a bit of ketchup off his lips. "That's going to be crucial if you're going to use the handcuffs to trap your keeper. She's an elf. They tend to be annoyingly quick."

Kenya stared at him. There was a lot to unpack there. She focused on the first thing. "I have super speed?"

"How do you think you ran so fast at the track?" Camilo asked, shoving another bite of hot dog into his mouth. "You used magic to enhance your speed."

The fire.

It made sense, but hearing it out loud felt like a blow to Kenya's gut. "So I cheated?"

She glanced at Camilo, hoping he'd say no and tell her that was silly. Magic wasn't the same thing as steroids.

But it's an unfair advantage.

Camilo shrugged.

"Perfect." Kenya crossed her arms and leaned back in her seat. She stared at the screen before her as the first advertisement lit up the display. "So even if I make it to the Olympics, I won't have actually earned it. Can I give these powers back?"

It was a childish comment. She knew the moment she said it. No one got a special ability and then complained.

But it wasn't the powers, it was everything that came with them.

The word *orphan* whispered in the back of Kenya's mind. Images of her parents flashed with it. Courtney and Reuben Davidson had dedicated their lives to their only daughter, whole-heartedly believing that she could be an Olympian.

And she wasn't even theirs.

Kenya's chest grew tight. She turned to Camilo, hoping that he was going to jump in with a criticism of some kind, tell her to grow up, or act like an adult.

He actually looked sympathetic.

Camilo gave her a small, almost apologetic smile. "I don't think it works that way. But if you can control them, you can make sure you don't end up cheating again."

He had a point there.

And Camilo was going to help Kenya compete at the Olympics, so her parents hadn't wasted their lives entirely.

She just needed to treat this new ability like any other skill.

Work hard. Train. Practice.

And her first task was looped around Camilo's shoulder.

"That's not entirely fair." Kenya pointed to the pouch. "The keeper didn't have the dagger tied around her."

"Seriously?" Camilo raised his eyebrows as he turned toward her. "You really want to try steal this today?"

"That's what we're here for, isn't it?"

Camilo snorted. "Fine." He slipped the strap over his shoulder and placed the bag on the seat between them. "We'll play on easy mode."

"Deal!" Kenya agreed, watching as his hand inched away from the pouch. She cracked her knuckles, trying to summon the flames again. "But don't say it doesn't count when I win."

———

Five attempts later, Kenya was feeling less confident.

The movie had started, but she wasn't watching. She wanted to prove that she could control her speed and get the pouch.

But that wasn't possible when Camilo had trapped her wrists.

Kenya grunted and tried to pull her hands free. Camilo held back a laugh at her attempts. It was completely unfair. He was ridiculously strong.

"You don't even need handcuffs," she muttered, clenching her jaw as she tried to break his grip. "You're basically a walking pair."

To her surprise, the comment made Camilo laugh.

Kenya stopped fighting and stared at him. It took a second for her to register why she was so surprised.

I've never heard him laugh.

It was loud and deep and surprisingly infectious.

A smile spread across Kenya's face. She started laughing too. "That wasn't that funny."

"No. I just like hearing that you know I'm winning." He switched his grip so that both her wrists were trapped in his right hand. With his left, he stole one of her starbursts, unwrapped it, and popped it in his mouth.

"That was one of the red," Kenya complained. "Those are the best."

"Obviously. That's why I stole it." Camilo grinned. "Now would you please watch the movie. I paid for this."

"Fine." Kenya had less than zero interest in the slasher flick, but maybe she could trick Camilo into relaxing his grip if she pretended to acquiesce.

Kenya leaned back. On screen, a couple wandered off into a cabin in the woods. There was some bad dialogue and a messy make-out scene. The back of her neck tingled, aware of Camilo's eyes on her as she watched.

Is he thinking about when he tried to kiss me earlier?

Because Kenya wasn't thinking about that. Or his strangely pretty lips. Not even a little bit.

The scene finally ended when the blonde starlet on screen went into the bathroom. She splashed water on her face and looked into the mirror.

A masked man appeared behind her.

Kenya screamed.

Or at least, she started to.

Her voice stuck. Flames rose from her chest and wrapped around her body. Her muscles burned and twisted.

And then her scream became a mewl.

She dropped onto the seat, tail rising in the air. Feeling it swish behind her felt unnatural. Kenya spun to bat at it with her paws.

Camilo scooped her up by the scruff of her neck. His face looked massive before her.

He grinned. "Figures a bit of fear would trigger your transformation. Why else would the term be scaredy-cat?"

14

CAMILO

The rest of the week, Camilo split his time into three parts.

Mornings for sleep. Afternoons for training Kenya.

And at night, he watched her bedroom window, turning away whenever she danced into view, often scantily clad and texting. One time, she'd been talking into a stuffed Wookie like an announcer.

It was cute. Not that Camilo thought so, obviously, but someone else might have. He wasn't paying attention to the changeling. He was waiting for the keeper.

Camilo had learned his lesson. He wouldn't attack out of nowhere. But he had the handcuffs now. If an opportunity arose, how could he not take it?

It wasn't like Kenya's training was progressing.

In the changeling's defense, conditions weren't ideal. The usually desolate Spook was invaded by a group of theater students. Kenya's parents banned him from her room. And there was no public space in Castor's Grove that hadn't been discovered by obnoxious preteens, worn out mothers, or hormone-fueled couples.

Any magical training session was frequently interrupted, and Kenya's progress was slow. Camilo may have guessed how to trigger her transformation quickly, but it hadn't proven the advantage he'd hoped.

Her shifting was tied to her emotion. When she was afraid, she transformed into a cat. Once her nerves settled, she relaxed into human form. Kenya could summon her speed with enough determination. But her control was lacking, and prolonged usage resulted in sharp headaches.

It didn't exactly inspire confidence.

But Camilo needed her to be ready when the keeper returned. He needed that dagger.

So he was forced to do the unthinkable—invite Kenya to his house.

Julia would not be impressed. Neither would Holly.

But Camilo had been careful. He'd hidden anything that could connect him to The Morgana Center in the compartment of his truck. There hadn't been much.

Anyway, he doubted that Kenya would explore the apartment. She always focused on stealing the handcuffs.

There was a knock on his door.

Camilo closed his eyes, said a silent prayer, and slid back the dead bolt.

Kenya stood in the corridor. Her smile was a little too big, eyes a little too excited. There was a large orange cat in her hands— Pumpkin. Technically, he belonged to Mrs. Donovan, whose apartment was two doors down. But Pumpkin was an equal-opportunist pet. He prowled the hall and snuggled whoever was willing to give him food. That meant he spent almost as much time at Camilo's apartment as he did his own.

"I found my twin." Kenya held him up to her face. "See the resemblance?"

Currently, there was little. But transformed, Kenya did bear a certain resemblance to a smaller Pumpkin, though with a few more white splashes. Camilo had noticed the similarity at The Spook.

"No. He's much cuter." Camilo took Pumpkin from Kenya. "Though it's nice to know you're starting to see yourself as a cat."

She wrinkled her nose in objection.

Camilo sighed. Magic functioned on faith. Until Kenya believed, her shifting wouldn't progress.

He rested Pumpkin onto the floor and the cat's fluffy tail vanished into the apartment.

"You going to let me in too?" Kenya asked "Or are we going to practice out here?"

If only that were an option.

Camilo stifled a sigh and stepped aside. "Don't touch anything."

"So this is the home of the mysterious Camilo Lopez." Kenya pulled her sneakers off and rested them beside his mat. He couldn't help but notice the lime green laces. She seemed to think the color needed to be present on all her shoes.

Kenya walked across the linoleum floor in a pair of socks. Her denim shorts highlighted her legs, and she'd tied a knot in the center of her white t-shirt so that a hint of her midriff was exposed. Dark curls bounced above her shoulders.

Camilo's eyes took her in. It was getting increasingly difficult to convince himself that she wasn't attractive.

She's a shifter. One of them. I can't forget that.

This was just a temporary alliance. Once Camilo had

the dagger, they'd go their separate ways. Kenya to the Olympics, hopefully, and him—

I'll have my father back.

He'd also finally get a proper date with Holly.

"I didn't expect you to be such a fan of pink," Kenya said, turning around the room, a smile spreading across her face.

Camilo's eyes darted around the familiar space: the blanket tossed over the old gray couch; the crocheted doilies on the coffee table; the paintings of flowers hanging from the walls. All pink. "My abuela decorated it."

"You live with your grandmother?"

"No, she moved to Spain after my abuelo died."

Camilo had been sixteen. She'd begged him to come with her, convinced that prayer and ritual could keep his curse at bay. But even if praying a daily decade of the rosary were enough to cure him, it would have made no difference. His father was here.

I won't abandon him. I'll save us both.

Even if Julia tried to keep Camilo away.

"Interesting," Kenya said, eyes narrowing as she studied him. "You'll have to tell us all about her at dinner on Tuesday. My parents have a million questions about you. And your family."

Camilo got the impression that it wasn't just Kenya's *parents* who were curious. But there were few topics he enjoyed discussing less.

"Gave up on ever getting these?" He pulled the strap of the black pouch over his shoulder and held it up in the air, trying to refocus Kenya's attention. Every other session, she'd rushed for the handcuffs straight away. Go figure she'd choose today to lose her competitive edge.

"No rush. My parents think I'm with Lily." Kenya's eyes

landed on a row of shelves in the corner of the room that displayed a variety of tchotchkes and keepsakes. "Is that a Lego version of the Millennium Falcon?" She ran forward, lifted the model and turned to him grinning. "Are you secretly a nerd?"

Camilo's jaw clenched. Hadn't he specifically told her not to touch anything?

"Careful with that." Camilo had made the model with his father when he was five, just before the curse had progressed and made such things impossible. He hurried forward, took the ship from her hands, and returned it to its proper place.

None of the blocks had been disturbed. Camilo breathed a sigh of relief.

The scent of magic—warm, spicy, and fresh—tickled his nostrils.

His head turned just in time to see the red and blue energy swirling around Kenya's hand.

She hadn't lost her competitive edge at all. Her interest in his belongings had been a ruse to catch him off guard.

Camilo didn't know if to be annoyed or impressed.

He caught Kenya's wrist just as her fingers brushed the pouch and redirected her force.

Thanks to her speed, the result was that Kenya was thrown onto the couch, her legs up in the air.

"But I— How did you—?" The frustration sizzled in her voice. Kenya didn't take losing well.

Camilo laughed while she pushed herself up right. She gave an annoyed pout for a moment before joining in. He liked the sound. It made him feel lighter.

He'd turned Kenya's training into a game because he knew how competitive she was. But Camilo would be lying if he said he wasn't enjoying it as well. Part of it was the fact that he kept winning. But it was also... fun?

Camilo couldn't remember the last time he'd had fun.

An old photograph on the shelf caught his eye: his parents on their wedding day.

The laughter died on Camilo's lips. His shoulders grew tight, and his stomach turned. What was he doing?

In the photograph, there was a slight bulge beneath his mother's dress, a sign that Camilo was already growing within. Diego's hand hovered protectively over his new wife's stomach, eyes brimming with pride behind thick square frames. They were all smiles for the camera.

They wouldn't have been so happy if they knew the fate that awaited them.

His mother had died from complications with pregnancy, her body unable to support triplets. His father kept his curse at bay only four more years. Now, he was a prisoner in a cage he'd designed.

What right did Camilo have to feel happy?

He was supposed to be saving his father. Not laughing because Kenya couldn't get handcuffs. His mother was still dead; his father still trapped. Camilo had done nothing to fix anything. He didn't deserve to be having fun.

Camilo's hands curled into fists. His shoulders trembled. He wasn't sure if he wanted to cry or scream, but either way, he needed to get control before he clenched the wrong muscle.

"Camilo?"

The sound of his name, soft and tender, barely a whisper on Kenya's lips sent a sudden shiver down his spine.

He hadn't noticed her rise from the couch. But now, she was right beside him.

Her hand brushed against his shoulder.

Camilo tensed. She was going after the pouch. He wasn't going to be fooled again.

Hand ready to block her, he turned.

"Those are your parents you're looking at, aren't they?" she phrased it like a question, but it was obvious she'd already deduced as much.

Clever. See your opponent in a weak moment and pounce.

Kenya was more ruthless than he'd realized.

"What happened to them?" she asked.

"Mum's dead. Dad's sick." Camilo shrugged, trying to disguise the quiver in his voice. He wasn't supposed to tell her about himself. But he couldn't just invent some happy make-believe life where his parents were on holiday in Madrid.

He focused his attention on Kenya's hands, waiting for the telltale flames that would show she was about to strike.

She raised both arms.

New approach.

Kenya usually only came at him with one hand, and she normally kept it low. They were rising too high now.

Was she aiming for the strap by his shoulder? And why wasn't she using her speed?

"I'm so sorry, Cam." Kenya's arms wrapped around his neck. She pulled herself toward him, and the warmth of her body pressed against his. He caught a whiff of the curious scent, like cinnamon and ginger, that lingered after she'd worked her magic.

Is she hugging me?

Camilo's hands hovered by the pouch, still anticipating another trick. No one had hugged him since he was a child. Even his grandmother had been too afraid after puberty hit.

But Kenya didn't know about any of that. She had no

idea that Camilo was something to fear. And this wasn't a trap.

He raised his arms, stiff and awkward. They hovered just above her back for a second as he contemplated what to do.

Then, shoulders suddenly heavy, Camilo slumped forward, collapsing into Kenya's embrace.

15
CAMILO

The next two days Kenya visited his apartment and attempted to steal the handcuffs. She wanted to control her super-speed. Her shifting was a different matter.

I'm a human, not a cat. Her voice repeated in his mind. *It feels weird having a tail. Anyway, how does that help me steal a dagger?*

Admittedly, Camilo didn't think Kenya's shifting was crucial for his purposes. But he knew the importance of being able to control magical transformations. It would be a disservice to let her ignore that aspect of her abilities.

Even if she wanted to.

Unfortunately, to convince Kenya to practice shifting, Camilo had to bribe her with answers about the items in his home.

On Sunday, she asked about the Millennium Falcon, then the many science trophies: gold, shining, and burnished. They were displayed on the bottom row of shelves. Diego's name was on all of them. He'd been a genius, a child prodigy. Abuela had begged God for a brilliant son, and from the moment she held him in her arms, she knew that her prayers had been answered.

Monday, Kenya searched the kitchen and discovered a recipe book. The pages were discolored, and instructions had been scrawled and edited as though there'd been a war between two chefs. Originally, it had belonged to Camilo's mother. She'd compiled it while pregnant, filling pages with meals she remembered from her childhood in Mexico. But after she'd passed, his abuela had been kind enough to modify and enhance the recipes, even adding a few traditional Spanish meals to the binder.

Unfortunately, Camilo could make none of them. His childhood had been focused on church and prayer, not learning to cook. He let that truth slip to Kenya without thinking.

He let a lot of truths slip.

Camilo was becoming almost comfortable around Kenya. It was very disconcerting.

He blamed it on her laugh.

There was something about the way Kenya's eyes grew wide and her lips pursed that warned Camilo it was coming. Whatever stress had been rising within him, tightening his shoulders and squeezing his chest, began to dissipate. The corners of his mouth twitched. He tried to keep his expression indifferent, but his smile always spread a fraction of a second too soon, already anticipating her response.

Kenya would throw her head back and laugh, loud and unashamed. It filled the small apartment, the happiest sound the walls had heard since Diego left.

Camilo was powerless in the face of such joy. It was impossible not to join in.

By Tuesday, he was looking forward to the moment she

expended her energy and was forced to curl up on his couch, bare legs tucked beneath her, and watch old horror movies with him. He liked the way her scream got squashed into a squeak and how her magic filled the room with the scent of warm spices as she transformed.

Camilo leaned against the wall beside his front door. He kept half an eye on Kenya, rubbing her eyes beside the couch.

She'd been trying to steal the handcuffs for over an hour. Using her magic must have taken its toll.

"Give up?" Camilo suggested, turning the pouch in his hands. A glint of dark metal flashed at him from within.

The zipper's broken.

Kenya must've gotten closer to it than he realized. Or perhaps it was his own strength that had knocked it off earlier.

Camilo didn't like the metal winking at him. It made him feel cold, wrong. He tried to press the silver edges of the zipper's teeth back together.

There was a flash of light.

Camilo's head snapped up.

It was his phone, resting on the corner of the coffee table. A message had come through, and the screen had lit up. Kenya was staring at it.

"Who's Holly?"

Shit.

How had Camilo been so careless?

I've gotten too comfortable the past few days.

The screen was locked, so that the message itself wasn't displayed. But Kenya seeing Holly's name was already more than Camilo would have liked.

"Friend," he mumbled, stepping forward to grab his phone and slip it into his pocket. Clutching the top of the pouch to keep it closed, he dangled the challenge in front of Kenya's face. "You coming for these or what?"

"My head's going to explode if I keep trying." Her voice was odd, flat. She must've really overdone it.

"Movie time then?" Camilo suggested. He dropped onto the couch, hoping she'd join him. His hand reached for the television remote.

With the last burst of her speed, Kenya grabbed it. She leaned against the arm of the couch, clutching the remote to her loose green crop top. "I have questions. Do you want to respond to Holly first?"

Camilo's shoulders tightened. He and Kenya locked eyes.

It would be easy to take out his phone, type a message, and return it to his pocket. Camilo was fast. Even if Kenya tried, she wouldn't be able to see.

But why was Holly messaging? Had she figured out a way to *neutralize* Kenya?

"I don't want to read it right now," Camilo admitted, a familiar weight sinking him into the couch. The past week with Kenya, it had been easy to compartmentalize. The Morgana Center, his curse, Holly—they were all hidden in his car. He didn't need to think about them or consider how much he was hiding from her.

I don't owe Kenya anything. She's a shifter, a Castor—one of them.

His insistence did little to soothe the guilt.

Kenya stared at the remote, twisting it in her hands for a moment before she giggled. It was strange and high-pitched, not her usual laugh. "She's your girlfriend, isn't she? You can tell me. It's not weird. I know we're not actually together. We're just pretending for my parents."

Camilo ran his hand over the top of his head. His hair

would need buzzing soon. The curls were longer than he liked. "Holly's not my girlfriend."

"But you like her," Kenya guessed, turning her body so that her socks were on the couch cushions.

Camilo's eyes flicked to the curves of her calves.

She's not a human. Not a human.

Kenya took his silence for admission. She gave another nervous giggle. "Why haven't you asked her out?"

Camilo's jaw clenched. He couldn't think of a lie. "Because I'm not in a position to date anyone right now."

"Huh." Kenya tapped her heel against the cushion. "That why you need the dagger?"

Camilo's muscles grew so tight, he was worried they might start to spasm. This was not a line of questioning he liked.

"Forget about practicing your shifting," he growled. "We're done for today."

Kenya didn't budge. "Are you a Castor too?"

The question was like a slap across his face. He felt the cold metal of the handcuffs, burning through the leather pouch, sending a cold chill through his fingers.

"Of course not." His voice was rougher than he intended.

"Okay." Kenya hopped off the couch. Camilo hoped she was heading to the door, but she stopped before the shelves and lifted the model of the Millennium Falcon. She raised it above her head, and—"Oops."

The Lego ship slipped from Kenya's fingers.

Camilo forgot about holding the pouch closed. With a single leap, he flung himself across the room.

Something small and silver fell to the ground. The light *ting* as it tapped the floor barely registered.

Camilo landed on his stomach, the handcuffs beneath,

digging into his abdomen. He didn't care. All that mattered was that he'd caught the model just before it shattered on the floor.

"Knew it."

He looked up to see Kenya grinning.

"Regular people don't have reflexes like that." She crouched down so that their faces were more level. "You're like me."

Camilo's jaw tightened as he saw the smirk on Kenya's face. She'd interrogated him about Holly, almost broken one of his most treasured belongings, and now she was accusing him of not being human?

It was too much.

He stood and returned the Millennium Falcon to its place of pride on the top of the shelves, arms trembling. "Get out, Kenya."

"Come on, I just want to know what you are? Can you transform too?"

Camilo's shoulders tensed. He closed his eyes. Memories flashed across the back of his lids.

A wooden bar clamped in his mouth; cords dug into his wrists; buckets of ice rained on his chest, trying to keep the burning in his muscles at bay. His grandmother made the sign of the cross and cried before an image of the blessed virgin. His father mutated until he was covered in hair, yellow eyes bulging, face twisting so that it was half-human, half-beast.

And there were Julia's eyes, staring at Camilo as she pulled his father away, and he felt the rage of the curse boiling in his stomach for the first time.

"I'm not like you, Kenya." His eyes snapped open, and his hands curled into fists. "I'm not some weird species."

The growl in his voice betrayed the lie, but he forced himself to believe it. "I'm human."

Water rose in the corner of Kenya's eyes. Her mouth tightened. "Well, I'd hate to force you to spend any more time with a *weird speci*es."

She turned on her heels, opened the door, and slammed it behind her.

Hostia!

Camilo collapsed to his knees, shaking.

"I'm human," he repeated the mantra over and over, fighting the heat rising in his veins. His skin rippled, his teeth burned, fur threatened to erupt. "I *am* human."

Which was why he was going to give Holly whatever it was she wanted.

16

CAMILO

"You're late," Camilo said, staring at a large flower shaped clock above the counter. The long yellow hand pointed to the three. He'd asked Holly to meet him fifteen minutes ago. "I'm supposed to be meeting Kenya's parents for dinner now."

"So you'll run." Holly shrugged, unconcerned as she stepped into the cramped entry to the flower shop. She shivered, rubbing her hands over her exposed arms. "Why'd you ask to meet here? It's freezing."

Camilo didn't have a jacket to offer. He shifted the brown paper wrapped bouquet in his hands. If Holly had arrived earlier, he could have purchased the flowers after she'd left.

"Oh. Are those for her?" The faintest hint of hurt cracked through Holly's voice. Or maybe it was the cold.

"We don't have to talk in here," Camilo offered. "You can walk with me to the restaurant." Kenya's family would be inside by now. There'd be no chance of them spotting him with another girl.

Holly stood still, blocking the door. "You're really going all out for her. You've never bought me flowers."

"I used to pick them for you all the time when we were kids."

"That's different. I picked some for you too, and those were free. This took effort."

"I need to convince her parents." Camilo rubbed the back of his neck, elbow hitting the wall as he raised his arm. The truth was that he hadn't purchased the bouquet solely to impress Mr. and Mrs. Davidson. He owed Kenya an apology for what he'd said to her in his apartment.

And maybe for whatever I'm about to agree to do.

Camilo's stomach turned.

"I'll buy you a bouquet later," he offered, gesturing to the door with his chin.

"How about now?" In a single step, Holly reached the counter and tapped the bell.

"No, I'm already late. And I thought you wanted to discuss—"

Behind the counter, a frosted glass door swung open releasing a wave of icy air and an explosion of floral scents. The florist, Olive, stepped out, adjusting a pair of gold framed lenses that perched on the tip of her nose. She patted a few gray strands back into her bun and offered them a coral-lipped smile. "Still here, Mr. Lopez?" Her eyes landed on Holly, smiling before the counter. "And this must be the girl you're purchasing flowers for."

"Yes," Holly lied faster than Camilo, slipping her hand into his with only the slightest wince. "But we'd love to purchase another bouquet for my mom."

"Certainly." Olive's smile grew bigger. She opened the top of the counter, inviting them through. "You can come into the icebox and choose what you'd like. More green?"

"I was thinking red."

Camilo glanced at the clock. He should argue. But Holly's hand was soft in his, a wicked smile playing across her lips as though the two of them shared some brilliant secret. When she pulled him forward, Camilo didn't resist.

The icebox referred to the massive refrigerated section where the cut flowers lived to extend their lifespan. Arrays of colorful roses, sweet gardenias, and bright bunches of hyacinth bloomed in buckets. A symphony of floral scents washed over Camilo like he'd taken a dip in a perfume sea.

"Choose what you'd like. I trust Mr. Lopez to remove them carefully." Olive winked. "I'll ring you up outside when you're ready."

She returned to a corner of the icebox where she was unpacking a box of delicately wrapped orchids.

Holly's teeth chattered as she walked down the first aisle of flowers. Her hand slid from Camilo's once Olive was out of sight, and she pressed her fingers beneath her arms. "You can't manage in a coffee shop, but you can manage here?"

"I'm breathing through my mouth." Plus, floral scents tended to be soft and sweet. Coffee had a bitterness his nose couldn't abide. But Camilo didn't have time to argue about the effects of different smells. "Why are we here, Holly?"

"To purchase flowers." She stopped before a bucket of red peonies. "Roses are too cliché. Let's get some of these instead. What are they?"

Camilo pulled a red peony from the collection. "You said you'd let me in to see my dad if I got you something from Kenya. What is it?"

She'd been reluctant to say on the phone, claiming it would be safer to discuss in person. Camilo had suggested a variety of times that wouldn't have interfered with his dinner plans. But Holly was insistent.

She knew about the dinner. Does she want me to be late?

Probably. Holly didn't want him making a good impression with the Davidsons.

"Three of these as well." Holly pointed at the red tulips.

"You're wasting time." Camilo ground his teeth as he retrieved them, trying to hide his annoyance. He should be happy Holly was jealous. It would've stung more if she'd been indifferent to his fake relationship.

"So leave if you're in such a rush."

Camilo spun the last tulip between his fingers, careful not to crush the stem. They both knew he wouldn't do that. "When have I ever left you when you said you wanted to talk?" He passed her the flowers.

Holly smiled as she took them, staring at the petals. "I want Kenya's blood."

Camilo inhaled too deeply, until the smell filled him. He coughed, choking on the scent of flowers. "Pardon?"

"Kenya's blood. I need it if I'm going to neutralize her. She has to give some to be tested anyway, doesn't she?"

When Holly phrased it that way, it sounded simple. Camilo had always intended to steal the blood sample that Kenya provided to the US Anti-Doping Agency, so he could replace it with a human one.

But it had been over a week, and no official had come to collect a new sample of Kenya's blood. It shouldn't have taken so long. Something was up.

"No one's coming to test her again," Camilo said. His chest tightened as he admitted it. He'd been denying it to himself the past few days, but saying it aloud made it real. How was he going to tell Kenya that he couldn't keep his part in their deal? It would crush her to learn that the Olympics was forever out of reach.

"So?" Holly traced her finger along the petal of a red chrysanthemum. Suddenly, her choice in color seemed more poignant. "Slice her with a claw and collect a few drops of blood on a paper towel." She laughed.

Camilo didn't. "You want me to hurt her?"

Holly sighed. "We're talking about a pin prick. I don't need a lot. Just enough to inspect her DNA."

"Why?"

Holly plucked three of the chrysanthemums loose, damaging one of the stems in the process. Her fingers tightened around her red bouquet.

What answer did Camilo want? He already knew what she'd say.

To neutralize her.

But what did that mean?

"Do you need more information?" Holly asked, lower lip pressing into a pout above the flowers. "You should trust me."

She was right. Camilo rubbed the back of his head. He might've apologized if Holly had stopped there.

But she didn't.

And her next remark sounded like a threat.

"And getting me a sample of Kenya's blood might be your only chance to see your dad again."

17
KENYA

Kenya crossed and uncrossed her legs, pulling down the tight red fabric of her dress as a server filled their glasses with water. Her eyes flicked from her mother, turning the gold embossed pages of the menu, to her father, cleaning his glasses on the edge of a blue button-down shirt, to the wooden door. It opened, and Kenya's heart stopped.

A couple with a round-cheeked toddler stepped in. A hostess in a red vest stepped from behind a podium to show them to an empty table. No one else followed them into the restaurant.

He's not coming.

Kenya twisted her phone between her fingers, keeping it out of her parents' sight beneath the table. She fought the urge to unlock the screen, and text her frustration at Camilo. What would be the use? He hadn't responded to the last three.

Screw it.

The temptation was too great. Kenya's fingers flashed across her phone as she composed her message.

Thanks for ditching me. So much for our deal.

No, that wasn't right. It wasn't only dinner that Kenya was upset about. She deleted the message and tried again.

Sorry I'm some weird species and not perfect like Holly.

She definitely couldn't send that one.

Her thumb tapped furiously, erasing each letter. No need to admit that there was a hint of jealousy underpinning her annoyance.

The phone buzzed in her hand as a message came through. Then another, and another. A couple at a nearby table cut their eyes toward Kenya. The tone cut through the soft flute music and chatter of the restaurant.

Kenya hurried to silence her phone as the messages continued. She didn't recognize the number.

Is it Holly?

It was a ridiculous thought. Camilo wasn't going to be talking to his crush about his fake relationship.

Kenya opened the barrage of messages. They were from someone who introduced themselves as Yasmin Gul. The name was vaguely familiar, but the last message was several paragraphs long. Kenya didn't have time to read that now.

"I trust that's Camilo with an explanation for his lack of punctuality."

Her mother's voice forced Kenya to look up from her phone.

Courtney made no effort to conceal her judgment. She tapped her sky-blue nails against the menu, staring at her daughter with an eyebrow raised. Tardiness was one of her pet peeves.

She's going to be even less impressed when she hears Camilo's not coming.

Kenya needed to stop procrastinating and tell her

parents that her boyfriend had ditched her. She opened her mouth, took a deep breath, and announced, "We should go ahead and order. I'll have a mango lassi."

I'm pathetic.

Her mother's lips pursed, and her nails continued tapping. She looked like she wanted to ask more, but Reuben rested his hand on hers.

"Sounds great, my little miracle." He waved to the waiter.

Kenya hid her face behind her menu It was another truth she couldn't face, another secret festering in her chest, burning in her brain like that awful word *orphan*.

Her head snapped back to her phone. She typed another message.

Sorry, I pushed you to talk.

Kenya was about to hit send when the restaurant door opened.

Camilo stepped inside.

He'd dressed up for the occasion, trading his shorts and t-shirts for a gray tie and red button-down. He wore long dress slacks that still managed to stretch too tight over his thighs. The black pouch with the handcuffs hung across his shoulder. There was a bouquet of flowers in his hand.

Kenya's heart skipped in her chest.

No, stop that. We're mad at him!

The past week Kenya had gotten swept up in the fantasy of her lie. Camilo's veil of indifference hid someone kind and competitive, who recognized every *Star Trek* reference she made, who snuggled his neighbor's cat under his grandmother's pink blanket, who trembled whenever her fingers brushed his skin. Combined with his soft lips and muscular thighs, what girl wouldn't have developed a crush?

Today had slapped her back to reality.

Camilo liked someone else. His interest in Kenya was purely selfish. They weren't together. They weren't even friends. He thought she was weird.

"I am so sorry for being late, Mr. and Mrs. Davidson." Camilo had mastered the puppy-dog look. His eyes were wide and apologetic as he slipped into the vacant seat. "It took me ages to find the right ones. Here, these are for you."

He offered the bouquet to Kenya. She saw the flowers properly for the first time. Their petals curled and frilled like coral from the ocean floor. But that wasn't their most striking quality.

"They're green." It was an effort not to smile as she accepted the flowers. "That's my favorite color."

"I know."

Liar. Kenya had never told him that. He'd just gotten lucky.

But her parents were impressed. Reuben clapped Camilo on the shoulder and commended his efforts. Courtney caught her daughter's eye and smiled, nodding in begrudging approval of the gift.

Kenya clutched the flowers to her chest. Were they an apology for earlier or just an act for her parents' benefit?

Camilo might manage to win them over even after being late.

But was that a good thing?

This relationship is becoming too real.

If Kenya couldn't remember that it was a lie, she was going to get seriously hurt.

18

CAMILO

Camilo's eyes fluttered over the knife beside Kenya's plate. What were the chances she'd cut herself during dinner?

He ran his thumb over the cutlery to his right. Dull. There went that wish.

"Ready to order?" Reuben asked from across the table.

Damn it. Why had Holly chosen right before dinner to make her request? The purpose was to impress Kenya's parents. Given that Camilo wouldn't be helping her with the Olympics, the least he could do was put some effort into their fake relationship.

"Hard to decide. It all looks so amazing." Camilo plastered a smile onto his face as he turned his attention to the menu. He'd never eaten Indian food before. His grandparents were both too proud of their own cultures.

"The sooner you decide, the sooner we can see who's faster, right, my miracle?" Reuben said, winking at Kenya as his hand slipped into the lining of his jacket.

Courtney groaned, hiding her face behind her menu. "Don't take that thing out in front of people."

The item in question appeared to be an old calculator.

"What?" Reuben pushed his wife's plastic shield down to offer a goofy grin. "Old Cassio is my lucky charm. I had him on me when we met, I'll keep him on me always. Anyway, it's tradition. In fact..." He turned to Camilo. "Would you care to join our competition, Mr. Lopez?"

Camilo glanced at Kenya. She didn't notice. Her eyes were glued to the menu, fingers twitching on her lap.

Clearly, she would be no help.

"What competition?" Camilo asked Reuben.

"Race against the calculator." Kenya's father grinned as though this explained everything.

Courtney sighed and leaned back in her chair. "Kenya tries to tally the items we're ordering before Reuben can add them with the calculator. He's been doing it with her since she was little. Hazard of having a math teacher as a father, I assume."

And another reason she's so competitive.

Kenya's concentration made sense.

"Are you adding already?" Camilo accused her, covering the prices with his hand.

Kenya's smile was guilty. "Only practicing. I don't know what everyone's ordering."

"But you can guess," Reuben accused, laughing as he wagged a finger at his daughter. "Camilo, you're the only wild card in this equation. Order something that will throw her off. What'll it be?"

Camilo called the name of the first item that mentioned lamb. The Davidsons each stated their orders aloud, more complicated than his own, and then Kenya and Reuben got to work, the former using her fingers to keep track while the latter tapped numbers methodically.

A lucky calculator.

Camilo's father would have loved that.

Is this what my life would have been like were it not for the curse?

Camilo hadn't inherited his father's genius. His mental arithmetic was atrocious. Maybe that would've been different if Diego had studied with him as a child, helped him create model volcanoes, turned math into a game. Instead, his lessons had been abuelo's physical training and abuela's prayers.

Something tightened in Camilo's chest. He stared at the menu, pretending to tally the prices, though he'd long forgotten half the items the Davidsons named. Even when the waiter arrived, and Courtney repeated the order to him, the words washed over Camilo without registering.

The lock on his father's prison was a calculator of some sort.

I deal in numbers and half absolutes...

Why had Holly said it was the last time he might see his father?

"Got it!" Kenya exclaimed, raising her arms and almost hitting the innocent waiter, attempting to fill her glass. She blurted out a number, and turned to Camilo with a massive grin.

Was any contest too trivial for her to delight in winning?

"Oh, yeah, I got that too." Camilo smiled and passed his menu to the waiter.

"Then you're both correct," Reuben said. "But Kenya wins by a hair. And the crowd goes wild!" He followed up his announcement with a cheer, much to his wife's embarrassment.

Camilo joined in.

Kenya's eyes caught his. She smiled, and tucked a curl behind her ear. Her finger trailed over the rim of her glass, now filled with water. The skin on her wrist was lighter, making the green veins visible.

The cost of admission to see his father. But how did he get it? And what would Holly—

"Dad!" Kenya's eyes widened, and her head snapped toward her father. "He doesn't have to answer that."

Reuben had asked a question. Camilo had missed it.

Dammit.

He needed to focus.

"Come on." Reuben laughed. "I have to make sure he's with my incredible daughter for the right reasons. What's wrong with asking which of your qualities drew him to you?"

Camilo frowned. He hadn't expected a question like that, and definitely before their food had even arrived. But he knew the answer. "Her laugh. It's contagious."

The Davidsons fell silent, eyes all on him as though they expected more.

Camilo cleared his throat, fighting the urge to tug at his collar. Hadn't that answer already been too honest?

"She's determined." Camilo addressed his compliments to his dinner plate. "More than a bit of a nerd. And beautiful, of course. I always feel happier when I'm with her. Even when I don't want to."

He was only saying all this to please her parents. But that didn't mean, it wasn't the truth.

Camilo's eyes betrayed him, flicking to Kenya against his wishes, catching sight of her thick curls and poorly concealed smile.

Why did she have to be so lovely?

We're not friends. She isn't human. I owe her nothing.

Maybe if he kept repeating it, Camilo could force it to be true.

19
KENYA

The table was filled with an assortment of chicken, lamb, and vegetable curries. A platter of garlic naan rested in the center of the table for them to share. Kenya dipped the bread into the golden-brown liquid in her bowl, watching Camilo throughout the meal.

He was distracted. His eyes kept focusing on inanimate objects—Kenya's glass, an elephant statue across the room, the spoon in his own hand—for a fraction of a second too long. There was a pause before he answered her parents' questions or laughed at their jokes.

Not that they'd noticed. Kenya's parents seemed quite impressed with Camilo. And why wouldn't they be? All of his answers were exactly what they wanted to hear.

It was torture.

Why did Camilo have to be so good an actor?

The compliments he'd given her earlier kept swimming in her head. Did he really like her laugh? Kenya had always been told it was too loud. Why had he chosen that of all things to focus on?

And he called me beautiful.

Kenya's fingers twisted around the cloth napkin on her lap, dusting any crumbs from her hands.

It wasn't just that Camilo had called her beautiful. That was an obvious compliment to offer if you wanted to pretend. It was how he'd glanced at her afterward.

What had that expression been? Embarrassment? Guilt? Did it matter? Was it a sign that he meant it? Or just further proof of his shockingly good acting skills?

Kenya wanted to shred the napkin. She'd been thinking about this for almost the entire meal. It was going to drive her insane.

This farce has to end.

Kenya's feelings for Camilo were getting too complicated and distracting her from her goal.

I get the dagger. He helps me fake the test results for the Olympics.

There was one way to speed the process along.

Dessert arrived. Kenya sunk her spoon into the mango ice cream. A bit dropped onto her napkin, but she hardly noticed. Her eyes were on the pouch by Camilo's hip.

He leaned forward, and a glint of dark metal flashed from within. The bag wasn't zipped.

Around the table, the topic of conversation switched to books. Camilo made the mistake of mentioning *Dune*.

Kenya's father latched onto it. He could talk about the sci-fi series for a shocking amount of time. Her mother knew better than to stay to listen. She excused herself to use the restroom.

Camilo was too polite to know better. He was trying to listen. Rookie mistake.

This is my chance.

Kenya dropped her spoon under the table. "Oh no!"

Neither her father nor Camilo so much as glanced her way.

Kenya crouched down under the guise of retrieving the fallen silverware. Her eyes were level with the handcuffs. She took a deep breath and concentrated on her goal, trying to summon the fire that brought her speed.

No, not yet.

Every time she used magic, Camilo caught her.

She needed to change strategy.

20
CAMILO

Camilo's chin rested on his palm as he watched Reuben's animated gestures. He was saying something about porous shields.

It was gibberish to Camilo, who'd never made it through the entirety of the first *Dune* novel. But listening to Reuben was soothing, like a white noise machine in a child's bedroom. Camilo's father had gotten excited about topics like this too.

I bet they would've been friends.

It was pointless to wonder. The two would never meet.

Camilo let Reuben's voice wash over him. He was tired of his thoughts spinning from his father's condition to Holly's request, to Kenya, to the dagger, back to his father. An endless loop he couldn't seem to escape.

Kenya kicked his calf under the table.

What's that for?

A massive grin spread across Kenya's face. She pushed aside the white tablecloth, using her eyes to focus Camilo's attention downward.

He followed the curve of her thighs toward her knees.

His heart froze.

Dangling from Kenya's fingers were the handcuffs.

Camilo's hand went to the pouch at his hip. It was empty.

That's impossible.

He hadn't smelled any hint of magic.

She didn't use any.

He had been that distracted. How pathetic. Kenya had been able to steal them like any common pickpocket.

Camilo's hands curled into fists. He wasn't sure if he was mad at himself or at Kenya. Perhaps both.

Courtney returned to the table. She tapped her husband's shoulder, cutting his explanation of fictional socio-politics short. There was a vase in the corner she wanted to show him, and the two excused themselves.

The moment their backs were turned, Camilo's lips curled in a snarl. He leaned toward Kenya, lowering his voice to a whisper. He hated the way it growled. "You cheated."

"Excuse me?" The smirk vanished from her lips. She raised her eyebrows. "How?"

"In every way." There were so many reasons that this didn't count, Camilo didn't even know where to begin. "The zipper's broken. You didn't use magic—"

"That wasn't a rule."

Was she joking? The entire purpose of the challenge was to ensure she'd mastered her abilities.

"You're just upset because I outsmarted you." Kenya grinned.

Camilo scoffed. Perhaps there was some truth to her statement, but he had every right to be frustrated. "Your keeper isn't going to be distracted by"—he floundered for a good excuse—"playing pretend boyfriend for you."

"She's not going to have the dagger in a locked bag either. You're just being a sore loser."

Had he not just said that the zipper was broken? "It wasn't—"

Kenya's parents returned, cutting their argument short.

Camilo sat through another few minutes of polite conversation, bending a spoon in his hand beneath the table.

I'm not being a sore loser.

There was a snap as the metal broke. Oops. Camilo tried to hide the broken spoon beneath his napkin.

Perhaps he wasn't being the most gracious loser.

But the handcuffs aren't a toy. How do I know she's ready to use them?

Kenya's parents paid for his dinner despite Camilo's protests, and the four of them left the restaurant together, stepping through the large wooden door to the parking lot beyond. His truck was on the opposite end to the Davidsons' jeep.

They said their goodbyes outside the restaurant. Reuben clapped Camilo's back and told him he looked forward to another dinner. Even Courtney gave him a hug farewell before following her husband across the lot. It was the parental stamp of approval that had been tonight's goal.

And I can't even enjoy it.

Kenya was still lingering before him, her weight on one leg. She fiddled with the zipper to an overstuffed silver fringed purse. The handcuffs must've been inside. "You want them back?"

Camilo's hand twitched forward.

I'm being childish. She needs to start training with the

handcuffs at some point. If I delay too long, she'll miss her
chance to get the dagger.

Plus, Camilo would be watching from the tree outside
Kenya's window. If the keeper returned, he would be there
to assist.

Camilo shoved his hand into his pocket. "Keep them.
You won."

"And you lost?" There was smile creeping onto Kenya's
face.

"Let's not push it."

Kenya's lips pressed into a pout. Her nose wrinkled.

And Camilo knew what was coming.

Kenya burst into laughter. The sound filled the air
around them, echoing under the eaves. It was impossible
not to join in.

"Thanks for training me," she said. "I won't let you
down."

Kenya turned to leave. Camilo reached out and grabbed
her wrist. She twisted so that their eyes met.

"We're not finished. You need to practice using the
handcuffs before you're ready to trap the keeper." Camilo
had messed up the first time. He couldn't afford for her to
make the same mistake. The dagger was too important. "I'll
see you tomorrow afternoon. Same time?"

Kenya hesitated. She sighed and slipped her hand from
Camilo's grip. "Okay. See you then."

Camilo leaned against the restaurant wall, watching
Kenya's figure retreat to her parents' car, all long legs and
toned dark curves. For a moment, he'd been afraid she
would refuse to meet with him again.

The apartment is going to feel lonelier when she does.

It was a stupid thought. By then, Camilo would have

the dagger, and he'd be cured. He could make real friends, human friends. Like Holly.

That was who he wanted to be spending his time with.

Wasn't it?

Camilo's phone vibrated in his pocket. He jumped and snapped his gaze away from Kenya, scrambling to retrieve the device.

It was close to ten. The only person who would call him so late was Holly. She couldn't think he already had Kenya's blood.

But it wasn't Holly's number on his phone. It was her mother.

What would Julia want?

Camilo hurried to answer as he went toward his truck.

"Three rings. Thought you were faster than that." Julia's voice was cold and curt on the other end.

"Sorry. I was with the changeling."

"I hope that isn't another lie."

Camilo's hands felt suddenly sweaty. He fumbled for his keys. "Of course not."

"Good. Once was too many times."

A shudder went through Camilo. He thought he'd escaped the worst of Julia's retribution, but he recognized his boss' tone. There was a punishment in his future, a reminder not to lie about anything relating to his mission again.

"Come to the old playground by your apartment," Julia said. "There's someone who wants to meet you."

21

KENYA

Kenya arranged the green flowers in a vase of water beside her bed. A smile tugged at her lips as she admired the bright hues of the petals.

What is wrong with me?

She groaned, covered her face with a pillow, and collapsed backward onto her bed.

I can't like Camilo. That's a recipe for disaster.

And they were still going to be spending more time together training?

Kenya should have refused. Once she had the handcuffs, she'd be ready to steal the dagger. That's what Camilo had said when he issued the challenge. Now, he was changing his own rules.

Maybe Camilo was reluctant to end their time together too.

Nope! He likes someone else. Holly. Whoever she is.

Kenya's stomach turned. It was probably a sign of indigestion from her earlier meal. It definitely wasn't jealousy.

Curiosity at most.

Would it be *so crazy* if she spent the rest of the evening

searching the social media profiles of every Holly their age who lived in Castor's Grove?

Her phone was still in her purse.

Kenya tossed the pillow off of her face and onto the floor before sitting up. Her walk-in-closet was open before her. The red dress from dinner lay crumpled on the floor, where it had been discarded when Kenya changed into her pajamas. The silver bag dangled from the door handle. Her phone wasn't the only thing within. The outline of the handcuffs bulged through the fabric.

Why do I even need to practice?

Using a pair of handcuffs struck Kenya as fairly self-intuitive.

An idea formed. Maybe she could find a better use for her time than hunting Hollys.

Kenya bounced toward the purse, shirt brushing against the tops of her thighs, and reached for the handcuffs.

A chill burned her fingertips.

Kenya flinched. She'd been expecting the peculiar sensation, but it still shocked her. Maybe that was why Camilo thought she'd need to practice.

But she could do that by herself surely. Did he think she wasn't capable?

Kenya took a deep breath and grabbed the thin chain in the center of the cuffs. Her fingers curled in a fist, ignoring the chill as she pulled the weapon free.

The cold sank through her skin until even the bones of her fingers felt frozen. But the feeling didn't spread beyond her wrist. Kenya could handle that.

She returned to the edge of her bed and held the handcuffs beneath the lamp. The metal absorbed the light, casting it in a shadowy aura.

Kenya practiced opening and closing the rotating arms, careful not to accidentally lock them. The metal numbed her fingers, but she stood by her initial assessment.

Pretty easy to figure out.

So why would Camilo suggest more training sessions? Maybe he didn't *like* Kenya, but was there a chance her company wasn't as off-putting to him as he claimed?

Or does he have some ulterior motive?

Kenya didn't like that option. But Camilo had appeared dressed in all black and a hockey mask trying to steal a dagger. It was worth considering.

She rested the cuffs on her mattress and tried to massage the cold from her right hand. The situation wouldn't seem as difficult if she could talk to someone. Kenya's usual go-to for a conversation about her family's lawn guy was Lily. They were even set to go hiking tomorrow morning. Camilo was sure to be a topic of conversation.

How can I get her opinion on the situation when she doesn't even know what it is?

Lily was as clueless as Kenya's parents. Camilo had insisted that the existence of magic needed to remain secret. He'd hinted that it could be dangerous for them to learn the truth.

But no one would need to know if Kenya told Lily. Maybe, tomorrow—

Two sharp taps came from the window.

Kenya's spine snapped straight. She turned toward the glass.

Had she imagined the noise?

The window scraped open, pushed by a pair of pale hands.

Kenya was too shocked to be afraid. Her body remained

frozen as she watched a tall figure with long limbs and pointed ears climb through her window. It adjusted a pair of baggy shorts, tossed a few strands of blonde hair behind its head, and waved.

The breath caught in Kenya's throat. Her mouth grew suddenly dry as she whispered—

"You're back."

22

CAMILO

The old playground was two blocks south of Camilo's apartment on Townsend Street. It was a small patch of enclosed foam floor in the corner of Little Elm Park. Two rusty swing sets creaked, rocking in a gust of strong summer wind. A row of yellow monkey bars extended from beside them, stretching toward a tower of colorful plastic tubes. A red slide, which had once seemed gigantic, twisted in a spiral beside the climbing frame. Both were shorter than Camilo.

At this time of night, Little Elm Park was typically deserted. But there were two lone figures seated on a wooden bench near the playground.

Julia wore a white lab coat over her jeans, unusual outside of The Morgana Center. One hand clutched the grip of a tranquilizer gun. The other tapped against a large purse. Her head bowed in unusual deference as she whispered to the man beside her.

Is he the one who wants to meet me?

Camilo stopped a few feet shy of the bench, hiding in

the shadows of an elm tree as he studied his boss' companion.

The stranger was old. Wrinkles furrowed his brow and pulled his mouth into a permanent scowl. His narrow chin and clean-shaven head gave his face the resemblance of an upside-down egg. It would have been easy to dismiss him were it not for his physique. A large neck with bulging veins attached to a pair of broad, square shoulders. His arms carried enough muscle to make even Camilo hesitate.

The old man's eyes turned—flat, green, indifferent. He snorted, interrupting whatever Julia had been whispering, and raised his gun. The barrel pointed at Camilo.

"Your dog, Dr. Nichols?" His voice was bored and unimpressed. He tapped a thin metal tube that dangled on silver chain before his chest. It resembled a whistle.

Camilo's jaw tightened as he approached. He'd heard the descriptor before, usually amid a group of hushed giggles from The Morgana Center's newest hires. No one had ever tried to use a dog whistle on him before. That was a new level of insulting.

Julia frowned. Her eye flicked to Camilo. Pity flashed in the cold, piercing blue.

Or perhaps that was wishful thinking.

"Camilo Lopez," Julia introduced them with a small, tight smile, flicking her wrist from one to the next. "Tobias Buckler, The Morgana Center's most illustrious donor."

That's who he is? How is this a punishment?

The Morgana Center's donors met two criteria. They believed in the value of scientific research, while being utterly disinterested in the topic. Only the most gullible wouldn't rescind their funding if they discovered that their charitable donations were going toward the study of magic.

But he called me a dog.

Tobias Buckler circled Camilo, appraising him as though he were a cattle up for auction. "A curious pup. You think he's capable of fetching my dagger?"

Camilo's jaw clenched. The old man was no ordinary donor. He knew about magic. But what did he mean *his* dagger?

Then, it clicked. Julia's sudden urgency. Her willingness to involve Kenya instead of retreating when their plan went awry. It had never been about his father.

"You want the changeling's dagger." Camilo spun with Tobias now, studying the old man in turn. Age had done nothing to stoop him. At a distance, he might be mistaken for a young man. Only his skin gave him away. Camilo could see only one reason why Tobias might be after the dagger. "Did a witch curse you?"

Julia's hand lashed forward, slapping Camilo's face. She wasn't strong enough to hurt him, but instinct took over. He snarled and grabbed his boss' wrist, trapping her in position.

There was a flash of panic in Julia's eye. Her gun was on him a second later, shaky with just her right hand to support it. "Release me."

Crap. What am I thinking?

Camilo opened his fist, dropping his hands to his side. A bruise was already forming on Julia's skin.

"You are not to speak that way to Mr. Buckler, do you understand?" She lowered the gun. "He is an indispensable ally. Most of our supplies are thanks to him. The tranquilizer. Those handcuffs."

Camilo's eyes flicked from the glowing white liquid in the gun to the empty pouch by his hip. Julia wasn't talking about money. Tobias had donated the actual items.

"I'm sorry." Camilo hung his head. But his guilt was for

hurting Julia, not how he'd addressed the old man. What politeness did he owe someone who kept comparing him to a dog?

None, but a bit of caution wouldn't hurt.

Tobias was engaged in the supernatural. It was etched in his appearance. And how else could he have obtained such items?

Camilo glanced at the pendant on the old man's chain. It wasn't a dog whistle though its cylindrical shape bore a resemblance to one. There was a button, and the cones beneath the silver mesh suggested the device was a speaker.

Curious thing for someone with access to magic to wear.

Tobias snorted, and his lips twitched. The ghost of a smile crinkled his eyes. He slipped the pendant beneath the collar of his shirt. "I see why you've been hiding him from me. My otoscope." The old man held his arm out expectantly.

Julia frowned. She was unaccustomed to taking orders. Camilo expected a battle of wills.

Tobias must have been providing more than tranquilizer and handcuffs. Julia plastered a smile on her face, nodded, and went to her bag waiting beside the bench.

So this is my punishment. I have to let this old man inspect me.

It was degrading. Camilo would give Julia that. Medical examinations always took him back to his childhood. But he'd suck it up. There was no limit to how many curses a changeling's dagger could break. If the old man was after the weapon too, their goals were aligned.

Julia placed the dark otoscope into Tobias' palm. There was a point at the end where a thin light shone from the tip of the device.

"Turn." The old man grabbed Camilo's chin before he could comply, twisting his head for him. A moment later, the light was shoved into Camilo's ear. "Sensitive?"

Camilo didn't want to give either the satisfaction of knowing how much the otoscope was stinging. He shrugged. "Only a bit."

Tobias grunted. He turned Camilo's head again and began his inspection of the next ear. "Tell me, boy, what do you know of the changeling's dagger?"

Camilo hadn't considered himself a *boy* since his grandmother left him on his own at sixteen. But the title was an improvement on *dog*.

"Only that it has the ability to sever any witch's spell, not just the one placed on changelings." Camilo rubbed his ears the moment the old man's back was turned. He could feel the hairs vibrating within.

Tobias dropped the otoscope into Julia's palm. "Tongue depressor."

She passed him a popsicle stick.

"Open your mouth," Tobias ordered.

Camilo dropped his jaw before the old man could shove his fingers inside and pry it open for him.

"And what do you know about yourself?" Tobias pressed the popsicle stick onto Camilo's tongue, peering into his throat. "You think you were cursed by a witch?"

Does he expect me to answer now?

"His father was," Julia answered. Her voice was sharp, harsher than she'd likely intended, because she softened her tone as she continued. "It spread to Camilo."

"Half-cursed, half-human. An unfortunate combination." Tobias removed the popsicle stick and dropped it back into Julia's bag. "He might serve. If I'm going to cleanse that wretched forest, I need someone capable."

"What for—?" Camilo started to ask, but a sharp look from Julia cut him off. Questions went only one way in this exchange.

"He won't transform," Julia said. "His muscles are for show."

Ouch. Camilo fought the urge to flex. Did she want the old man to think he was weak?

Tobias smiled. "Let's test that, shall we?"

23
KENYA

Kenya's keeper had returned.

"Unless I hear your stalker return," the elf muttered, tugging at the oversized shorts, which fluffed like a skirt above her knees. She leaned out the window, the tips of her ears vibrated, like she was listening for something. Satisfied with whatever she heard, she nodded and stepped toward Kenya. "I'm afraid our introduction was cut short before. I'm Briony."

The elf offered her hand.

Kenya didn't know how to react. The timing was too perfect. Was this a sign from the universe?

The dark aura of the handcuffs winked beside Kenya's pillow.

She could use her super-speed, grab them, and capture the elf. Easy.

Before Kenya could collect herself enough to act, Briony's hand swept toward the bedside table instead. She plucked a flower from the vase, eyes narrowing as she inspected the color.

"I already know who you are, of course, Kenya Davidson." Briony pointed toward her with the stem. "I slipped you into a crib in the ICU when you were just a few months old." Her tone was pleasant, like they were two old friends discussing pastries.

Kenya forgot about the handcuffs. She stared at the elf, trying to process what she'd just said.

An ICU crib.

Kenya didn't remember being four months old, obviously, but she'd heard the story. After contracting a bad flu, she'd been rushed to the hospital. Her vitals were low, and she was roasting with fever. The doctors said she was lucky to survive.

It was the reason Kenya's father called her his miracle baby.

But that's not my story.

"I wasn't the one who got sick." Kenya's throat was dry. Her voice barely a whisper. She didn't want a response unless it was to tell her she was wrong.

Briony shook her head. For some reason, the elf was still smiling. "That was the original Kenya Davidson, who unfortunately didn't survive."

The original...

Kenya's stomach turned. She felt like she was going to throw up.

Even after Camilo's explanation for how she'd been slipped into a crib, it hadn't occurred to Kenya that her parents had once had another child.

A real child.

And she'd died.

Kenya was a fake, a parasite, an imposter. Courtney and Reuben had been forced to raise her, unaware that their true daughter was gone.

They're going to hate me.

Kenya's chest started heaving in heavy dry sobs. She covered her mouth, afraid her dinner might return.

"Oh dear, don't look sad." Briony patted her knee.

Kenya was too shocked to pull away.

"We were able to connect a child who needed parents with parents who needed a child. Changeling babies are a blessing. You've lived up to all their dreams much better than a human child would have."

Kenya shook her head. That couldn't be true.

Unless...

A whisper of hope slithered into her mind. What if Camilo was the one lying? What if he did have some ulterior motive?

She latched onto it, staring at the woman before her with wide, desperate eyes.

"I can still compete in the Olympics?"

"Oh, definitely not!" Briony held up her hands and straightened to almost her full height. "I've spent most of the past couple weeks ensuring the officials forgot about trying to test your blood again. We don't want them discovering anything—er—unusual about it. That's part of what we need to discuss. The magical world survives through secrecy. Competing against humans now that they test these things could expose all of us. You'll have to stop, or we could both get in a lot of trouble."

The elf continued speaking. Her words sloshed through the air like waves, thick and meaningless and suffocating.

Everything that Kenya had been trying to avoid threatened to drown her.

My parents aren't my parents. They were tricked into raising me, tricked into loving me, tricked into dedicating their lives to me.

"Take it back." Kenya stopped heaving. Her fists

clenched, and she stared into the elf's pale gray eyes. Who cared about Camilo's quest for the dagger? He'd never even said why he wanted it. "My powers, my memory of all of this. I don't want any of it. Take it back."

"I'm afraid that's not how this works."

"Why not?" Kenya couldn't keep sitting anymore. She jumped to her feet. "Your dagger undoes magic, right? That's its thing. Use it to undo mine."

"There's no spell allowing you to use magic. You're a shifter. It's simply who you are. The changeling's dagger can't—" Briony cut herself off, mouth pulling into a line, points of her ears rising. "How do you know what the dagger does?"

Shit.

"I'm just assuming," Kenya tried to cover her mistake. She wasn't going to betray Camilo's identity to some stranger.

Briony's eyes shifted toward the bed. Her ears rose until the tips pointed to the ceiling. "What is that? On your sheets?"

Kenya stepped backward, trying to block the handcuffs from view. "Nothing. Just a toy." Her hands scrambled over the mattress feeling for the weapon.

"I don't know who you've been talking to or what lies they've been filling your head with." Briony's eyes locked on Kenya. "But I'm your keeper. My task is to guide you into the magical world now that you're an adult. We're on the same side."

Somehow, Kenya doubted that.

A good person wouldn't force my parents to raise a child that wasn't theirs.

Kenya should never have doubted Camilo. Maybe he was holding his motives close to his chest, but that didn't make him a villain. She should never have tried to take the easy way out and abandon him. They'd made a deal.

And Kenya intended to keep it.

For Camilo. And any other changeling that Briony had hidden.

No one should have their lives, their realities, their very identities, suddenly cut from them.

"Do you understand?" Briony took a step back, inching toward the window as she spoke.

Kenya's fingers brushed against the icy sting of the handcuffs. This time, she didn't flinch. Her fingers curled around the weapon, and her jaw clenched. Kenya summoned the flames in the soles of her feet and rushed toward the elf.

Briony spun to the side.

Kenya was moving too fast to change her course now. She hurtled toward the open window.

A scream rose to her lips.

I'm going to fall.

24
CAMILO

Tobias' test proved little different to the ones Camilo had suffered at the hands of The Morgana Center's scientists, who'd been curious to test the boundaries of his strength.

He stripped down to a sleeveless white undershirt and black boxers so that his limbs weren't restricted by his dress clothes from dinner. Tobias barked orders.

Push-ups. Pull-ups. Burpees. Sprints. Leap from one piece of playground equipment to the next and back again.

Camilo hung from the climbing frame and lifted his knees to his chest. He stood on his hands for five minutes. He jumped and squatted and twisted. Three hours with no breaks. His lungs burned and his muscles ached.

This has to be enough.

Camilo had been waiting for Tobias to stop him, clap him on his back and assure him he'd passed whatever this test was. But the old man leaned against the red slide, watching unimpressed. Julia fidgeted beside him, adjusting her eye patch, then her hair, then the bag around her shoulder. Her fingers tapped the butt of her gun.

Does she want me to do well or to give up?

Camilo couldn't tell. But everyone, even the accursed, had their limits, and he was reaching his.

"Tate's breakthrough was exactly what you wanted," Julia said. "We'll have all the demons infected in time. There's no need—"

Camilo's arms slipped from the monkey bars, and he fell to the playground's soft foam floor. Spots spun before his eyes; his stomach growled. He'd used up all his fuel.

"Less efficient than I thought," Tobias' voice echoed through the empty park as he drew closer. "Perhaps you're right, Julia. I could best him." He pressed the toe of his shoe into Camilo's side.

I'd like to see you try, old man.

A growl rumbled in Camilo's chest. It escaped his lips a mere whimper.

"Should he fail I'll have to send his father instead."

"Tobias, please," Julia's voice was trembling. "There are other options."

The old man grunted. "None loyal nor mad enough to attack their own without supervision."

Camilo's eyes fluttered, fighting between his need to watch and their own desire to close. The outlines of Tobias and Julia flickered at the corner of his vision.

"You can't, please." Her hand reached toward the old man, grabbing his arm in a desperate bid. "Diego's mind is gone. It'll kill him if you send him in."

My dad... He wants my dad to fight for him?

Panic flooded Camilo's brain.

"A heroic death." Tobias pushed Julia's hand away, annoyance creeping into his voice. "You forget who's been paying for his upkeep these past five years. I own him. And in two weeks, Diego will—"

"No." Camilo forced himself to sit up, ignoring the pain that pounded through his abdomen. He had no idea what *it* was that might kill his father—a demon perhaps? It didn't matter. "You can't send him on a suicide mission."

Not when I'm about to get the dagger. Not when I'm finally close to saving him.

Tobias' eyebrows rose. "You are a stubborn dog, aren't you?" He crouched, bringing their faces level. "How about this. One last test. If you can pass, I won't need your father. I'll know you can manage the task on your own. Are you up for it?"

"Yes." Camilo clenched his jaw and forced himself to stand, blinking away the spots swimming before him.

Tobias' lips curled as he pulled a lighter from the top pocket of his shirt. A click of his thumb summoned a bright red flame.

The old man held the fire to Camilo's palm and issued his final challenge. "Don't burn."

25
KENYA

This is going to be a problem.

Kenya leaned her head against the wall and stared out the open window. The first traces of sunlight brushed the sky, painting it pink and gold. It was a perfect summer morning.

And she was trapped.

Last night, as she was hurtling toward the window, petrified that she was about to fall to her death, Kenya had transformed. She'd dropped the handcuffs, and her body had started burning and shifting. As a ball of orange fur, she'd flown into the night.

Until a hand grabbed her tail.

Briony had pulled Kenya back into the room. The elf seemed eager to flee, but she wanted to teach her *unruly changeling* a lesson before she did.

Now, Kenya was shackled to her own bed post. The handcuff stung her left wrist. It seemed to have shrunk to the exact size necessary to trap her.

That didn't stop Kenya from attempting to break free. She gritted her teeth and tugged. The dark metal scraped her skin, rubbing it raw. There was a growing layer of dried blood forming on the cuff.

Kenya winced and glared at her silver purse, still hanging on the handle of her closet. Her phone was in there. She needed to call Camilo.

Why didn't he give me a key?

A bird whistled in one of the willow trees outside. Lily would be arriving soon. Kenya's parents might try to come into the room before that. They couldn't find her like this.

There was no alternative. She'd have to involve Camilo.

Kenya stretched across the bed. She could almost reach the silver purse with her toes. If she could wiggle her hand just a bit further down in the handcuffs—

"Ah!" Kenya gasped as the metal sliced deep into her wrist. Tears formed in her eyes from the pain, like someone had shot an icicle into her palm. Hot blood trickled toward her elbow.

But it had worked. Her toes clasped the strap of her purse and pulled it toward her.

Kenya got her phone free and stared at the blank screen.

What exactly was she going to tell Camilo?

26

CAMILO

Something warm and wet licked Camilo's cheek. He opened his eyes and found a Corgi lapping at his face.

"Fenton, here! Come back," the dog's owner called in a panicked voice from a few feet away.

Camilo pushed himself up and shooed the corgi. Night was fading from the sky. Indigo mixed with the pink and gold that rose from the east. Only the earliest bird hopped through the blades of grass, hunting for its worm.

The soft foam playground floor was springy beneath Camilo. Had he fallen asleep there?

No, he'd passed out from the pain.

The memory of the previous night brought a wave of heat to his palm. Camilo lifted his arm. The skin on his hand remained raw and red, a first-degree burn. It had been worse before he fainted. Camilo's quick healing was not enough to make him fire-proof.

I failed Tobias' test.

What did that mean for Camilo's father? Did some horrible fiery fate await him?

Camilo was alone. The dog walker had run off the moment the corgi had gone back to them.

Trembling, Camilo forced himself to stand.

Julia and Tobias had been nice enough to leave his clothes. The red button-down shirt, gray tie, and matching slacks were folded on the bench.

Camilo didn't care enough to put them back on. He shoved his feet into his shoes and limped toward the parking lot where he'd left his truck. His muscles burned in protest.

He needed food and a long nap in a proper bed.

But there wasn't time to worry about either. In two weeks, if he didn't get the dagger, Tobias Buckler would send his father to cleanse some magical stronghold and be killed by a monster.

Camilo couldn't let that happen.

He searched the pockets of his dress pants for his keys.

There was no need to panic.

Kenya's keeper was sure to return at some point during the next two weeks. That would give Camilo a chance. He could save his father.

The keys dropped from his pants and onto the ground. His phone fell with them.

Camilo caught the device in midair. There were several unread messages. One was from Holly. He went to open it, and his thumb froze.

Does she know what Buckler's planning?

Holly's words at the flower shop had sounded like a threat. What if they'd been a warning? She liked to learn as many of her mother's secrets as she could. She must have had at least an inkling of what the old man wanted

But then, why not tell Camilo outright?

There was a new message from Kenya as well. Camilo opened that one instead. His eyebrows rose as he read.

Handcuffed to my bed. No key. Can't break out. Please come before my parents find me?

Wait. Where was the—dammit!

Camilo recalled the *plink* when he'd dove to save his model of the Millennium Falcon. The key was on the floor in his apartment.

He'd have to go for it now.

Camilo climbed into his truck, shaking his head. How the hell had Kenya managed to trap herself? He'd assumed she'd need more training, but this was impressively inept.

Unless she didn't trap herself.

Camilo's body went cold as he started the engine.

What were the chances that the one night he'd been absent, the keeper had returned?

Pretty high if she knew I was in the tree.

But that couldn't be the case. Camilo refused to believe it.

Because if Kenya had been trapped by her own keeper that meant she'd tried to get the dagger and failed. It meant the elf was angry with her changeling and wouldn't return soon.

It meant Camilo's father was doomed.

27
KENYA

For the second time in twenty-four hours, someone climbed into Kenya's room.

Camilo was all olive skin and bulging muscles. A sleeveless white shirt had his arms exposed, and a tight pair of athletic shorts accentuated his thighs as he landed in a crouch beneath her window.

They'd never been alone in her bedroom.

The cold ache in her hand wasn't enough to stop the rest of Kenya's body from growing hot. Her breath caught in her throat. She shifted higher on the bed, trying to position herself in a flattering pose against her pillows.

It was a pointless endeavor. Mostly because of her outfit.

Why do I not own cuter pajamas?

Kenya was wearing a pair of ratty old shorts, which had once been green. They were barely visible beneath her oversized gray t-shirt. The sleeves reached almost to her elbows, and in the center, in thick white font, it asked the question: *Who's the king of the pencil case?* Beneath was a picture of a cartoon ruler, illustrated with a smug human face. Her father had chosen it for her.

She tried to block the illustration with her right arm. At least she wasn't wearing the bonnet that normally protected her curls.

Camilo pushed himself up from the floor. His limbs trembled, and his movements were slower than normal.

"You're hurt," Kenya said, forgetting to hide her shirt as she sat forward to get a better look. Had Briony visited him last night too?

"And you're trapped." Camilo grunted. He leaned over her, holding the corner of the mattress. His breath was sharp with alcohol and mint, liked he'd just gargled mouthwash. Red lines rose like cracks in his eyes. A yellow hue circled his pupils, the edges of the sun during an eclipse. "Tell me you're just a moron who did this to herself."

Well, that would've been a rude way to phrase it if that had been what happened.

"Obviously n—" Kenya began to defend herself, but she cut herself off as she saw Camilo's reaction.

The yellow streaked like lightning through his eyes. Veins popped from his arms, angry rivers rushing from his wrists to his neck.

He snarled and pushed himself from the mattress. Shreds of her sheets flew into the air.

Camilo spun so that his back was to her, raising his arms to block his face. "Dammit, Kenya. Do you understand what you've done?"

"Will you keep your voice down," Kenya whispered, her heart pounding. "My parents might hear." She glanced at the corner of her mattress. There were great rips in the fabric, as though it had been raked by claws.

Camilo dropped to his knees. His shoulders rose and fell with heavy, shuddering breaths. Was his skin darker than it had been before?

No, it was his body hair. Kenya had never noticed it before, but the early sunshine streaking through her window accentuated it.

"It wasn't my fault," she said, hoping that the truth might calm him down. "Briony saw the handcuffs on my bed and realized what they were. I tried to stop her from leaving, but she grabbed them and trapped me instead."

"How stupid do you think I am?" Camilo's voice was deep, almost a growl. His body trembled, a few more deep breaths. When he spoke next, he sounded defeated. "You didn't listen. You saw the dagger, and you went for it. Why are you so impulsive?"

"That's not fair," Kenya objected. "I just told you what happened. It's the truth. What more do you want me to say? That you were right? I need training. I know that."

At least she did now.

Camilo's shoulders slumped forward. His head bowed, and his hands rested on the floor as though in prayer. The light changed, and the black hair that had covered his body a few moments prior was invisible again. His muscles seemed to deflate.

Something's wrong.

Kenya had never seen Camilo sapped of energy. This couldn't just be because her first try at the dagger had failed.

"Please, tell me what's happened?"

Without thinking, Kenya stood and tried to cross toward him. The chain of her manacles stretched tight, and the teeth within the metal cuff sank into her wrist again.

She swallowed a squeak as the fresh blood dripped to the floor.

Camilo's head lifted. He jumped to his feet and turned, staring at Kenya's wrist. The yellow in his eyes had retreated.

"What's happened," he muttered, "is that you failed to live up to your end of our bargain." He retrieved something small and silver from his pocket—the handcuffs' key. Camilo pushed it into the hole and twisted. "And now in two weeks, my father—"

The dark metal manacles clattered to the floor.

Neither Kenya nor Camilo looked at them. His eyes were on the blood dripping from her wrist. She had eyes only for the boy before her.

What was he saying about his father?

Before she could ask, Camilo yanked his shirt over his head.

Thoughts about parents, hers or his, vanished from Kenya's mind. She stared at the smooth pectorals and rippling abs. Was there an ounce of fat anywhere on Camilo's body?

"Here." Camilo took Kenya's hand and pulled it toward him. His fingers were soft, his grip gentle as he held her arm in place. Brown eyes wide and sad, he pressed his shirt against her cuts, letting the blood soak into the white fabric without concern.

He does care about me.

Kenya studied his lips. They were too pretty to belong to a boy with all that muscle.

"I'll do better next time," she said. "Promise. After some training, I think—"

"There is no next time. You failed. That's it."

"What do you mean?" Kenya had competed enough to

know that you didn't give up after one failure. "You failed your first time too. Then you came back with a new plan—"

"Yeah. You." Camilo wouldn't let her speak. He kept dabbing at her blood. "And look how that turned out? Your failure is a million times worse than mine. Your keeper isn't going to return in the next two weeks. Not after her own changeling attacked her." His jaw clenched, and his grip grew tighter.

It was starting to hurt.

Kenya yanked her arm free.

The movement caught Camilo off guard. He stepped back, clinging to his bloody shirt.

"You didn't say anything about a time limit," she objected, shaking her arm in an effort to return the heat to her hand. "We can come up with a new plan."

"We can't."

"Of course we can. I'm going to get the dagger for you. Or else our deal—"

"Is off," Camilo snarled. His eyes glowed yellow again. When he opened his mouth, his teeth were large and sharp. "You can't get me the dagger. And you running in the Olympics is the last thing I care about. I was a fool to think you could help me."

His body trembled, veins bulging and black hair returning again.

"You're shifting." Kenya couldn't keep the realization to herself.

"I am not," Camilo's voice was a growl. His jaw was stretching, elongating into a muzzle. He slammed a large, furry fist into the wall.

"Kenya? Is that you?" Her father's voice came from out in the hallway.

"*Hostia!*" Camilo jumped away, shaking still, but human

once more. He ran to the window. Before he disappeared from the ledge, he turned to Kenya. "We're done. Get that through your skull. And consider this our official breakup."

28

CAMILO

Camilo stared at the bloody shirt, lying beside the sink.

He was back in his apartment, standing in the middle of the kitchen with his thumb poised over his phone. Holly's contact information was open on the screen. One push and he'd call her. It was the obvious next step.

Camilo had visited The Morgana Center a hundred times as a child. He knew the layout well enough. But things had changed over the past five years, and he'd never studied the facility with the intention of planning a heist, especially not one which involved escaping with a massive, dangerous beast. He'd assumed his father was safe in Julia's care. Now, he knew better.

I have to get him out.

If Camilo failed, there would be no second chance.

I act once. Carefully and correctly. Assess my father's prison first, then plan, then execute.

He had Kenya's blood. Holly would happily take him to see Diego.

So why am I hesitating?

Pumpkin leaped onto the counter, interrupting Camilo's thoughts for a moment. The cat sniffed the blood-soaked shirt and lifted his nose in disdain. He crossed toward the microwave. Tins of tuna were piled on top.

"You have no consideration for the fact that my life is currently in chaos, do you?" Camilo sighed, grabbed one of the tins, and peeled it open for the cat.

Pumpkin mewled—half gratitude, half complaint about how long the meal had taken—and buried his face in the tuna.

Camilo lifted his arm as much as it would allow and stroked the cat's back. His eyes wandered to the bloody shirt, then down to his phone.

Dammit, he needed to stop wasting time.

Camilo slammed his thumb against the green call symbol.

Holly answered on the third ring.

"Hold on." There was the sound of a chair scraping and papers shuffling as she stood. A door closed, and her voice, soft as though she were afraid someone might overhear, spoke again. "This better be an emergency."

"I met Tobias Buckler last night." That hadn't been how Camilo planned to begin their conversation, but the words slipped out before he had a chance to process what he was saying.

Holly was silent on the other end.

"You know him, I presume." *Otherwise, you'd be asking questions.*

"We've met. He's quite brilliant." There was a hint of reverence in her whisper.

Camilo ground his teeth. Tobias Buckler, wealthy as he might have been, was tainted by magic. It was obvious in the way he moved. Yet, neither Holly nor her mother would ever dare to call Camilo *brilliant.*

On the counter, Pumpkin licked the last scraps of tuna from the tin. Camilo focused on the cat, trying to keep his voice calm. Perhaps he was reading too much into an off-handed compliment. "Apparently Tobias Buckler pays for my father's upkeep and is threatening to pull his funding."

He waited for a gasp, a loud *what,* or an argument that he'd misunderstood. Anything that would have indicated shock.

"I'm sorry, Cam." Holly's voice quivered. It might've been sympathy, resignation, maybe even nervousness. But there was no hint of surprise. "But maybe it's for the best. Taking care of Diego is costly. We've knocked him out to run diagnostics now, but it's obvious—I mean—he's been in this condition so long that even with the dagger..."

Camilo let his phone fall to the counter. Holly's voice became a dull whine, barely audible on the other end. Pumpkin hissed and batted the device with his paw.

The cat had never been fond of Holly, even when she was younger.

He likes Kenya though.

Camilo's shoulders tensed as his eyes landed again on the blood-soaked shirt.

Holly was still on their call. She was talking about Diego's declining quality of life and increased expenses like he was an old dog that needed to be put down. Even having known him as a small child, Holly couldn't see the creature locked in the cage as a human.

What is she planning for Kenya?

Nothing good. But if Camilo wanted to save his father, Holly would need blood.

Pumpkin watched him with large green eyes. There was an accusatory expression on his orange face.

Wait. Could I—?

An idea blossomed in Camilo's mind. It made his stomach turn with that familiar sense of guilt. There was no escaping it.

"*Lo siento, gordito.*" Camilo scratched the top of the cat's head and grabbed his phone. "I have what you asked for. How soon can you let me in?"

29
CAMILO

Diego Lopez had carved The Morgana Center beneath the shell of his grandparents' old restaurant. The wooden sign that once read *Tapas de Madrid* had been slapped with a coat of white paint and replaced with the words: *Private property. Keep out.*

The foreboding words were in direct conflict with the warm, buttercup yellow walls and bright red door that passersby would notice at a glance.

Closer inspection of the building revealed state-of-the-art security. The silver behind the windows was metal panels, not curtains. A digital keypad locked the door. The air would have found it impossible to enter were it not for a series of small vents just beneath the roof.

Camilo shifted the strap of his duffel bag as he approached. Within were the handcuffs, back in their usual pouch, and a blood-soaked shirt, stuffed into a plastic bag and sealed. He stared at the keypad beside the red door.

This might be the craziest thing I've ever attempted.

If there was a code to unlock the door, Camilo had never seen anyone use it. Instead, the employees scanned their cards against the flat surface or unlocked it from the computers in The Morgana Center.

Camilo's key card had been confiscated five years ago. But perhaps there was a way to cause the lock to short circuit?

The door swung open before he could investigate further.

Tate Barron stood before him, greasy brown hair poking at strange angles from his head. His eyes looked like dinner plates beneath his glasses, sitting on dark half-moon shelves that indicated a lack of sleep. The stubble on his chin hadn't grown in the past twelve days.

"Camilo! I thought it was you on the camera. Impossible to miss those shoulders." Tate grinned, reached forward, and pinched near Camilo's neck, as if trying to feel the muscles. "Did Julia call you in for testing? I'd love to see how the handcuffs affect you. And I can show you what I'm working on."

"Absolutely not." Camilo stepped away from the keypad. He was already on edge. The last thing he needed was Tate experimenting on him and prattling in his ear. "I'm here to see Holly."

"Oh." Tate's smile faltered for a second. "She's in our office. I'll take you."

"Great." Camilo didn't bother keeping the sarcasm from his voice. He didn't want company while he was walking through the facility trying to find its weak points. But if he had to be saddled with someone—why Tate? Julia's favorite was obnoxiously observant.

Camilo tried to walk a few steps behind Tate as they weaved through a series of wrought iron tables and chairs. These, a broken stove in the kitchen, and a large chalkboard menu were the remnants of the former restaurant. They'd been saved as a precaution against an intruder who managed to breach the first floor.

Though, short of breaking down the front door, Camilo couldn't see a way in.

"You look drained," Tate said, unnecessarily chipper as they reached the back of the restaurant where the elevator waited. "Training with Kenya last night?"

"No." Camilo's jaw clenched. He had no desire to talk about anything that had happened the previous night. With himself or Kenya.

Tate seemed to get the message. The scientist swiped his card against a second keypad, and the elevator's metal doors opened.

The true heart of The Morgana Center was underground: six levels of sterile white rooms, science labs, office spaces, and holding cells. Holly's office was on level four.

Tate pushed the appropriate button, and the elevator began its descent.

They were passing level two when a loud wail rose through the shaft. It enveloped the metal, encasing them in a scream. The sound was anguished and desperate, raking Camilo's inner ears. He covered them with his hands.

Tate stared at him from behind his large frames. "Sometimes noise travels through the ducts from the lower levels. It's extra loud to you, isn't it? One of the side effects of your curse?"

Without taking his eyes from Camilo, the scientist began digging in one of the pockets of his lab coat.

If he takes out an otoscope now, I swear to God, I'm going to punch him.

"We got new demons a few days ago. They're not settling well. Keep trying to escape. Don't know why. I've been working with their DNA. One of them is quite different, not a fire-starter like the others. He can change his face. It's quite...Ah!" Tate pulled a pair of orange foam earplugs from his coat and offered them to Camilo.

They weren't sealed in plastic, which meant there was a high possibility that they'd been in the scientist's own ears.

"That's disgusting." Camilo scowled at the offered plugs. It wasn't Tate's bizarre offer that had him annoyed though, it was what the scientist had said. "What do you mean you don't know why they'd try to escape? Wouldn't you try to break free if someone caught you and trapped you like a zoo animal?"

Camilo regretted the questions the moment they left him. He would never have dared to make such a comment to Julia or Holly. The implication that a demon and a human shared any commonalities would have infuriated one and offended the other. If Tate mentioned his response, they'd wonder why Camilo was taking the side of the monsters they contained.

They might think I've turned against The Morgana Center.

But he hadn't. Using science to overcome magic was his father's dream. It was only Tobias Buckler who Camilo was betraying.

No, that wasn't quite true. There was one other person.

Camilo tried not to think about the bloody shirt in his bag.

The elevator stopped at level four, and they stepped into the corner of a long hallway. It made no difference which path they took. The Morgana Center was a circle. Evenly spaced white doors lined the perimeter while the inner walls were made of glass, allowing a view of the floors above and below. All were identical except the third. An iron box hovered in its center, attached by metal rods and a single pathway.

I'm coming, Dad.

Scientists passed alongside them as they walked through the sterile, white hall. Most were strangers to Camilo—an old woman with wispy gray curls, a short man with a dark mustache, a pair of narrow-nosed twenty-somethings who must have been twins. When had Julia hired all of these people?

They stared at Camilo, some more openly than others. He turned from their eyes, hoping Tate would mistake the movement a sign of his discomfort. Camilo studied the distance between the levels. Could he jump from here to the third floor?

Not if I'm dragging my father.

Tate scratched his stubble, looking like a child playing scientist in his large white coat and oversized rubber boots. "You know, most animals in captivity have significantly longer life spans. There's no scarcity of resources like in the wild, so..."

Camilo fought the urge to slam his fist against his own forehead. Tate didn't let things go. The scientist had a memory like an elephant. Though his emotional awareness seemed more akin to a fish.

"We're not talking about animals," Camilo said. He kept his tone even, trying to choose his words more carefully this time. The other scientists might be listening. "They're..."

What word could he use for the creatures imprisoned below? Not animals, not humans.

"Demons? Castors? Magical beings?" Tate offered the suggestions with a smile as he stopped before the door to his office.

"Whatever they are, it's obvious they don't want to be imprisoned. Even if it's necessary for the safety of humanity."

Tate's brow wrinkled. He seemed lost in himself, tapping his keycard to his chin before remembering to scan it and unlock the door.

The space that Tate and Holly shared was half-office, half-science lab. Shelves full of glass test tubes, beakers, and burners lined the far wall. Acids, chemicals, and substances with curious colors shimmered on the rows beneath, scrawled labels taped beside them. Closer to the door, two desks faced opposite walls. Each surface was large enough to fit a computer, as well as a microscope with its tray of slides.

Holly sat at the desk facing the right wall. She was the picture of a scientist, hair pulled into a ponytail behind her, lab-coat buttoned to just under her neck, scribbling formulas on a notepad while glancing back at whatever strange equation was displayed on the screen.

At the sound of the door opening, her head popped up. She flipped the book shut, hiding her thoughts, and beamed at Camilo. He smiled back, trying to hide his discomfort.

Maybe he was overreacting to Holly not warning him about Tobias Buckler. It did seem as though she wasn't privy to the old man's plans. And she'd always seen Camilo's father as a tragic horror story. Perhaps her earlier lack of surprise had less to do with hiding information and was instead the result of Holly's own preconceived assumptions about Diego being confirmed.

"Do you want to see what I've been working on?" Tate asked, slipping in behind Camilo and crossing to his desk. He grabbed a sealed test tube and lifted it in the air. It was empty. "I think you'll like it. It's a modification of your father's work, and once injected, the demons—"

"He doesn't care, Tate. And your research is classified."

Holly rolled her eyes. She tiptoed toward the door, stopping a few inches shy of Camilo.

For a moment, he thought she was going to hug him.

"Did you bring it?" Holly whispered.

Camilo's shoulders tensed. Uncertain if he was betraying a friend or a stranger, he unzipped the duffel bag and handed over the blood-stained gray shirt.

Holly grinned, pulling it to her chest for a moment before hurrying to lock it in the top drawer of her desk. "You have no idea how invaluable this is going to be for The Center. I'm on the verge of a breakthrough."

"Good." Camilo had no way of knowing if that was true. But, mistake or not, he couldn't take back what he'd done, so he put all thoughts of the shirt out of his mind. Only one thing really mattered. "Now, take me to my father."

30
KENYA

"Are you sure you still want to go hiking?" Lily asked, twisting the straw of her smoothie as she stared at Kenya. "We could get our nails done, or go shopping, or just stay here and rant about Camilo?"

The two sat at opposite ends of a pink plastic table outside a juice shop. Doc lay on the warm concrete at their feet, panting beside a collapsible bowl. The goldendoodle had gotten restless in the car. Though they were almost out of the city, Lily had been thrilled for an excuse to stop.

I think she's hoping I'll change my mind about the hike.

The point of climbing Bear Mountain was to help Lily train for the upcoming Castor's Grove Marathon. But it had been Kenya's suggestion.

The two had barely seen each other since the qualifiers. Lily's summer had been full of beach days and late-night hangs with their former classmates. Kenya had been in attendance only as a topic of conversation. Her performance at the qualifier, the photograph in the newspaper, and her inconclusive drug test had yet to exhaust themselves as fresh gossip. Kenya's absence at all the parties, and the continued lack of a clean drug test, continued to feed people's curiosity.

Maybe I can transfer to a different city after my first semester at university.

Kenya sighed. Maybe she should give up on the hike. It was approaching midday. They would sweat their asses off if they climbed Bear Mountain now.

The late start had been Kenya's fault. She'd been a sobbing mess after Camilo left. Lily had found her upstairs, still in her pajamas, plucking green petals from the flowers.

It was pathetic. Kenya was acting like this was a real breakup. She couldn't let a boy, who she hadn't really been dating, ruin her day like this.

Kenya had insisted that they go on the hike. She'd pulled herself together, changed into her favorite white sneakers with her lucky lime green laces, grabbed Doc's matching leash, and hopped into Lily's car. No more being sad about Camilo.

What Kenya hadn't realized was that crying about him had been distracting her from everything else.

"I'm sure whatever happened, it was one hundred percent his fault," Lily assured her, spinning the bright purple straw that had come with her blueberry blast smoothie. "Cause Kenya is the best, right Doc?" She leaned down, braid swooping over her shoulder, and scratched the goldendoodle's head.

Doc's eyebrows rose. He glanced up at Kenya with an accusatory gaze. The few times he'd interacted with Camilo had made it clear that the goldendoodle was a fan. Kenya wasn't so sure Doc would be on her side in this situation.

But it wasn't Camilo that had her staring at the green smoothie before her, lifting her straw in and out without sipping.

"What would you think if I quit competitive running and forgot about the Olympics?"

Lily leaned over the table and swatted Kenya's shoulder. "Don't be overdramatic. Just because your first serious boyfriend turned out to be a jerk doesn't mean you give up on your dreams. Did that Yasmin girl reach out to you?"

Kenya grimaced. "Don't remind me."

After reading the short novella worth of messages, she'd realized why the name sounded familiar. Yasmin was the intern for the Grover's Gazette who'd snapped the picture of Kenya and Camilo leaving the alley. Somehow, the snake of a photographer, thought they'd be willing to do an interview with her.

Kenya had responded with a short, but emphatic **NO**. Yasmin had sent another five messages afterward before attempting to call. Her number was now blocked in Kenya's phone.

"You should do an interview for the Gazette," Lily said. "It'll be a total comeback story, and Camilo will realize what a massive mistake he made dumping you." She tapped her temple like she'd just said something brilliant.

Except that Camilo was never my boyfriend. And my parents were never my parents. And I was never Kenya Davidson.

I'm some strange species that stole her place.

Camilo had been right when he called her weird.

A sob rose in Kenya's throat. She squeezed her eyes and swallowed it down. The tears wet the backs of her eyelids despite her best efforts. But she couldn't start crying in front of Lily again.

"I'm going to buy a bottle of water for Doc." Kenya pushed her chair back and stood. She tried to disguise the fact that she was wiping her eyes as she hurried into the smoothie shop.

Air conditioning blasted inside the bright pink and green interior. A group of younger girls giggled at one table, and a woman argued with her toddler near the bathrooms. No one cared enough to notice Kenya.

Good.

I am a human. Not anything else.

She rubbed her nose and wiped her hand on the edge of her gray tank top, gaining control of her tears.

There was a red-headed woman behind the counter, washing a blender at the sink.

A man with similar hair sat on a pink stool beside her, trying to get her attention.

Is he harassing her?

Kenya was no stranger to uncomfortable interactions with customers. She'd worked part-time as a waitress for the past two years. The only reason she'd given in her notice before summer was because she was so confident that she'd be focusing her energy on the Olympics. Now, she'd probably have to beg for it back.

I am not starting to cry again.

The bottle of water she'd come in for was in a fridge behind the counter. She patted her cheeks dry and slunk closer, hoping to give the worker an excuse to ignore her belligerent customer.

But neither noticed Kenya as she approached.

"Come on, Daisy," the man said, clasping his hands together, voice pleading. "Just let me steal a couple pieces for the plane. No one's going to know." He leaned across the counter and reached for a banana.

Daisy swatted his hand away and glared at him. "The manager will."

Something about the interaction made Kenya pause. She looked at the two again, same bright red hair, straight noses, splash of freckles on the cheeks. Her initial assessment had been wrong. This wasn't a disgruntled customer and frazzled worker. These two were siblings.

Kenya stopped a couple feet away, hovering by the counter. She fiddled with a plastic wrapped cookie on display beside the cash register. It was rude to eavesdrop, but she didn't want to interrupt them either.

"You *are* the manager!" The man gave an overdramatic sigh. He crossed his arms and leaned back, giving her an accusatory look. "You're still mad that we're leaving."

"Of course I am, Ivan," Daisy said, spinning toward him. "The Western Woodlands will be unprotected."

Kenya's head snapped up at the name. She'd only heard it once before.

Camilo asked me if I knew where it was.

"Oote is staying." Ivan tilted his head, seeming to reconsider it. "Okay, he's not much good without Fran, but one of her dads is sick. We have to go visit. And there's dozens of protective spells." He grinned and leaned forward again. "So give me some blueberries."

Did he say spells?

Forget being polite.

"Hi, sorry, but did you say something about the Western Woodlands?" Kenya hurried toward them. "What is that? Is it magical?"

Two freckle-spattered faces snapped toward her.

Daisy groaned and slapped the side of Ivan's head. "Do you have any idea how much I've spent in amnesiac powder because of you?"

He held up his hands a second too late to block her. "Relax. Not like she can do anything about it." Ivan turned his seat toward Kenya and pointed a finger at her face. "You a knight? Legally you have to tell me."

"Uh..." Kenya paused. She had no idea what he was talking about.

Which means it's definitely something to do with magic.

Kenya hadn't thought about the Western Woodlands since Camilo asked. But her mind latched onto it now, a lifeline to distract from the current state of her thoughts.

There was only one way these two strangers might tell her the truth.

"I'm a changel-uh." Kenya hated the way the word felt in her mouth. It conjured images of cloaked elves, spirting off with poor, sick infants and replacing the innocent baby with a dangerous imposter. *Shifter* wasn't any better. What was the third thing Camilo kept calling her? "A Castor."

That didn't sound as terrible.

"You should've started with that." Ivan grinned and patted her shoulder. "The Western Woodlands is a block west of here. Officially, it's a protected wildlife park, but the yale painting is a door. No problem entering for any Castor."

"How do you know she's telling the truth about being a changeling?" Daisy slapped her brother's head again.

Kenya didn't care. She was already retreating. "Thanks!" She pushed the door open and hurried back to her plastic table on the patio.

Doc barked as Kenya approached, sensing her excitement.

Lily raised her eyebrows. "Where's the bottle of water?"

"Forget that." Kenya waved her hand in dismissal. She slipped Doc's leash out from under the chair and grabbed her friend's hand, pulling Lily to her feet. "There's been a change of plans. We're going to the woods."

31
CAMILO

A pair of glowing yellow eyes burned from within the darkness as Holly closed the heavy metal door behind Camilo.

She'd accompanied him to the end of the bridge and scanned her card to admit him. "Five minutes. That should be enough time to say goodbye." It wasn't an empathetic desire to allow Camilo a moment of privacy with his father that stopped Holly from entering with him.

Diego scared her.

He scared most of the scientists.

Even in the pitch black, the yellow eyes tracked Camilo. Fear crept up his spine and into his throat. It was irrational. He knew the glass was there.

I'm going to need to be a lot braver than this if I intend to sneak him out and start caring for him myself.

Camilo fumbled for the switch beside the door. A dim light flashed overhead, cooling some of the darkness.

Before him, his father came into view.

Diego Lopez was more wolf than human now. He prowled on all fours behind the glass, body covered in dark gray fur. His mouth stretched into a short, pointed muzzle and a tail swished between his legs. The only hint that he'd once been a man was a series of black markings around his eyes, their shape vaguely reminiscent of his square-framed glasses. His back was curved. The bones of his spine rose through the fur.

"Dad," Camilo whispered, taking a step closer.

Diego's lips peeled back, sharp canine teeth below. The glass blocked the noise, but he leaped forward, gnashing his jaw, eyes pinned to his son. A white haze clung to their glow.

Don't you recognize me?

Julia claimed he couldn't, but surely, there was some part of Diego still within.

Camilo drew closer and rested his hand on the glass, trying to get a sense of the depth. It was bullet-proof and tempered. Difficult to obtain in a large quantity without someone asking questions. He'd need to make his father's new cage of mainly metal.

That will be the easy part.

Camilo looked over his shoulder toward the door he'd entered through. Hanging on the wall beside it were three large tranquilizer guns. Another two were attached to the ceiling beyond. In order to clean Diego's cage and bring in fresh supplies, Julia had to shoot her former partner with the glowing white liquid.

It wasn't a standard tranquilizer.

They'd used something different when Camilo was younger. Julia had needed to use massive amounts and mix it into Diego's food for it to take effect. The Morgana Center originally had a division dedicated to creating it, and the cost of supplies had been exorbitant. Tobias Buckler's donation had simplified things.

Camilo would need to steal some of the glowing white liquid to start. He could figure out an alternative method to feed his father later.

Maybe walk into the room with him and trust that he won't hurt me.

Diego's head tilted, studying his son with big yellow eyes. He leaned back his head and opened the short muzzle.

Camilo watched the silent howl. The last time he'd heard his father was fifteen years ago. It was the same day that his father's curse reached the point of no return.

Originally, Diego's body had shifted between forms—a wolf one night, a human the next. Then, he'd become stuck.

Diego had been at work when it happened, but he'd run before Julia, or anyone else, could stop him. He had been half a beast, mind addled and twisted, but they guessed at once where he'd fled—back to his parents' apartment, searching for his son.

Camilo's memories from that day were full of the confused, murky impressions of a child. He recalled his father telling him that they were going to live in the forest. But the memory was false. Diego's curse had cost him the ability to speak.

Moving to the woods must have been the whimsical invention of a five-year-old's imagination, Camilo inventing stories as he packed a bag full of his toys in preparation.

Abuela had found them together and screamed. She'd been reciting prayers when the team of scientists arrived.

Julia, leading the other four, had attempted to reason with Diego, using logic to coax him back to The Morgana Center so they could contain him before the madness advanced. It was as she was leading him away that the curse revealed its last cruel secret.

Camilo transformed for the first time.

His memories became moments—scents, sounds, sensations. Perfume mingled with chemicals in his nostrils. Abuela's shrill voice, begging every saint she knew for mercy. The smell of iron as Julia's eye burst, and hot blood trickled onto his paw.

Camilo shook his head, trying to erase the memories.

I'm not here to dwell on past mistakes. There's still a chance we can make things right.

Kenya may have failed to retrieve her changeling's dagger, but there were others. Camilo just needed to make sure both he and his father survived long enough for him to obtain one.

"And no old man is going to stop me."

A secure holding cell. Tranquilizers. Sufficient quantities of meat. Camilo could handle all of it.

"I just need to get you out."

Camilo walked the length of the glass, letting his hand trail along the smooth surface until he reached the door.

His father followed, gray wolf ears twitching.

The keypad was just as Camilo recalled—a curious calculator. There were no letters, and the numbers were comprised of dashes. Additional symbols surrounded the ten digits. Some were obvious: addition, subtraction, division. He remembered using brackets in the order of operations, and pi had been all too common in geometry. But what were the upside-down *U* and *T,* or even the vertical line?

There was a camera in the corner of the room. Holly might be watching.

Camilo adjusted his stance so that she couldn't see him trying combinations, as he recited the riddle. "I deal in numbers."

Perhaps that meant the mathematical symbols were a distraction.

"And half absolutes."

He typed his mother's birthday. The door gave no response.

"Nothing's enclosed if you flip the truth."

The date of his mother's death proved just as fruitless.

"Theirs ends with them. His starts with mine."

Who was *they*? Who was *he*? Camilo didn't even know if *mine* referred to his father. But he kept typing all the significant dates he could think of for his family.

"Do deviations recess," he came to the end of the riddle, just as confused as he had been when he started, "Or follow the line?"

Camilo's finger hovered over the vertical line. Something dark slammed against the door from the opposite side of the glass.

The sound was blocked, but the impact was enough that the entire prison trembled.

Camilo stumbled back. He stared in horror as his father flung himself against the glass.

The madness was upon him.

Diego gnashed at his own limbs, tearing at the massive paws that had replaced his hands. Blood dripped from his jowls. He rose onto his hind legs, taking the shape of a man for a second before launching forward again. His claws raked against the door, leaving red streaks dripping down the glass.

One of the guns mounted to the ceiling of the prison fired six darts. Four found their target.

White liquid sank into Diego's limbs, and he tottered to the ground.

Holly rushed in a few seconds later. "Dammit, Camilo, what did you do?"

"Nothing." He held up his hands, already a few feet shy of the door lest Holly get suspicious. "I don't know what set him off."

Maybe he doesn't want me to free him.

But that was only because Diego didn't know the future that awaited him otherwise.

"Jesus. If he were to have escaped..." Holly rested her hand to her chest. Her body was trembling. Even with Diego knocked out, she hadn't dared to venture too far into the cell. "That glass won't hold forever. I know it hurts to see, Cam, but Mr. Buckler might be saving us all by—" She cut herself off.

"No, by doing what, Holly? Finish your thought." Camilo crossed toward her so that they were both standing before the metal door. "Clearly, you know what the old man is planning."

Holly stepped back, trying to keep space between herself and Camilo. She was still shaking, but her gaze was defiant. "By sending your father to fight a dragon."

32
KENYA

Doc sniffed the grass as they walked the perimeter of what Kenya assumed was The Western Woodlands. Massive trees towered within a border of painted wooden panels. They depicted colorful images of wildlife: bumblebees sipped from massive pink blooms, a family of raccoons devoured a basket of berries, a bird with snow white plumage spread its wings amid a halo of sunshine.

But so far, there'd been no sign of a yale, which according to Kenya's phone, was an *antelope- or goat-like creature with the tusks of a boar.*

"Are you sure we're allowed in?" Lily chewed the end of her braid, glancing from the painted panels to the storefronts on the opposite side of the street. "I can't imagine the mayor put wooden panels with no entrances around a public space he wanted people to explore."

"I told you there's a door by the—"

Doc barked and tugged at the leash, refusing to move further.

Kenya turned to find him wagging his tail at one of the panels.

"That's not a real deer, Doc." She rubbed the golden-doodle's head. "Do you think you're a hunter? Silly dog, you've never even caught a mouse." Kenya tried to pull him on.

"Please, let's do something else," Lily said, wrapping her arms around herself and shivering despite the heat. "I won't even complain about hiking."

"Doc won't budge," Kenya said. It was odd. The golden-doodle was well-trained.

What about this image had so captured his attention?

Kenya looked at the large brown eyes of the creature in the panel's painting. At first glance, she'd assumed it was a deer, but there were tusks protruding from its jaw, and its antlers twisted in a shell-like spiral.

"This is it. This is the yale." It was prettier than Kenya had expected. She kissed the top of her dog's head. "You found it, Doc."

So where's the door?

Kenya reached forward. Her hand slipped through the panel.

Lily screamed.

"Don't freak out." Kenya retracted her arm and reached toward her friend, trying to comfort her. "I know it's a lot, Lil, but I have to tell you something. I'm not who you think, I—"

"Stop, you're being weird." Lily pulled away. She squeezed her eyes shut. "I don't feel well. I'm sorry, girl, I have to go."

"Wait," Kenya shouted, but it was too late. Lily was already running back toward her car. "You're my ride."

The tears that had been plaguing her all day began to

pool once more as Kenya stared at her friend's retreating back.

I was going to tell you the truth, about magic, about me.

Kenya pressed the heel of her palm against the corner of her eye, trying to stop her tears. It wasn't like she was really stuck here alone. She could catch up to Lily.

I am a weird species with super-speed after all.

But that was exactly why her friend had fled.

Seeing just a bit of magic had panicked Lily. What would she do if she learned that Kenya wasn't even Kenya?

Doc barked. His nose was still pointing toward the panel.

The yale watched them with its big, brown eyes. There was a challenge in its gaze.

Maybe Kenya wasn't who she'd always assumed, but she was someone. It was time to decide who.

Can I follow Lily and pretend that none of this ever happened? Just continue life as though I never learned the truth?

Kenya tightened her grip around Doc's leash, took a deep breath, and ran forward.

Her sneakers landed on soft, springy earth. Before her eyes, a forest stretched, full of every type of green she could imagine. Towering trees rustled in the wind, sending a rain of leaves cascading to the grass beneath. Colorful fruits dangled from twisting vines, and blossoms opened to the sun. The air was full of their sweet, floral perfume.

"Wow." Kenya's breath caught. She'd never entered a magical forest before. Heart pounding, she turned. From this side, the wooden panel with the depiction of the yale didn't exist. Instead, she could see the cars on the street beyond, pedestrians milling on the distant sidewalk, shopfronts behind.

Doc ran up to the nearest tree, cocked his leg, and released a stream.

"Smart, claim the woods as your own." Kenya giggled, but the joke only amused her for so long.

These woods must have belonged to someone. Were there more people within, like the red-headed siblings she'd encountered earlier?

Kenya stared into the darkness of the trees beyond. The trunks were large, but spread wide, leaving enough space for an elephant to pass. It made the deeper woods appear like a series of twisting caverns.

Something magical waited beyond. Kenya wasn't going to run from it.

"Come on, Doc. We're going on an adventure."

———

Kenya's heart pounded as she wove around the trees, jumping over roots and slipping on patches of moss. Doc bounced beside her, nose sniffing the air. Pockets of sunlight fell through the leaves, creating golden puddles to guide their path, and birds serenaded them from the distant branches, their music whistling through the woods.

The rhythm felt familiar. Kenya couldn't explain how, but she hummed with them.

Doc caught the scent of something and pulled her deeper into the trees. His tongue lolled from his mouth, and a thin trail of drool dripped onto the grass. The goldendoodle's version of Hansel and Gretel's breadcrumbs.

The smell that had captured Doc's attention wafted toward Kenya a few paces later.

Bread. Someone's baking bread.

How was that possible in the middle of a forest?

There was only one way to find out. Kenya just hoped her fairytale analogy wasn't too apt. She didn't want to run into a cannibalistic witch who was trying to lure in unsuspecting strangers with a house built from baguettes.

The trees grew taller and stranger the further they traveled into the woods. Trunks twisted in strange ways, making Kenya's path on the forest floor narrow while opening wide spaces in the canopy above. It was almost like someone had used magic to carve a path for a very large creature.

Above her, the branches moved. They stretched and eased, closing the gaps. Kenya's breath caught. Maybe she was being a bit too brave.

Doc, who shared none of her fears, continued leading the way, tail flouncing to either side. He stopped to sniff the air and loose an excited bark every few feet, and soon, the shadows of the trees gave way to a sunken grove.

Kenya gasped as she saw it.

Within, was a brilliant garden surrounded by a village. Painted wooden homes in a variety of shapes and sizes circled the perimeter and climbed the sides of nearby trunks. Bridges hung from the canopies, connecting the trees. People walked on stone pathways, tended to the garden, shouted to one another from windows.

But they weren't humans.

Kenya sank onto a raised root, speechless as she stared into the sunken grove. A pair of massive butterfly wings, full of bright pink swirls, fluttered at the corner of her vision. They were attached to a small person, about a foot high, who whizzed past her ear toward the garden. Kenya watched as they attempted to pull a carrot from the dirt.

A few feet away, shouting to someone at a higher level, was a man in gray sweats and a tropical print shirt. His skin was orange, and his pointed ears stretched to the back of his skull. Skipping up a stone path, toward where Kenya sat, was a young woman with leaves woven into her long black braid.

"Don't you know it's rude to sit on my roots," she said, shaking her head at Kenya before sinking into the trunk.

Kenya's mouth fell open as she scrambled to her feet. "Sorry," she said, and heard a sound like a *humph* from within the tree. It was bizarre.

And amazing.

There's another world within our city.

"How is this—?" Kenya turned to Doc, bursting with thoughts. But the goldendoodle was busy making friends with a rather bold chipmunk.

Kenya had just made the most incredible discovery of her life, and she had no one to share it with. No one she cared about had any idea that magic was real, and it might ruin their lives if she told them.

There was only one exception. And he currently hated her.

Kenya was going to change that.

33
CAMILO

Camilo positioned a large pane of glass in the doorway of his abuela's old room. The interior was empty. He'd shoved the old bed and dresser into the living area, squishing them behind the couch and against the shelves full of tchotchkes.

The floor was layered in metal beneath Camilo's feet. He took ten steps backward into the room before his heel hit the wall. This was it.

Camilo closed his eyes, made a silent prayer, and charged. His shoulder slammed into the glass. Was it enough to hold?

Crack!

The glass shattered beneath his weight, and Camilo tumbled forward. He managed to catch himself on his hands and knees instead of planting face-first onto the living room floor.

"*Me cago en todo lo que se menea,*" Camilo cursed at the broken shards that surrounded him, slamming his fist down in a fury. The expression was another of his abuela's curses. It translated roughly to *I shit on everything that moves.*

Camilo had broken through over four inches of glass. There was no way it would be enough to contain his father.

The entire room will have to be encased in metal.

He'd suspected as much, but it wasn't ideal. A solid door meant that Camilo wouldn't be able to check on his father without entering the room. He'd hoped he could find a way. But bulletproof glass had proven difficult to obtain. Everywhere that sold it within the city either worked only with businesses or insisted on doing the installation themselves. Camilo could just imagine the questions if they discovered a nineteen-year-old Latino building a prison cell in his grandmother's old bedroom.

Plus, he didn't want witnesses. Even in a city, secrets could spread. When Diego disappeared from The Morgana Center, Camilo would be the obvious suspect. But no one was likely to assume that he'd hidden his father in his apartment. It would be easier to release Diego into Castor's Woods, the sprawling forest to the north, where deadly beasts were already rumored to roam. None of the scientists would risk trying to track him within.

Blood dripped into Camilo's eye. He reached up and pulled a shard of glass from his forehead. More had embedded themselves in his palms and knees.

So much for this being shatterproof.

Camilo stood and immediately regretted not wearing shoes. Angry chunks of glass grew like stalagmites on the floor of a cave. He tiptoed through their maze, wincing every time his eyes failed to notice the light glint off their clear surface.

A trail of bloody prints marked his progress to the kitchen.

Camilo grabbed a bowl from above the sink and a pair of tweezers from the junk drawer.

Pumpkin lay on the counter above, flicking his tail. There was a white bandage wrapped around the cat's front leg and an empty tuna can in front his chin. He batted it onto the tiles with his paw, then turned his gaze longingly toward the food atop the microwave.

"Nice try," Camilo informed the cat, sitting on one of the kitchen stools. "But you can't keep milking my sympathy. I'm injured too." It wasn't a fair comparison. Camilo's cuts would heal in a matter of minutes.

There were some advantages to being cursed.

Camilo pulled a shard from his palm using his teeth. He spat the glass toward the sink. A few feet away were two books. His father's copy of *Dune* was open to the riddle on the back page. Beside it was a notebook with a to-do list, each item more daunting than the last.

Number one. Build an unbreakable cage.

Number two. Steal a keycard.

And then, the worst of all: number three. *Solve the code for Dad's door.*

Camilo ground his teeth, using the tweezers to pull the glass from his legs and shoulders.

Pumpkin watched the shards fly across the kitchen and land in the sink.

"Don't suppose you're secretly a sphinx who solves riddles?" Camilo asked, removing the last piece of glass. He scratched the top of the cat's head. "Or do sphinxes only give riddles? Either way, suppose I can't ask more of you."

Pumpkin lifted his orange chin, tilting to get Camilo's fingers where he wanted and mewling in agreement.

A high-pitched squeak came from the living room.

Pumpkin's fur rose in objection. He hissed, jumped from the counter, and retreated to the bedroom, proving more agile than Camilo when it came to dodging glass.

Another desperate squeak came from the apartment's doorbell. It was soon drowned by someone pounding against the door.

"Please, let me in," Kenya's voice called from the other side.

Oh God. Camilo stared at the door. *What is she doing here?*

After freeing her from the handcuffs yesterday morning, he'd assumed that was the end of their relationship—fake or real. Kenya would be safer away from him, outside of The Morgana Center's sphere of influence. And Camilo needed to focus on his father.

Yet, he found himself with the strangest desire to go to the door. But that was silly. He could wait for her to go away.

"I know you're in there. I saw your truck outside," Kenya shouted. "Please. Cam, I'm so sorry about the dagger. I messed up, and I feel terrible."

Now she was apologizing to him?

Camilo groaned and stood. He couldn't have her yelling about magic in the hallway. Most of his neighbors were only half deaf.

"It's fine, Kenya." Camilo pulled the door open and found her standing on the mat. She'd dressed in all the shades of green—lime sneakers and matching hair tie, sage shirt, and shorts the color of the forest. "You don't need to apologize, okay? You did your best. I shouldn't have let you take the handcuffs. Or yelled at you. I'm just—not having the best few days."

"I have something to show you that might make you change your mind." Kenya's hands fluttered in the air before her, a nervous smile spread across her face. "I found the Western Woodlands."

34
CAMILO

Camilo's blood raced through his veins, the pulse in his neck quaking like he'd just run a marathon.

But all he was doing was staring at a painting.

The yale watched him too—a deer with large brown eyes and ivory tusks. It seemed to be beckoning him forward. Camilo's arm raised.

"...and then Lily just left," Kenya finished telling him what had happened with her friend. "Do you think I scared her?"

Camilo froze. The question burned in his ears. How many times had he wondered the same thing?

The truth was that most humans didn't handle magic well. Camilo had been used as a demonstration once for The Morgana Center. He'd seen the fledgling scientists faint before him or grow violently ill. Their brains couldn't comprehend the supernatural. When they'd finally managed, their emotions had ranged from anxious to petrified.

But they'd seen him. Not Kenya.

She transformed into a cute little house cat. And her magic smelled like cinnamon and ginger.

Camilo reached out and grabbed Kenya's hand the way he'd often wished someone would grab his. She stared up at him, caught off guard.

"Of course not," he assured her. "This woods is probably protected by an enchantment. Most Castor strongholds have wards around them that prevent humans from entering."

"Oh." Kenya still looked sad, but she'd latched onto Camilo's hand with a surprisingly strong grip. "I suppose that means my parents also..." She sighed and looked at her shoes. "Not that I would've brought them. I know they're better off not knowing. I just feel..." A forced smile spread across her face. "But I'm not alone. Because you're here."

Camilo pulled his hand from Kenya and rubbed the back of his neck with an uncomfortable laugh. He hadn't exactly come here out of the goodness of his heart.

Holly asked about the Western Woodlands. And Tobias has plans to attack a dragon in a Castor stronghold. That doesn't sound like a coincidence.

"You said you saw goblins, pixies, nymphs." Camilo recalled the descriptions that Kenya had given him. "Anything else?"

"I don't know. You're the one who gave me all those names."

But she'd recognize a dragon.

Maybe Camilo was wasting his time. Once his father was safe, what did he care if Tobias slayed a dragon? They were deadly beasts who hoarded gold and burned innocents with their flames.

Camilo wondered what excuse he could offer. He needed to get to the hardware store.

Kenya's eyes were wide and hopeful.

The excuse caught in Camilo's throat. He couldn't run off the way her friend had. That would be cruel. And it was barely past midday. The hardware store would still be open in a few hours.

You're just making excuses to spend time with her. You enjoy her company too much.

Julia wouldn't approve. Neither would Holly.

Camilo didn't care what either of them thought. He grabbed Kenya's hand again. "Come on."

Together, they stepped through the painting.

———

A new world of scents and smells erupted before Camilo— sweet fruits, soft flowers, warm earth soaked in sun. Animals played in the trees, the taps of their footsteps the rhythm to the birds' song.

It called to him.

Curiosity compelled Camilo to walk further into the woods. He didn't know which direction to turn his head. The flora mimicked the eclectic buildings of the city. Tropical plants blossomed alongside deciduous elms and oaks, all far larger than they had any right to be.

"You don't have a problem in here." Kenya followed him.

Camilo stopped, staring at a papaya tree four times his height. A pair of black squirrels balanced on its leaves, attempting to shake loose a massive papaya. "Am I supposed to?"

"You said humans couldn't enter."

It was like the squirrels had dropped the papaya onto

Camilo's head, and the force of it flattened him to the ground. His body stiffened, yet he felt himself sinking.

"Forget it." Kenya pushed a curl behind her ear. "I'm sorry I said anything. I'm sorry for everything. And I'm going to make it up to you."

But it wasn't that simple.

Humans can't enter Castor strongholds. Julia's told me as much.

No enchantment had compelled Camilo to leave or banished him from the area. But the curse interacted with other magic in strange ways. That wasn't what panicked him.

Why did I just assume that I could enter?

Was it the painting of the yale's eyes? Was it Kenya?

Or was it Camilo himself? Did some part of him know the truth?

No matter how many times I say it or insist otherwise, the curse means that I'm not really—

"Listen," Kenya's voice cut off his thoughts. She positioned herself so that she was before him. Camilo's gaze latched onto her, an anchor of reality amid the panicked swirling of his thoughts. "I, Kenya Davidson, because I'm pretty sure that's still my name—"

What is she talking about? Why would that not be her name?

"—swear to fulfill my original end of our bargain. I will get the changeling's dagger for you."

She held up her pinky finger.

Camilo stared at it. He recalled when he was twelve, making a similar promise with a girl.

Holly said that she would be with me when we were older. And I promised that I'd cure my curse.

This time, Camilo didn't have anything to offer. He

stared at Kenya's proffered finger. "I can't live up to my end of our deal."

Faking Olympic test results wasn't exactly in Camilo's wheelhouse. He assumed Tate, or even one of the other scientists, could find a way. But no one at The Morgana Center would help Camilo after he broke his father loose.

Kenya didn't flinch. "I don't care. I'm making you a promise. I want to help you."

Not a deal. Just...a kindness.

Camilo took her hand in his, pressed her pinky finger into her fist. "You're crazy. You don't have to help me."

"Yes, I do." Kenya refused to let him push her arm down. She stared at him, eyes rimmed with red. "Because, like it or not, Camilo, we're friends. Or at least, I'm your friend. But I hope you're mine too because I could really do with one right now."

Friends.

When Camilo was younger, his grandparents had kept him apart from other children as much as possible. The only friend he'd ever had was Holly. Because, afraid of him or not, she was the only one who knew what he was, the only one who could choose to spend time with him regardless. Any human would've been ignorant to the risks of a friendship with Camilo.

He stared at the trembling orange fruit, unable to meet Kenya's eyes though her hand was still clasped in his. "You don't know what I am."

"So tell me."

Kenya stood close, unafraid. Telling her would change that.

As it should. She trusts me too much. I don't deserve it. I haven't even told her the truth.

Camilo's gaze turned to the grass. With an effort, he

summoned, the words. They came in a voice that was soft
and low and openly ashamed.

"I'm a werewolf."

35
KENYA

For the next week after Camilo's confession, Kenya distracted herself from her ongoing identity crisis with a new routine.

Morning training sessions with her parents were unavoidable. Each time she mentioned the Olympics, her father started cheering or her mother began talking about professional coaches. And the words Kenya wanted to say stuck in her throat. No amount of rehearsing was going to prepare her for their reactions when she informed them she was quitting.

But how was Kenya feeling about it?

Competing at the Olympics had always been her dream. Hadn't it? So why was her biggest concern disappointing her parents? She should've been screaming into her pillow and holding back tears whenever she thought of the shiny gold medal that would never be hers. But when she searched for despair, Kenya mainly found indifference.

Not only was she a biological imposter, but an emotional one. Did Kenya really share her father's love of mathematics and science fiction? Did she actually enjoy shopping with her mother? Was she a fan of the romcoms she and Lily watched every month?

Or would those aspects of her personality fade too?

The moment she could escape, Kenya fled from those thoughts. Straight to Camilo.

The werewolf.

He'd only spoken the word once when he first confessed in the Western Woodlands.

Kenya had laughed. She didn't understand why Camilo was so anxious to tell her. After a magic dagger, an elf, and flames that turned her into a cat, Kenya could handle a werewolf. No amount of Camilo insisting that he was dangerous had convinced her otherwise. Not even when he'd explained the situation with his father.

Diego Lopez was locked in his wolf state, safe for the moment, but he needed to be moved soon.

Perhaps saying Camilo had *explained* things was a stretch. He'd been sparse on details. The conversation seemed to pain him.

But it was enough for Kenya to know that she'd made the right decision by promising to help him.

Camilo occupied most of her days. She spent mornings at his apartment, holding metal panels as he bolted them to the wall with an ear-screeching drill. When the work of building an unbreakable cage exhausted him, they drove together to the Western Woodlands.

He's the perfect distraction.

Camilo's gray shorts showed the muscles in his thighs, and the tight sleeves on his white t-shirt made his bicep bulge as he turned the wheel. Kenya indulged in the memory of him removing his shirt earlier when the heat of the apartment had overwhelmed him. Sweat had made his muscles glisten, and it had been impossible not to stare as he'd returned to work. There was something undeniably attractive about Camilo using power tools.

"What are you thinking about?" Camilo asked, flicking his eyes away from the road.

Heat swept over Kenya's face. Had she been staring?

She leaned forward and fiddled with the radio, switching through the stations until she found one playing music. Answering Camilo's question honestly seemed a definite way to get a lecture on what *friendship* meant.

"Training," she lied.

Camilo shifted the black pouch on his shoulder. He never left his apartment without it. Kenya didn't know why. The handcuffs were no longer her target.

"Huh." Camilo's eyes narrowed, and for a moment, Kenya worried he'd call her out, but then a smile tugged at his lips. "You must really want that mango. Cause you've been lost in thought most of our drive."

Is he teasing me?

Kenya adjusted the lime green scrunchie holding up her curls. If he'd somehow guessed that she was fantasizing about him, she might never be able to meet Camilo's eyes again. Perhaps she should stop indulging in her one-sided crush so obviously. Training was a safer distraction.

And anything would be better than letting her thoughts drift back to herself.

———

The largest mango hung near the top of a massive tree, round and untouched. Two days had brought over a dozen failed attempts. But today, finally, Kenya was going to reach it.

She used her magic to propel herself through the

branches. The lower rungs were the most challenging, requiring the most speed to clear the distance. Kenya had struggled to even get her feet off the grass on her first few tries.

But now, she'd learned the secrets of the tree—where the branches were strong, where they grew thin, where she needed to place her weight.

Blue and red flames twisting around her legs, Kenya leaped and clung and climbed until she reached the final limb. It shuddered, but held, beneath her weight as she found her footing. The mango hung before her.

With a quick twist, she plucked it free.

"Victory!" Kenya waved the fruit over her head. "The crowd goes wild! They say Kenya Davidson is the absolute GOAT of mango retrieval!"

Camilo's voice called back, "You still have to make it down."

Down?

Kenya hadn't considered that aspect of the climb. She clutched the trunk as she stared at the grass below. It was a thirty-foot drop. Her head started to spin. Her heart raced. A familiar flood of warmth spread through her muscles, forcing them to contract.

Oh no. I don't want to—

Too late.

The blue and red flames emerged from within her, and a moment later, Kenya was a cat.

A week of training, and she still hadn't learned to control her shifting.

She hated it. Even the word *shifter* made her skin crawl. She remembered Camilo labeling her a *strange species*, imagined what her parents might think.

No.

Kenya Davidson might not have been a human, but she was still a person. Not a cat. Not a *shifter*. This fur, with its many shades of orange and peach, was only an outfit. She might be forced to wear it on occasion, but it wasn't *her*. Neither was the tail that trembled behind her with its fluffy white tip. Nor the vibrating whiskers by her nose.

Kenya sank her temporary claws into the branch. *"Get me down! Get me down!"* Her cries sounded like loud mewls.

Camilo's laugh was loud and deep, rising with the wind to shake the leaves. "Give me a second."

Kenya stretched as much as she dared, peering over the side as Camilo jumped onto the lowest branch with enviable ease. His white tank and small gray exercise shorts had his muscles on full display as he climbed, glittering with a light sheen of sweat.

Drool dripped from the corner of Kenya's mouth. It was harder to control as a cat.

Her claws were buried too deep into the tree. She had to twist her head to wipe her mouth against her shoulder, using the orange fur as a napkin, before Camilo arrived.

"Show off." Kenya's words were a hiss.

Camilo grinned as he pulled himself up onto the branch beside her. He kept his back pressed to the trunk. "You're looking awfully cat-like for a goat." He laughed at his own joke, leaned forward, and scratched behind her ears.

It was even more offensive because of how good it felt.

To Kenya's horror, she found herself purring. Her eyes closed, her claws retracted, and her head nuzzled toward his fingers.

Heat spread from her chest to the back of her eyes and tip of her tail. Her body stretched, morphing back to normal.

Kenya's cheek pressed against something firm and

warm. She opened her eyes and discovered that her head was now in Camilo's lap, resting against the exposed muscle of his thigh.

Her body felt hot again. It had nothing to do with magic.

Kenya sprang up, and her grip on the prize mango loosened. It slipped from her fingers.

Camilo leaned over, caught it, and returned to his seated position in a single fluid motion. He brought the fruit to his mouth and tore the skin with his teeth.

Kenya watched with more than a little awe.

He caught her staring, and his eyebrows rose. "I came to rescue you. Least you can do is share, right?"

"Are you sure you want to break your curse?"

Camilo lowered the mango. His lips pulled together, and he stared at her in sullen silence.

Perhaps Kenya was overstepping, letting her own feelings cloud her judgment, but...

"I know you're afraid that one day you'll lose control of your transformation and be stuck as a wolf, but what if that's not a guarantee? You have super strength, and speed. You heal fast." Kenya tried to recall the many abilities she'd noticed. "You understand me when I'm a cat. Do you really want to give all that up?"

Camilo turned his head; a distant glaze came over his eyes. He was sinking into one of the silent, sullen moods that plagued him when he first started work on the cage.

I should've kept my thoughts to myself.

"I scratched someone's eye out."

The fact that Camilo had spoken surprised Kenya more than the words themselves.

"It was the day my father started to morph. The woman who came to get him was a family friend. She was trying to help him, but I didn't understand. I got so angry, I trans-formed and—" His voice broke. It was the closest to tears Kenya had ever seen him.

It gave his face a vulnerability—parted lips, wide gaze—that made him even more attractive.

But there was something tortured about the way his grip tightened on the mango. His fingers broke the skin, and juice oozed onto his hand.

"Hey." Kenya reached forward and rescued the fruit from his grip. She squeezed his hand, letting the juice stick their fingers together. "You can't blame yourself for some-thing that happened when you were a child."

Camilo's gaze flicked to where she touched him. "I'm dangerous, Kenya. If I had the chance to use the dagger, but didn't, how could I live with myself if I hurt someone again?"

He addressed his question to the trees.

Kenya followed his gaze.

A large, snow-white bird, perched on the distant branch of a willow. The plumage of its tail hung below, patterned like an albino peacock. It was the one of the most beautiful creatures she'd ever seen.

"Being a changeling is a type of curse. I get stuck as an animal sometimes."

"That's just a different form you can take, Kenya," Camilo corrected her. "It's not a curse that's going to consume you, it's natural, like clenching a muscle." He flexed his bicep in demonstration. "You're only struggling because you don't believe that. And magic isn't science. It thrives on belief."

And I refuse to believe that I'm some strange species.

"Forget about my transforming," Kenya said. "What I'm saying is that I've lost everything I thought defined me. My dreams. My identity. Even my name was supposed to belong to someone else. But even with all that..." Kenya watched as the snow-white bird took flight through the trees. The branches twisted to allow it passage. "I don't think I'd take it back."

Kenya was in an enchanted forest. She'd spoken to nymphs and pixies and fairies. Maybe she didn't enjoy turning into a cat, but her powers allowed her to do things most people couldn't comprehend.

It didn't matter that her parents had been duped, that they'd been tricked into loving a child that wasn't theirs. Kenya was starting to like magic.

How selfish does that make me?

Kenya bit into the orange flesh of the mango. It was sweet. Juice dripped down her chin.

Camilo leaned forward and pressed his hand to her cheek. His thumb wiped the juice from the corner of her lip.

Kenya's heart stopped. Her breath caught. She stared into his deep, brown eyes.

How is his skin so soft?

"You're not cursed, Kenya," he said, voice soft. His hand hovered on her chin. "And you're not lost. I know exactly who you are."

Camilo brought his arm lower, resting his hand on the small of her back. He pulled Kenya toward him.

She had to remind herself to breathe. *Is he going to kiss me?*

Kenya closed her eyes as Camilo pulled her against him. Her hands pressed against his chest. She waited to feel his lips.

Instead, his breath brushed against her ear. He whispered, "You're a scaredy cat who needs rescuing from a tree."

"I'm not—" Kenya started to object, but the words died on her lips as he pulled her closer toward him. Her body pressed against his. All that separated her skin from Camilo's muscles was the thin fabric of their shirts.

"Hold on," he instructed. He tightened his grip around her waist as she wrapped her arms around his neck. Then, Camilo jumped.

Kenya's heart pounded as he carried her to the forest floor. Only when her shoes were on the grass did her words return, and she muttered a breathless objection against Camilo's shoulder, too soft for him to hear.

"I'm not scared. And I'm not a cat."

36
CAMILO

Four days remained before the deadline for his father's rescue.

The new cage was as secure as Camilo could manage, but the other two items remained unchecked on his to-do list. He should have been sweet-talking Holly to steal her keycard or hunting through the boxes of Diego's old things to find a clue to his cage's code.

Instead, Camilo was in the Western Woodlands again. Playing games with Kenya.

His bare feet pounded across the spongy grass. The wind whipped at his face as he twisted between trunks and ducked under branches. A blur of blue and red flames moved in the corner of his vision, sneaking ahead of him.

Oh, absolutely not!

Camilo gritted his teeth and pushed himself toward the red-leafed maple that was their finish line. He slapped his palm against it a split-second before Kenya, keeled over onto his knees, and let his chest fall to the grass.

His lungs burned. His head spun. He felt light and giddy, adrenaline flooding his mind.

A sound escaped from Camilo. It was one part laugh, one part gasp of a dying man. "I won!"

"That was at least a tie."

He turned his head, and his eyes rose from the lime green shoelaces to Kenya's legs, long and toned. They lingered over the curves of her calves, the muscles in her thighs, her flat stomach, visible in her cropped gray tank, before finally arriving at her face. She hadn't even broken a sweat.

Kenya grinned, an amused flicker in her eyes, taunting Camilo to object. She looked so cute, so pleased with herself. It was impossible not to smile back.

What am I doing here?

Camilo had no illusions that Kenya would be able to obtain the dagger. It might be months before her keeper returned, and the element of surprise would always be in the elf's favor.

But Kenya wanted to help. That meant more than Camilo could put into words.

Plus, it wasn't like he was wasting his time. Training with her was good for him too. Camilo needed to be at his best to pull off this rescue mission. Kenya pushed him to run faster, made him want to show off his strength.

And spending any more time alone might cost him his sanity.

Camilo could only stare at his father's riddle for so many more hours before he ripped out his own hair. He didn't dare post the entire poem on the internet, lest Holly be on the watch for it, and searching in pieces had proven futile.

He needed help.

Camilo reached into the black pouch slung across his

shoulders. The chill of the handcuffs bit his fingers as he searched for the paper within.

"I was thinking," Kenya said, holding her ankle behind her as she bent forward to stretch her leg. "That once we have the dagger—What's that?"

Camilo held up the two folded pages. He'd ripped them from *Dune* a few nights ago, after he'd forced himself to read the entire novel and found no clues within. "It's a puzzle."

Kenya moved closer. Her leg brushed his arm, and Camilo found his eyes tracing her curves once more.

"What kind? My dad made me do math puzzles when I was younger. I used to like them. Who knows if I still do?"

Kenya folded to touch her toes. She was angling her head to see the paper. But her position suggested a number of less wholesome things to Camilo. He tried to keep his eyes from glancing at her ass, and he shifted so that her face wasn't so close to his thighs.

He cleared his throat and unfolded the pages on the grass between them. "I don't *think* it's a math puzzle. But there is a calculator. Sort of."

Kenya took her stretching to the ground, touching the bottoms of her feet together and pressing her knees down. She leaned forward. Her lips mouthed the riddle as she read, and her eyes flicked to the calculator. "Interesting."

"You have an answer?"

"No, but there's a couple hints. We know the answer must be numbers, but it also mentions *half absolutes*. So maybe just one of the symbols." She pointed to the vertical line on the hand drawn calculator. "And *nothing's enclosed* might mean not to use parentheses, or just to use one?"

Camilo nodded. He'd wondered if that line was a hint to the bracket before too. But he didn't remember learning about an absolute symbol. "What about *flip the truth*? Any idea what that means?"

"Maybe you have to enter the answer backwards." Kenya lifted the drawing of the calculator and examined the symbols. She mumbled the riddle as she studied it, eyes on the paper with a studious focus. She pulled her curls loose, twisting one with her finger.

How does she look beautiful when she's concentrating?

Camilo rested his chin on his palm and let his shoulders slump forward. He watched her with a smile. "I think we can safely say you like puzzles. Not surprising given you sleep in old Star Trek t-shirts and have a stuffed Wookiee in your room. You're kind of a nerd."

Kenya pursed her lips as she passed the pages back to Camilo. He expected a quip—something about the Lego model in his apartment.

"You shouldn't rush to stab yourself with the dagger," she said, voice soft. Her fingers held fast to the riddle. Against the folded pages, their thumbs locked in a kiss.

Just the slight touch, the sensation of her skin against his, was like a jolt running through Camilo. His eyes latched onto hers.

"After you heal your father, I could keep it. And we could—" Kenya released the paper and turned her eyes skyward to the canopy of leaves. "You wouldn't have to just give up your powers. I'll keep an eye on you. And *if* your symptoms progress, I can break the curse before you lose control but—I don't know. What do you think?"

There was a nervous smile on Kenya's face. Her eyes flicked from the trees to Camilo.

But he didn't know what to say. She'd hinted that he shouldn't break his curse before, but this was different. She was offering to be his failsafe. Give him a way to embrace his powers without fear of losing control.

It would be wrong to accept, and yet...

A future that Camilo had never dared to imagine unfurled across the back of his eyes. He saw himself as a middle-aged man in his forties, running through the trees, abilities still intact. He could leap between branches, fall without fear, smell the symphony of scents that the forests wore as perfume. At his side were his family—his father, children, a wife.

For the first time, it wasn't Holly filling that role in his thoughts.

Camilo's ears grew hot as he stared at Kenya. She was beautiful. Loyal. Kind. Impulsive in the best way. The only person in his life who'd ever known what he was and not recoiled.

But they didn't—and might never—have the dagger.

Kenya deserved better than a man who might snap and go mad at any moment.

"Listen, I know you promised, but—" Camilo cut himself off, head tilting as he followed his own advice. There were footsteps, light but fast approaching. Someone trying not to be heard. "Shit."

Camilo shoved the riddle back into his pouch, grabbed Kenya's arm and pulled her to her feet. He stepped forward, placing himself between her and whoever approached. They weren't likely to be sneaking around with good intentions.

A thin, pale shape with bright blue wings dodged behind the trees, before stepping into the light.

The fairy couldn't have been more than sixteen, with freckles splattered across her nose. She wore her red hair tied in two buns atop her head. The color with the sunshine yellow dress that draped her body, shapeless as a sheet.

"Excuse me," she said, giving them a large toothy grin as she waved. "Have you two seen a dragon?"

———

It was a hoax. Camilo could see no other explanation.

There was no dragon in the Western Woodlands. Nor were there demons, or vampires, or witches, or anything that The Morgana Center could consider a threat. The locals were mainly nymphs and pixies, with a sprinkling of fairies—standoffish perhaps, but not dangerous.

The few pixies who'd spoken with them had made their rules clear. No killing any living thing within their woods. Even visitors had to abide. Once Camilo had learned this, he'd set all concern for the location from his mind. This couldn't be the target for Tobias Buckler's ire.

A dragon would destroy such a place.

She's just trying to waste our time.

Camilo stared at the back of the girl's wings. Thin black lines streaked through the shimmering blue. They belonged on a giant insect, not someone who looked so human.

The fairy, Poppy she'd called herself—though Camilo had his doubts about that being her real name—claimed to have been playing hide-and-seek with a dragon. A ridiculous story, but Kenya had gotten excited and offered to help look. Now, they were trekking through the trees on a pointless quest.

This girl probably lives here and is getting annoyed with us visiting so often.

All the locals likely were. The few who passed Camilo and Kenya never waved, and he doubted it was words of welcome that they muttered beneath their breath. Only a few pixies enjoyed watching them from afar. And Camilo suspected the tiny creatures were mocking them whenever he turned around.

Perhaps they'd sent Poppy to play this prank.

"You said he's purple, right?" Kenya asked, twisting her neck as though she wanted to search in every direction.

"With big gold eyes," Poppy confirmed. "He's this big —" She stretched her arms as wide as she could. "Bit bigger than a horse. If you think you see a twisting purple snake in a tree, it's probably his tail wagging."

Camilo didn't bother scanning the forest. The only creatures nearby were a pair of rabbits and a lone squirrel. He could smell the faint musk of their scents. There was no hint of a dragon in the air.

Not that Camilo knew what a dragon smelled like.

Like a snake or fire. Maybe.

Whatever. It would be something distinct, and Camilo would notice. There was no reason to worry. None at all.

But an irrational fear gnawed at his stomach.

"Seems like your dragon would be too large to hide in these woods," Camilo said, stepping forward to walk alongside the fairy.

Poppy glanced at him. "Oote's not *my* dragon. I'm only helping watch him while Fran is away."

Camilo snorted. The fairy was a terrible liar. Dragons had names like *Skullfire,* and *Flamesong,* and *Starfall.*

"He loves to play hide-and-seek, but he always cheats," Poppy continued, kicking a pebble with her toes. "Ivan should never have taught him how to turn invisible!" She cupped her hand to her mouth and shouted the answer into the trees as though she thought this imaginary, invisible dragon was before them now.

This is getting increasingly ridiculous.

What little uncertainty Camilo had entertained shrank to a negligible speck. There was no dragon in the Western Woodlands.

The trees were too close; the branches too crowded; the story too far-fetched. It would've burned the whole place down or starved to death long ago.

Tobias Buckler had no reason to be interested in the Western Woodlands. Holly must've heard its name somewhere else.

"Oh, no, look at the time!" Camilo looked at his wrist. He didn't have a watch, but given the nonsense the fairy had invented, he didn't see why his lie needed to be believable. "We have to go, but good luck finding your invisible Hoot."

Camilo grabbed Kenya's hand and pulled her away before either she or the fairy could protest.

"That girl was lying," he muttered, explaining the situation to Kenya under his breath as they left the woods. But, despite his relative certainty, Camilo's eyes darted in every direction as they walked through the trees.

He couldn't shake the feeling that an invisible dragon might be watching.

37
KENYA

"Look at this menu." Kenya's father lifted the plastic covered sheet as he sat at the table. " More like Somewhat Okay Food."

He made the same joke every time he visited the restaurant.

Very Good Food specialized in cheap, greasy meals. A squashed dining area consisted of wobbling, plastic-covered tables and cheap chairs that were too small for most of the restaurant's patrons. Kenya had spent her last two years of high school working in the kitchen as a waitress, or chef's assistant, or whatever title her boss, Ed Healey, wanted to assign.

The restaurant had once been Kenya's favorite, mostly because of its burgers. Less so now. Not because of Ed or any of the staff. It was the patrons. A block away from Very Good Food, there was a massive manor with a family of unsettling aristocrats. After an incident—which Kenya was now beginning to realize had likely involved magic—she'd been less comfortable at the restaurant. It was part of why she'd quit.

But Kenya had never mentioned that to her parents. As far as they knew, Very Good Food was still her favorite. They wouldn't have brought her tonight if they didn't want to discuss something serious.

"Ed says the name is ironic," Kenya said, lifting up the plastic menu as a shield. She didn't bother reading the items. Outside of the daily soup, the menu never changed.

"That would suggest he has bad food," Courtney muttered. She tapped her fingers in disapproval as she scanned the specials. "It's certainly unhealthy. What would you recommend?"

Kenya shrugged. The excitement of almost seeing a dragon, followed by the disappointment of learning the creature didn't exist had put her in an unfortunately pensive mood.

The kitchen door swung open. Ed Beasley's stomach appeared, followed by the man himself. There was a blue apron tied around his waist with the establishment's name in block letters. A baseball hat in a similar style declared him the manager. Ed had become a fervent believer in identifying himself as the boss the day after he noticed a bald patch near the top of his head.

"Huh." Ed scoffed as he approached. "If it isn't my ex-waitress come to steal my kitchen's new secrets. We're out of burgers."

"That would be impressive given the number he kept stocked in the freezer," Kenya said.

Ed finally cracked a smile. "They're lasting longer with you gone. Guess that's the plus side of losing my fastest waitress to the Olympics."

"Oh, I don't think that's likely." A weird, high-pitched laugh bubbled up from Kenya's stomach. She clamped her mouth shut and avoided looking at her parents while they gave in their orders.

Ed returned to the kitchen without writing any of them down.

The moment the door swung closed behind him, Courtney leaned across the table, expression serious. "Why would you make a comment like that? I didn't raise you to cut yourself down."

Kenya reached for the menu only to find that Ed had taken it with him. She had nothing to hide behind.

"What your mother means is that you're our miracle baby." Reuben leaned over and squeezed Kenya's chin. "You are the most talented kid. You're destined to be an Olympian." He did his usual cheer.

Oh God.

Kenya's legs twitched. Her feet burned. Wisps of flame swirled beneath her chair. She wasn't a baby, or a kid. She wasn't even theirs.

"That's not..." Kenya tried to find the words. Her parents' eyes were wide, full of love, worried about the girl they thought was their daughter, their miracle child who'd almost died. But in reality—

The repetitive ring of Kenya's phone trilled in the pocket of her jeans. She reached around to grab it and saw the name on the screen: *Unknown Caller.*

Is she ever going to quit?

There was only one person it could be. Yasmin Gul. Since realizing that Kenya had blocked her number, the newspaper intern had been using burner phones to try get in contact. Perhaps ignoring personal boundaries and bombarding people with overly wordy offers had gotten Yasmin interviews in the past. It was only making Kenya fantasize about the intern falling into a septic tank and having her picture taken as she crawled out, preferably covered in feces.

"Is it *Lily*?" Courtney put on a high-pitched sarcastic tone as she said the name. "Can't remember any summer where you've spent so much time with her."

Kenya cut the call and lowered the phone. If her mother knew she was spending time with Camilo, why couldn't she just come out and say it? Kenya shouldn't even have to lie. She was eighteen!

But I do have to lie. About everything.

"Which is fine," Reuben said, giving his wife a look before resting his hand on his daughter's wrist. "But we're concerned you're losing yourself a bit."

So they could tell.

Did that mean they were also going to notice that Kenya wasn't really theirs?

Tears pooled in her eyes. She needed to focus on something else.

But Camilo wasn't here to distract her.

"You haven't been pushing yourself this past week," Courtney said. "Your practice times have been slower than ever, and you haven't seemed to care."

"It's like, you've lost your spark for running," Reuben agreed.

"That's not true," Kenya interrupted. She never felt more alive than when she ran. It just wasn't when she slowed herself down to human speeds during 400M dashes.

Racing Camilo through the forest and almost winning had made her giddy.

And that would be gone too once he had the dagger.

Why didn't he say anything about my idea to wait before breaking his curse?

Had he forgotten or was he offended?

"That is not the face of someone happy." Courtney pointed a finger at her daughter. "You need to remember where your focus is supposed to be."

Ed stepped out of the kitchen, carrying their plates. Kenya's mother fell silent, straightening her gold necklace, and smiling as though they'd been having a normal conversation. Her eyes fell at the sight of her salad, hastily constructed from burger toppings.

Once they were alone again, Courtney turned back to her daughter. "Your father and I think you should compete in the marathon."

Kenya's eyebrows rose. Her mother couldn't be serious. "On Saturday? That's two days. I haven't been training." She didn't need to explain to her parents that dashing 400 meters and pacing yourself for twenty-six miles were two drastically different skill sets.

"Lily can run alongside you. It's not like she won't love the opportunity to chat, and maybe you'll remember just how capable you are."

"No one expects you to win," Kenya's father reassured her.

But I probably could.

Maintaining her magic for twenty-six miles straight would be impossible, but Kenya could manage enough bursts to set her ahead. She could just imagine the newspaper article then.

Briony would be thrilled. Secrecy seemed to be the one thing the elf and Camilo agreed on.

If I won a marathon, Briony would probably come back to chuck me out the window for real this time.

Kenya's eyes widened.

"At least think about it," Reuben said, chuckling and

adjusting his collar. He pulled his calculator from his pocket. "A little late, but you up for the challenge, miracle girl?"

"Sure, Dad."

But while her father stole a menu from a nearby table and began crunching the numbers, math was the furthest thing from Kenya's mind.

I know how we can get the dagger.

The idea didn't fill her with excitement, but dread. She didn't want to lose Camilo.

Kenya didn't want to break her promise to him either.

38
CAMILO

A large solitary oak marked the turn off Sylvanwood Avenue that led to the home of Drs. Nevil and Julia Nichols.

Camilo's four days were dwindling to three. And two items remained unchecked on his list.

The riddle required another pair of eyes, or at least a fresh perspective. Holly couldn't be trusted to help. But she did have a keycard.

Camilo lifted the hood of his jacket and slipped down the street, hugging the stone wall of the property beside. This small sub-section of the city was known as Professor's Nook. The collection of three-story homes was less than five blocks from the university and occupied almost exclusively by its senior lecturers. Each house was separated from its neighbors by low stone walls and wrought iron gates.

As a child, Camilo had assumed it was one of the wealthiest areas in the city. But he'd had only his grandparents' rent-controlled apartment for comparison. Professor's Nook was, at best, upper middle class. Julia may have come from money, but she'd sank it into The Morgana Center, not real estate.

The white gate to the Nichols' house was open at the end of the street. Light shone from downstairs, and there were voices within.

Camilo hadn't expected that.

Dr. Nevil Nichols, a decade and a half older than his wife, was the head of the university's biology department. He'd taken a sabbatical over a year ago to study a rare algae they'd discovered in a Swiss lake. Camilo had heard nothing about him returning.

Julia spent more nights in The Morgana Center than her home. When she did return, it was typically because she'd missed her bed.

But that was her voice downstairs among the group. Camilo picked it out. There was Tate's laugh a second later. And a third voice he recognized.

Tobias Buckler.

A gust of wind carried strange scents—smoke, ash, a sour note of sulfur. Demons. How was that possible? What was the old man up to?

Camilo stood to the side of the gate, hidden behind the wall. From this distance it was impossible to make out what was happening inside. Should he risk approaching the house to catch a glimpse? Curiosity made him inch closer, but what if he was caught?

A soft smell, like rose-scented soap, freshened the air, erasing concerns about demons. Camilo knew the fragrance well. He leaned against the wall, listening to Holly's cautious footsteps as she tiptoed across her yard and through the gate.

Her hair was loose, falling in waves to her shoulders,

and she'd wrapped herself in a blue robe that shimmered in the moonlight. She stared into the sky before turning.

Holly jumped as she spotted Camilo, standing in the shadows of the wall.

"You could've made a noise to let me know you were there," she said, resting her palm against her chest. Her brows and lashes were darker than normal; her lips had been painted red. Beneath the robe, she wore a black lace dress. "Why did you bring those?"

She pointed to the black pouch across Camilo's shoulder. The handcuffs had remained within since he'd released Kenya.

Camilo tightened his grip on the strap. "Why didn't you warn me that your mother was entertaining?"

"Excuse me?" Holly's darkened eyebrows rose. "You're the one who *told* me you were coming here. You're lucky I even came out to see you."

That was true. Camilo had wanted to avoid another coffee shop meeting, but he also knew what Holly liked. A little assertiveness excited her, and the desperation of a late-night visit would play on her sympathy.

Camilo hated trying to be so strategic with his movements. Was asking a friend for a favor supposed to feel manipulative?

If Kenya had a keycard, she'd lend it to me without even asking why.

But was that a good thing? Camilo hadn't done enough to deserve the trust she placed in him. He hadn't even told her about The Morgana Center, or its mission. Or that Holly had wanted her blood.

The thought made Camilo's shoulders tense.

A frown creased Holly's lips, and shadows danced across her cheeks. There was no sign of the round-faced girl who'd lectured him about scientific principles with starry eyes and a dream of making the world safer for humanity. She was the image of her mother.

No, part of the Holly he'd loved must still have been there. She was his friend, even if she expressed it differently. Otherwise, she wouldn't have come outside to speak with him.

"Can you hear what they're saying?" Holly asked, flicking her eyes toward the house.

"No, but I can make out Buckler's voice."

And smell demons.

Were they the ones from The Morgana Center? Had they been released? Or was it dead bodies Camilo smelled.

A horrible thought struck him. "Has Tobias done something to my dad?"

"Jesus. Not everything is about your father. He was invited to showcase *Tate*." Holly didn't disguise the bitterness in her voice. She paced in a circle, hands waving before her face. "My mother is trying to persuade Tobias that her new genius's work is the answer to all his problems. Meanwhile, I try to mention my discovery and get sent to bed like I'm twelve. Do you know how embarrassing it is to have your mother banish you while all of your coworkers are networking? They already think I'm only at The Center because of nepotism. Now, she's basically confirmed that my research is worthless. But if she knew what I've managed to create, Tate wouldn't be the only one she's calling a genius."

Holly stopped pacing. She looked toward her house.

"We should go closer. You can eavesdrop for me. I tried, but I couldn't hear anything through the doors."

Curious as he was about Tobias' plans, Camilo could

think of little that would bore him as spectacularly as Tate blabbing about his research.

He grabbed Holly's wrist. She turned, and her eyes flicked from Camilo's face to the moon. It was a waxing crescent. He knew without looking. But an innate sense of lunar cycles was all that accompanied Camilo's curse.

"You know it doesn't have an effect."

Holly's hand trembled in his grip. "It enhances your abilities. All our experiments show it."

Camilo's jaw twitched. They both knew it wasn't his enhanced healing that frightened Holly. He was talking about his transformation. It wasn't like the movies where a full moon made him lose control. She shouldn't be afraid.

But now wasn't the time to fight. Camilo was here with a purpose. "I'll eavesdrop for you, but I want to borrow your keycard in exchange."

Holly stared at him, face unreadable. She was reminding Camilo of her mother again.

"I just don't want the image of my dad throwing himself against the glass to be my last memory of him, you know?" He released her wrist.

Holly sighed. Her expression softened now that she was free. "I'm sorry, but I think you know I can't give you my keycard. Maybe I can sneak you in to see Diego one last time. Come help me and we'll figure it out later."

That wouldn't work. Holly could watch him on the cameras and sound an alarm when he opened the glass.

"Keycard or nothing." To emphasize that this was the end of the debate, Camilo pulled his phone from his pocket. He wasn't expecting a message to have come through.

The sight of Kenya's name beside it made him smile.

Holly ground her teeth. She hated being ignored. "You're being rude. It's a ridiculous request."

No less so than asking for someone's blood.

Camilo opened Kenya's message. His heart stopped.

**I know how to get the dagger before you move your dad.
Call me.**

Whatever he'd been expecting, it wasn't this.

"Seriously?" Holly's eyes flicked to the screen. "You're messaging the changeling? Is that supposed to make me jealous?"

Camilo shoved the phone into his pocket before she could read more.

"You think I'll feel insecure and agree to your deal. But I'm not worried." Holly's smile grew sweet, her voice tender. "You asked me if I could ever love someone like you right here when we were thirteen. Do you remember?"

She knew he did. The spot was two feet away, near the corner, where ivy grew on the stones. He'd tried to bury his face in it when he'd first started to cry, embarrassed to let Holly—older, smarter, and beautiful to Camilo's twelve-year-old eyes—see his tears.

"You swore you were going to break your curse one day so we could be together. And I thought that was so brave, I kissed you."

She stepped forward, letting her fingers brush against his. She stood on the tips of her toes. Her pale eyes sparkled with some mixture of excitement and fear. They started to close as she tilted her head back.

Camilo pulled away.

Holly stumbled forward. She hadn't expected him to move. Her eyes widened, and she crossed her arms beneath her chest, collecting herself as she turned to him.

I've embarrassed her.

In the past seven years, Holly had summoned the courage to kiss Camilo so infrequently, he could count the occasions on his fingers. Never had he rejected her.

But the thought of kissing Holly now felt wrong. There was only one girl whose lips had been on his mind the past week.

"Fine. Act aloof." Holly flipped her hair over her shoulder and shrugged "But we both know you're not the kind of guy who breaks promises. Feel free to message me again when you're out of whatever mood this is."

Her smile was confident if a bit forced as she turned.

Camilo watched her disappear. Holly didn't know him as well as she thought. He'd broken a deal with her in just these past couple weeks.

What's one more broken promise?

Camilo walked away and pulled out his phone to call Kenya.

39
CAMILO

He still had no keycard, no answer to the riddle. His four days had turned into two. And yet, he was feeling optimistic.

"Kenya's plan might actually work," he said, swiping a razor across his chin.

Pumpkin meowed in response, tail swishing as he stared through the open bathroom door.

The Castor's Grove Marathon was on Saturday—twenty-six miles in a massive loop around downtown. It was open to the public. Prizes were awarded and winners had their names published in the paper. It was the exact type of attention the city's Castors wanted to avoid.

If Briony thought that Kenya was planning to compete, there was a strong possibility she'd resurface and attempt to stop her. An interview in the Grover's Gazette was the perfect way to send a message to the keeper.

Camilo had helped Kenya work out the details yesterday. It all came down to Yasmin Gul. The newspaper intern had been thrilled when they'd called, though she'd attempted to cover her excitement with a layer of overly formal professionalism. She was more than willing to do an interview.

Kenya had just one stipulation. Camilo needed to be there.

Julia would be furious. Having a stray photograph in the newspaper was different to being the subject of an interview.

"But once I use the changeling's dagger on my father, Julia won't be in charge anymore." Camilo washed off the last of the shaving cream and grinned at his reflection. "And I can..."

His smile faltered. What did he want? To be free of his curse? Or to give the dagger to Kenya and keep his abilities?

Pumpkin pushed against his leg, leaving a line orange fur against the gray pants.

Camilo sighed and scooped the cat up, careful to avoid his bandaged front paw. "Continue to give you tuna, yes? You did earn it."

———

The black pouch rode shotgun in Camilo's truck. The handcuffs should've been safe in his apartment, but he preferred to keep them on him, just in case Kenya's keeper appeared unannounced. He'd left with time to spare. Being early would earn him points with Kenya's mother.

Camilo turned up the radio, singing as he drove. He kept mixing up words and laughing, almost like he was nervous.

It's an interview, not a date. And you literally just saw her yesterday. What's the difference?

Maybe it was Yasmin. The newspaper intern was bound to ask questions about their relationship. Camilo would need to play the part of a devoted boyfriend.

What if instead of *pretending* to be in a relationship with Kenya, he asked her out for real?

His phone vibrated in the cup holder.

Camilo answered. "Don't panic, I'm on my way."

"On your way where?" Julia's voice came through the loudspeaker of his truck.

Camilo's eyes widened. Why had he assumed it was Kenya? Just because he was thinking about her? He knew wasn't a genius, but he ought to be smarter than that.

"We're outside your apartment building." Julia's voice was cold and brusque. A faint quiver beneath betrayed her own uneasiness. "Are you on your way back?"

Something strange was happening. Julia never came to the apartment, not since she'd lost her eye.

"I was going to see Kenya," Camilo admitted. Whatever was going on, it felt safer not to lie. The closer to the truth he stayed, the less suspicious he would seem. "I'm still supposed to get the dagger, aren't I?"

"I should think." A man's voice grunted from the other end.

A chill went through Camilo. Tobias Buckler was outside his apartment building. What if the old man broke in and found the makeshift cage?

"Should I turn around?"

There was a pause. Camilo got the sense that they were talking on the other end.

Julia responded a few seconds later, "No. We'll collect you. Stay outside the changeling's home till then."

"No, that's—"

Julia hung up before Camilo could finish.

Her phone went straight to voicemail when he tried to call her back.

———

Camilo parked his truck across the road from the Davidsons' house. He stared at the willow tree on their property, watching the leaves fall. They were the bane of his existence whenever he dealt with the lawn.

His muscles twitched, desperate to make a move. But what?

I should've come straight here.

Camilo had turned around after his conversation with Julia. It felt safer to meet at his apartment. But she'd never answered her phone and there was no guarantee that he'd pass her on the road.

She might drive Tobias Buckler to Kenya's house anyway. What would they do if Camilo wasn't there? Would the old man insist on meeting the changeling who was supposed to steal his dagger?

The thought made Camilo's stomach turn.

So he'd gone in a circle, turning back around to reach the Davidson's house. There was no sign of Julia or Tobias, but they couldn't be far behind.

Camilo's hands twitched for his phone. He started to compose a message to Kenya, deleted it, then started again. He'd never told her about The Morgana Center, or Julia, or Tobias Buckler. Springing it on her by text right before her interview felt selfish.

And did he need to warn her?

Kenya wasn't a demon or a dragon. She shouldn't have been in danger.

It's me Julia wants to meet with.

Camilo wished she'd said why. Did it have to do with his father? The dagger? Tobias Buckler's mysterious dragon?

Whatever it was, Camilo hoped it was quick.

Yasmin would be arriving soon. Kenya's interview was scheduled to start in about fifteen minutes. Camilo's chance at arriving early was gone, but maybe there was a chance he could be on time.

A car's engine hummed in the distance. In the reflection of Camilo's rearview mirror, a long black vehicle spun onto the road with little regard for the residential limits. It jerked to a silent stop, blocking the street.

Camilo doubted it was Yasmin Gul behind the tinted windows.

He turned his engine off, climbed from his truck, and approached.

The back window rolled down. Julia and Tobias sat at a ninety-degree angle from one another, taking advantage of the large interior's circular seats. Her hair hung like a curtain across her missing eye, obscuring her face. But the old man had positioned himself so that he stared straight at Camilo. He held a glass with two large ice-cubes in his left hand. In his right was a tranquilizer gun. The butt pressed against Tobias' shoulder, his finger on the trigger.

Why is he—?

Before Camilo could process the question, Tobias raised the gun and fired.

The dart was a glowing white star, shooting across the short distance in record speed. It slammed into Camilo's chest, and he felt the warm liquid spread beneath his skin.

La madre que—

Camilo's vision blurred. He stumbled forward.

His mind slipped away. In his last second before the tranquilizer overpowered him, Camilo was aware of three things: the scent of lavender; the sound of a car slamming on its brakes, and the feeling of his key, slipping through his fingers.

40
KENYA

Kenya knelt on the white carpet in the living room and adjusted Doc's bowtie. There was no reason to think the goldendoodle would be in any pictures, but if everyone else was dressed up it didn't seem fair to leave him out.

"Are you wearing jeans?" Courtney's voice rose as she stepped into the living room.

Kenya tugged at the sleeves of gray button-down she'd been instructed to wear before her mother noticed that she'd had them rolled. "Would you have preferred leggings?"

Courtney scoffed, and her disapproval turned to Doc. "Why is the dog in a bowtie? They'll think we're ridiculous."

"Who cares what they think?" Reuben came from the kitchen, carrying a platter of sliced fruit and cheese. He dropped it onto the glass coffee table with a sour expression. "These are the same people who came up with the story about Camilo being a drug dealer and our daughter taking steroids. We shouldn't even let them in our house."

Trust me, if Camilo's apartment didn't look like a metal factory, I'd have insisted we meet there.

Courtney sighed. She fixed the display of cheese, which had been jostled by its move, crossed to her husband, and straightened his tie. The blue was the same shade as her dress. "That's exactly why we can't give them any more ammunition. We will be the picture of black excellence." She patted his chest before turning to her daughter with an accusatory glare. "Where is Camilo?"

"On his way," Kenya said. There was at least fifteen minutes before the interview. Plenty of time for Camilo to arrive.

Still, there was an uneasy feeling in the pit of Kenya's stomach that she couldn't quite shake. She checked her phone. No new messages.

Should I call and make sure he's on his way?

The doorbell chimed.

Thank God!

Kenya rushed to the door and pulled it open.

Yasmin Gul stepped into the hallway without invitation. A massive smile stretched across her face, pushing her cheeks to their limits. She wasn't looking at Kenya, instead, her eyes scanned every inch of the room.

Maybe I shouldn't have worn jeans.

Despite being a year younger than Kenya, Yasmin looked like a middle-aged woman who'd stepped straight out of the eighties. Her long hair was clipped behind her head, and she wore a white pants suit. The padding of the jacket squared her shoulders.

Her notebook was the only thing that betrayed Yasmin's age. It was bright yellow, covered in sunflowers. The tip of something silver and metallic marked a page near the middle.

Kenya turned toward her still open door and stared out into the street, looking for the official newspaper reporter who'd come for the interview. Instead, she saw an old white car parked opposite their driveway. A girl with a long black ponytail sat in the driver's seat, talking on a cell phone. She looked suspiciously like Yasmin.

There was another vehicle a few feet ahead. It was large and silver with flecks of mud on the wheels.

Camilo's truck.

But there was no sign of him nearby. What could have happened to make him run off without a word?

Yasmine cleared her throat. "It's a pleasure to officially meet you, Ms. Davidson."

Maybe Briony returned and Camilo followed her?

That could mean Kenya was about to suffer for nothing. Holding back a sigh, she turned and let the door close.

"I'm Yasmin Gul," the newspaper intern said, stating the obvious. Her hand was outstretched before her. "Thank you for agreeing to let me interview you."

"Well, you did call fifty times." Kenya's smile was sarcastic as she shook Yasmin's hand. "This interview is for the Gazette, right?"

"Oh no! Last time, Mitchell stole my idea and published everything under his name without giving me any credit. Can you believe it?" The moment Kenya broke the handshake, Yasmin snapped a picture of the nearby trophy cabinet with her phone. "This is going straight on my blog."

Kenya could no longer sustain a smile, not even a sarcastic one.

"You've been harassing me for an interview because you want to post it on your blog?" Kenya just managed to avoid shouting. Getting the interview into the Grover's Gazette was crucial if they wanted Briony to see it. "How many people even read your blog?"

"Right now, numbers are a bit low, but don't worry. This piece is going to attract a ton of traffic. I can feel it."

I've made a terrible mistake.

Camilo was going to be furious with her. Again.

Maybe he already was. If he'd realized that the interview wasn't for the Gazette that might also explain his absence.

"Did you talk to anyone outside?" Kenya asked. Once she knew what had happened, she could get Yasmin out and find Camilo to apologize.

Yasmin coughed and walked further down the hall, oblivious to—or purposefully ignoring—all the hints that Kenya wasn't going to invite her in further. "So where can I set up?"

The would-be interviewer was already turning into the living room.

"There's been a misunderstanding." Kenya hurried behind, grinding her teeth. "Perhaps you can call your boss and—"

"Oh my gosh!" Yasmin was staring at Kenya's parents, who'd positioned themselves picture-ready before the fireplace. "You're *the* Courtney Davidson. I've watched all the lectures you gave at the university. The number of tax loopholes you found for your clients was inspiring."

Courtney's face lit up.

It's too late to stop this interview.

Kenya stifled a groan as she watched the apprehension melt from her parents. Reuben couldn't hold grudges against teens; Courtney was a sucker for a compliment.

And Yasmin was spewing them out like an active volcano.

"The photographs of you two are going to look phenomenal. You match perfectly. And that blue has your skin glowing. And can I just say what a credit you are to your profession? I help my father with all of his taxes, and the resources you and your team have created are just incredible."

Journalist, blogger, and aspiring accountant. What didn't Yasmin want to be?

Courtney beamed as she directed their interviewer to a chair. Reuben made a joke about cheese as he offered her the platter, "Wondering if our cheese is good, ah? It might brie."

Yasmin laughed as she took one of the toothpicks.

Maybe Briony should've stolen her to be their daughter.

"Are you hoping to be an astronaut too?" Kenya asked, from where she'd been forgotten by the doorway.

All three looked at her confused. Perhaps the question didn't make sense without the context of Kenya's previous thoughts.

"You know, because you seem to be everything else." The comment didn't seem as clever now that Kenya was having to explain it. She tucked and untucked one of her curls, tapping the heel of her shoe against the carpet

Her mother looked horrified. Her father still seemed confused.

"I can't be an astronaut," Yasmin said, her face serious. "I have terrible motion sickness." She inched forward on the armchair and pulled her phone out. "Do you mind if I record this?"

———

Yasmin started with the easy questions.

"When did you first start running?" "Are there other athletes in your family?" "What inspired your Olympic aspirations?"

Kenya knew the answers she was expected to give.

The moment I could walk. Mum played volleyball; Dad's a runner too. I've wanted to compete since I was seven.

But the words caught in her throat. They were the responses of someone else, someone she had been, or someone she never was. Kenya wasn't certain.

Either way, that person's Olympian dream was dead, killed with the twist of a dagger. It was buried in an enchanted woods, alongside a host of other secrets. Kenya didn't mourn it.

I have magic and super-speed. Beating Camilo is more of an achievement than an Olympic medal.

But Reuben and Courtney didn't know that. They answered on their daughter's behalf, and Kenya's stomach twisted with every word.

She could embrace the good parts of being a changeling, but her parents couldn't see magic, couldn't visit enchanted places, couldn't know the truth.

They would look at Kenya, and all they would see was a disappointment.

———

About twenty minutes into the interview, Courtney and Reuben left, on a quest to find their old trophies for a picture.

"So, let's get to the real meat of the story." Yasmin leaned forward, pen poised. There was no sign of her overexaggerated grin. "What's going on with you and the boy from the photo?"

"Glad you asked." Kenya's eyes flicked to the window. She could see the back of Camilo's truck through the curtain.

Is it a good sign that he hasn't driven off yet, or does he want to yell at me?

Kenya wouldn't blame him. She wanted to scream at herself. Forcing a smile, she addressed Yasmin, "The Gazette's story was borderline libel and definitely racial profiling. Camilo's not a drug dealer. We're dating."

"Really?" Yasmin's eyes narrowed. A thin smile—at once more genuine and more sinister than her exaggerated grins—made it clear she thought otherwise. "Care to explain who it was that collected him outside your house then?"

Kenya straightened. For the first time, the Yasmin had her full attention.

"An old man and a woman with an eye patch, being driven around in a black limousine with tinted windows," Yasmin studied Kenya's face, searching for a sign of recognition. "You know who I mean."

I definitely do not.

Wait. There was one person who might wear an eye patch—the woman Camilo had attacked as a child, the one who had his father.

But why would she have come for Camilo?

"If you tell me, I'll give you his car key." Yasmin had the nerve to smirk as she lifted the silver item from her notebook. "Otherwise, I might have to search myself."

Oh, you have got to be joking.

First, Yasmin ruined Kenya's reputation with a picture. Then, she harassed her for blog material. Now, instead of showing concern for someone who might be in trouble, the wannabe-journalist-blogger-accountant was trying to extort Kenya?

I am so done with this girl.

Kenya took a deep breath and summoned her magic. Her body grew hotter than it ever had, wisps of flame flying from beneath her skin, curling around her fingers. She was lightning.

In a single blink, Kenya had snatched the key from Yasmin's hands.

"Huh?" Yasmin stared at where it had been, eyebrows twitching. Her breathing became ragged, unsteady. She rubbed her forehead as if it were aching, and her eyes flicked to where Kenya now stood, towering over her. "You were just—how did you—?"

"No more questions." Kenya glared at Yasmin. She didn't have time to worry about what witnessing a brief stint of magic had done to the girl's brain. "Tell me everything."

41
CAMILO

Camilo's cheek pressed against the cool leather interior. The scent of whiskey made his head spin. He couldn't feel the black pouch across his shoulder. Where were the handcuffs?

"... now that you've seen Tate's work in action, don't you think..." Julia's voice was soft and muffled, like she was under water.

Ice clinked in Tobias' glass, too loud. It echoed in Camilo's head. "You can't reverse it. That's what he is."

There was a pause. Camilo could imagine the two staring at one another across the car. Julia folded first. "Block it then. If you prefer that terminology."

Tobias snorted. "You're talking about the opposite of what you've achieved. Forcing the magic to overreact in demons—"

"Not only demons," Julia interrupted. "Diego obviously —and you saw Holly's research on the changeling girl."

She means Kenya.

Camilo forced his eyes open.

Tobias' face was a few inches shy, pale and wrinkled, watching him. "Waking up already, boy? Perhaps there's more magic in you than I thought." He pulled a needle from the top pocket of a white shirt and continued speaking with Julia. "Blocking magic would be near impossible. And not to my needs, there are only two creatures in the Western Woodlands I would deign to spare, and neither is receptive."

Camilo blinked, eyelids heavy as he tried to keep up with the conversation. They'd gone from Kenya to the Woodlands, to—the needle jabbed his wrist. Tobias' pendant-speaker fell free, swinging like a pendulum.

Back. Forth. Back.

Warmth spread through Camilo again, and his eyes closed.

———

The car screeched to a halt, jerking Camilo's mind back to consciousness.

"Couldn't walk the few feet on your own?" Tobias asked.

Camilo was groggy enough that he thought the old man was talking to him.

"Dr. Barron's going too," Julia's reply was clipped. "You didn't think I'd leave you alone with him."

"I'm not in the habit of spurning a trained dog. Unless he misbehaves."

"Exactly."

The door opened, and the scents of the city drifted into the leather interior. With them was the sharp, chemical smell of bleach, a bit too strong, like someone had been overzealous with their cleaning.

There was a shuffle as Julia climbed out and someone else got in.

Camilo was too weak to attempt an escape. He kept his cheek pressed to the leather, resisting the urge to peep. He didn't want Tobias jabbing him with a needle again.

When their new companion spoke, Camilo was glad he'd kept his eyes shut. Tate's voice was as recognizable as always.

"I didn't realize that—um, well, I'm not ready—I don't think." Camilo couldn't know, but he swore he could feel the scientist's eyes on him throughout the stuttered protestation.

A drawer beneath the seat opened. Someone unscrewed a bottle, and the liquid began to flow. More whiskey judging from the smell. "Relax, boy. I'm not the monster. He's in no danger, providing he's able to see reason."

Tate released a sigh. He leaned forward, and his coat brushed against Camilo's leg. "That's a relief because it really isn't ready yet. I know I've studied Camilo's genetic sequence for the past few years, but I still haven't managed to isolate—I don't know how Diego managed. Or Holly for that matter. But she refuses to show me, which is its own problem. And the demons are entirely—"

"Drink." Camilo was relieved when Tobias' order forced Tate to stop his nervous babbling. Nothing he was saying made sense. "What is it you think that you've created for me?"

There was a loud gulp as Tate swallowed. "For The Morgana Center, you mean? It's the first step of a cure, I suppose, isn't it."

"You think you're curing the demons?" Tobias' voice was amused.

The whiskey sloshed in the glass as the car turned.

Tobias tried a different question. "Do you know what I want to use them for?"

"Holly said she overheard that you wanted to kill a dragon."

"Not in this instance. A dragon is a tool, providing it has a rider to keep it under control." Camilo could hear the bottles move as Tobias refilled his own glass. "I happen to have a granddaughter who's in possession of a dragon."

Tate's already magnified eyes must have grown wider, for Tobias then asked. "Does that surprise you?"

"Oh—I don't—I guess, I haven't—er—haven't heard of dragon riders."

Camilo hadn't either.

"They're not Castors," Tobias voice was harsh. The whiskey scented his breath. "But my granddaughter has been seduced by a fairy. Normally, she hides from me in a magical stronghold called the Western Woodlands. But at the moment, she's away, and her dragon is little use without her."

He paused to take another sip. "With the dagger, I can slice through the enchanted barrier. The demons will be my army. At my command, they can raze the trees, and capture the dragon. My granddaughter will have no choice but to join me when she returns."

Camilo tried to keep his face impassive as he listened. He wasn't sure how much to believe. It felt like too much of a stretch to think that, beneath the cruel exterior, Tobias Buckler was a concerned grandfather.

But whatever his motivation, the old man wanted the Western Woodlands destroyed.

Camilo's body tightened. The forest's inhabitants might not have been the friendliest, but they didn't deserve to lose their homes. Or worse.

Tobias might not have the demons stop at trees, but that brought Camilo to a different question.

Why would the demons follow Buckler's orders?

"My mother was killed when I was seven years old."

The sudden change in topic made Camilo's brow furrow.

Tate's reaction was more sympathetic. "That's terrible, Mr. Buckler. I'm sorry—"

Ice cubes clinked in Tobias' glass as he waved away the sympathy. "She had unfortunate taste in men. One night, it was a vampire. A hungry one. He sank his teeth into her neck and drained her blood, leaving her cold and shriveled on the floor when he departed. My sisters and I saw everything."

For a moment, Camilo's heart twinged. He knew what it was like to lose a parent to magic.

"My older sister called 911. She told them what happened. You can imagine what they thought, hearing a ten-year-old girl talking about a blood-sucking demon.

"An agent for the city came to collect us the following day. I didn't want to abandon the only home I'd known. So, I hid in a set of bushes outside.

"The agent was squat, dark hair, I'll never forget her face. I peeked through the window as she pulled a white powder from her pocket and blew it into both of my sisters' faces. It made them forget everything. The coroner's report said our mother died of a drug overdose. They believe that now.

"I escaped, fleeing before the same could be done to me. But I found the agent years later. Do you know what she was?"

The old man didn't pause long enough for Tate to answer.

"Not a demon or a vampire or even a witch. She was a fairy." Tobias slammed his glass onto the leather seat. Ice flew into the air. Camilo knew because the melting cubes rained onto him, sending cold rivers streaking over his shirt. "It's tempting to assume every Castor is vile and evil. I did for some time. But the truth is more complicated. Magic corrupts. Those with its power stampede across the world, those without ants beneath their feet. The Castors do not care how their actions affect humans because we are nothing to them. That is why it is our moral duty to purge magic from this earth. Even if it means that we must use it ourselves."

Whether that way of thinking was hypocritical or not, the old man's voice burned with passion. There was no doubt he believed his own words.

And it confirmed Camilo's initial suspicions about Tobias Buckler.

He's been twisted by magic himself.

"That's quite a paradox," Tate said. He giggled. It was so high, it hurt Camilo's ears, before dropping back to its deep baritone. If science didn't work out for him, Tate might have a promising career as an opera singer. "Magic corrupts, but it can't be defeated without magic, so—not that it matters, I suppose. The Morgana Center has always used science. Though perhaps if you combined—no, er, never mind. It was kind of you to share all of that with me, Mr. Buckler."

Tobias snorted. The passion was gone, his usual wry tone returning. "It wasn't for your benefit."

A hand gripped Camilo's shoulder. His eyes betrayed him, fluttering open in a panic as the old man pulled him upright.

Tobias Buckler leaned closer, green eyes cruel and cold amid the wrinkles. "You really think I didn't know you were awake?"

42
KENYA

Kenya searched Camilo's truck, hoping for a clue about what had happened to him. Adrenaline pumped through her, keeping her thoughts focused only on the task at hand.

The truck's interior was clean—a sign Camilo had stopped his gardening work the past couple weeks. A case full of plant seeds and a pair of unworn rubber boots rested in the backseat.

There were no clues. She could've let Yasmin search the truck.

Kenya almost climbed out, but her eyes landed on the cubbyhole. *I'm a moron.*

She opened the compartment. Books and papers erupted onto the passenger seat. The name *Diego Lopez* appeared on almost all.

Kenya flipped through them. One was a piece of paper with a number of sketched logos. The largest had been annotated. It showed a conical flask dripping acid onto a cauldron and causing the sides to melt. Beneath it was a name: *The Morgana Center.*

Other papers mentioned a different location: *Tapas de Madrid*. It sounded like a restaurant.

Kenya was no detective, but she was willing to bet Eye Patch and Oldie were the same people who had Camilo's father. They were more likely affiliated with the cauldron-melting Center than a place that served Spanish cuisine.

"What are you doing?" Her mother's voice floated through the open door from a few feet away. It trembled with the high-pitched singsong of someone annoyed, who was trying extra-hard to appear otherwise.

Kenya looked up to see her parents marching toward her across the street. Yasmin followed, rubbing her fingers together before her nose as though the truck's key might materialize in them again.

"You can't run out—" Courtney started her sweet-toned lecture before she was near the truck.

But Kenya didn't stick around to listen. She slammed the door, climbed into the driver's seat, and started the engine.

The truck spluttered to life and lurched forward.

A second later, Kenya was off. She tried not to notice her parents in the rearview mirror. Both were shouting and waving at her.

It didn't matter. Camilo had been abducted. Kenya needed to get him back.

Her heart pounded in her chest as she drove. She was moving west, heading toward Camilo's apartment on instinct. But what direction should she be going? There was no address scribbled beneath the melting cauldron.

Kenya fumbled for her phone, ignoring every lecture she'd received. She opened the map and started typing, eyes darting from the screen to the road. There were few other cars around, but she was still panicked a cop might pass by.

Entering *Morgana Center* into the search bar yielded no results.

So where am I going?

Kenya's chest tightened. Her eyes kept flicking from screen to road and back again. What was the name of the restaurant?

She started trying to type. *T-A-P*—Was that a police car behind that bush? If an officer stopped her, Kenya was in trouble.

And what about Camilo?

What if the people who took him want to lock him away? What if he gets hurt? What if—oh no!

The adrenaline that had kept Kenya focused fled as her anxiety rose. Fear reached in and seized her chest. Its grip was hot, burning with orange and blue flames. They wrapped themselves around Kenya.

No, stop! I can't transform. I'm not a cat. I'm a person. I'm a person!

Kenya's desperate pleas to her own magic were futile.

Her legs rose from the gas pedal. Her arms slid from the wheel, limbs shrinking as she shifted.

This is not good.

Cats couldn't drive.

No one was pressing the gas, but the truck didn't seem interested in stopping. Kenya's small orange form hovered, suspended in the air, for a fraction of a second. It was enough time to realize that she was careening straight toward a tree.

There was a loud thud, and Kenya launched forward.

43
CAMILO

The building before Camilo appeared to be a residential home, thin and tall, squashed between a restaurant and a convenience store. Its gray stone façade was better suited to a castle than a house in a city, but Castor's Grove was known for its unusual architecture. What stood out was the door.

Someone had burned a sword into the wood. The hilt was less than a foot shy of the front step while the tip of the blade threatened to pierce the ceiling.

This was not what Camilo had expected when Tobias had ordered him out the car.

The old man pulled a large ring of keys from his pocket. He tapped and turned them, opening a line of locks that guarded the door.

Camilo and Tate watched from the step below.

I ought to run.

But the effects of the tranquilizer still lingered in Camilo's system. His body swayed, and his thoughts moved in light-headed loops. He felt mesmerized by the sight of Tobias releasing the locks.

The door creaked open.

Camilo was pushed inside before he could object.

Within was a dark, narrow room, dimly lit by the bulbs overhead. Suits of armor lined the walls, like remnants of an ancient history. Old scrolls, letters, and paintings hung from the walls or sat in display cases.

Camilo stared at a woven tapestry that depicted an army charging at a dragon. "Is this a museum?"

"In a manner." Tobias' words were accompanied by his usual snort.

"Wow." Tate sounded impressed. He went at once to a glass display case that showed an old notebook. "*The Mischief of the Fey Folk and the Dangers They Present.* This is dated from the fourteen hundreds. Did you know that back then, they believed..."

Camilo zoned out the scientist's chatter and stared at the old man. What game was Tobias playing? He hadn't drugged and abducted Camilo for the sake of a history lesson and a heart-to-heart. There was some other goal, hidden beneath the surface.

"Why am I here?" Camilo's head was spinning. he didn't have the patience for another riddle. "I should be with Kenya. We have a plan to—"

"Get the dagger. Yes, I'm aware." The corner of Tobias' lips twitched. He stood with his arms clasped behind his back, staring at an oil painting of a bleeding chimera. "We've had people keeping an eye out to see if Kenya's name began generating attention. Castors only survive because of their secrecy. The keeper will be forced to reveal herself if Kenya fails to comply. Very clever of you both to figure that out."

Tobias' bored tone cut through the compliment. It

made Camilo feel as though it was an obvious solution that he should've recognized earlier.

"Pity, you couldn't be trusted to bring your plan to completion." The old man turned from the painting and toward a narrow passage, disappearing into darkness.

Camilo glanced toward the exit. Tate stood beside it, a guard of sorts, but not one likely to pose a threat. Even weak and giddy from the tranquilizer, Camilo liked his odds.

He should run.

But the old man's voice echoed from the room beyond. "You should know the dagger won't work. Not how you want anyway."

He's lying.

But there was no hint of deception in Tobias' flat tone.

Camilo's legs moved without his consent, carrying him toward the old man. The passage was longer than he'd expected. His fingers trailed the smooth wall, legs unsteady.

Maybe I couldn't have escaped Tate after all.

He stumbled into what must once have been a kitchen. Checkered tiles covered the floor, and a sink was mounted in the corner. Above it, massive murals transformed the walls. Where the center of the room was shadows, lights illuminated the display.

It told the story of a war, though not one Camilo had learned about in school.

Fairies, pixies, and nymph-like creatures brandished cruel hammers, spiked clubs, and bronze swords. Their host charged forward, rushing toward a group of women with dark eyes, huddled around a cauldron. Witches. They were cloaked in the rich indigo hues of night, fingers clutching locks of fur, pieces of iron, and chains of woven leaves. A full moon shone into the center of their potion.

When the hosts met in the next panel, it was not the witches that the army fought, but a group of wolves. The largest bore streaks of gold in his brown fur. He battled in the center, surrounded by a wall of fairies and elves.

The third panel was carnage. Blood stained the snowy pelt of a dying wolf. Its stomach had been sliced open, leaving a pattern of entrails mixed into the paint. The upper half of an elf stared into the center of the room with his mouth open in a permanent shriek. His torso ended in a jagged red explosion of guts as though he'd been bitten into two. Even the witches, once safe behind their beasts, were among the pile of corpses.

Which side had been victorious, it was impossible to say. But the losers were clear.

In the background of every panel was a village. It had blended into the scenery so that Camilo's eyes dismissed it. But in the final panel, the creatures were among the houses. Witch, wolf, fairy, pixie, elf, and nymph met in the center, circling a fountain made of bones. Blood ran from empty skull sockets instead of water, and they dipped their hands into the flood. Littered at their feet were more bodies. Only this time, the dead were human.

"What is this?" Camilo's voice was so soft he was surprised Tobias heard.

"A warning. And a choice." The old man's eyes glowed in the shadows, the glittering green of snakes. "Keeping the dagger from me, so you can stab your father with it will only kill him. I assume that's what you were hoping to achieve with Holly's keycard?"

Camilo felt dizzy. Between the snake-like eyes and tragic paintings, he didn't know where to look. This new information meant he didn't know what thoughts to focus on either. "She told you."

"Luckily for you. Though I don't think she grasped the severity of the situation. She's rather naïve when it comes to what you are."

Camilo shook his head. The movement made stars flash before his eyes.

Holly knows what I am. Better than most.

But not better than anyone.

Kenya's laughter rung from Camilo's memories. He saw her nose crinkle, and her head tilt back in joy. Would she find his truck and wonder what had happened to him?

"There's no curse." Tobias walked toward the third panel and placed his fist on the pelt of a dark gray wolf with a crushed skull. The creature looked disturbingly similar to Diego.

"Werewolf"—Tobias' lips curled around the word in disgust—"is simply what you are." He drummed his fingers against the walls, working his way backwards through the murals. "Perhaps, centuries ago, your kind were humans. But you might as easily be a demon of a different kind, which the witches lifted from the underworld through their spells. I've heard the tale of your origin many ways now." He stopped at the first panel, staring at the cauldron. "Whatever the truth, your father's keeper told him the version where your ancestors were humans that the witches enchanted to fight for them."

Camilo's heart stopped. The weight of that one word pressed against him.

Did he say my father had a keeper?

That would mean...

"He was a changeling," The words cracked on Camilo's

lips. His mouth felt dry, like he hadn't had water for the past three days.

But the moment he spoke, Camilo knew his words to be true.

Diego had been a genius, like his mother always envisioned. His transformations started when he was eighteen, the age keepers returned to lift a changeling's spell.

"His current condition is due to his own creation," Tobias continued as though Camilo hadn't spoken. There was a hum in the old man's voice. This part of the tale pleased him. "A virus intended to block his magic. Only magic doesn't like attempts to thwart it. It overreacted, and your father ended up trapped as a wolf instead. His notes on the subject have proved more than a little helpful. Though Tate has taken it to a level I doubted could be achieved."

The old man's fingers fluttered to the pendant outlined beneath his shirt.

If he's telling the truth, then this whole time...

The thing Camilo had been most afraid of, his curse progressing beyond his control, had never even been a possibility?

Julia must have known.

Holly too.

Camilo's knees finally gave out. He fell forward, stomach heaving, breaths coming in ragged gasps as though he wanted to be sick.

Tobias watched him with his cold, green gaze. How was it that the cruel old man was the one finally telling Camilo the truth?

"It's good that this knowledge disgusts you." Tobias started to pace again, though this time, his eyes were on

Camilo and not the mural. "Werewolves are a plague. But unlike your father, you're only half beast."

The old man stopped before the final panel. An ocean of human corpses surrounded him. He raised his hands like Moses parting the sea.

"Join me. Use the power at your disposal to destroy the very magic that taints you. I've no doubt you'd be better suited to capturing a dragon than any of the demons."

Camilo trembled as he stared at the old man. The room was spinning, and he didn't think it was the tranquilizer.

"So what will you be? Are you dog or boy?"

44
KENYA

Kenya's body throbbed as the nurse wheeled her through the broad corridor in the Accidents and Emergencies area. The foam seat stuck against the exposed skin on her thighs and back. She shifted, trying to wiggle the edges of the imposed white gown closer together. Her limbs ached in protest, but she didn't dare ask for help.

You wouldn't be in so much pain if you'd been wearing your seatbelt.

The nurse's snarky comment replayed in Kenya's mind.

I'm sorry, but I can't exactly help it if cars aren't designed with cats in mind.

Lighter than normal and with nothing holding her in place, the force of the collision between truck and tree had sent Kenya flying through the windshield. She'd landed on a young couple's lawn among a pile of glass. Luckily, pain had consumed her fears before anyone found her. Otherwise, Kenya might've found herself at a veterinarian instead.

"When can I get my phone back? And my clothes?"

Kenya's voice was clipped. It wasn't only because she disliked the nurse—the woman hadn't even offered her pain killers. Focusing on her frustration kept Kenya human.

"Never if you end up in jail."

"It was my boyfriend's car." The police had come to question Kenya about why she'd been driving Camilo's truck earlier. The nurse had obviously been eavesdropping. So she ought to know that, despite Kenya's feigned lack of recollection, the officers had seemed unconcerned. It was the insurance company who wanted Camilo to call sometime that week and confirm she'd had his permission.

Which he won't be able to do if he's being held in a cage somewhere.

Kenya's stomach gave a nervous flutter. She pushed the fear away, repeating the mantra that had gotten her through the past few hours.

I am a human. I will find Camilo. It will be fine.

The nurse pushed Kenya through a swinging blue door into the waiting room. Children's artwork decorated the white-tiled walls, brightly colored scribbles at odds with the tense people knotted around the blue chairs. Some paced. Some tapped their toes in time with the ticking clock above the receptionist's glass window. Some were injured themselves, pressing cold compresses or blood-stained towels to various body parts while they struggled to fill out forms.

Courtney Davidson was one of the pacers. Her hands twisted in her flat-ironed hair, sweat making it frizz so that stray curls rose around the edges.

Reuben sat, eyes tracking his wife. The blue tie, carefully chosen to match her outfit, was undone, fallen in a crumpled mess onto his lap. There was a clear bag with Kenya's things at his feet. Her phone screen flashed before her, messages coming through. She couldn't read them from such a distance, but there must have been more than a dozen. They kept coming, causing the device to vibrate and lighting the screen with a fresh bubble of unreadable text.

That wasn't normal. Something serious was happening.

Was it Camilo?

He might've broken free from his captors on his own. Or perhaps he'd managed to send messages asking for help. Or maybe it was Eye Patch and Oldie, and they wanted a ransom.

Kenya's imagination would run wild if she didn't get to the messages soon.

Reuben spotted her first. He stood, grabbed his wife's arm and forced her to turn. Their expressions shifted from worry to relief and back to worry once more as the nurse approached.

"How is she?" Courtney asked.

"Excellent considering." The nurse scowled at Kenya, like she thought she'd wanted to end up in the hospital. "The MRI machine malfunctioned while she was in it, and the CT scan picked up some abnormalities. But no broken bones. No fractures. No internal bleeding or any severe physical injuries as a result of the accident. At least as far as we can tell. She shouldn't be in much pain."

Oh good. I'll just let my body know it shouldn't be aching despite flying through glass and being covered in cuts and bruises.

Kenya had spent hours training and never felt this sore.

Courtney's relief turned to annoyance. But it wasn't directed to the nurse.

"What were you thinking?" She crouched down so that she was level with her daughter. "Driving Camilo's truck? Not wearing a seatbelt? And Yasmin said you leaped up in the middle of the interview. Have you any idea how rude that is?"

Kenya stared at her mother. Courtney couldn't be serious.

I was in a car accident, and you're worried that I offended Yasmin Gul?

The nurse cleared her throat, an annoyed *ahem* that made it clear she hadn't finished. "As I was saying, your daughter is very lucky. However, she has bruising, a rather nasty cut on her left hip, and is showing signs of a concussion. She's unable to remember anything to do with the accident: why she was driving, where she was going, what caused it. If she goes home, she'll need monitoring. Someone has to check on her every three hours. She needs quiet, not questions, no bright lights, and absolutely no screens."

Kenya's head whipped up toward the nurse, sending pain shooting through her neck.

She has to be joking.

Without a phone and with her parents' constantly monitoring her, how was Kenya supposed to know who was messaging her or find a way to save Camilo?

45
KENYA

Kenya had been home less than an hour before she started pulling open the kitchen drawers. Her mother's favorite hiding place was behind the expensive silverware that they never used.

"What are you doing?" Courtney stood in the doorway, arms crossed, eyes intense, and hair wild, like a beautiful, dark-skinned medusa in a silver robe. Her voice was loud and annoyed. She answered her own question. "You're looking for your phone."

Why ask if you already know?

They stared at one another over the cream island countertop. A vein on Courtney's forehead bulged. She seemed to interpret Kenya's lack of objection as an admission of guilt.

"What is wrong with you?" She walked forward and began rearranging the items on the countertop, which had been moved in Kenya's mad dash to check every location. "You're already limping. Do you want a serious concussion too? Because forget about running a marathon on Sunday, you could be out of commission for months."

Kenya's mother made it sound like a threat. Did she forget that the marathon had been her idea? Racing was the furthest thing from Kenya's mind.

"How about forever?" she suggested, pulling the tray of silverware out. The phone wasn't behind it.

"Don't be overdramatic." Courtney pushed a ceramic blue cookie jar against the wall. "You'll be fine once you don't make it worse. But we need to talk about that boy."

Kenya closed the drawer, staring at her mother over the countertop. "You know his name."

"I don't believe for a second that you don't remember why you took Camilo's truck today. Yasmin told us he got into a car with some strange people. I don't want you getting involved with anything shady. You have a future to think about. You can't race in the Olympics if you're locked up behind bars."

What do you think I would be involved in? Don't you know me?

"That's not—" Kenya shook her head. Tears welled in the corners of her eyes. Maybe she did have a mild concussion.

Or maybe her mother's words hit too close to home.

If something did happen to Camilo and he disappeared, the girlfriend who suddenly had his truck would look mighty suspicious.

Kenya squeezed her eyes shut. She couldn't be afraid.

I am a human. Camilo is my friend. I will help him, and he will be fine.

Kenya just needed her phone so she could figure out her next move. Those messages had to be a clue. She just needed her phone.

But her mother was hiding it because she believed some grumpy nurse over her own daughter.

Well, her fake daughter.

"You keep talking about the Olympics like it's the only thing that matters in my life." Kenya's frustration trickled into her voice, making it grow louder than she'd intended. "But that's not my future. Camilo—"

"Oh please, stop right there." Courtney raised her hand. "I did not raise you to be the type of girl who wraps her future up with some boy. You think you're quitting running? What happens when you lose your athletic scholarship then? I'm not paying your tuition because you decide to throw away your future."

That wasn't fair.

"You think I have no future if I don't go to the Olympics?" Kenya was shouting now. All the things she'd been avoiding saying to her parents bursting from her. But she had to embrace the anger, otherwise the fear would set in. "You have no idea what's going on. Who are you to judge?"

"Excuse me?" Courtney's back straightened. Her voice rose to meet her daughter's with each word. "Who am I? Who am I? I am your mother. And I have every right to be concerned when my daughter starts acting like a completely different child."

That's exactly what I am.

Kenya's hands fell to her sides. Her mother's words had been ice. They'd left her cold, shivering, numb.

Reuben appeared a moment later, drawn by the noise. His duck slippers quacked with each step as he ran down the stairs toward his wife and daughter. The calculator bulged in the pocket of his robe. "What's happening down here? My miracle girl, are you okay?"

"No." Kenya's voice was flat, lifeless; her eyes stayed

glued to her mother. "You're right. I am a different child. I'm not the baby you gave birth to."

Reuben's brow furrowed. He stared at his wife, bewildered. "What is she talking about?"

Courtney's mouth opened, stuttering for a few seconds before she blurted out a response. "She's giving up running. That's what."

"She's concussed, Courtney. She has a concussion." Reuben's expression changed as he turned to his daughter. "You're going to heal, baby. You'll be fine. You'll still be our first ever Davidson Olympian." He walked toward her, arms outstretched for a hug.

He didn't understand. Neither of them understood.

I'm not your child. I'm not a future Olympian. And neither of those facts have anything to do with Camilo. Who is missing. And I'm the only one who cares.

"I'm going to find my phone." Kenya pushed past her father, hurrying out of the kitchen.

Her mother grabbed her wrist, stopping her in their dining area. The wooden table gleamed. It was seldom used.

"That boy doesn't care about you," Courtney snapped. There was an unfamiliar desperation in her voice, making the pitch rise and crack, interspersed with anxious breaths. "There are over a hundred messages on your phone now. Yasmin posted about your accident and everything else that happened during your interview on her blog, and evidently every single one of your former classmates has seen it. Everyone is asking if you're okay, if she's lying about you, if the whole thing is just a joke. But there is not a single message from him."

Because he's been abducted, and he's in a cage, and he needs me, and I don't know what to do, and you're not listening.

A lump rose in Kenya's throat. She couldn't be afraid. But she couldn't keep yelling at her parents either.

It was pointless. They'd never understand. They couldn't.

Kenya pulled her arm free and fled up the stairs. Her parents began to argue as she climbed.

"Why now?" Her father was annoyed. "You couldn't wait?"

"Something is going on, Reuben. Ever since the qualifier."

Kenya didn't linger on the steps to listen. She hurried into her bedroom, locking the door behind her so that her parents couldn't follow. Her hip ached as she attempted to pace. Nurse be damned. She should've grabbed painkillers.

I'll buy some when I leave.

Because there was no way Kenya was staying home tonight. Not when Camilo was missing.

But where do I look?

The Morgana Center clue was a bust. But what about that restaurant? *Tapas de Madrid* sounded like a common name. There was bound to be one in Castor's Grove.

Where was a different question. Kenya's parents had confiscated both her phone and her laptop. Without the internet, she had no idea how to find a map of the city. The ones posted in public parks only showed portions. She could drive around and take pictures to try to piece one together.

No, because how would she take pictures?

Then it hit Kenya. She had another device. It was an old tablet from when she was a little kid. The parental controls blocked any messages, even emails, except from specific, pre-approved numbers. But it had a camera and, even better, might be able to access a map.

Kenya crossed her fingers as she went toward her closet. The light shone from beneath the door. Funny. She didn't remember leaving it on.

Her hand froze just shy of the handle. There were soft, shuffling noises coming from within.

Someone was hiding in Kenya's closet.

46
KENYA

I'm a human. It's fine. Don't get scared.

Maybe the noises were just Doc. The goldendoodle liked making a nest in Kenya's clothes. Perhaps the door had swung shut behind him.

Now that she thought about it, of course, it was her dog.

Occam's razor. Simplest solution is always right.

Fear under control, Kenya grabbed the handle and pulled.

A figure in black stood in the center of the small walk-in closet. They faced the wall opposite, leaving Kenya staring at the back of a dark hoodie. There was something in the intruder's hands: green and silky. The corner of the fabric waved beside them.

My robe.

The closet door creaked as it widened.

The figure turned.

A spark of flame crackled beneath Kenya's ribcage, the first hint of fear starting to activate her magic. It extinguished the moment she saw the face.

"Camilo?" She didn't know why his name slipped from her lips as a question. There was no mistaking his features: pink lips, thick brows, soulful puppy dog eyes. And slung across his shoulder, as always, was the pouch with the handcuffs. Kenya burst into a smile. "You're okay! Thank God!"

She rushed at him, ignoring her hip's objection as she wrapped her arms around his waist. He felt smaller beneath the hoodie, like he'd been starved for days. "What happened to you? Why are you going through my closet?"

"I'm not." His voice was slow, deliberate, like he was testing it out after a period of disuse.

Kenya's eyes flicked to the many t-shirts and dresses tossed on the floor. Were those all really from her? She had been indecisive with her outfits the past few days and returning clean clothes to hangers wasn't her strong suit.

Camilo was going to think she was a mess.

"I crashed your truck," Kenya said. A nervous laugh escaped her lips. Horrible timing. "Which isn't funny at all. I'll pay to fix it. I also messed up with Yasmin, and..."

She trailed off as she noticed Camilo's eyes scanning her.

Was it because she was rambling or had something else caught his attention?

Kenya glanced down at her outfit.

I have to get cuter pajamas.

After she'd returned from the hospital, she'd changed into a pair of running shorts—an inoffensive gray, thank goodness—and one of the old t-shirts she often slept in. It featured a massive cartoon depiction of *R2D2*.

Kenya crossed her arms, trying to cover the Star Wars droid. She waited for Camilo to call her a nerd. But no taunt came.

Maybe because your outfit isn't important right now?

"What happened to you?" Kenya asked. "Yasmin said you got pulled into a car by a woman with an eye patch and an old man? They're the ones who have your dad, aren't they? Did something happen to him?"

Camilo frowned. The expression didn't suit his lips.

Kenya ran a hand over the top of her curls, feeling a few of the smaller ones frizz at her touch. It didn't matter. They were already a mess from the accident and the hospital. She'd need to spend tomorrow resetting them all with curling cream.

"They wanted..." Camilo trailed off, and his eyes fell to his feet. "It's difficult to explain."

Back to being secretive.

Kenya bit her lip, uncertain what to say. She'd thought Camilo was finally trusting her. He'd told her about his father, their curse, the reason he needed the dagger.

But nothing about Eye Patch or Oldie.

"Your interview's online," Camilo said. "It's gone viral. At least within the city."

Which meant Briony might have seen it. At least something good could come out of all of this. "Did Yasmin mention I was going to run the marathon?"

"Maybe." Camilo shrugged, like he'd forgotten to check for the most crucial piece of information. "It was more focused on my disappearance and what we might be up to. Your keeper won't be pleased."

"So my plan worked." Kenya smiled as she stepped from the closet. She stretched her arms and felt the muscles protest. But she didn't care. She spun back to Camilo. "You think Briony is going to come tonight?"

"Briony?" He seemed confused by the name.

Kenya was certain she'd said it before. Had he really forgotten? "My keeper. The elf with your dagger?"

"Ah." Camilo's eyes widened. He nodded a few times, fingers twisting before him for a moment as he studied her again. "I'm glad you're not at the hospital still. This is better."

"How'd you know I was at the hospital?"

"It was in the article." Camilo followed her from the closet. He peered around her room, eyes searching for something. "Do you have a sound system of some kind?"

Not what I was expecting.

Kenya couldn't place what, but there was something off about Camilo. Whatever had happened with Eye Patch and Oldie had affected him more than he was saying.

"I just listen to music on my phone," Kenya admitted. "Lot of dead weight to carry a speaker running."

"That could work." Camilo frowned and his eyes narrowed as he considered it. The expression wasn't one Kenya had seen on his face prior. "Never thought I'd have something in common with an elf, but I suppose noise is now both our banes."

"Huh?" Kenya had no idea what he was talking about.

Camilo leaned forward and took her hand. The skin on his fingers was rough and calloused. "We're something special, you and I, aren't we?" He whispered the question into her ear.

Kenya shivered. It was a meaningless word, some small part of her knew that, but the way Camilo said it, drawing out each syllable, letting his breath tickle the side of her cheek, drowned out her ability to reason.

"I need your help to get the dagger. I've learned a lot since we last spoke. Please, Kenya, will you do what I tell you?"

47
KENYA

Does anyone actually find this relaxing?

The high croon of whale song rose from the phone's speakers, floating through the room. Kenya shifted, covering her ear with a pillow. But the sounds played on Camilo's order.

He'd advised her to sleep while they waited. Between the whales, her father's hourly check-ins, and a general pounding of anticipation, that seemed impossible.

Kenya lay with her eyes closed. Her breathing mimicked the slow, steady rhythm of sleep. If she let her mind race, she might grow nervous again, and that could lead to fear. She counted seconds and sheep until she grew bored. Then, she counted fairies and goblins and dragons.

A hand grabbed her shoulder and shook her awake.

Kenya expected to see one of her parents, or perhaps Camilo.

A pair of pale gray eyes studied her. Briony leaped backward, one hand clutching something in the pocket of her loose black shorts. Her ears stuck out from her hair. The pointed tips quivered like an arm carrying too much weight.

"Hands where I can see them."

Kenya lifted her arms from beneath the covers.

"Turn off the noise."

Camilo had warned Kenya to avoid that if possible.

"I can't. Or my parents will come check on me. They'll be back soon anyway. They think I have a concussion."

"Not surprising." The elf's ears continued trembling. "You created quite the stir today." Her eyes flicked around the room. She tiptoed toward Kenya's door and twisted the lock. "Perhaps I didn't emphasize the importance of secrecy. Running races is bad. Going to a regular hospital for treatment is worse. But giving a blogger reason to write that you're taking drugs that give you super speed? I've had changelings try and fail to muck things up that badly."

Kenya's elbows dropped as she watched Briony creep around the room. "Is that what Yasmin wrote? That I'm taking something that gives me super speed?" It sounded insane. What would have given her such a wild idea?

Me using my powers in front of her.

Right. That could've been it. Still, a power-giving tablet was an imaginative leap.

"No one's going to believe her," Kenya assured the elf.

"You'd be surprised." Briony didn't look up as she answered. Having inspected the length of the room, the elf had arrived at the closet. Her hand hovered before the knob.

Kenya's breath caught as it creaked open.

Camilo was in there. The elf would see him and try to run. That wasn't part of the plan.

Kenya stumbled out of bed, ready to run and block the window.

She froze as she saw the closet's interior. Her clothes still lay on the floor, but there was no sign of Camilo among them.

Where is he?

Kenya hadn't seen him since climbing into bed, but she'd assumed he was hiding in the closet. There was nowhere else to hide in the room.

The moaning whales filled the silence as Kenya's eyes searched for him.

Briony's ears quivered, but she seemed more relaxed when she turned. "Some humans can stare at a griffin and convince themselves it's a statue or a light show. But if they were all like that, secrecy wouldn't be so crucial. The ones who recognize the existence of magic are seldom friendly." The elf moved toward the end of the bed. Her eyes were on Kenya, her back to the window. "Who gave you those handcuffs?"

Over Briony's shoulder, Camilo's face flickered into view. He stood just by the curtains. But he hadn't been there before. Kenya was certain of it.

Where did he come from?

His lips opened and closed without a sound, mouthing at her, *now, now, now.*

Kenya was forgetting the plan.

"Ow!" She shouted, grabbed her hip, and dropped to the bed. The bandage rose above the elastic band of her shorts. She pulled her shirt up to ensure that it was visible and continued to whimper. "Ow! It hurts. Ah!"

Am I taking this too far?

If she was, Briony didn't notice. The elf grabbed the post at the base of the bed and leaned closer. "What happened? What cut you?"

Kenya was too busy whimpering to answer. Her exaggerated moans mixed with the whale song.

The tips of Briony's ears curled, like leaves hiding from an overexposure to sunlight.

Camilo approached, lithe but slow, as though afraid to use his speed. Dark metal glinted in his hand.

A cuff latched around the elf's wrist, trapping her to the bedpost.

Camilo's hand disappeared into the pocket of Briony's overalls and produced the dagger. He held it before him, one hand on the black hilt. The silver glinted in the light.

"You can't," Briony said. "You don't understand what they'll do with that."

"Believe me, I know perfectly well. But my freedom is worth a hundred of you tree lovers. And one shifter." Camilo's lips moved, but the voice wasn't his. It was high, something of a whisper. He turned to Kenya, and his brown eyes melted into a steely gray.

Something was very wrong.

This isn't Camilo.

Kenya needed to run.

But fear seized her insides, faster and more desperate than when she'd had the accident. Flames rose around her. They weren't the type that gave her speed.

Camilo's features slid from the face until its features were a pale, blank canvas—nondescript and unimpressive, the type that would go unnoticed in a crowd.

Kenya's screams turned to desperate cries as she shrunk. Her paws landed on the springy mattress.

Before she could run, a pale hand grabbed the scruff of her neck and jerked her upward once more.

Kenya was helpless as the face-changer carried her

toward the door. She turned, hoping to find an escape, a plan.

There was only Briony, chained to the bed. The elf's jaw was clenched; her ears curled into fists. She spat at the face-changer's back and, as though it was a curse, she muttered a single word.

"Demon."

48
CAMILO

Dog or boy.

Those were the options Tobias offered. Neither sounded appealing.

Camilo hadn't thought of himself as a boy since his abuela left him on his own. He'd never been a dog.

But he knew the answer the old man wanted to hear, and Camilo wasn't stupid.

"I've been with The Morgana Center since I was a child. It was my father's dream to cure curses. Why would I ally with the beings who can cast them?"

Tobias snorted. "Stand up then, boy. You'll come with me at dawn. We'll strike the Western Woodlands then. My army is made up of cambions, fire-demons. Their flames are deadliest in the day." A cruel smile curled the edges of the old man's lips.

Camilo pushed himself to his feet. He stared at the portrait behind the old man, with its mass of human corpses trampled beneath the magical creatures. How would the opposite prove better?

A pattering of footsteps jogged in an awkward gait

down the passageway. Tobias turned his head at the same time as Camilo.

Tate rushed into the room, glasses askew. His phone was in his palm. "The message just came through. The face-changer is in position. To get the dagger. And the changeling—"

Kenya.

Camilo turned to a statue, unable to so much as breathe as he waited to hear what more the scientist had to say.

But there was no more.

Camilo had mistaken Tate's pause for a sign that he was starting a new sentence about Kenya. But the exertion from running down the passage had left the scientist panting. It was one sentence.

"Why is a demon after Kenya?" Camilo's voice rose. He stepped forward. The portraits swirled around him as he tried to remember the snippets of whispered conversation he'd heard in the car.

A hand wrapped around his shirt's collar and pulled him back.

Tobias Buckler was as strong as Camilo had suspected.

"Now why would you worry about the changeling if you're on our side."

Shit.

Camilo had forgotten the lie he was telling. He swallowed the panic that was rising in his throat, trying to keep his voice soft, his expression calm. "The demons are our enemy. Why would I be happy about them obtaining anything?"

"No, the demons work with us now," Tate said, scratching his stubbly chin with a nervous giggle. "Wasn't Tobias explaining it all to you? The virus that we created is highly sensitive to certain auditory stimuli. Under the right conditions, it triggers an aggressive attack against the magic in their genetic sequence, which in turn creates—"

"I could almost be fooled into believing that," Tobias cut Tate off without any acknowledgement that the scientist had been speaking. The old man's hand and eyes were on Camilo. "Except that you weren't worried about the dagger. You were worried about the girl."

"I—" Camilo's mind wasn't clear enough to think of a lie. "Kenya's not our enemy."

"You're as bad as my granddaughter." Tobias sighed. "They're all the enemy. Yourself included. It's a pity how few of your kind accept the lifeline I offer."

The old man shoved Camilo to the floor with a force that should have been impossible.

He won't be happy until we're all dead.

For the first time, Camilo counted himself among the Castors.

Something heavy buried itself into his chest. It was Tobias' boot.

Perhaps undrugged, Camilo could have bested the old man, but now he struggled to breathe.

"Stop! You can't hurt him!" Tate ran forward, arms waving. "Camilo's our friend."

Coming from the stubble-chinned, bespectacled scientist, the words sounded like a joke. Camilo bit back a wheezing laugh. He was in no position to turn away an ally, and yet—perhaps it was the drugs or the anger of humiliation—he couldn't accept Tate's kindness.

All this time, I thought he was working to cure my father, but he's been learning how to control demons. How to control all of us. And he's known the truth about me the entire time.

Camilo wouldn't have held Tate to the same level of accountability as Julia or Holly. But that was because there was nothing between them beyond mild disdain and clinical curiosity. The suggestion otherwise was just another insult.

"We're not friends, Tate," Camilo choked the words out. "You've been using me. Keeping me in the dark. All of you have."

The pressure from Tobias' boot cut off Camilo's air. Water pooled in his eyes. In the teary world it created, Tate's face looked almost hurt.

"That's not—I thought you'd approve." The scientist ran his fingers through his hair. The strands grew more disagreeable, porcupine bristles rising in panic. "It was an accidental discovery. I was trying to find a cure for your father, a way to undo the virus, if that's what you want to call it. I had no idea my tweaks with the demons would allow us to turn it on and off. I've never seen anything like it. Certain frequencies trigger an auto-immune response in the demons. Their magic flares up, only inside of them. The effect is... unpleasant."

Camilo tried to piece together the scientist's rambling.

The virus causes magic to attack the host from within. That's why my father is trapped as a wolf.

For the fire-wielding demons, it must've been like burning from within. No wonder there were so many screams from The Morgana Center's holding cells.

And Tate modified it so that the scientists control the effect somehow.

"We placed trackers in the demons. So now, we can monitor them and stop them from doing harm. They can go free," Tate continued his rambling. "Isn't that what you wanted?"

Being tortured for failing to comply with an old man's hateful whims isn't freedom, genius.

Camilo gasped his objection. Tobias was cutting off his supply of air.

"Stop. He can't breathe." Tate's voice rose to a drum-beat frenzy as he shouted at the old man. "Julia's orders are that Camilo be kept safe. If you kill him, our deal is off."

"You think I take orders from Dr. Nichols? You've already given me the device I need to control the demons." Despite his dismissal of the threat, Tobias' boot eased on Camilo's chest. "No, I won't harm your dog. Not so long as you keep him under control tonight."

There was a thick, throaty sound as the old man summoned his saliva. He spat.

Camilo's jaw clenched as the thick glob slid across his cheek. No longer choked by the old man's boot, his simmering anger rose to a boil.

Who was Tobias Buckler to spit on those with magic when he himself was transformed by it?

Who was Julia to lie to him? Holly to betray him? Tate to pretend to be his friend?

Camilo's body trembled, muscles bulging and expanding beneath his skin. The beast within him wanted to break free.

For once, Camilo didn't suppress the urge. He would give in to the wolf.

And he would get revenge.

49
KENYA

The demon's fingers dug into the scruff of Kenya's neck. He shook her body, sending her organs rattling within. The passageway spun as they left the bedroom.

"Kenya, is that you?" Her mother's voice was softer than normal.

In an instant, the face-changer's features melted. His skin grew dark; his eyes turned brown; his lips plumped.

He's wearing my face.

A chill went through Kenya.

The rest of the face-changer' body remained masculine beneath its dark clothes, but that would have been difficult to notice from afar. The black hoodie was wide and baggy, obscuring most of his form.

"Are you okay?" Courtney wrapped her robe tight around her body and turned on the light in the corridor. Her room was at the far end.

The face-changer nodded. When he spoke, his voice was a perfect replica of Kenya's own. "This cat jumped through my window. I'm going to take it outside."

"No, Mom. Don't believe him." Kenya's warnings were desperate meows. Her mother wouldn't understand.

"I don't think that's..." Courtney's voice trailed off as she drew closer. She stopped before the demon, studying his face. Her eyes narrowed before growing wide. She stumbled backward, apprehension clear on her face. "You're not my daughter."

She knows.

Kenya meowed, trying to warn her mother again. *"Run! Get out of here!"*

"And I thought I was nailing the mannerisms." The face-changer sighed, voice masculine once more as it stepped closer to Courtney.

"Reuben," she shouted for her husband.

His head appeared through the door. "What—?" He broke off, following his wife's gaze.

Kenya twisted in the face-changer's grasp, trying to break free. She had to help her parents, but her heart was beating too fast. There was no way she could calm down enough to transform again.

The face-changer's features melted. He became Camilo. Then Courtney. Then Reuben.

Kenya's father screamed. Her mother collapsed to the floor.

The face-changer sighed, features returning to their nondescript, pale form. "Is there anything as easy to break as a human mind?" He hurried down the stairs.

"What do you mean break? What did you do?" Kenya's questions were mewls. She fought against his grip.

He slammed her against the wall. Pain shot through her hip. Her mewls turned to whimpers.

"Don't cry. This isn't fun for me. I've no feelings toward shifters in either direction," the demon muttered. With his free hand, he pulled a phone from the pocket of his jeans. It was old, the kind that didn't have an internet connection. "But they want you. Particularly the girl."

He flipped the phone open, pressed a button, and held it to his ear. "I have them both. Bring the car." There was a long pause, then the face-changer's lips twisted in frustration, and he added. "Please."

50
CAMILO

Red rage painted the room. Flashes of it, like furious lightning cracked from Camilo's skin. The fabric of his clothes sank into mounds of dark fur, brown bordering on black, with streaks the color of blood. His mouth stretched into a muzzle; his ears rose pointed to the ceiling.

Tate's shriek was loud and desperate, like how Abuela had shouted her prayers to God on similar occasions. Fear kept the scientist frozen.

Tobias shoved something into Tate's hands and jumped toward the passageway. "You might want to shoot him. Otherwise, it's your funeral. Good luck." There was a sick snicker that cracked the old man's bored tone. He disappeared through the passage before Camilo could attack.

A metal door scraped behind the old man, sealing the other two within: a petrified scientist and a creature that no one in their right mind would describe as a dog.

Camilo was a wolf, massive and dangerous. He could smell Tate's fear, rising like tendrils of sugary sweat.

The scientist pressed his back against the wall. Trembling in his fist was the hand-gun version of the massive tranquilizer that Tobias had used to get Camilo into the car. Only a splash of white liquid glowed within. Small and inconsequential.

Camilo was over three-hundred pounds as a wolf. Where his head had spun, and his muscles had felt drained before, he barely felt the effect of the tranquilizer now. He doubted this little bit more could do anything.

"Go on. Shoot me." Camilo snarled, creeping closer to the scientist. *"Give me a reason."*

"Please, Cam. Don't. Calm down. We're friends. Or maybe we're not friends. I know you don't really like me, but I swear, I don't want to hurt you. I was just trying—"

Camilo pounced at the scientist.

Despite his words, Tate fired.

The dart shot Camilo in the shoulder. He wobbled for a few seconds before ripping the needle out with his muzzle.

Tate's shirt was the next thing in his teeth. It was a stupid bright Hawaiian blue. Camilo would enjoy ripping it to shreds.

First one scientist. Then the others. Then Tobias Buckler.

They would all regret their lies.

The scent of fear increased. Tate sobbed and trembled, dangling from Camilo's jaws. He'd given up trying to fight back.

In the red haze of his vision, Camilo's eyes landed on the portrait behind him—a story of death, of pointless bloodshed. Who had emerged victorious from this battle? Not the creatures that bound themselves together in the human blood.

The wolf in the scene was large and gray, standing on two legs, his tongue lolling out, his front paws like hands. There was something uncanny about it.

That was when, amidst the scent of Tate's fear and the sounds of his desperate sobs, it struck Camilo. This mural, this story, it had been painted by humans.

And so had his.

All his life, Camilo had been cautioned that when he transformed, he would become a beast, angry and vicious, unable to control himself. He'd been afraid of what he might do, who he might hurt.

Didn't I tell Kenya that magic is all about belief?

Camilo was done listening to what other people said about him.

Tobias Buckler was out for vengeance. He'd taken one cruelty and used it to fuel a lifetime of hatred toward an entire group of people.

Camilo wasn't a monster. He didn't want to be out for revenge.

Wolf or man, he was better than that.

The scent of urine mixed with fear. Tate's sobs had turned silent.

Camilo rested the scientist onto the floor. Other than the large holes in his shirt, Tate was fine.

Their eyes met, and Camilo saw his gaze reflected in the scientist's glasses. Two large pools of liquid amber, not red, not angry, just sad and confused.

Behind his spectacles, Tate's eyes didn't look so different.

He's not the enemy.

Whatever mistakes the scientist had made, Camilo could forgive. There were more important things to deal with now.

Kenya was in trouble. He needed to save her.

Camilo turned from the trembling scientist and slammed his weight against the metal door.

51
KENYA

The sound of Doc's barks, anxious and confused, peppered the night.

Kenya hung limp, a stuffed toy in a demon's hand, tail swishing beneath. Her brain rattled, and her vision blurred from his shaking. Her hip throbbed with pain. She tried to take slow deep breaths. Sobs, or the closest thing she was capable of making as a cat, blocked her throat.

Camilo had been abducted. Her parents were hurt. Even Briony was trapped by the handcuffs.

And Kenya had no idea why any of this was happening.

The limousine's engine was quiet, a soft purr as it turned onto the street. No headlights guided its way. It stopped before them, a solid, glinting wall that blocked any hope of escape Kenya might have harbored.

"Finally," the face-changer muttered.

The door opened. A woman in black boots and dark jeans stepped onto the street. Two guns were strapped to her hips with a belt. One was a handgun, the other glowed with white liquid. Blonde hair hid half her face, but a gust of wind tossed it to the side, revealing an eye patch beneath.

Fantastic. Just what I need to stop being afraid.

This was the woman who had come for Camilo, the one who was holding his father hostage.

And I'm next.

The woman's one sharp blue eye flicked over Kenya before rising to the demon. "You have the dagger?"

"Right here." The face-changer pulled the weapon from the pocket of his hoodie. He held the handle with care, pale eyes staring at the silver blade.

"Put it on the pavement and step back." Eye Patch's tone suggested she was used to giving instructions.

The demon hesitated.

She reached toward her belt. Instead of a gun, she pulled a small speaker from her pocket, brandishing it before her. "Should I activate it?"

The face-changer bent over, keeping his grip on Kenya as he complied. "Not like I have a use for it. Witch's magic doesn't last long."

"It only needs to last until tomorrow morning." Eye Patch kept her eye on the face-changer and her finger on the device as she retrieved the dagger. She tucked the device into her belt.

"What's the interest in those woods anyway? Nothing dangerous within. Or did you get tired of experimenting on us and want to torture some nymphs instead."

"Hardly your concern." Eye Patch glanced at Kenya. "Our changeling. You have her subdued. We hardly need a virus."

"Think she's too weak to transform." He flicked his wrist, and the world blurred before Kenya. A mewling cry, high-pitched and desperate, escaped her.

"Stop that." Eye Patch pulled Kenya from the face-changer's hand.

"Not like your people won't do worse."

The woman, who held Kenya both more coldly and more gently than the face-changer had, frowned at the accusation. "You murdered a man and stole his identity. Or did you forget what you were up to when the knights found you?"

"Man was a crook. I did the world a favor." He shrugged and pressed his hands together, eyes on the phone. "Now, about our deal."

"In a moment." Eye Patch turned to the car. "Take her, Holly."

Even in her state of anxiety, Kenya recognized the name. She'd gone on her phone to search for it more times than she cared to admit the past few weeks.

A pair of hands stretched from within the limo. They latched around Kenya, pulled her into the dark interior, and shoved her in a cage.

Kenya was too weak to protest.

A pale round face appeared before her, a cruel parody of the moon with blue eyes and a close-lipped smile.

Holly.

And not just any Holly. This was the one who'd called Camilo, the one he'd avoided talking about ever since, the one he liked.

Kenya had wondered what she looked like, who she was, and what her interests were for weeks. This wasn't what she'd pictured.

Holly looked nothing like Kenya. She was blonde, and thin-lipped with a pointed nose. But she was pretty, unfortunately, even with her hair pulled into an unkempt bun, and the white coat hiding most of her figure.

She's also trapped me in a cage.

Which screamed red flag. Camilo had very questionable taste in girls.

"It's a pleasure to finally meet you, Kenya," Holly said. Her tone was patronizing, like she was an adult talking to a child. There was something off about her smile. It was taunting, yet it felt forced. "Camilo's told me so much about you."

There. In the way her eyes tightened as she said *Camilo*. *Is she jealous of me too?*

Or maybe that was wishful thinking on Kenya's part.

Given that I'm trapped, I should probably save my wishes for something more useful than hoping Camilo's been saying nice things about me.

A voice rose outside. The face-changer?

Through the tinted window behind Holly, Kenya saw him drop to the grass. Julia drew the handgun from her belt.

Kenya jumped in the cage as she heard the bullet fire. *Did she just—?*

"I imagine he's said nothing about me though," Holly continued speaking as though her companion hadn't just murdered someone. "But we've been working together this whole time to make a gift for you."

The fur on Kenya's back rose. She curled her tail into the cage, stepping backward until she felt the iron on the backs of her legs.

Whatever the gift was, she didn't want it.

Holly reached into her coat and pulled out a syringe. The liquid within was red.

"It's made from your blood," Holly explained, tapping it against her thigh. "Camilo got me a sample. Once I inject you, it'll cure your shifting problem. You'll be stuck in this form. Fitting since your DNA is more cat than human."

Kenya shook her head. That wasn't true. This girl was bluffing.

Camilo had his secrets, but he wouldn't keep Kenya in the dark about something like that. And he definitely wouldn't help!

Would he?

Camilo had feelings for Holly. He'd admitted as much. And he'd wiped the blood from Kenya's wrists when she cut herself on the handcuffs.

But still, it couldn't be true. Camilo couldn't have been working with these people the whole time.

Holly unwrapped a needle. She screwed it into the syringe and pressed the bottom until a drop of red liquid blossomed at the top of the silver point.

The door opened, and Eye Patch climbed inside. On the grass behind her, the face-changer lay in a pool of blood.

Kenya wanted to throw up.

"Drive," Eye Patch ordered, tapping on the limousine's glass partition. She looked at the needle in Holly's hand. "Either wait to show Mr. Buckler or do it now, don't dawdle."

Seeing them together, the resemblance was obvious.

Holly leaned closer to her mother. "You have the dagger?"

There was no hint of the cold, patronizing tone she'd used with Kenya. Instead, Holly sounded younger, more hopeful and excited. It wasn't the voice of someone who'd trap another in a cage and threaten to transform them into a cat.

She has to be bluffing.

Kenya was a human. Nothing could change that.

Except right now, she undoubtedly had four paws, a tail and a variety of orange shades in her fur. None of which sounded very human-like.

Eye Patch pulled the changeling's dagger out and passed it to her daughter. The blade sparkled in the light.

"Where is Camilo?" Holly asked.

It was a small comfort to realize that she didn't know either.

"Tobias insisted he be out of the way for the night." Eye Patch held up a reassuring hand, there was a look of relief on her face, quite at odds with the blood splattered on her white shoes. "But don't worry, I sent Tate along too. He'll tell us where Camilo is, and we can stop on the way."

Kenya had no idea who any of these people were. She'd thought she and Camilo were friends, but there was so much he hadn't told her.

Were we ever really a team, or has he been working with these people the entire time?

"So by the end of tonight," Holly said, voice trembling and a wild look in her eyes, "Camilo will be human." Then, the smile on her face turned cold and vicious. She wiped the drop from the needle, and her eyes landed on Kenya. "All the more reason to ensure you're not."

52
CAMILO

The echo of a muffled gunshot made Camilo's ears tremble.

He'd broken free of Tobias' warped museum. Whatever metal the door was made from, it wasn't strong enough to stop a wolf with a goal.

Camilo had no idea at what point it had become night, but the stars were out when he'd emerged. Only one person on the street had noticed the massive wolf burst onto the steps. It was a teenage boy, maybe fifteen. He'd screamed, and Camilo had ducked into an alley.

By the time he'd returned, human again, the boy had been convinced that the dark beast was only a stray dog.

Camilo moved as fast as he could, transforming from wolf to human and back as he moved between crowded streets and dark alleys. He was less cautious than he should have been, trusting that the odd human who caught sight would convince themselves otherwise. It would've been worse not to take the risks.

The Morgana Center had sent a demon after Kenya.

Camilo needed to get there before anything terrible happened.

Holly is behind this.

No one had said, and yet, Camilo felt certain. She was the one who'd been so concerned about neutralizing Kenya.

And she wanted her blood.

Everything Camilo had learned about The Morgana Center's virus rushed through his head. He didn't trust the old man, but Tate's ramblings had corroborated that the demons were now under their control.

The gunshot sounded like it had come from Kenya's house.

Camilo needed to pick up his pace.

He loped across mowed green grass, paws crushing garden beds full of summer blooms. The air was rich around him, a thousand smells. Every flower petal, every tree, every house seemed to have its own scent. Camilo sniffed the air, searching for Kenya in the aromatic mist.

Another smell tickled his nostrils, faint, but unforgettable: lavender mixed with magic, leather, and whiskey.

Julia's car.

It was too strong a scent to have been from earlier when she'd come for Camilo.

He kept his eyes peeled for it as he ran.

Doc's barks, confused and desperate for help, rose through the night like a beacon from a lighthouse. Something had happened. Camilo just had to hope he was in time.

The hot smell of iron and sulfur twisted in the air. It concentrated above a dark body, face down on the grass outside the Davidson's house. Blood pooled around the head, sinking into the grass and staining it red.

Kenya?

Camilo's limbs froze for an agonizing second. But it couldn't have been her. The smell was all wrong.

He flipped the body with a push from his nose.

A white face with small features and pale eyes stared up without blinking.

Camilo didn't know the demon, but his head craned upward to the waxing moon. And he howled, some instinct insisting he mark the tragedy.

Voices came from within the house.

"Reuben, Reuben, wake up! What was that?"

"I—I don't know. What happened? I think I had a nightmare, and— who the hell are you?"

A third voice answered, a woman. "Briony. We met before. You just don't remember."

Camilo didn't wait to hear the rest of their conversation.

He found the leathery scent of the car's interior somewhere beneath the demon's blood and followed its trail. Julia was moving in the direction of The Morgana Center.

Kenya must've been with her.

53
KENYA

The silver point of the needle pressed through the bars of the cage.

Kenya hissed. It was not a sound she was accustomed to making. Hearing it coming from her mouth made her ears twitch in discomfort. Her tail flicked, and she batted at the encroaching hand with her claws, trying to force it to flee.

This can't be happening.

But it was.

The needle found the flesh of Kenya's neck. Her orange fur offered little protection from the sharp metal. It felt cold.

No, I'm not a cat. I'm a human. A human.

Kenya closed her eyes, trying to slow her breath, to transform right now. No heat spread through her muscles. No orange and blue flames rose from her chest.

The needle withdrew, and the syringe was empty.

Holly tossed it into one of the limo's compartments. There was a cold smile on her face, a flash of victory around her eyes. She turned to her mother. "We could make the changeling The Center's pet. She'll be quite harmless. Impressive, isn't it?"

No, it's horrible and sadistic.

This whole thing had to be some horrible nightmare. Kenya wasn't a pet. She was a person.

Her legs gave out beneath her, all four of them, and Kenya sank to her belly. Her tail curled around her. She stared at the white tip as it flicked up and down, up and down. It belonged to someone else. Not her.

"Diego was the genius." The soft voice woke Kenya from her trance. That was the name of Camilo's father.

Holly's hands gripped her lab coat, bunching the fabric in her fists. She let out what might've been a laugh. But it was cold and unhappy. "Tate modifies the sequence to fit demons, and you call him a genius. But I modify it for a shifter, and not a single compliment?"

She expects to be praised for this?

Kenya's claws extended. She wanted to slash one of Holly's bright blue eyes and give the scientist an eye patch to match her mother.

That was justice, wasn't it? An eye for a—what had this girl taken from Kenya?

A life. An identity. Her very humanity.

"Don't be childish." Holly's mother stared out the window, arms crossed, blood splattered sneaker tapping against the floor. "Tate found a way to control the effects. You could've done likewise if you'd worked with him. But I doubt your endeavor had such pure intentions."

Holly grabbed the cage, lifting it into the air and rattling Kenya within. "She could've been a threat to The Morgana Center. If Camilo let anything slip—"

"He doesn't know enough to worry about that. The only

thing you were concerned about losing was Camilo's interest. You've done the bare minimum to keep it."

Holly slammed Kenya's cage back to the seat. "I've been working on a cure for his father. That's all he cares about. That's all either of you care about."

Did she just say there's a cure?

Kenya's mind latched onto the possibility. That meant, if she could just get out of the cage, she could find a way to fix herself.

While Holly's voice rose and cracked in frustration, her mother's was an indifferent chill. "I won't apologize for trying to save my friend. And you hardly win points for doing the bare minimum of your job. I would fire anyone else who insisted a cure was impossible as much as you do."

"But it is impossible. You know it is! Even your precious Tate can't solve it. Diego is a wolf. And Kenya is a cat. Forever."

Those five words were another needle. They sank into Kenya, seeping all the way to her center and seizing her chest with a metallic crunch.

Her body went numb. She stared through the bars, no longer hearing the two women before her.

Kenya was a cat.

What would her parents think? Or her friends? They couldn't know about magic. Would they think that Kenya had run away from home? Or believe some worse theory that the awful Yasmin Gul was certain to invent?

My parents will hate me.

Her last interaction with her mother had been a fight. Kenya had told them she was done with the Olympics. Her father would probably insist she'd been kidnapped, but her mother would assume the worst.

She'll think I was always doing drugs, and that I threw my future away to run off with Camilo.

The metal fingers squeezed tighter around Kenya's chest. She didn't want to think about Camilo.

Whatever was happening here, this was all because of him.

Kenya had been so stupid to think they were friends or that he was starting to care for her. Had he been faking it every time he laughed? Every time he opened up to her about his family and his curse? Had Kenya just believed what she wanted because she liked him?

I should never have trusted him. I should—

Kenya's thoughts were thrown into silence as the limousine skidded to a stop. Her cage flew through the air, crashing onto the floor, and her side hit against the metal bars.

Pain shot through Kenya's back hip, spreading through her left side until it reached her neck.

"What the hell happened?" Eye Patch pulled the glass window open.

"Julia, I mean, Ms. Nichols." The driver forgot to be polite in his panic. "It's a wolf. A massive black creature. Came out of nowhere. Doesn't seem to be moving. I—what should I do?"

54
CAMILO

How does a wolf extract a cat from a vehicle?

Because there was no question what form a terrified Kenya would be in now. Julia wouldn't have sent a demon there to extend a polite invitation to visit The Morgana Center.

Camilo paced before the limousine, large paws silent against the asphalt street. There was no red tint blurring his vision now. Logical thinking was as possible for a wolf as it was a man.

But there was a sense of impatience within Camilo, a longing to act.

He rushed the car, pressing his weight against the side. Perhaps as a human, Camilo couldn't lift a vehicle. But as a wolf, he could knock one over.

Shouts of objection came from within as the wheels lifted. Julia. Holly. Their driver.

And soft anxious mewls.

Kenya.

Camilo stopped pushing, and the car dropped to the

road. What was he thinking? If he knocked the vehicle to the side, she could get hurt.

So much for wolves thinking logically.

The car door opened on the opposite side. A blonde bun and a white lab coat emerged.

Holly turned, clutching a tranquilizer gun in her hands. She pointed it at him, and the white liquid shone in the moonlight.

It was larger than the pathetic one that Tobias had handed to Tate. But Camilo had seen his father withstand five shots before falling.

Do your worst.

But Holly didn't pull the trigger.

"I know that's you, Cam," she said. Her voice trembled, but her eyes were focused. "And I know you're angry, but you don't have to be. Please, I need you to be a human."

Camilo snorted. So she knew that the tranquilizer wasn't enough to damage him in this form too. What else did Holly know about werewolves that she hadn't told him?

"I'm here to make a deal." Holly licked her lips. Slowly, she lowered the tranquilizer.

That was unexpected.

Camilo's head tilted.

"Either you can have Kenya or this."

Holly pulled a blade from within her coat. The metal caught in the moonlight, glittering with the promise of a broken curse. It was everything Camilo had longed for these past fourteen years.

"Which one will it be?"

55
CAMILO

Tobias Buckler said the dagger wouldn't work. But the old man was also dreaming of some sort of magical genocide. He wasn't the most reliable source of information.

Camilo shrank into his human form. He still wore the dark jeans he'd put on to attend the interview with Yasmin. But he'd ditched the collared shirt about thirty blocks prior. It had been drenched in sweat and doing more to encumber his movements than help him blend in.

Holly's eyes lingered over his chest, tracing the muscles down to his abs and back to his shoulders as they drew closer.

Another day, Camilo might've reminded her that she found his body an off-putting reminder of his strength. Now, his focus was on the dagger. Light flashed along the edge of the silver blade. It sang: *your father or Kenya?*

But it wasn't only Diego who might've benefited from Camilo taking the dagger.

Tobias Buckler intended to use the weapon to cut his

way into The Western Woodlands. He'd destroy the woods, burn everyone within.

Camilo needed to take the dagger. But he also needed to save Kenya.

"Why is everything always a trade with you?" He stopped on the sidewalk, just beside the back of Julia's car.

"Because you can't have both." Holly stopped at the opposite corner. The tranquilizer hung loose in her right hand. Her left fist latched around the dagger's hilt, even as she held it forward.

"I could just take it, you know."

"Then what will my mother do to Kenya?" Holly smiled, but her voice was tense. "I didn't think it would be so difficult a choice. You should know what you want."

Both.

But if it was a choice between Kenya or hundreds of innocent creatures, perhaps including Camilo's own father... the decision should have been easy. He'd been focused on saving his dad for as long as he could remember.

And yet, the thought of never hearing Kenya's laugh again made Camilo's muscles tense to the point it hurt to breathe.

The blade glinted in Holly's hand.

"This is a trap." It had to be. "Buckler wants the dagger."

Holly rolled her eyes. "You think I care about Tobias Buckler? The point has always been to save you. We promised, Cam. Do you not remember? You swore you'd find a way for you to become human again."

Her voice cracked. Holly paused for a moment, blinking back tears.

"Well, the dagger's right here. Don't you want to lift your curse?"

There was something about her voice, not as cold or callous as it had grown these past few years, but sweet and desperate. She was the little girl Camilo had known, the one who'd listened to his fears, his only childhood friend.

"I'm not cursed, Holly." Camilo's voice was soft. He didn't believe most of what Tobias had told him, but that much he felt was true. "This is just who I am."

"Stop." Tears dripped onto Holly's cheeks. She wiped them with the back of her hand, and the dagger disappeared in the shadow of her face. "This is about her, isn't it? You're choosing her over me."

Is that what Holly thought this was? A choice between her and Kenya?

It was egotistical in a way Camilo couldn't believe.

But, in another sense, Holly wasn't wrong.

I am choosing Kenya. Over everyone.

"Keep the dagger," he said. "Just release Kenya." Once she was safe, Camilo could figure out another way to thwart Tobias' plan and save his father.

Holly choked out a laugh, bitter and cruel. She didn't move to open the car door. "You fell for a cat, Camilo. The blood sample you gave me showed it plain as day. She's not even close to being human. And now, she's just like your father. Trapped in her true form, forever."

What does she mean? Did they infect Kenya with their virus?

Camilo's chest tightened. He stepped closer, and Holly raised the tranquilizer gun in defense. The dart pointed at Camilo's heart.

He glared at her over the barrel, a low growl rising in his throat. "What did you do?"

"Neutralize the threat. I told you a changeling could be

dangerous. She's messed with your head, and now you're making the wrong choice."

Camilo wrapped his hand around the gun's barrel. He didn't dare grow too aggressive for fear that Holly would signal to her mother. "You told me to choose. I have. Give Kenya to me."

"No." Holly answered as her finger pressed the trigger.

The tranquilizer shot straight into Camilo's heart. He stumbled backward, trying to pull it free before the silver liquid shot through his veins. If he transformed again, he wouldn't feel its effects. He just needed to act fast.

Camilo closed his eyes, trying to concentrate through the impending fog.

Something sharp pressed into his chest, right where the dart had hit.

"You'll thank me later." Holly's voice was whispered steel.

Camilo's eyes opened in time to see the point of the changeling's dagger at his heart. Panic shot through him, interrupting any hope he had of transforming. The blade would take away his abilities. Or worse if Tobias Buckler had told him the truth.

"Holly, don't—" Camilo lifted his arms to push her away.

But he was too slow.

She plunged the dagger into his chest.

Blood rose in his Camilo's throat as he tried to scream.

56
KENYA

The latch on the cage door was broken.

Iron bars pressed into Kenya's side. The force of the collision had sent her prison crashing to the opposite seat, and up had become right as she'd hurtled through the air.

Fresh pain spasmed through her previously good hip to the point Kenya wondered if the bone had shattered.

But the cage had suffered too. Its door was dented, the lock pulled loose.

She could break free.

No, I can't.

Julia sat beside the cage. Beyond her were the sealed doors and windows of the limousine.

Kenya lacked the opposable thumbs to open them.

She might forever.

That was likely why Julia was paying her no attention.

The older woman leaned forward, peering out the tinted windows at whatever was happening on the street between Camilo and her daughter.

They're probably celebrating their success or making out.

Kenya didn't want to think about it.

"This better work." Julia licked her lips. She fumbled in her pocket and produced a phone. It lit up and a moment later a male voice, deep and powerful came on the other end.

"He escaped."

"Yes, I see that." Julia adjusted her hair, blocking the eye patch, still studying the window. "Why?"

"Camilo transformed and Mr. Buckler locked me in a room with him, and I thought Camilo was going to kill me, but then he put me down and ran into a metal door instead. The hinges were rusted. He broke it clean off."

"Not how, Tate. Why?"

"I think he didn't like what we'd been doing." There was a pause. "Is he really cursed?"

"Let's hope so." Julia ended the call.

Kenya tried to make sense of the conversation. Would this be her life now? Trapped in a body that wasn't hers, eavesdropping on strange scientists, and trying to make sense of their plots.

It couldn't be worse than watching herself become an urban legend—the almost-Olympian who'd run off with a drug dealer. Her parents would hate even her memory.

Julia's eyes widened. She moved across the limousine, bringing her face toward the back window. "What is she thinking? If he loses control..." Anxiety radiated from her body like magnetic waves.

Kenya lifted herself from the iron bars. Her hips trembled in protest.

What was happening outside?

Julia wouldn't go closer to watch her daughter having an intimate moment with a boy. At least, Kenya hoped not. It must've been something else.

But do I want to know what?

Yes.

It was like being a changeling. There were difficult truths, parts she didn't want to face. But knowing was better than living in the dark. Magic was worth it.

Kenya couldn't settle for life in a scientist's cage.

If she was to become an urban legend, so be it. Maybe she could play into the myth, find a way to send letters to her parents and Lily, make use of her power.

Being a sentient cat was a type of magic.

And who's to say that I'm not one with super speed?

Kenya had never used her power in this form before, but she'd never remained a cat long enough to test it.

Julia gasped. "Did it—No. No. What?"

She moved toward the door.

This was Kenya's chance.

Maybe I'm a cat, but I'm still a magical one.

She closed her eyes and focused her will.

Blue and red flames lapped at Kenya's paws. Her shoulders lowered, back arching to send her hips higher as she crouched in preparation.

The door flew open before Julia reached it.

Holly trembled as she stared into the limousine. She held the changeling dagger before her. Blood dripped from the blade, staining her hands a murderous red. "It didn't work. I don't understand. I think he's de—"

A rock flew through the open door. Two more clattered onto the roof.

It was raining stones.

"Get in the car." Julia grabbed her daughter's hand, pulling her in.

Kenya didn't intend to stay with them.

She lurched forward, orange fur blending into the magic, and turning her into a ball of fire.

The dented door yielded against her force, springing open.

Kenya flew through the air and into the night, landing on the sidewalk. Her paws kneaded the ground in a drumbeat of victory. Until another stone nearly took off her tail.

"Wait, she—"

"Forget the changeling. Tobias has the connections to shield you from a murder charge, but he won't help without the dagger. If we save Diego, he can never know how we failed his son."

The door slammed shut, and the limousine sped off as another set of rocks began to hail.

Whatever was attacking, Kenya needed to run.

But the sight of Camilo's body stopped her.

The limousine had blocked it from her view, but now he was exposed, an unmoving mass in the center of the street.

Kenya's breath caught.

They'd left the safety of her neighborhood. Nothing moved in the empty shops and offices that lined the road. The lights were from the sidewalk lamps and the stars. There were no headlights to signal an approaching car.

Camilo would be truly alone if she left.

Their friendship had been a farce the entire time. He'd helped Holly trap her in this state. Kenya owed him nothing.

But her paws carried her toward Camilo.

Kenya's body was numb. She couldn't feel her heart. Her eyes scanned the olive chest, darkened by the rivers of blood that rippled through the muscles. A trail of red dripped from the corner of his mouth as well.

Is he really—

There was the faintest movement of his limbs, a fluttering of breath.

Holly's pronunciation was premature, but Camilo would die soon if he didn't get help. He was losing too much blood.

Kenya needed to stop it somehow. But fluffy orange cats didn't have cell phones or the ability to shout for help. Nor did they have access to cloth or fabric.

It couldn't be hygienic to plug a stab wound with fur.

But options were limited.

"*It's your fault.*" Kenya's words were a meow. She hopped onto his chest, hating the way he shuddered at her weight. It was lucky cats didn't seem capable of crying. Otherwise, she was afraid water would be streaming from her eyes, adding salt to the iron rivers of Camilo's blood.

He didn't deserve her tears.

"*You're the one who trapped me like this.*"

Trembling, Kenya wrapped her tail tight and curled into a ball in the center of Camilo's chest. Tears or not, lumps rose in her throat. Cold dread threatened to break through the numbness.

"*Don't you dare die. I can't be angry with you if you die, and I deserve to be furious.*"

It didn't occur to Kenya that the rocks had stopped raining until a shadow with large, pointed ears blocked the streetlight.

57
KENYA

The black van that came for Camilo was not like the ambulance Kenya had traveled in earlier that day.

It materialized about ten minutes after Briony called, and two women rushed from within to admit Camilo into the back. Kenya wouldn't call them doctors.

The first had short brown curls and pale skin. Her rolled gray sleeves displayed tattooed pink petals swirling from her palms to her elbows. She opened the van while her companion approached.

"Werewolf?" the second woman asked. She wore a silver dress with long flowing sleeves, like something from a renaissance film. Her dark hair was flecked with gray that shimmered in its woven knot.

Briony nodded.

"Tricky. Very tricky." The woman's hand disappeared into her sleeve. When it returned, there was something flat and white within, a bit like a deflated balloon. "What caused the wound?"

"I didn't see. Just a regular blade." Briony's answer contradicted itself.

The renaissance woman didn't seem to notice. She bent down and pressed the balloon against Camilo's lower abdomen. His body began to rise.

Kenya jumped onto the road. Her hips throbbed from the impact, but she ignored the spike of pain. Why was Briony lying about the changeling's dagger? What if that was crucial information that they needed to save Camilo's life?

The elf's head twitched, and she glared at Kenya as if warning her to keep quiet. "What does it matter? You can save him, can't you?"

"We'll see." The renaissance woman blocked Camilo's wound with a white cloth before guiding his floating body toward the now open van.

There were no machines on board. Instead, a large black pot was anchored to the corner of the floor, and the far wall had been equipped with shelves. They displayed an assortment of pots, seeds, and strange bottles. One clear liquid was labeled *fairy's tears*. Within another, *demon's shadow* writhed. A third was full of glowing green lights. Kenya couldn't see what was written on its side.

The woman with the flowing sleeves rested Camilo onto a makeshift bed in the center of the truck and turned at once to the shelves. She searched through the bottles, stopping to pluck leaves and petals.

It didn't feel right to look away, not when Camilo's condition was so vulnerable. But the tattooed woman approached and blocked Kenya's view.

"Myrtle," she introduced herself. A pair of pointed ears, much smaller than Briony's own, peeped through her brown curls. "Is there a reason you're still a cat, ma'am?"

"Because boys are jerks, who betray you and then die."

Kenya mewled a response, trying to step around Myrtle's ankles to peer into the van.

"Just why I've never been fond of men. But I'm going to need you to be a bit more specific."

Kenya's ears twitched, and her tail snapped behind her as she turned to Myrtle. The woman's expression was serious, arms crossed. The petals shifted on them. Perhaps they weren't tattoos.

But that wasn't what surprised Kenya. Even though she was a cat, Myrtle had understood her. Just like Camilo could.

———

Myrtle had never heard of a virus that affected magic. Certain spells had the ability to block it. Those could be broken if one could determine the weakness. She claimed there was no reason to think there wasn't a cure for Kenya's condition.

But Myrtle's breath had caught at the word *scientist*, and she'd flinched at the description of the needle. Her reassurances were empty, meant only to soothe Kenya's fears.

"Inhale," Myrtle instructed. She listened to Kenya's heart through a small stethoscope.

The mundanity of the object was almost disconcerting given the situation. Kenya kept waiting for the metal to glow or announce her vitals.

"No signs of anything internal." Myrtle nodded as she curled the stethoscope and slipped it into the pocket of her long black pants. "Just some bruises and your hip bone might be cracked. Easy fix. If the only major problem is that you're permanently shifted, you've come out of this lucky. I'm just not clear on how this happened."

"I told you," Briony answered before Kenya could. "My changeling got discovered by the knights and they attacked. The werewolf happened to be passing and saved her."

The elf gave Kenya a look that clearly meant *don't contradict me.* Briony had been not so subtly sending that message for the past few minutes. Despite the twitching muscles in her legs suggesting that she'd prefer to be pacing, the elf had remained present throughout Myrtle's examination.

Briony's fake story and silencing glares made it obvious that she didn't want anyone learning she'd lost the changeling's dagger.

But is that because she's worried about me or herself?

Myrtle's eyes narrowed. She didn't seem to be buying Briony's explanation. But a shout came from the van, grabbing all of their attention.

Camilo's body arched upward as though he'd been possessed. Green liquid bubbled from his wound.

"Mother and Crone. Myrtle, I need you," her companion shouted. "He's rejecting the spell."

What does that mean?

Kenya's heart stopped. She would never forgive Camilo if he died.

Myrtle rushed into the van. Kenya made to follow.

"Oh no you don't." A hand grabbed the scruff of her neck.

Kenya's paws rose from the ground. She hissed and her tail flicked in protest. *"Put me down!"*

"Hush. My ears are only just starting to recover from your little stunt." Briony spun her around so that their eyes were level. "You need to tell me what happened. Who were the people that took my dagger? Where did they go?"

Camilo was the one who should be answering the elf's questions. Kenya twisted, trying to see him, but Briony had stepped away so that they were to the side of the ambulance.

"*Maybe they went to a restaurant. Ever heard of Tapas de —*" Kenya's meows were squashed as a palm engulfed the entirety of her head.

That wasn't fair. Her whiskers vibrated, protesting being pinned down. Kenya considered biting the elf's hand, but she couldn't get her mouth open wide enough.

"I said hush. I can't understand you. We need a different communication strategy. Maybe..." Briony moved her hand, searching in her pocket. She pulled out her phone, pressed the button, and scowled. "Dead. Figures. That's the problem with temporary protections. Doubt you can type anyway."

Kenya flexed the toes on her front paws. She didn't like the elf just assuming her incapable.

I bet I can still type.

Kenya wondered how she could prove that to the elf. Maybe if she broke free and grabbed the phone. Only the device was dead, and someone holding the scruff of her neck seemed to be cat-kryptonite.

A familiar bark distracted Kenya from her plot to text. Her ears twitched.

What was Doc doing out on the streets?

The goldendoodle stepped beneath one of the lights a few buildings shy. Kenya's parents were behind him.

"Do you smell her, boy?"

"He's not a bloodhound, Reuben."

They didn't seem to notice the black van full of glowing

lights that was stopped suspiciously on the side of the road, nor the elf and orange cat standing to its side.

We must be hidden by magic.

Doc was immune to its effects. His eyes latched onto Kenya, and his tail rose in excitement.

Arf, arf, arf!

The goldendoodle tugged on his leash, pulling them forward.

"Wander to hell. This is just what I need. They'll wake the whole neighborhood if we don't let them in." Briony's gray eyes flicked to Kenya. There was a hint of sympathy in them. "Unfortunately, there's no telling how they'll react when I do."

58
KENYA

Reuben and Courtney sat on the sidewalk. There was no talk of chairs or blankets or the germs that would get on their robes.

The night was warm, but they huddled together, eyes following a passing car. Perhaps they wondered why it hadn't stopped or seemed to notice them at all. Briony hadn't explained whatever magic shielded them from notice for the moment.

Kenya's parents had been overwhelmed by the information that the meowing orange cat was actually their daughter.

They'd sunken into states of slack-jawed shock, sliding onto the sidewalk as though their souls had slipped free. Their goldendoodle lay loyally with them, his head on Reuben's lap, and his eyes full of concern.

Kenya could only look at the scene for so long before her heart grew tight. Their inability to accept who she was, even when a magical elf explained it to them, was worse than if they'd believed she'd been kidnapped or run off with Camilo.

That bastard.

While Briony was distracted with Reuben and Courtney, Kenya took the opportunity to go the van.

She was so low to the ground she couldn't see anything but glows of magic within unless she stood on her hind legs. It wasn't a position that came easy.

Instead, Kenya jumped into the ambulance. Only her hip had protested. The women were oblivious to the small orange mass staring at them from beneath Camilo's bed.

There were some perks to being a cat.

Myrtle had whispered to seeds and pots of soil, and plants blossomed forth at her command, glowing with warm green hues.

Silver-sleeves plucked their petals and snapped their stalks, closing her eyes and whispering before adding each ingredient to her cauldron.

Wisps of blue and silver smoke rose from within, and bright iridescent bubbles burst from the surface. They filled the space with the scents of aloe and honey.

It would have been amazing in any other context. Kenya had taken in as much knowledge of the magical creatures as Camilo was willing to share over the past few weeks, but he'd hidden truths. What she had was a few pages plucked from a book and read out of context.

Cat or human, there was an entire world Kenya had only just begun to explore.

She just wished she wouldn't be alone on the adventure.

When the potion was finished, the Renaissance woman scooped clear salve from within.

Please work. If he's okay, I'll—

What? Forgive him? Kenya wasn't sure she could keep that promise.

The women carried their concoction toward Camilo. Kenya backed away before either of them noticed her beneath the table.

Myrtle's companion closed her eyes and pushed the salve into Camilo's stab wound.

His mouth opened in a silent scream, and his body grew tense, muscles tightening into a ball. He shook as though trying to repel the salve.

But the woman refused to pull her arm away and end his torment.

Or maybe Kenya was the one to blame.

If she'd promised to forgive him—

"Daughter. Is. Shifter," Briony's voice was loud and slow as though she were talking to a bag of bricks instead of two humans. "Changes shape into cat. Daughter, orange cat. Orange cat, daughter. Understand?"

Doc's head tilted to either side, watching the elf's hands as she brought them together, trying to combine *cat* and *daughter* by interlocking her fingers.

Reuben and Courtney continued to stare at the empty street.

"I give up." Briony threw her hands in the air. She turned to the ambulance. "I need amnesiac—" Her eyes landed on Kenya, tucked against the corner. In two strides, the elf hoisted her into the air once more.

Kenya's eyes narrowed as Briony brought their faces together. *"Let's not make this a habit."*

Being picked up without warning was a nuisance Kenya hadn't anticipated.

"Why aren't you helping me? I'm trying to explain this to them for your sake. I have no issue wiping the last twenty-four hours from their minds."

Kenya understood the threat. It meant her parents

would have no idea that she was a cat. They'd be confused about what had happened to their daughter and what horrible event had occurred that had caused them to repress an entire day. It couldn't be healthy for their psyches.

But it wasn't like the truth was helping them much now.

"*Go for it,*" Kenya meowed.

Briony may not have understood the words, but she must've gotten the general sentiment. "You're the most difficult changeling I've ever had the displeasure of dealing with."

She released Kenya from her grip.

"*Wait, don't just—*" Kenya mewled in panic. Was the elf trying to kill her by dropping her almost six feet in the air?

There was a gasp, and a flurry of footsteps.

Kenya's tail extended, and her body twisted in midair guided by a subconscious instinct. She lifted her back right paw so that she landed on her three good legs.

Well, her *better* legs. Her left hip wasn't pleased to have absorbed part of the shock.

Still, not a bad landing. Kenya pawed at the road and shook out her fur.

I might be getting the hang of this cat thing after all.

"Oh, thank God!"

Huh?

That wasn't Briony's voice.

It was Kenya's mother. Both she and Reuben were on their feet, running forward. Doc chased their heels.

"You're okay!" Courtney choked back a sob as she collapsed onto her knees beside Kenya. The silk hem of her robe pressed into the road, and her flat-ironed hair stuck up at odd angles around her head. Tears flowed down her cheeks.

Was that a further effect from her exposure to magic?

Kenya had never seen her mother cry.

Courtney wiped her cheeks with the back of her hand and sniffed. She turned her red eyes up to Briony, who towered above them all. "What are you doing dropping my daughter onto the street." She paused and some of the indignation left her as her gaze turned to Kenya. "That is you in that form, she's not lying?"

She was hearing Briony's explanation.

Which meant it was no magical side effect making Courtney emotional. She was crying because her daughter was a cat. And maybe she'd realized something else too.

Like that I'm not really her child.

"It is her, Reuben!" Courtney turned to her husband, who was stumbling forward, eyes blinking out his daze. "I'm sure of it. She's really a cat!" A high, shrill laugh escaped her lips, and she slapped a palm to her forehead. Her lips pursed, and she turned her displeasure to Briony once more. "Why is she a cat right now? You said she could change forms."

"Yes, well..." Despite her height, the elf managed to shrink beneath Courtney's gaze. "She's stuck."

"As a cat."

"Well, I'm not a mouse." Kenya tried to make a joke. It fell flat, mostly because no one understood it.

"I do apologize, Mr. and Mrs. Davidson. This was not what you agreed to when I approached you eighteen years ago." Despite saying she was apologizing, Briony sounded relieved. "I'll be happy to wipe the events of tonight from your memories, and if you're willing to allow it, we can replace them with new ones. As far as you'll know, Kenya will be attending university somewhere in Europe, to escape—"

"What?" Reuben stood beside his wife, one hand on her shoulder. His eyes had been fogged still when he'd come running up, but they were clear now as he stared at Briony. "How will we see her if we don't know that she's a cat?"

Doc barked as though to accentuate Reuben's question.

Kenya's head tilted to the side as she studied her father. Did he really want to see her still, even though she was covered in fur? Even though she wasn't really his?

"You won't." Briony shrugged. "Not until she's human again. Trust me, it'll be much easier for your lives if you're not constantly struggling to accept the existence of magic."

"But you think we can accept the fact that our daughter's disappeared somewhere in Europe?" Courtney crossed her arms, voice growing deep and serious. It was the tone she used when discussing court cases. "Absolutely not. I will not live a lie again. Your system is terrible. If we'd known what she was—"

Kenya's head sank lower as she saw the tears well once more in her mother's eyes. She could guess what Courtney would say next.

You'd never have wanted me.

"—we'd have been prepared for when she turned eighteen. She kept trying to tell us that something had changed, and we had no idea. We didn't listen." Courtney's voice broke. She stretched her arm forward, hand trembling as she rubbed the side of Kenya's cheek. "Can you ever forgive us?"

She's apologizing to me?

No, that wasn't right. Courtney Davidson didn't apologize. Not to her daughter at least. The magic must've gotten to her head.

But Courtney's eyes were clear. Rational.

A tension Kenya hadn't noticed eased from her limbs. She pressed her cheek against her mother's fingers, unable to respond in any other form.

"There's nothing wrong with the system," Briony muttered, rubbing her elbow. She frowned at her feet, avoiding eye contact with the Davidsons. "It's not unusual for an eighteen-year-old to become more independent and start making their own decisions. Less than five percent of changeling parents ever need their initial memories restored."

"Well now we have ours back, you're not taking them again," Reuben said, stepping forward and placing himself between Briony and his wife. It was a curious sight, a man in an oversized gray bathrobe and duck slippers facing off with a six-foot tall elf. "When you came to us that night in the hospital, we agreed to take in and raise Kenya. It doesn't matter if she's a shapeshifter or a changer or a cat. She's our daughter."

"Exactly," Courtney agreed. "Even if she's a cat. She's still our child."

Kenya's mother was still on her knees, her father standing. But they were a united front as they stared at Briony in defiance. It may have taken Reuben and Courtney Davidson a while to process what their daughter was, but now they had. They knew the truth. Kenya would never live up to their dreams for her. She wasn't the child they'd given birth to. She wasn't even human.

And they were still here.

A sob rose in Kenya's throat. It came out as a long, sad purr. She leaped into her mother's lap.

Courtney stared down, surprised for a moment. Then, she wrapped her arms around Kenya, pressing their foreheads together. "I love you, baby. And if you're a cat, you're going to be the very best cat that ever lived."

"She already is. Look at this fur." Reuben crouched beside them, putting an arm around his wife's shoulder and rubbing behind Kenya's ear. "It's like fire. I bet you'd dominate if you competed in a cat show."

Doc barked in agreement.

Kenya would have laughed. *"I'm not entering a cat show. Ever. How is that the first thing you two think of?"*

"She's talking." Reuben tapped his wife's shoulder. He looked up at Briony. "Can you translate?"

The elf sighed. "I don't speak cat, but if you can find a phone that'll turn on or happen to walk with pen and paper..." She waved her hands as though they should fill in the rest.

"Wait." A smile spread across Reuben's face as he reached into his pocket. "I have something here that might work."

59
CAMILO

The taste of iron was hot in Camilo's throat. His chest burned as though someone had taken a star and shoved it through his ribs.

Not a star, the dagger.

Holly had stabbed his heart. And Camilo had bled.

There was no curse for the enchanted blade to cut, so it had torn through the sinews of his flesh instead. Camilo recalled his last thought before everything turned black.

Kenya.

With a desperate gasp, his eyes fluttered open. Above him was a low black ceiling.

What happened to her?

Camilo inhaled. He caught whiffs of aloe, honey, basil, thyme, rose water, feathers, fur, too many strange scents to count. Among them was the warm, spicy tingle he'd come to associate with Kenya. She was here, and she was using magic.

I need to find her.

"Kenya," Camilo's voice was weak as he tried calling to

her. Placing his weight onto his elbows, he pushed himself upright, ignoring the protests from his chest.

He was in some strange van, lying on a makeshift pallet surrounded by glowing potions and plants. There was a cauldron in the corner.

"Sorry to disappoint," a voice spoke from behind him— a woman, more than a bit annoyed judging from her tone. "But my changeling is preoccupied. You and I need to have a chat, however."

Briony stood near the edge of the van. Her height made it impossible for her to straighten, so she was forced to slouch into a scowling hunched-back figure. Her position blocked most of Camilo's view of the road beyond.

"But where is—"

Briony grabbed his shoulders and pushed him back on the pallet. The elf hunched lower, bringing her face before his.

"Kenya is safe. Little thanks to you." Briony's nose twitched on each word, accentuating her annoyance. "Where did your friends take you-know-what?"

Camilo raised his hand, trying to push the elf off of him. The movement sent a spasm through to his chest. He gasped.

"Nightingale's spell stopped the effects of the dagger enough for you to activate your own abilities. But even with accelerated healing, it's going to take a while for you to recover." Briony smiled, but only half of her mouth moved. "Now, where is it?"

Camilo tried to decipher what the elf was saying. "Nightingale is a witch?"

"From the Nightingale coven, yes." Briony waved her hand. "She works with my friend Myrtle. They run an emergency healing service. Off the record sort of stuff. They're napping up front now, but we need to talk while they're gone. The people you're working with took something very important."

"The changeling's dagger."

Camilo's voice was soft and strained, but Briony covered his mouth with three long, pale fingers.

"Not so loud. Do you have any idea the damage that weapon can cause in the wrong hands? They weren't exactly keen on giving it to a wandering elf. Took a lot of convincing to get the position. If anyone learns that I lost it..." Briony raised her eyebrows, giving him a look that suggested the implications were obvious.

At least some of them were.

"I know where it is." Camilo managed to push himself upright once more. This time, the elf didn't stop him. "And what they're planning. We need to get to the Western Woodlands before dawn. You'll need my help to retrieve it."

His chest burned. Camilo clasped his hand to his heart, wincing as he held back a groan.

"I don't see that you can be of much use," Briony noted. Her voice was blunt though not unkind. "And I appreciate the information if you're being honest, but I can't trust you enough to take you with me. She's stuck because of you."

Camilo turned, following the direction of the elf's gaze.

From his position on the pallet, he made out an orange tail with a white tip, twisting from the sidewalk onto the road then leaping into the air like a circus performer.

Kenya's tail. Explains why the air smells of her magic.

Had the elf said she was stuck?

"At least that's what she claims," Briony continued, crossing her arms and hunching forward for a better view of the sidewalk. "Not exactly an easy changeling. Probably the most trying since that one— gosh what was his name.

I'll fail my licensing exam if I can't remember. Whole reason we changed the rules about permission. Vanished to Mexico just over twenty years ago. Adoptive parents were the hyper religious sort."

The elf was speaking to herself. She waved her fingers, trying to think, and her eyes stared upward as though the answer might appear on the van's ceiling.

"Diego Lopez?" Camilo guessed.

"Yes. That's it." Briony snapped. Her brow furrowed, and she turned to Camilo. "How do you know his name?"

Because a demented old man told me.

Twenty-two years ago, Diego had fled to Mexico, seeking a cure for his curse on the advice of his parents.

He'd been eighteen, the exact age when changeling curses were lifted.

And a genius.

The very thing that his parents had wanted. Or rather, his adoptive parents.

"Theirs ends with them, his starts with mine," Camilo whispered the lines of his father's riddle as they began to whisper in his mind. "Do deviations recess or follow the line?"

Briony's eyes narrowed. "Did you hit your head as well?"

It must have seemed that way. Camilo suspected his grin looked half mad. But he didn't care. He pushed himself from the pallet bed. His legs were in better condition than the rest of him.

My dad hasn't lost his mind.

When Camilo had tried to enter the code, he'd thought his father's actions were a sign that there was no man left within the wolf. That was wrong. It had been a message. Another clue.

The answer to the riddle.

Blood.

That was the line the poem referred to; the deviation was being a werewolf. Diego was questioning if it was genetic and would pass to his biological son.

But there were no letters on the prison's keypad. How did Camilo enter the word? And what did the next four lines of the riddle mean?

The rest of the solution came to him the moment he reached the edge of the van, turned his head, and spotted Kenya.

Reuben and Courtney were with her, kneeling on the sidewalk and staring at something on the ground between them and their daughter. It was a calculator.

Briony followed his gaze. "Odd, isn't it? Her father had it in his pocket for some reason. But he insists it can spell words if she types them backwards then flips the device. Pretty limited vocabulary though. It's missing a lot of letters."

"And the *D* and the *O* would look the same if you didn't find a way to differentiate them."

Briony took a moment to consider it. "I suppose. There's also no *J* or *U*. Took ages to guess she was trying to spell Julia. Are you sure you don't want to lie back down? You seem giddy."

Camilo was. Because a plan was unfurling in his mind.

"Forget the Western Woodlands. We're going to steal the dagger before they make it there."

And more importantly, Camilo was going to rescue his father.

60

KENYA

Kenya tried to avoid looking at Camilo as he peered out from the van. It was difficult. Her eyes kept flicking from the old calculator toward him.

The glowing colors within the ambulance outlined Camilo's body. Betrayal had done nothing to make him less attractive. If anything, his shoulders seemed broader and more muscular from her current perspective. And even the swollen red scar in the center of his pectorals had a certain appeal.

Briony stood beside him. The elf's body was stooped like the crone from a children's movie, and for the first time, her ears made Kenya think of a bat.

Their lips took turns moving, their voices soft.

What are they talking about?

Camilo's eyes landed on Kenya.

Her cheeks grew hot, and her whiskers twitched. She snapped her head down toward the calculator. She'd been trying to spell something. What was it?

Oh right.

The large gray buttons taunted her. Its digital numbers

and mathematical symbols hadn't been designed for spelling. Kenya had to get creative. She pressed *0, 1,* then paused. How the hell was she supposed to make an *R*?

There was a way to do this entire thing with shortcuts. Kenya wouldn't need to turn the calculator upside down and type backwards if she knew them either.

Too bad cats can't get math degrees. I'm sure how to spell on your calculator would've been day one of undergrad.

Kenya would've laughed at her own joke, but her current form didn't seem capable. Instead, her body trembled in a low rumbly purr, and her eyes narrowed as she pressed the square root sign.

By the time she finished her first word, the calculator read .

Her parents stared at it from the opposite direction.

"What word has a double I?" Courtney's lips pursed as she tried to sound out what letters she thought she recognized.

Reuben was faster to understand. "No, it's an *M*. Mad... id. Madrid!" There was a strange gleam in his eye as he stared at his daughter. His chin shook up, down, left-right, a bobble-headed doll waiting for confirmation.

He's finding this a bit too fun.

"Why would she be typing Madrid?" Courtney clicked her tongue, giving her husband a frustrated look.

"Maybe the people who did this to her are Spanish."

"No, it's a restaurant," Kenya meowed, tapping her paw against the sidewalk, careful not to clear the calculator by mistake.

"Oh, there's more!" Reuben put his hands on his knees and leaned forward, grinning at his daughter. "What's the next clue? I'm great at this game."

"It's not a game!" Kenya wished they'd check if their

phones were working again. But she suspected her father would try to make her type with the calculator even when they were.

"I think the effect of magic is starting to take its toll." Briony's voice came from high in the air as the elf approached. "You two should get some rest. My friends will take you home. We'll see to Kenya."

Camilo's black sneakers stepped into view.

Is he going to apologize for betraying me to a group of insane scientists?

He ought to! He should be groveling on the sidewalk with tears in his eyes, telling Kenya that he was a fool for ever having feelings for his precious Holly. Instead, he was holding back a smile.

Kenya wanted to scratch his ankle.

She also wanted to cry. Camilo was okay. He was alive.

It was annoying how relieved she'd felt seeing him sit up, how grateful she still was underneath her anger, how her brain kept betraying her by finding him attractive whenever she glanced at him.

Or maybe it was her heart that was the traitor.

Either way, Kenya was done wasting her time on Camilo.

"Home does sound good," Courtney said, pushing herself up. Doc, who'd been dozing beside her lifted his head at the suggestion. "But Kenya should come with us."

"Yes. I want to go home too!" Kenya literally leaped at the suggestion. She was aiming for her mother's arms.

Camilo caught her instead. He slipped his hands under her forelegs and held her out before him. His lips tried and failed to conceal a smile. "She said she wants to stay with us."

"That is not what I said!" Kenya hissed, paws flailing. *"I'm going with my parents."*

"She says that we need to discuss how she's going to adapt to life as a cat now." His smile slipped free a little more. "She wants my advice since I transform too."

"I definitely do not want any more advice from you! You're the reason I'm stuck like this, you absolute piece of—"

Camilo brought Kenya closer, snuggling her against his chest.

Her whiskers pressed against his muscles. She felt the warmth from his skin against her cheek, then her entire face. The musky scent of cologne still clung to him.

Kenya should've taken the opportunity to scratch him and break free. Instead, some horrible instinct—that she was certain had everything to do with her being a cat and nothing to do with still being attracted to the boy who'd trapped her in this state—kicked in. Kenya found herself rubbing her head against Camilo, amazed by how firm his muscles felt.

Maybe I could get used to being a cat.

No! Aghh!

Kenya's brain was betraying her again.

"Fine then." Her mother sighed. "But not too late. It's almost two hours past her curfew."

"Do you think a midnight curfew is really still necessary?" Her father's voice grew more distant. "Given that she's—no, of course. We should keep the curfew."

"No, wait!" Kenya pried her face from Camilo's muscles in time to see Briony guiding them into the ambulance.

"Stop. We need to talk," Camilo said.

"A bit late for that, isn't it?" Kenya stared up at his chin. She wanted the apology she knew was coming, but Camilo needed to understand just how royally he'd messed up.

Kenya wasn't sure she could ever trust him again. *"Can't talk my way back into being a human since you gave my blood to the people holding your father prisoner. If that's even true seeing as you've been lying to me this entire time."*

Camilo winced. "I never lied about my father."

"So then why would you help those people?" Kenya's meows grew high, catching in her throat. *"Because your girl-friend worked there? You have terrible taste."*

"You're focused on Holly?"

Maybe Kenya was a little. But only because it added an extra layer of embarrassment to the situation. This whole time, she'd been developing feelings for Camilo, and he'd been scheming with another girl to take advantage of her. *"I'm focused on the fact that we're supposed to be friends, but you've been lying to me for weeks."*

The ambulance's engine started. Briony waved as it rumbled off.

"Listen." Camilo knelt down, taking the chance of releasing Kenya onto the sidewalk now that her getaway vehicle had gone. He didn't know she'd figured out how to use her speed in this form. She could take off. He probably couldn't catch her in his current condition.

But Kenya turned back to face Camilo with his puppy-dog eyes and too pretty lips. She wanted to give him the chance to apologize, to explain. Because, despite every-thing, she wanted to forgive him.

"I'm not going to apologize for you being stuck as a cat."

Kenya's claws extended, and her tail snapped up like a whip. Seriously? Was the universe trying to mess with her? She'd just admitted that she wanted to forgive him, and Camilo doubled down on being a jerk?

"Holly asked for your blood before we found the

Western Woodlands and became real friends. Otherwise, I wouldn't even have considered it."

Kenya sat down, tail flicking behind her. It wasn't an apology, but this seemed like the closest thing she was going to get.

"This whole time, I've been in the dark too. I'm only just starting to understand everything. And I want to share it with you. All of it."

"Okay."

"Briony and I are going to the place where Holly and Julia went. We're going to infiltrate, get the dagger back, and free my dad. But it would be a lot easier if you're there to help."

Kenya wished she could laugh.

"So now you're willing to share information with me? To get me to volunteer to help you again. Yeah, sorry, I already made that mistake. Hasn't worked out too well. But really, I wish you and Briony all the luck. Hopefully your both still human-shaped when you return."

Kenya stood and turned, searching for a street sign to orient herself so she knew how to get home.

"Please, it's not just me who needs you," Camilo called out as she bounded toward the curb.

No, it's your dad, who may not even be in danger, and Briony, who was threatening to take my parents' memories less than an hour ago.

"If we don't get the dagger back—"

Kenya didn't even glance over her shoulder. Nothing Camilo could say could convince her to make the mistake of helping him again.

"—the Western Woodlands will be reduced to ashes."

Kenya froze.

The universe really was enjoying messing with her.

61

KENYA

"You want me to crawl through there?"

Kenya stood near the edge of the parking lot of Tapas De Madrid, hiding behind a menacing sign that cautioned intruders to keep out.

Camilo, crouched on the ground beside her, pointing at an open metal vent. Several of them were hidden beneath the roof's cookie cutter trim. Too small for any human to squeeze through.

But just big enough for a small orange cat.

After learning that the Western Woodlands was at risk, Kenya'd had no choice but to accompany Camilo and Briony on their mission to retrieve the dagger. She was as much to blame for its loss as they were, maybe more. Kenya couldn't let the enchanted forest or its inhabitants suffer because of her mistakes. She had to stop what she'd set in motion.

Though it had given her a perverse sense of satisfaction to inform Camilo that they couldn't take his truck to their destination. He gave her blood to a mad scientist; she crashed his vehicle. It was a small, but sweet, bit of justice.

Briony had driven them instead. Her car was only a few blocks away from Kenya's house.

It had felt somehow absurd watching the elf fold herself into the driver's seat. Even more bizarre had been noticing a brush, foam ear plugs, and a bucket hat stuffed in the center console and the loose change on the floor.

Kenya had envisioned the elf as a shadowy figure, always on foot, leaping into nurseries and swapping babies. This seemed too normal.

"Such a clever disguise." Briony's voice was so soft, Kenya almost didn't hear her. The elf was in a runner's starting position beneath the restaurant's sign, fingers steepled on the asphalt and knees bent. Her eyes scanned the building.

According to Camilo, there was an entire secret laboratory beneath the sunshine walls and quintessential red door of Tapas de Madrid. Kenya wouldn't have guessed either.

"I can toss you up," Camilo continued explaining his plan with the vent. "It would only be dangerous if you weren't in control of your shifting."

Turning into a human in a space she couldn't fit did seem potentially disastrous. *"Lucky, that's not an option thanks to you."*

Kenya didn't think her meow conveyed the sarcasm she'd intended.

"Does she think she can do it?" Briony looked to Camilo to translate.

"Yes." He responded without turning from Kenya. "Once you're in, you'll need to find the second exit. Most of the scientists are on that floor. One will have their keycard out beside them, you—"

"Steal it, make my way up on the elevator and come let you

in. I got it." Camilo had explained all of this already in the car.

Kenya just hadn't expected the vents to be so high, or so small, or so dark.

"Okay, then let's go."

62

CAMILO

It felt like he was supposed to make a motivational speech or offer words of encouragement. But Camilo's jaw was locked too tight. He felt as though everything in his life had led him to this moment.

He was going to save his father.

Once they were inside, Briony and Kenya would go after the dagger. Camilo would create the distraction. His father breaking free would gain everyone's attention. All the scientists would come.

Camilo intended to already be in control of several tranquilizer guns.

Success hinged on one thing.

They couldn't be discovered until the moment was right.

Camilo tried not to look at the cameras—little eyes peeping out from beneath the eaves—as he paced the perimeter of the walls. The Morgana Center's security was state-of-the-art. But that didn't mean there was always someone watching.

The clock in Briony's car had read 3:08 AM when they'd

arrived. Given Tobias Buckler's intended time of attack, Camilo estimated that meant the old man and his convoy of infected demons would be leaving in a little under an hour. Any scientists at The Morgana Center would have been there to assist. They were hopefully too busy with tasks to concern themselves with glancing at the outdoor security cameras which seldom showed anything.

"Would you choose a vent?" Briony hissed in his ear. The elf followed inches behind Camilo. Her long limbs tapping in an agitated dance—fingers to palm, heels to floor, wrist to hip.

Camilo stopped. He'd walked the entire length of the building trying to find a vent that was out of a camera's eyeline. But his father had designed The Morgana Center. Diego was too clever to have made a mistake like that.

All I did was make sure we appeared on all the cameras.

Himself and Briony, at least. Kenya was too close to the ground for the lens to pick up.

Maybe we should all have crawled.

"This one will do," Camilo muttered.

Kenya was by his feet, staring up at the vent.

Does she know her fur is standing up straight?

It wasn't a bad thing if she was afraid. If anything, it comforted Camilo.

But he ought to offer some words of reassurance. *I believe in you*, maybe? It felt cliché, and it barely brushed the surface of what he wanted to say to her.

The fact that Kenya was helping meant everything to Camilo. Yet, at the same time, he'd never doubted that she would come.

Kenya was brave, and kind, and loyal to a fault. The kind of person who climbed trees without considering how to get back down, the type that was a bit too quick to volunteer to help a stranger. Even if she didn't believe Camilo about his father, she would never have let the Western Woodlands burn to the ground.

And she's a lot more capable than she realizes.

There were a hundred other things that flashed through Camilo's mind as he looked at the orange ball of fur at his feet. Memories of her laugh, the way she'd purred against his chest, her insisting they race again every time she lost.

Camilo knew what he wanted to say. What he needed her to know in case something went wrong and he didn't see her again.

He crouched down to lift her. His hand felt clammy. Camilo wiped them on his pants, wishing the elf wasn't tapping a few inches away.

Kenya's eyes were on him, round and green with slitted pupils. They had the same vibrant spark as her human ones. Camilo would have recognized them anywhere.

"You know, whether you're in cat or human form, Kenya it doesn't matter. I lo—"

The thud of a door silenced Camilo before he could finish. Music full of heavy bass and angry drums blasted from within.

"Run," Camilo ordered.

Only Kenya bolted.

Briony's ears had curled into tight balls, and she'd collapsed onto the ground. He tried to pull her up, but his chest spasmed at the attempt.

Behind him, a deep voice spoke. "I was hoping you'd show back up."

63
KENYA

Kenya trembled beneath the hedges that bordered the parking lot as she watched Camilo and Briony. They'd been caught before she'd even made it in.

Their assailant was a short scientist with a rat's face and an owl's eyes. Round spectacles perched on his nose. A device around his neck blasted music, and a pair of guns sparkled in his hands. They were full of a white liquid that glowed like magic.

Why aren't they running?

But the answer was obvious. The deep bass affected Briony worse than the whale sounds, crippling her while she attempted to plug her ears.

And Camilo didn't want to abandon her.

What did it say about Kenya that she'd run?

I have to save them.

But how?

The device around the scientist's neck. Kenya just needed a clear run, and she could snatch and break it.

Before she could move, the man aimed his guns. One

barbed tip prodded Camilo's back, the other aimed at Briony's neck.

If Kenya leaped from the shadows, the scientist would shoot.

Then what would she do?

Kenya didn't know, but she had to do something. She rushed forward just as the scientist marched the others through the bright red door.

It swung shut, almost catching Kenya's whiskers.

She was on the wrong side.

"Wait! You missed one of us!" Kenya mewled, standing on her back legs to scrape her claws along the metal. It was even worse than the scientist's music.

If we couldn't hear the noise until he opened the door, what are the chances he'll hear me scratching?

Low.

Kenya would need another way in. There was an obvious one.

Her eyes climbed the building until they reached one of the vents, almost seven feet in the air. Kenya had never jumped that high. Definitely not as a cat.

But she was going to have to. Otherwise, Camilo and Briony and everyone in the Western Woodlands was doomed.

I can do this. I have magic. I just have to believe.

Kenya walked backward, lowering her front paws and lifting her hips—a cat's version of a starting position. Her tail stiffened. She gathered her will, letting the flames of magic wrap not just around her paws but her entire body.

And then, Kenya leaped.

64
KENYA

I did it! I made it.

Kenya purred in elation as her back legs scrambled into the vent. She had to crouch to fit, but it wasn't as dark as she'd feared. Now, she just needed a plan to find Camilo, Briony, and the dagger.

The metal was slippery. Kenya skidded forward and found herself shooting downward through the vent.

Kenya screamed as her legs lifted into the air.

She was going to crash to her death.

Kenya spread her limbs, claws extending and scraping along the metal as she tried to slow her descent. Five exits flashed by. She failed to catch any of the ledges.

The tip of Kenya's tail brushed against cold metal. She'd managed to stop just shy of the bottom.

Right. As I always intended.

Kenya dropped to her feet and shook out her fur. She tried to recall the map Camilo had sketched for her in the car. The bottom two floors were mainly cages, with an experimental test room on the sixth.

A shiver ran through Kenya. What if she was captured and turned into Holly's test subject?

But there was no going back up. The only way to find the others and get out of the vents was to move forward.

Her fur prickled as she crept through an opening to her left. Her heart pounded in her chest; her tail was almost afraid to move. There was a grate a few feet away.

An escape?

Anguished screams rattled through the vent. The force of them made Kenya's ears quiver. She buried her head beneath her paws, trying to drown it out.

Now I know how Briony felt.

With a deep breath, Kenya pushed forward.

Maybe it would be better if she didn't find Camilo and Briony on this level.

What was he about to say before he got captured?

Kenya's mind had started filling in words. But she didn't trust her brain when it came to Camilo. Maybe she'd imagined the *luh* sound. Or maybe he'd been about to say something innocuous like *I luh-eave it for you to decide what's best.*

It didn't matter anyway.

Even if Camilo had magically decided he liked her, Kenya couldn't trust him. Not after everything. She had to be smarter than that.

A smart person wouldn't be thinking about dating a boy when crawling around in the vents of evil scientists who want to destroy magic.

The grate looked into a padded cell with soft blue walls, the color of waves. A sprinkler system sprouted from the floor, and there was nothing to hint at the location of the door.

Kenya wouldn't be any closer to freedom if she jumped in there.

She continued through the vents, searching for an escape. More vents looked into more blue padded cells. One had walls fused from smooth reflective plates.

A different cage for a different sort of demon.

Like the face-changer.

Kenya's ears lowered, and her chest tightened in sympathy for the demon who'd captured her.

Camilo had explained the scientists' virus. It trapped people like Kenya in their animal forms and caused fire-wielding demons to turn their flames inward. What had it done to the face-changer?

More screams echoed through the vents, paralyzing Kenya. She covered her ears as the metal quaked beneath her. She was getting closer to the source.

Kenya's stomach turned as she crept toward the next grate.

"I trust that's a satisfactory demonstration for you all now?" The speaker was an old man judging from the deep grizzled tone. "Anyone fails to follow orders, and you'll all find your insides on fire for much longer than a minute."

Despite the threat, his voice was flat, almost bored. There was no reason to doubt the truth of his words.

A shiver went through Kenya.

This old man had to be the one Camilo mentioned on their drive. The one who wanted to destroy the Western Woodlands.

The one who wants the dagger.

Did Tobias Buckler have it already?

Kenya took a deep breath, steeled her nerves, and pressed her face flat against the bars.

The room beneath curved in the shape of a closing bracket. A pane of glass, reaching from floor to ceiling, split the space into two sections. Kenya's grate was on the side with the door.

Decorations were sparse. One long window, set in half the curved wall, looked out at something gray. Tranquilizer guns hung like paintings, and there was one long table with chairs, all arranged on the same side. It was the sort of set up you'd expect to see in a play.

But there was nothing entertaining about the scene beyond the glass. Rows of thin people lined up, their clothes loose and baggy. All bore the appearance of someone who hadn't showered in weeks, hair flat and lifeless, skin slick with oil and sweat. Their eyes were all pupils, no hint of an iris or any whites.

The fire demons. We have to rescue them too.

Three people watched behind the table.

Holly was at the far end, staring down at a tablet like a child who'd been told to entertain herself. There was no sign of Camilo's blood on her hands, and she'd changed into a clean coat.

Julia stood a few feet to her daughter's right. Her foot tapped against the smooth, white tiles. There were still flecks of red on her shoe. Her head was turned toward the old man.

Tobias Buckler was just as Camilo had described. His pale scalp bore the darkened spots of age, the folded wrinkles. But his arm, resting against the table, rippled with sinewy muscles. There was a microphone on the table before him. He held his chain before it, thumb roving along the pendant on the end.

But it was what was in his other hand that caught Kenya's attention—the changeling's dagger.

Tobias tapped the flat side of the blade against the table.

Kenya's whiskers twitched as they rubbed against the grate, warning her that she couldn't fit through the bars. She pushed her face closer just the same.

How do I get it?

"They understand," Julia said, answering on behalf of the thin, silent demons beyond the glass. "We'll have people at the ready with guns if any of them are foolish enough to flee."

"Good. Shoot anyone that emerges from the Western Woodlands. The entrance is somewhere to the north. That's how the fire's survivors will try to flee." A dark smile pulled at the old man's lips. He leaned forward, resting the dagger flat against the table as he pressed a button on the microphone. "Fire up. Let me see what we're working with."

Behind the glass, the pupil-eyed army raised their hands. Balls of dark flames rose to life, blazing above their palms.

Kenya's breath caught.

"Out." Tobias commanded, and the flames vanished. He chuckled as he leaned back in his seat. "Can't beat an army of cambions to destroy a forest."

"I trust our funding will continue without issue then," Julia said, arms crossed.

"Depends what you consider an issue." The old man leaned back, turning toward Julia.

None of them were paying attention to the dagger

Kenya took another two steps forward, her front paws resting on the slats. It was right there. She had a clear opening.

If I could just get down, I could use my super speed and—

"We have company," Holly said, standing suddenly. She

stepped forward, showing her mother something on the tablet.

Julia sighed. She pressed the screen.

The grate dropped beneath Kenya, sending her falling.

Jokes on you, this is exactly what I want.

65
KENYA

K enya twisted in the air, angling herself toward the table. She landed on all fours, tail poised. The dagger was at her paws.

But there was something she hadn't considered until now.

How am I going to lift it?

The pommel was too large to fit in Kenya's mouth, the blade too dangerous. She fumbled at the weapon with her paws. Someone grabbed her tail, lifting her in the air.

At least it wasn't the scruff of her neck this time. Kenya almost wanted to give her captor points for creativity.

Until she realized how much more painful it was.

"Jesus! That hurts!" Kenya cried in protest, trying to slash at the old man through his white coat. The muscles in the base of her tail stretched and burned. Twisting made things worse.

"Your changeling, I presume?" Tobias sounded bored. "Ought to kill her before she becomes a nuisance."

"We've had enough deaths for the day." Julia plucked Kenya from the old man, cradling her against her lab coat.

It might've been infantilizing if dying wasn't being pushed as the alternative.

"She's a cat. Not a monster. Aren't you?" There was the hint of a threat in Julia's last question. She rested a finger against Kenya's head.

Tobias grunted. "She might be stuck, but that's no cat. A shifter is a shifter is a Castor."

"No, I'm a cat. A cat who's going to scratch all of your eyes out and free my friends and get the dagger when you drop your guard." Kenya banked on the fact that they couldn't understand her meows.

"See?" Julia said, raising the one eyebrow that was visible at the old man.

Tobias narrowed his eyes at Kenya. His mouth was set to respond, but the door banged open behind him.

Camilo marched inside. The owl-eyed scientist and his massive gun were still at his back.

Kenya's breath caught. But this was good. He was alive, and she'd found him.

But where's Briony?

Tobias' lips twisted into a scowl. The indifference in his voice turned sour as he saw Camilo. "Not so many deaths after all it would seem."

"Oh, thank God," Julia's voice was so soft, Kenya wondered if she imagined it. But when she glanced up, there was a tear resting on the scientist's cheek.

"You're alive!" Holly's words came out in a mad, desperate rush—half-gasp half-shout. She dropped the tablet and raced forward. A foot away, she stopped, blocked by an invisible barrier. She raised her hand, and her fingers trembled as though afraid they'd slip through his body if she tried to touch him.

If Camilo noticed her, he didn't show it. His eyes were on Kenya, wide and anxious.

"Surprise. I came to rescue you," she meowed.

Camilo's eyes narrowed. His head twitched. He was probably trying to tell her that this was not the time for jokes. Or maybe he wanted her to run again.

Not without him. And not without the dagger.

There was a way out of their situation. Kenya just needed to figure out what.

66

CAMILO

Why is Kenya here?

She was supposed to be outside, safe and hidden in a bush somewhere or, better yet, making her way home.

Camilo should never have gotten her involved. He'd thought he needed her help to get into The Morgana Center. But getting taken prisoner had proven just as effective.

It may have been a quick recalibration, but he had a new plan.

Kenya's presence changed everything.

"I could stab him with the dagger," Tate suggested, pressing the sharp tip of the needle deeper into Camilo's spine. "Make sure he's actually dead this time."

"Tate, what are you saying?" Tension frayed the edges of Julia's voice. Only a few weeks ago, Camilo would have been tempted to believe it was out of concern for his well-being. He knew better now. The only emotion behind her words was shock. Her subordinate wasn't supposed to make those suggestions without her approval.

Tate continued to address Tobias as though Julia was a shadow. "I made the mistake of trusting him before. Not again. Camilo made his choice. He was trying to break in here with an elf. I tossed her in a cell. But Camilo's different. He won't be easy to neutralize."

"Indeed." Tobias ran his thumb over the curved silver pommel of the changeling's dagger. There was a cruel tilt to his lips.

A lump rose in Camilo's throat.

Before he'd stepped through the door, he'd have been thrilled. Tate getting the dagger was exactly what he'd wanted. Camilo could grab it from him, transform into a wolf, and—

It didn't matter now.

Julia had Kenya. One wrong move on Camilo's part, and who knew what his former boss might do. It was too risky.

"We'll cage him overnight like we agreed," Julia said, turning to Tobias as well. "He won't be a threat to your plans." Her eyes flicked to Camilo, and her hands tightened around Kenya.

Message received.

Camilo caught Kenya's eyes. They were wide, a spark of determination burning in the pupils and igniting the green with fiery streaks. But behind the strength, worry rippled. She was afraid.

And she still came in to try to rescue me?

Camilo's chest tightened. He was thinking too highly of himself. Kenya was joking when she said that. She'd come to retrieve the dagger and save the Western Woodlands, maybe Briony too. Camilo probably hadn't crossed her mind until he'd marched through the door. Kenya was understandably furious with him.

Whatever her motive, I should've guessed she would sneak inside. It's not like she's patient about following instructions.

"Camilo had that option," Tate said, turning his deep voice into a snarl. "He almost ripped me to shreds. My clothes are in tatters. He needs to be dealt with. Properly. Please, let me do the honors?"

Tate had to move one hand from the gun's trigger to stretch it toward Tobias.

Camilo took the opportunity to pivot, holding his hands high in surrender as he turned to the scientist. "There's no need to kill me. I swear. One stabbing tonight was enough for me to learn my lesson. I'll cooperate. Just don't hurt Kenya. Please."

Tate frowned, lowering his gun for half a second. The scientist hadn't been expecting the sudden request. His lips mouthed a silent response.

Camilo would have tried to make out what, but a high noise, half-sob half-shout of frustration rose from Holly. She'd run forward when he first stepped in, but even standing only a couple feet away, Camilo had barely noticed her.

"That's the reason you—" Holly's voice broke into a strangled laugh. Trembling, she leaned forward, and her hand wrapped around Camilo's wrist.

Now she's not afraid of me?

But of course, she wasn't. If anyone should have been afraid, it was Camilo.

"You stabbed me."

It was almost funny.

"I'm so sorry, Cam," Holly said, and every part of her quivered—her fingers, her voice, even her eyes. She looked like a child, playing dress-up in her mother's white lab coat. "I thought the dagger would break your curse. I didn't think—I didn't know—" Holly pulled her hand away to wipe a stream of snot and tears with the sleeve. "We're still on the same side. The only problem is her."

Holly lifted her hand and pointed toward Kenya, still trapped in her mother's arms.

The person who stayed behind to keep me alive?

Briony had told Camilo how she found him on the road. Kenya had curled on his chest to stop the bleeding. It had probably saved his life, giving him just enough blood to keep alive until he could be healed.

Camilo doubted Holly had expected the dagger to hurt him. It didn't change that she'd left him to die after the fact. Both of them had.

"Quaint as this all is," Tobias Buckler said, standing from the long table and starting to approach. "I don't fund this center hoping for soap opera quality entertainment. Time is creeping on, and I have a forest to burn."

Tobias' hand tightened around the dagger, knuckles glowing white. He brandished it, slicing the air, a dangerous glint in his eye as though he wanted an excuse to use the blade.

Camilo's upper body ached. He didn't like his odds against the old man.

I won't survive if he stabs me.

"I'll fight for you," Camilo offered. "Help you with the Western Woodlands. If that's what you want."

Kenya lifted the one paw she still had free, waving it at him. *"You're bluffing, right? You can't do that. Just get the dagger and run. I'll find a way out on my own."*

Julia's hand smothered Kenya's meows.

"That's an interesting offer," Tobias mused. He slowed his approach, lowering the dagger. He didn't loosen his white-knuckled grip. "What do you think?" The old man looked at Julia.

Her eye flicked from Camilo back to Tobias, down to Kenya muzzled in her arms, then across the room, to the rows of demons waiting beyond the glass. "You have an army that will obey. Taking Camilo is too risky. It'll be safer to leave him here."

"Hmm." With an agility that defied his age, the old man spun toward Julia. He crossed the short space between them. "I wonder whose safety it is that you're referring to there."

Tobias plucked Kenya from Julia's arms and lifted the dagger once more.

He was going to stab her.

Camilo tried to run forward, but a spasm shot through his chest. His steps were as slow as any human. He only managed to take two before the old man reached Holly.

Tobias shoved both Kenya and the dagger into her hands. "You've got more mettle than your mother, girl. And you'll know just where to cut your new pet if my dog doesn't listen."

Holly stared at the blade in her hand, then the struggling cat. One last chance for redemption. If she did the right thing here, Camilo could forgive her.

She didn't.

"Understood, Mr. Buckler." The tremble was gone from Holly's voice. Her lips drew into a thin line, and she pressed the blade against Kenya's neck.

Camilo's muscles tightened, spasming again, almost as though they wanted to escape the confines of his skin. Julia would have used Kenya to keep him in line. Holly might slice her prisoner to teach Camilo an entirely different lesson.

But the old man made a mistake.

Kenya was now in the perfect position to get the dagger.

How can I tell her—?

Bright flashing lights and a wailing siren broke Camilo's train of thoughts.

67
KENYA

What the hell was happening now?

Kenya squeezed her eyes shut, trying to block out the flashing red warning. The noise was a different issue.

She'd assumed the siren was another outcry from the pupil-eyed army beyond the glass. But their only reaction had been to cover their eyes.

The source of the alarm was Holly's tablet.

"It's Diego," Julia's voice was loud, frenzied enough to rise above the noise. "He's broken free."

Is she talking about Camilo's dad?

Kenya risked opening an eye. In the center of the flashing red, Julia unlocked the tablet, finger flicking the screen even as she turned to grab one of the loaded tranquilizer guns from the wall behind.

"What are you all waiting for?" Her head turned from her daughter to her assistant to whatever Tobias Buckler was to her. "We have to secure him before he escapes and hurts himself."

"Keep that gun aimed at him, boy," Tobias snapped the order to Tate before turning to Holly. "The dagger too."

The cold metal returned to Kenya's cheek. Her whiskers trembled, buzzing against the blade. Breathing could have been dangerous. It was a damn good thing Holly had steady hands.

Or a bad one if she decides to hurt me.

Tobias blocked Julia as she ran toward the door. The alarming tablet was tucked beneath her armpit.

"I told you to put him down long ago and end all of this," Tobias pulled the tablet free and flung it against the far wall.

Glass shattered as it collided, passing through the window and into the gray scenery beyond. Red light continued to flash through, but the speaker was broken.

The only sound was Tobias, voice rising to a shout as he glowered at Julia. "How do I get my army out without your mad wolf killing one of them?"

"Your army—?" Julia pulled her hair out of her face, revealing her eye patch. She waved the gun before her. "Your army only exists because of Diego's research. I need your funding to keep him alive, to find a way to cure him. If he dies, what do I care about your army or a dagger or any of this? Tate, come with me. Holly can handle Camilo."

Tate's head turned toward them, glasses slipping down his nose.

Julia pushed past the old man. She didn't stop to see if he was following as she ran through the door, vanishing from sight.

It didn't make sense. Julia had killed a demon, but was worried about saving a werewolf. Though Holly had transformed Kenya into a cat and now threatened her with the dagger, she'd sobbed when apologizing to Camilo.

Their feelings for the Lopez family were complicated to say the least.

No wonder Camilo was confused about who to trust.

"Don't move, boy." Tobias' fingers hovered over his pendant. Now that Kenya was closer, she could see the silver mesh of the speaker. "You're going to open that door so I can get my army out, then go to the third floor and fetch whoever was smart enough not to run at the sound of these alarms. I have a forest to destroy."

Tate hesitated as though he hadn't yet decided whose commands to obey. His eyes flicked between Camilo and the old man.

"Keep the dog still, Nichols." Tobias snapped the instruction. "Are you deaf?" He grabbed Tate's arm and dragged him around the table toward the glass door. The owl-eyed scientist struggled to cling to the gun. Behind the glass, the pupil-eyed army had become the spectators. They shifted in their positions, leaning closer so that their lined formation grew less obvious.

Kenya couldn't say how, given the nature of their eyes, but she could tell that all were looking at Tate and Tobias.

"Don't move." Holly pressed the flat of the blade against Kenya's neck, turning toward Camilo.

He'd been inching closer.

So much for him being controlled by Holly threatening me.

Or maybe he had a plan. If so, it better be a good one. All Kenya could come up with was scratching Holly's wrist.

Then pray she drops me instead of stabbing me with the dagger.

Holly couldn't risk the latter option. Right? Kenya was all the leverage they had to control Camilo.

Killing me is out of the question.

Assuming Holly was a logical, sane individual. Kenya

wouldn't put money on that. The scientist also seemed liked the type of sociopath who would enjoy maiming someone.

This cannot be how I die.

Thanks to how Holly had positioned herself, Kenya now faced Camilo. She twitched her whiskers, trying to grab his attention. If they were going to get out of here, they needed a plan.

Camilo's gaze was fixed on Holly. He raised his hands, looking like a little boy who'd been caught stealing cookies, not a grown man facing a borderline insane scientist.

To his right, Tobias ripped the gun from Tate's hands and pointed toward a scanner on the glass cage. It needed a fingerprint.

"I'm not afraid of you, Holly," Camilo said. "No one should be."

Is he saying that for my benefit?

Because Kenya wouldn't describe her current stress as being caused by Holly. The culprit that was making her scared was the dagger pressed to her throat.

"I don't want you to be afraid of me," Holly said.

"Good. Cause I don't think your work is all that impressive." Camilo's hands were open, palms outward to show they were empty. "You needed the blood sample I gave you to infect Kenya. You couldn't have done that without my assistance, could you?"

Holly shifted, out of offense, confusion, or general discomfort, it didn't matter. The dagger moved with her. Still, too close for comfort, but at least the air could pass between Kenya's neck and the blade. It was a short relief.

"Would you hurry up, boy?" Tobias' voice was loud from over by the glass.

"I'm sorry, my thumb must be sweaty."

Holly spoke to Camilo over Tate's frantic apologies. "Are you trying to bait me into getting annoyed for some reason? You know I needed the blood sample. The virus had to be sequenced to fit her DNA, otherwise, it wouldn't work. But it's damn impressive that I did that. So what is it really? Because if you're hoping for an apology or some admission that I was wrong, it's not happening. The changeling is a problem. I don't regret trapping her like this." Holly lifted Kenya higher.

"I don't regret it either."

Kenya was enjoying feeling the space between her and the dagger increase. But her brief glimpse at relaxation fell short as she heard Camilo's response. He'd refused to apologize earlier as well, but did he need to keep hammering in the point? And to Holly of all people?

"Because," Camilo continued, "I never gave you Kenya's blood."

Wait. What?

Kenya's eyes snapped to Camilo. Of course he had. They'd both said—

"I took a sample from my neighbor's cat, Pumpkin. He was happy to donate. I kept waiting for you to realize and get angry, but you never even questioned why her genetic sequence would be identical to a cat. It suited what you wanted to think of her too well."

Holly had said that, hadn't she? That Kenya was more cat than anything else.

"You're lying." Holly's arms dropped as though the muscles were giving way. The dagger was a healthy distance from Kenya. "The virus wouldn't work if it wasn't coded to her profile. It has to be sequenced to match. She wouldn't be a cat."

"No. Not unless..." Camilo's eyes dropped to Kenya. He

raised his brows. There was a hint of a smile tugging on his face.

Not unless I believe.

Kenya's heart stopped. Could she really have been that foolish? This whole time, she'd assumed a virus had her trapped. What if it was just her own mind?

Since getting injected, she'd started telling herself that she was a cat. Just like Kenya had refused to think of herself as anything but human before.

But Kenya was neither.

I'm a shifter.

And that was what Kenya needed to do.

She closed her eyes, trying to tune out whatever was happening between Tobias and Tate. There was no reason for her to be afraid of Holly. Or any of these people.

Kenya had magic.

Something eased in her mind, a muscle within her brain. She'd been tensing it without knowing. Heat rushed into her as it relaxed. Flames danced along the backs of Kenya's eyes—blue and red. Her body stretched.

Holly shouted and stumbled backward. She'd been forced to release Kenya. All she held now was the dagger.

Not for much longer.

I'll be taking that.

68

CAMILO

A stream of expletives erupted from Tobias. He'd noticed Kenya transform. But there was little he could do. He was too slow.

Or rather, Kenya was too fast.

Camilo blinked, and she was gone.

Holly's head spun in circles, trying to find where Kenya had vanished. She waved the dagger before her. But Holly wasn't a fighter. She had no idea how to grip the pommel or do more than swipe at the air and hope to get lucky.

Kenya grabbed her arm from behind.

We're actually going to make it out of here.

"What are you doing, boy?" Tobias' anger grew louder. "Are you trying to steal my controller?"

Oh no.

Tate had finally made his move. After capturing Camilo and Briony, the scientist had taken them into the old kitchen of Tapas de Madrid. There was a blind spot by the stove.

Tucked into the corner, Tate had lowered both the gun

and the volume on his music and apologized for the farce. Julia had Holly and some of her other employees on watch for an attack. Tate needed to make sure it looked like he was on their side still if someone looked at the cameras.

"I had to find you first," Tate had said. *"I figured you were coming to free your dad. I can help you. But—but I want to free the others too."*

He'd been talking about the demons, the very creatures he'd helped to infect.

Apparently, a brush with death in the jaws of a werewolf and the subsequent life reevaluation that followed had led Tate to conclude that he'd been working for the wrong people. He wanted to make amends.

To prove it, the scientist broke the speaker around his neck. Julia had entrusted him with The Morgana Center's device. Only one other remained.

Their new plan, quickly conceived, had been simple enough, if risky. Briony had snuck off on her own to free Diego. Camilo told her the code.

It seemed wrong, letting the elf be the one to type it in and release his father. But that was precisely why it had to be Briony. So no one would suspect.

Camilo hadn't known about the alarm system.

Just like he hadn't been expecting Kenya. Tate was supposed to get the dagger so that Camilo could take it from him. In the fake fight that would follow, Tate was going to shoot the tranquilizer at the old man.

Once Tobias was knocked out, they could break the device around his neck that gave him control of the demons. Tate would free the army from captivity, and they'd escape. Briony and Diego would be waiting for them just outside his prison.

But none of that had happened. And Tate, after stalling to open the door as long as he could, had tried to lunge for Tobias' frequency emitter.

He'd missed.

"What are you doing?" The old man lifted his leg. His boot collided with Tate's stomach, sending the scientist flying toward the wall. "Traitor. Secure the dagger, Nichols."

Just a few chairs from where Camilo stood, Holly was trying. But Kenya was taller, stronger, and supernaturally faster.

Enough blows to her wrist and Holly's grip failed her. She dropped the dagger.

It was in Kenya's hand before it hit the ground.

"You shifting bi—" Tobias cut off his own curse as he fired the tranquilizer gun.

"Kenya, look out," Camilo shouted.

But he needn't have bothered.

In an explosion of fire, Kenya shrunk into a small orange ball of fluff. The changeling's dagger shifted with her. Just like her clothes, the weapon had melded into Kenya's cat form, and would only reappear when she was human.

The dart from the tranquilizer would have hit a human's chest. It flew high above the head of a cat, crashed into the wall and clattered to the floor.

On the opposite side of the table, Tate had pushed himself upright. He was limping toward the keypad again. The demons watched his every step, no longer pretending to be an army at attention. Their faces pressed against the glass.

"*I did it. We did it.*" Kenya meowed, stepping toward Camilo. Her eyes opened and closed in heavy blinks. She seemed unsteady on her feet as she approached. Using so much magic in such a short span had an impact. *"Where's Bri—"*

"Give me back that dagger!" Tobias lunged toward Kenya.

Against a regular human, even worn down, she could have escaped. But the old man was something different.

Camilo jumped in front of her, lifting his arms to block Tobias as he flew over the table. The two fell, and a chair clattered to the floor with them. Another crashed against Camilo's side as they rolled. He needed to gain the upper hand, pin Tobias down and break the device. Then, Tate could release the demons.

They would take care of the old man from there.

Every muscle in Camilo's upper body burned as though it were being ripped from within. Tobias bested him in mere seconds.

"That all you got, dog?" Tobias spat into his face, forcing Camilo to close his eyes. "You would've been useless to me after all. Ought to put you down and out of your misery. Just like your beast of a father. This will have to do."

Tobias moved one of his hands from off Camilo's wrist. The dart from the tranquilizer gun lay inches away. It was no mystery what the old man wanted it for.

The frequency emitter slipped from Tobias' shirt. It dangled only a few inches from Camilo's face.

I just have to break it.

Camilo clenched his teeth. The muscles in his arm popped, but he couldn't give in to the pain.

With the last bit of magic he could muster, Camilo grabbed the emitter and squeezed. The device cracked, breaking to pieces beneath the force of his fingers.

"You idiot! You blasted cyst on humanity!" Tobias

stabbed the tranquilizer dart into the soft flesh of Camilo's temple.

The glowing white liquid hit him worse than ever. But in his last moment of clarity, Camilo managed to shout two words.

"Now, Tate."

69
KENYA

Several things happened either simultaneously, or in such rapid succession it was difficult to recognize that one had led to the other.

Camilo destroyed the pendant while the old man stabbed him with the glowing white liquid. Tate—seemingly at Camilo's order—pressed his ring finger to the glass cage.

"You're free. I'm sorry. Be free," Tate spoke as a crack rose in the glass, sliding open.

At the same time, Tobias sprang off of Camilo. "You idiot. You've doomed everything." The old man grabbed Holly's hand and pulled her from the room. They vanished before Kenya had fully processed any of it.

Why couldn't my brain have super-speed?

Shouts, laughs, and screams filled the room as the glass opened, releasing the demons into the room with them.

Kenya crossed to Camilo. His eyes were closed, his breathing uneven. But at least there was no giant stab wound in his chest.

"How is he?" Tate's deep voice only a few inches away

made Kenya jump. He was crawling beneath the table, moving toward Camilo's feet. "Not good. We'll need to carry him to the third floor. Briony and Diego are waiting there. But estimating his weight at about two hundred and—"

A burst of dark red flames flew across the edge of Kenya's vision. It wasn't her magic.

She turned, and her heart stopped. One of the chairs beside her was ablaze. Another fireball ignited another seat, then the next went up, like candles on a cake. Only it was no one's birthday, and the flames could be deadly.

"Stop, you don't understand." Tate stood. "We're all on the same side. Camilo is like you. We need your help carrying him out. Ah—" Tate's deep voice turned into a high squeak as a fireball flew by his head.

A cruel nasal laugh rose from the mass of former prisoners. Soon a chorus of voices joined it, some deep, some nervous, some grizzled with age.

"You think we're going to help you, scientist?" one asked.

A deep bellowing laugh responded. "No, let's burn this place to the ground."

"And hope they all go with it."

Smoke spiraled from the chairs, rising toward the ceiling as the temperature rose. Camilo wheezed on the ground.

"No, wait," Kenya mewled, trying to stop them. Maybe she could talk to the demons and have them listen to her in a way Tate couldn't. She at least had to try.

Kenya relaxed her shifting muscle, letting her own fire transform her. The changeling's dagger was in her hand once more, back from whatever shifting interdimensional portal her magic hid it within.

"Stop, please! You don't understand. Our friend will die."

One of them, the last in the room stopped. He was short, gray flecks in his hair, He turned, and something about his nose was reminiscent of a snake. "Good. Anyone who knows what you've done here is better dead. That way, no one can figure out how to control us again." He lifted his hand and hurled a ball of fire toward the table.

It burst to life.

The demon cackled and slammed the door. It transformed into a wall of fire, red hot and solid.

"He's trapped us in." Smoke filled Kenya's lungs. She coughed and fell to the floor.

She had never experienced heat this intense. Sweat pooled around her temples and her fingers. Her grip was sticky on the changeling's dagger. She slipped it into the waist band of her shorts as she looked at Camilo.

This was not good. That pupil-eyed asshole had locked them in here to roast to death.

I'm not going to let that happen.

"This is all my fault." Tate lay flat on the floor, wheezing as he stared up at the smoke. "I thought I could make everything right, but I was too late. When I found out the truth, looked through that strange, weird museum, I realized it just didn't add up. Camilo wasn't a monster. But now I've gotten him killed."

Kenya had no idea what the scientist was talking about, or how he was continuing to talk even while he struggled to breathe. But he needed to focus.

"We're not dead yet," she said, covering her mouth with her elbow as she searched for another way out. There was only the one door, now magma death. No other entrance to the room.

But there was a window!

It was already cracked from the tablet Tobias had thrown.

"We will be soon," Tate said. "At least I will be. Do werewolves and shifters have higher heat tolerances than humans? That's what I should've been testing. I never cared about viruses."

Kenya needed something to break the window. Everything was on fire.

No. Not everything.

There was one chair that the demons had missed. It had fallen onto the ground when Tobias and Camilo grappled. Despite the heat and sparks leaping and twisting from the table's inferno, this one chair had yet to be swallowed into the fire.

"It was Julia who begged me to specialize in them," Tate continued. "Discovering the way that magic interacted with them and transformed them into something that could be manipulated was an accident. I didn't know—" A fit of coughing cut him off.

Kenya stood, covering her mouth with her shirt, grateful that it was oversized. She grabbed the chair. The wood was hot, but she couldn't drop it.

"If there's an afterlife, do you think I could go to the good one after all of this? Or at least reincarnate?" Tate choked out.

You at least have to admire his lungs.

It was too hot for Kenya to summon her speed. The warmth from her own flames would be enough to make her pass out.

Summoning a burst of strength instead, Kenya flung the chair at the window. Already cracked and weakened, the glass shattered, leaving a jagged pointed hole, just large enough for a person to fit through.

We're going to make it.

Kenya crouched beside Tate, resting a hand on the scientist's knee. She didn't know him, but right now it was very important that they work as a team. Which meant he needed to pull himself together.

"You did some bad stuff, okay? But you're trying to make it better. That's all you can do," she reassured him.

Comforting a scientist who'd essentially attempted to enslave a group of people—be they demons or criminals it didn't matter—was not something Kenya had ever imagined herself doing. It twisted her gut in a way that felt very wrong.

But the room was on fire. The demons had tried to kill them. And Tate was her only hope.

"Now if you want to keep making amends, help me lift Camilo."

———

Kenya was the last through the window.

Smoke clouded her vision, and her lungs burned. She gasped for fresher air.

The courtyard at the base of the Morgana Center was just as gray and fiery as the room they'd escaped. Screams came from the floors above, panicked footsteps. Scientists ran, hectic white blurs beside the glass, as they tried to flee. A ball of fire fell toward the poured concrete and crashed a few feet from where they stood.

Within the flames was a charred corpse in a lab coat.

Kenya's stomach turned. She looked away, focusing her eyes on Tate instead.

The scientist's arms were locked beneath Camilo's armpits, holding his upper body from the floor. His owl eyes stared up at the fiery explosions on the floors above.

"Where do we go now? How do we get to the stairs?" Kenya asked, taking hold of Camilo's ankles so that he was suspended in the air between them.

"Nowhere. There's no doors into or out of the courtyard."

He had to be joking.

"There must be one." Kenya looked around the gray circular area, trying to ignore the screams from the floors above. Her heart pounded in her chest. She couldn't give in to fear.

I'm a shifter. I'm in control of my form.

She kept her mind relaxed even as her panic mounted. Tate was right. The walls were smooth, gray and unpainted in this section. The only break was the window they'd just climbed through. Going back in would be a dead end.

Could we jump?

Maybe, if Kenya used all of her speed, she could make it high enough. But she couldn't carry the others.

She dropped Camilo's feet and moved to his face.

There was a howl from a floor above. More screams.

"Wake up. We really, really need you to wake up." Kenya poked Camilo's cheek. "Please."

"Ken. Ya." Her name slipped from his mouth in two slow syllables. But Camilo's eyes remained closed.

A heavy thud boomed from the concrete behind Kenya. Even in the heat from the surrounding fires, a cold shiver ran down her spine. Only something very large could have made that sound.

Tate's mouth fell open. For once, he was silent.

Kenya turned and found herself staring at a giant wolf

—taller than a horse and twice as wide. Black shadows rippled through its gray fur, and its eyes were dark and yellow, burning with power. Its lips curled backward, revealing canines like knives.

The wolf growled, and within the deep rumbling, Kenya made out its words.

"Need some assistance?"

70
CAMILO

The first thing Camilo noticed whenever he came to was the smells.

Smoke mixed into the air, blending with the usual scents of Castor's Grove—magnolia and cherry, hints of gasoline, and whichever spices were most popular in the nearest restaurant. There was the warm cinnamon and ginger that lingered on Kenya.

One scent stood out among the others, earthy like soil but with a chemical tang. It should have been at odds with itself, but the two profiles harmonized in a manner that spoke to the impossible taking life.

The sharp, rich smell reached into Camilo's memories, conjured images of rainy days, snuggled on a couch with his father while Diego put on episodes of Battlestar Galactica.

It's him.

Camilo's eyes opened to the sky.

A wolf's head rose before the moon.

Rich yellow eyes stared at Camilo. Diego's massive mouth opened in a toothy smile.

Tears pooled in Camilo's eyes, threatening to fall. He held them back as best he could, staring up at the furry face of the wolf above him.

"Mijo. Estas bien."

Camilo heard the words in his father's soft whine.

You can speak.

This whole time, Camilo had thought that his father was gone, mind lost to the transformation. But Diego had always been himself.

That's why I got my things together for us to move to the woods when you showed up transformed. You told me to.

How could Camilo have believed Julia when she'd insisted that packing his bags had only been a childish whimsy? And yet—

"You flung yourself at the glass," Camilo's voice was soft, brain struggling to believe what his senses showed. "You covered it in blood. You were—"

"Out of my mind?" Diego suggested with a growl. *"I wanted to give you a hint to the passcode, but there was tranquilizer still in my system. It addled my thoughts, or I'd have found a better way."*

All these years, the scientists swore Diego was deteriorating. Why hadn't they questioned Tobias' tranquilizer?

Why hadn't Camilo?

He opened his mouth, trying to find the words to apologize to his father. But it was too much. The tears came instead.

Diego's tongue rolled free. He licked the length of his son's cheek.

Camilo wrapped his arms around his father's neck and sobbed into the fur. His shoulders objected, trembling as they were forced to rise. So what? Camilo deserved the pain.

"I failed you," he said, voice muffled by his father's fur.

"No, you saved me."

"You were trapped for fourteen years. And I didn't—I took too long—I'm sorry, I—"

"Don't apologize." There was a tone of command to Diego's voice. He pulled his head away so that he could once more look his son in the eyes. *"You have done nothing but make me proud, Camilo."*

For a moment, the pain vanished. Light twinkled in the depths of Diego's eyes, and Camilo could feel the warm air of his father's breath, sweeping across his forehead. Everything felt right.

He released his father's neck and pushed himself up.

They were in the corner of the parking lot. A bush to Camilo's left delineated the property from a neighboring convenience store. To the right, the shell of Tapas de Madrid looked as normal as it ever did—walls still bright and cheerful, even in the moonlight.

Beyond Diego's shape, near the sign that warned intruders to keep out, were the very three people Camilo hoped to see.

Briony's lips pursed as she spoke into the phone she'd left in her car. Inches from her, Tate stared at the elf's ears with obvious fascination.

But it was the third person in the center of their trio who made Camilo's heart skip.

Kenya's curls rose like pineapple leaves from the top of her head. A sheen of sweat made her calves gleam. Her legs looked extra-long in a pair of tight gray running shorts.

She's human again.

Kenya's eyes landed on Camilo, and a grin exploded across her face.

It was the most beautiful thing he'd ever seen.

Camilo responded with his own shaky smile. He waved. For a moment, he thought she might come over, and his heartbeat quickened in excitement. He wanted to introduce her to his father.

But Briony tapped Kenya's forehead and stole her attention.

Camilo rubbed his eyes and turned to his father. "How did you—How did we—What happened in The Morgana Center? The last thing I remember, Julia was going to stop you, and Tobias knocked me out with the tranquilizer."

"Your elf friend, Briony is it? She entered the code. I'm so proud of you for figuring it out, Mijo." Diego paused for a moment, and Camilo wondered if to expect another lick. *"Once the alarm started, we figured someone would be arriving soon, so Briony armed herself with two of the guns from the wall. She shot Julia. But by that time, we'd started to hear the shouts from below. I figured you might be in trouble. So Briony carried Julia to safety while I moved lower, searching for you.*

"It was chaotic. The Center's employees were shooting whatever weapons they had or barricading themselves in rooms, and the demons were flinging fireballs at everyone, including each other. Some of the smartest of them fled to the elevator. They may have made it out. The rest are still stuck in all the madness. I was worried I wouldn't find you.

"But I caught your scent, rising from the courtyard down below. I was able to carry the three of you and leap to safety. The elevator just made it to the top before it gave out beneath my weight. I was surprised it made it at all with all of us in it. It's lucky she can turn into a cat, or it might've faded sooner."

Diego's eyes flicked toward Kenya.

"I gather she broke a window to save you all from burning to death. Seems like quite an impressive girl."

Somehow, that new information didn't surprise Camilo at all.

He smiled. "You don't know the half of it."

71
KENYA

Camilo was awake.

There had been no reason to worry. It was only a tranquilizer keeping him unconscious. Tate had said as much.

But a tension Kenya hadn't been aware of eased from her limbs. A grin spread across her face. She wanted to race to Camilo and wrap her arms around him.

Finally, I can say that we did it.

"After everything you've put me through, you have the audacity to smile?" Briony tapped the center of Kenya's forehead twice in rapid succession. "My dagger?"

The elf held out her hand, eyes on the bulge of pommel just visible through the oversized t-shirt.

Why couldn't I have transformed while wearing something else?

In the midst of trying to escape with all of their lives, Kenya had forgotten that she was wearing pajamas.

She pulled up her shirt and retrieved the dagger from the waistband of her shorts. The blade glinted in the moonlight, a quick goodbye, before Briony plucked it from her.

With a flourish of the elf's hand, the dagger disappeared into her pocket.

Kenya's eyes narrowed.

Why'd she bother holding out her hand so nicely if she was just going to grab it?

"At least that's sorted." Briony sighed. Her face seemed more relaxed now that the dagger was back in her possession. "Now, I trust that when I try to teach you in the future, you'll listen to me instead of trying to steal my belongings?"

"I think I can manage that," Kenya agreed, reaching for the base of her oversized t-shirt. It made her a shapeless mass when it was loose like this. Camilo probably thought she looked like a blob on two legs.

Not that Kenya cared. He'd betrayed her. She was done being interested in him.

Only...

He may have kept me in the dark about the scientists, but he didn't give Holly my blood.

Which meant it wouldn't be the craziest thing in the world to forgive him. Right?

Kenya wrapped her hand around the excess material and twisted the shirt so that she could tie it above her stomach.

"Good. First lesson." Briony tapped Kenya's forehead again. "Don't steal things from strangers because the boy you like asks you to."

Kenya dropped her shirt. That was a gross oversimplification of what had occurred. Did Kenya have a crush on Camilo? Sure, but that wasn't why she'd agreed to help initially.

"It's not her fault. It's basic biology," Tate said, eyes focused on Briony's ears. He'd recovered from his breakdown in the fire. "She was attracted to Camilo, so she trusted him." The scientist said it so calmly, like he was rattling off the equation for photosynthesis.

"Okay, that's not true," Kenya objected. She wanted to bury her head in her shirt. Wearing pajamas in the middle of the parking lot was embarrassing enough. Did Tate have to make his absurd statement so loudly? Camilo and his dad were only a few feet away.

Imagine if that's the first thing Diego hears about me. That I helped his son because I thought he was attractive.

"We—Camilo and I—we made a deal," Kenya stuttered. "Mutually beneficial. It wasn't like…"

She was arguing with no one. Tate's interest had shifted.

He stared at the elf's ears. "Your hearing is quite astounding. How do you manage to survive in a city when your sense is so attuned?"

"Earplugs." Briony's eyes narrowed. "Why?"

"You haven't got them in now."

"No, I've been taking them off when I go on missions. After Camilo managed to sneak up on me"—she glanced in his direction—"I thought it would be safer to be able to hear any impending threats. Evidently, I was mistaken. I might've sustained permanent damage after your stunt." The points of her ears twitched.

In the corner of the parking lot, Camilo stood. His bare chest seemed to glow in the moonlight. It emphasized his broad shoulders and chiseled muscles. He turned to Kenya and smiled at her with his too pretty lips.

I think my heart just stopped.

Camilo looked like he belonged on the cover a trashy romance novel. If he had been, Kenya would have bought it, and not as a gift for Lily.

And I'm still in my pajamas.

Kenya tied her shirt up and focused her attention on the stars. If Tate or Briony caught her staring it wouldn't disprove either of their accusations.

They might not be entirely wrong about my motivations.

Kenya's feelings for Camilo had driven at least part of her desire to help him. And she couldn't deny that teaming up with a ridiculously attractive boy her own age sounded more appealing than studying under the middle-aged Briony.

But who cares why I decided to help Camilo?

The important thing was that, as Kenya watched him approach, smiling and laughing with his now-freed father, she was happy she had.

72
KENYA

The five of them squashed into Briony's car for the drive back. It was no easy task. Diego was almost as large as the vehicle. Even with the back seats folded flat, his muzzle and tail stuck out the windows. Camilo and Tate rode with the werewolf pressing them flat against the doors.

Kenya was in the front, which sounded like a good deal, until they'd pushed the seat so far forward that her knees knocked against the compartment.

This is what a pretzel feels like.

"What about Julia?" Camilo asked, wriggling so that his head was against the back of Kenya's seat. His arm reached into the front and stole a stick of gum from the elf's center console. "My dad is asking."

Briony frowned as she started the car. "The one with the eye patch? I left her hidden beneath the bushes. The police will come for her and whatever's left of the rest of them. I sent an anonymous tip."

"That's who you were talking to on the phone?" Kenya

couldn't hide her shock as the engine started. "I didn't think you dealt with the police."

Briony smiled. She looked almost amused. "The Castor's Police. They're mostly werewolves." The elf gave Camilo a pointed look over her shoulder before returning her eyes to the clear road. "You'll find we have our own versions of most things you're familiar with. Including races."

"Like the Olympics?"

"They're called the Fabled Games. But yes. I would have told you that when we first spoke if you'd given me the chance."

In hindsight, maybe Kenya should've considered that possibility. "I suppose you could also have reassured me that my parents wanted me. You asked them to raise me, didn't you?"

Briony nodded. "Of course. After they lost their first daughter, I approached them with the offer, and they agreed, memory wipe and all. We don't just sneak babies into unwilling families." She glanced into the back of the car and muttered something. It was difficult for Kenya to hear, but from the way the elf's lips moved it looked like *anymore.*

A whole other version of the Olympics. Wait until my parents hear that.

Kenya could already imagine her mother arguing with an orange-skinned goblin referee. Her father would tell every creature there—elf, fairy, pixie, werewolf, whatever— that his daughter was the fastest being in existence.

Though, was she?

Kenya had seen how Briony moved. Camilo as well. And as a wolf, Diego was even faster than the two of them.

It would be a real challenge.

If Kenya wanted it.

She wasn't sure. Maybe she did. Or maybe, she'd be just as happy exploring the hidden areas of Castor's Grove. Either way, it was nice to have the option.

"I suppose I'll have to give lessons to all of you about how the magical world operates," Briony said, stopping at a light and glancing at the trio squashed into the backseat.

Tate's owl eyes emerged from beneath a mass of fur. His glasses had been pushed askew. "Even me?" he asked.

Briony frowned. "It's against protocol. Humans get their minds wiped. That's what will happen to all the other scientists, at least, the ones who survive."

"Oh." Tate's expression fell.

"But," the elf continued, and the scientist's brow lifted hopefully once more. "That virus you created. It concerns me. Few with any sway are fond of demons, but... if it could affect anyone else...I think, the need for a cure would lead the king to grant you clemency."

Did she say king?

There was a palace in the center of downtown. Kenya should definitely ask about that. But not now.

Her thoughts kept wandering to Camilo. She could feel him pressed against the back of her chair, could see the outline of his arm at the corner of her vision. Perhaps, if she twisted, she'd have been able to see all of him, to talk.

There were a million things they needed to discuss. He hadn't given her blood to Holly. So why had he let Kenya think that he had? And what did that mean about how he saw her compared to how he saw Holly? What had he been about to say to her before she'd jumped through the vent?

The questions burned in Kenya's mind. But she didn't

dare turn to ask him. What if Briony or Tate made another comment?

And Camilo just got his dad back. He needs time, not me bombarding him with questions about his feelings.

That was the least important thing. Kenya wished her brain would listen when she told it that.

"First stop. Davidson residence." Briony stopped in front of Kenya's house. "Go on then. Your parents have probably woken up by now and are worried sick."

"Yeah. Of course." After everything that had happened, walking through her front door to have a chat with her parents over an early breakfast felt anticlimactic.

That's probably why they end most stories before this point.

Kenya exited the vehicle and walked up the pathway. She fought the urge to hide the frayed ends of her shorts. At least she'd be able to change into something that wasn't heavy with smoke once she got inside. She hoped her parents had known to leave the door open. Kenya didn't have a key.

Footsteps bounced along the pathway behind her.

Kenya didn't dare turn around. It was probably Briony, and her heart was speeding for no reason.

"Wait." Camilo's fingers wrapped around her hand, blocking Kenya from opening the door.

She turned and found herself lost in his puppy-dog eyes —warm, and sweet, and pleading. Whatever he desired, she wanted to give it to him.

"I thought we should talk first, you know? Given everything." He gestured to Kenya, and his eyes landed on her shirt. His lips curved into a smile. "And here I thought you were a Chewy fan."

Was he referring to the stuffed Wookiee on her dresser?

Camilo had been in her room so briefly, Kenya didn't think he'd have noticed.

She crossed her arms over *R2D2*, trying to act like his teasing didn't fluster her. The others were likely watching from the car. Tate might be monitoring her reactions for signs of attraction. Kenya wouldn't put it past the scientist to relay those to Camilo.

Though I'm pretty sure he knows I find him attractive.

Kenya's eyes drifted down Camilo's exposed muscles before she caught herself.

"You wanted to talk about Star Wars characters?" she asked, pulling her eyes back to his. "Or explain why you lied about giving Holly my blood? No wonder you kept refusing to apologize."

"I am sorry about deceiving you though. Again." He gave a nervous laugh. "I was worried you'd lose control and shift in the middle of the vent if you knew the truth. But I should've given you more credit. You mastered your power."

Yes, sure, I'm amazing.

Now that Kenya had the answer to her first question, she was more concerned about the others.

"What were you going to say? Before I went into the vents?" she blurted it out before she could think of a good transition.

I am a master of subtlety.

Kenya tried to cover the awkward shift in topic. "Guess it wasn't *I lied to you about giving your blood away*?"

It wasn't funny. Kenya didn't think it was. So why was she laughing at her own terrible joke?

Couldn't I have been the one who got shot with the tranquilizer?

That way, she could have been rescued, carried home, and placed into bed. She'd have woken up in a few hours with nary an awkward interaction to stress over, and plenty of time to plan their next conversation.

Camilo laughed with her. Probably in pity. "I don't think I've ever known anyone as beautiful as you are, Kenya."

Wait, was he complimenting her?

Kenya swallowed her laughter.

"I mean inside and out," Camilo continued. "You're loyal to a fault, and determined, and compassionate."

Those are all on the inside.

Camilo wasn't hitting on her. He was giving her the same compliments that her dad sometimes did. Probably because he felt bad.

"It's okay, Cam," Kenya assured him, crossing her arms tighter across the cartoon droid on her shirt. "I'm not mad about you lying. You don't need to butter me up."

"That's not what I'm—" Camilo shook his head. "Since we first met, I've given you so many reasons to be skeptical of me. I didn't tell you about The Morgana Center, or what I was, or the situation between me and Holly. I thought I liked her, but I think my feelings were for someone she used to be, when we were little and she was my only friend."

Oh good, now we're talking about Holly.

Kenya would have preferred the anticlimactic ending. "You don't have to tell me this. Honestly. I get it."

She reached for the door handle.

Camilo grabbed her hand, intertwining their fingers, and stopping her from leaving. He spun her back toward him, bringing them closer together this time. "No, you don't. I've been so closed off. I told myself that I had to be to protect you from The Center. But I think really, I've been so busy hating myself, I haven't been able to recognize love. I see it now though."

Shoot me with the tranquilizer gun right now. Another scientist in the bushes. Please.

Kenya couldn't hold Camilo's gaze. What the hell had Briony and Tate said when she got out the car? They must've said something about her having feelings for him if he was confronting her like this? How? It had only been a few seconds.

"Let's not overreach here." Kenya held back a nervous laugh. "*Like*. Like a lot, even, maybe."

Camilo's eyebrows lowered. He didn't look like he believed her.

There came the laugh. Kenya's chest felt tight. She remembered how giddy she'd been that night when Camilo had given her the bouquet of green flowers. He'd been stuck in her mind since then. Her skin tingled whenever he brushed against her. Thoughts of him snuck into her dreams. The sight of him made her smile.

He was everything he'd called her and more: handsome, loyal, determined, compassionate, brave, resilient.

Oh God. He's right. I am in love with him.

Which was insane. She'd vowed never to speak with him again just a few hours ago.

"No, Kenya," Camilo said, closing the space between them. His hand rested on her shoulder, sending goose-bumps down her arm. "I love you."

That was when it finally clicked for Kenya, and she realized what Camilo was trying to say. She stared into his warm brown eyes and felt her stomach flutter. Once again, she came back with the brilliant response, "What?"

"I told you. I've never met anyone as incredible as you. You're gorgeous and smart."

Kenya hadn't known it was possible to simultaneously feel weak in the knees and like she could sprint an entire mile without magic. A smile spread across her face. She leaned closer to Camilo, bringing her hand up to rest on his cheek. She ran her thumb down his jaw and onto the muscles of his neck.

Camilo continued listing all the things he loved about her. "Competitive, brave. A bit impulsive—"

Kenya's lips cut him off as they crashed into his.

His mouth was soft and sweeter than she'd expected, like fruit eaten fresh from a tree.

Camilo didn't hesitate to return the kiss. His teeth pulled at her lower lip. The slight prick of his canines sent a shiver of excitement through Kenya.

She pressed herself closer against him, or perhaps he pulled her into position. All Kenya knew was that she could feel the muscles of his thighs pressing against the outside of her own. Her hands ran down his shoulders, over his biceps, over to his chest. His fingers tracing her spine, following the curve of her back.

He pulled away, eyebrows raised, and gave her the same smile he did whenever he teased her. "Did you just kiss me in front of my father? I thought that was highly improper."

Kenya's eyes widened. Crap. How had she forgotten?

She turned and saw Diego's head hanging from the window. His dark yellow eyes were turned to the sky as though trying to look elsewhere. Tate was pressed against the window too.

"Can we go now?" Briony called to Camilo. "She's not going anywhere. You can her kiss again tomorrow."

"Come by like usual this afternoon," Camilo said, grinning as he dashed off. "We can discuss what level of PDA is appropriate."

I am never going to live this down.

Kenya wanted to sink into the ground. But she also wanted to grin.

So what if she'd embarrassed herself? Kissing Camilo had been worth it.

73
CAMILO

Camilo stared through the high canopy of trees. The sun had yet to appear though its rays painted the Western Woodlands in a glowing pink. Butterflies in vibrant blues and yellows fluttered between the trees. They were pursued by a pair of black squirrels.

"Five, four..." Camilo muttered a countdown to himself. "...three, two—"

Right on cue, an orange ball of fluff sprung through the entrance, pouncing toward him.

Camilo spun and caught Kenya against his chest. "Got you again."

She hissed, but her head burrowed against his chest in an affectionate manner. He was never sure if she intended to rub herself against him like that when she was a cat, but she always did. Camilo liked it.

Flames rose from Kenya, and her body stretched into human-form.

Likely she was trying to break free, but Camilo adjusted his grip, so that she was stuck being held in his arms.

"How do you always know when I'm approaching? Can you smell me?"

Sometimes. The cinnamon and ginger scent of her magic often clung to her, but that didn't pass through the Western Woodlands' barrier. It was something else.

"I just have a sense of where you are," Camilo said. He had for the past month, ever since they'd kissed. It was difficult to explain.

And, judging from Kenya's narrowed eyes, not an answer she was going to accept.

"Or maybe you're really bad at sneaking up on people," Camilo offered, grinning at her.

Kenya pursed her lips. "Briony says I'm better at it than you."

Camilo scowled, remembering their last lesson with the elf. Tate had insisted on running tests at the end. Kenya was the one who'd made it into a game, having them each take turns sneaking up on one another.

"She cheats by having enhanced hearing," Camilo said, starting to walk. Despite insisting her ears had sustained damage, Briony heard every tap of someone's toe.

"Agreed." Kenya wriggled, trying to get loose for a moment before deciding against it. She wrapped her arms around Camilo's neck and rested her head against his chest. A soft, rumbly sound slipped from her lips.

"Did you just purr?"

"No."

Camilo grinned. She definitely had.

The scents of fruits and herbs tickled his nose as he carried Kenya further through the trees. Birds stretched their wings, waking in their nests and unleashing a morning warble. The Woodlands came alive with their song.

"Where's your dad today?" Kenya asked. "He and Tate working on their new project?"

Diego often accompanied them to the Western Woodlands. The impossible mix of plants had led him to hypothesize about whether the magic was impacting the particles in the surrounding air. He swore he could feel the climate shift as he walked.

Camilo had no idea. He hadn't inherited his father's sensitivity or his love of scientific discovery. Sometimes magic was just magic.

But he liked seeing his father free and happy. Camilo didn't even mind having Tate around so much.

The scientist and his father had struck up a fast friendship. They had more in common than could be healthy. Together, they would either accomplish great things or waste their days hypothesizing about the most meaningless of minutia. Together, they'd founded a new project: *The Merlin Core*. Its goal was to combine magic and science.

Their first mission was to create a cure for both viruses: the one that trapped Diego as a wolf and the modified version that affected the demons. Curing a disease without a sample or a test subject would be Tate's biggest challenge. He kept trying to hire Camilo to track down one of the demons who'd escaped: *"Not to force any of them to participate in the study, of course, but maybe you could persuade them. They'd be more likely to listen to you."*

Camilo had been afraid to ask if that was because of his looks or because he was a werewolf.

But The Merlin Core—despite having no location beyond the Lopez's living room—was closed on Sundays. Diego wasn't with Tate.

"He's gone to visit Julia." She was at Castor's Care, the

magical hospital where they'd wiped her memory. As Camilo understood, it had been a difficult task. Julia had known about the existence of magic for most of her life, and it had informed a lot of her actions. She'd lost a lot of herself in the memory wipe.

But she remembers my dad.

Diego couldn't go into the room. He was a giant wolf, and the point was to make sure Julia forgot about magic. But the cover story was that he'd moved to Switzerland for work. They spoke every three days on the phone.

Well, Julia spoke to a warlock who mimicked Diego's voice while a nymph translated his growls and whimpers.

It was quite the system.

"And still no news of Tobias or Holly?" Kenya asked

Camilo shook his head. The Castor's Police had found several dead in the charred remains of The Morgana Center. Other escaped scientists had been rounded up and memory wiped like Julia. But there was no sign of Tobias Buckler or Holly Nichols on either list.

"Get a room you two," a high-pitched voice shouted at them from the trees.

Camilo looked up and spotted a trio of pixies standing on one of the branches and giggling at their own joke.

Kenya climbed from his arms and made a face at them. The pixies grew excited at the provocation. They responded with their own series of rude gestures.

"Jerks," Kenya muttered. She leaned closer. "Bet they'd be nicer if they knew we saved them and their forest from destruction."

"I don't think Briony would like that somehow."

"No. And it might not impress them seeing as we're also the reason it was in danger." Kenya laughed at her own joke, eyes crinkling as her mouth opened.

It was the greatest sound Camilo had ever heard. He pulled Kenya toward him, lowered his head, and kissed her.

She melted in his arms.

Kenya tasted like her magic—warm spice that made his lips tingle. Her body pressed against him, and his hand wandered lower than her back.

There was a flutter of wings in the air as the pixies flew off.

Kenya pulled away, grinning at their retreating backs. "Guess that's one way to get rid of them."

Camilo would have smiled too, but the hair rose on his neck as another smell came to him, something like a bonfire. He had the strangest sensation that he was being watched still.

But when he turned there was no one there.

"Race you to the peach tree?" Kenya suggested, pointing at a spot far in the distance.

"Training for the Fabled Games?"

Kenya grabbed her ankle, stretching her legs as she prepared to run. "Maybe. I haven't decided yet."

She would. Camilo knew Kenya. She liked to compete, and she wasn't going to find a better challenge elsewhere.

"You just don't want your parents to nag you about training," he teased, rolling his shoulders.

"They're already on me about starting classes next week. My dad keeps insisting shifters still need math." She smiled, dropping into a crouch on the ground. "Ready?"

"Almost." Camilo closed his eyes, flexing the muscle in the core of his body. His limbs tingled as his muscles stretched.

"No, that's cheating," Kenya objected.

But she was too late, Camilo was already a wolf.

"All's fair in a magical competition," he growled and shot off through the trees.

Kenya was right behind him, the scent of her magic filling the air. "They still say go."

Yeah, but then you might have won.

Camilo bounded toward the peach tree. Something flapped above his head.

It wasn't a bird. Or a pixie. The sound was too loud.

He looked up and his breath caught. Above him, the trees were parting. Their trunks and branches bent and curved into strange positions, as though allowing something large to pass through.

"I won," Kenya announced. "Why did you sto—?" Her voice broke off.

In the sky above them, a massive purple dragon winked into existence. The inside of its wings glittered like the inside of a treasure chest. It twisted its long neck so that it stared down at them, blinking two huge pools of liquid gold.

A gurgling sound came from deep within its throat—an invitation?

Camilo took off again. Kenya fell in at his side.

Together, they raced through an enchanted forest, running in the shadow of a dragon.

And Camilo had never felt more alive or more grateful.

Above them, the dragon hooted. Camilo howled as Kenya laughed in delight at the sound.

"How incredible is this?" she shouted. "Imagine giving this up."

Camilo couldn't. There was no doubt in his mind. He and Kenya were the lucky ones.

PLOTWORKS PUBLISHING

Thank you so much for visiting the magical city of Castor's Grove!

If you enjoyed *Changeling's Dagger*, please tell your friends, or leave a review in the place where you purchased it. It would mean so much to me!

Please visit Plotworks Publishing to keep exploring the Castor's Grove universe! Sign up for the newsletter and get a discount!

You can also follow me on Instagram: @aj.renwick

Now turn the page for a sneak peek at *Dragon's Wisp*, the next title in the Castor's Grove universe—

DRAGON'S WISP

Yasmin Gul stood by the entrance to the cafeteria, eyes hungry as they hunted for her next story.

She'd been back at Folkstone High less than two weeks, and she already had a couple of leads. Some of the wealthier students had managed to get pizza after it had run out on Friday. Was one of the lunch ladies taking bribes?

And why had all the seniors on the football team decided to take the same six subjects as the ones last year? Yasmin had long suspected there was a cheating scandal to break among the sports team. She could be the one to expose it.

But as she scanned the cafeteria, Yasmin's eyes skipped over the corner tables that the footballers dominated. The growing lunch line, snaking its way through a row of metal rails, earned only a precursory glance.

Yasmin couldn't focus on high school drama. Her aspirations were bigger than that.

A thin boy with large glasses and unfortunate skin

slunk through the cafeteria doors, a few feet behind a group of freshmen.

Perfect!

"Excuse me!" Yasmin rushed toward him, clicking the cam of her pen. The ballpoint tip sprung out, poised above an open notebook. "Can I have a moment of your time to ask you a few questions?"

The boy froze in the center of the doors as a wave of students rushed past. His eyes grew wide, a bit like a deer that found itself facing a wolf.

Yasmin launched into her question before he could decide to flee. "How long have you lived in Castor's Grove?"

"Um... all my life." His voice was a nervous squeak. "Are you doing a report on freshmen for the Folks News?"

Yasmin's eye twitched at the mention of the school newspaper. She forced a smile. "I'm an independent reporter. Have you ever noticed anything strange happen in the city?"

"Huh?"

"You know, like an unnatural phenomenon that you couldn't explain?" It was a longshot, but Yasmin readied her pen just in case.

A hand reached over her shoulder and snatched the ballpoint from her fingers. "Look at that, Kal. I've got super speed!"

The joke, which had never been that clever to begin with, was on its fifteenth delivery—Yasmin was keeping count. It did not deserved the loud guffaw that followed.

Sensing an opportunity to flee, the freshman lowered his head and scurried toward the lunch line.

Yasmin spun to face the two idiots who'd ruined her interview.

Zachary Wilson was short, buff, and pale; Kalvin White his opposite. But both were equally obnoxious.

"Hilarious, Zach." Yasmin's smile stretched further across her cheeks, and she poisoned her voice with sugar. "Have you ever considered coming up with your own material?" She reached for her pen.

Zachary tossed it toward Kalvin. The taller boy caught it in one hand and waved it in the air before Yasmin. The moment she tried to grab it, Kalvin would pull his hand back and make the same, stupid joke.

Super speed. Ha. Ha. Ha.

It wasn't funny.

Over the summer, Yasmin had found the perfect story. There was a runner, a year older than her, who was faster than humanly possible. Yasmin had seen it with her own eyes.

Breaking the story should have made her career as an investigative journalist. And for a blissful twenty-four hours, Yasmin thought it had. Traffic to her blog reached an all-time high. Strangers from other schools shared her post on social media. It was as close to viral as any of Yasmin's stories had come.

Until her success crashed and burned in a sea of laughing emojis, comments mocking the concept of super-speed, and reports of bullying. The post was removed for *violating terms and conditions*, and Yasmin received a message prior to the start of term that she'd lost her position as the school newspaper's editor-in-chief. Apparently Folkstone High condoned neither bullying nor inventing *tall-tales*.

But I didn't make it up.

And when Yasmin unveiled the truth and became a local celebrity, everyone who mocked her was going to fall to their knees groveling for her forgiveness. She would take joy in withholding it.

"Keep it." Yasmin shrugged, refusing to let her smile falter as she looked at Kalvin. Who cared about a pen?

Yasmin did. It was one of her nicest ones. She lunged forward, swiping for the ballpoint while he wouldn't expect it.

Her fingers brushed the barrel before it was pulled out of her grip.

Kalvin and Zachary laughed. A third voice joined them.

The corners of Yasmin's lips twitched, smile threatening to collapse. She should have known the third member of Kalvin and Zachary's idiot trio would be nearby.

Mason Wick, their unofficial leader and the one who'd first thought to steal Yasmin's pen and make a joke about having super-speed, stepped forward. He wore faded jeans, a gray shirt, and the signature crooked smile that hid most of his teeth. *Shy* was how most of the other girls described it. But they'd invented a strange mythos around Mason, painting him as sweet and friendly and kind—a golden retriever disguised as a man. Yasmin knew better.

Just because a boy acted nice, didn't mean he was. There was something wicked about Mason's smile. Like he was hiding something.

"Come on, guys. Give it back." Mason ran a hand through his hair, sweeping the brown strands away from his face. "It's not Yasmin who has super speed. You can't expect her to get it."

Sixteen times. Yasmin added to her mental tally. Were they too stupid to think of new material?

Kalvin chuckled. Instead of returning the pen to its rightful owner, he tossed it to Mason.

Yasmin's fingers clenched around her notebook. If they

started playing pass the parcel with her pen again she was reporting all of them to the principal.

"Working on your next story?" Mason asked, a hint of amusement in his eyes as he offered the ballpoint. "Good luck."

He didn't say it, but the *you'll need it* was implied.

Yasmin snatched her pen. "Don't need it. Already have something brilliant I'm working on."

His crooked smile returned. There was nothing sweet or nice or golden-retriever-esque about it. "Can't wait to read it."

Kalvin and Zachary burst into more laughter as the three strutted toward the lunch line.

Yasmin leaned against the wall, jaw quivering as her smile collapsed. There was a *squelch* from her backpack— the sound of an overabundance of mustard escaping her sandwich. She knew she'd added too much that morning. Hopefully the foil would stop it from leaking over her books.

The flood of students entering the cafeteria diminished to a slow trickle until Yasmin stood out like a warning sign, standing alone by the doors. What a day to have worn red.

She tugged the long sleeves of her shirt, scanning the cafeteria with a new purpose as her stomach rumbled. There had to be a friendly face somewhere in the crowd. Yasmin wasn't popular, but she had friends—didn't she?

Her usual table was near the back of the room. Most of the writers for the Folks News ate together there.

Jeremiah Quick sat on the edge of the table, spider-long limbs sprawled over the bench. The pompous snot had been a pain in Yasmin's butt since they started high school. His writing was technically sound but hackney-ed and cliché. Him ending up as the newspaper's editor instead of her was something straight from an absurdist comedy.

Yasmin bet the snot had leaped at the chance.

Jeremiah caught her staring. He raised his hand.

Was he extending an olive branch? As a writer himself, perhaps he understood that Yasmin was suffering for her story.

Jeremiah raised his middle finger.

Charming.

Yasmin would remember this moment. When she got her big break as editor of a *real* newspaper, she'd remind Jeremiah of it too when he came begging for a job. Maybe she'd hire him as an unpaid intern.

Sitting in the cafeteria was overrated anyway.

Yasmin marched out of the doors back into the Folkstone halls. She held her chin up, refusing to feel upset. This wasn't a retreat. She was just, going somewhere to think. There was no sense gathering information on lunch ladies or football players yet. She needed to plan first.

The classrooms were locked or occupied by teachers preparing for their next class. Eating in the bathrooms was a level of depressing that Yasmin refused to accept. Her quest for privacy forced her through the back-exist and out onto the football field at the back of the school.

Across the grass, peeling paint covered with students' signatures, was the old gymnasium. The school had been begging for money to renovate or knock it down for the past three years. It wasn't a glamorous lunch location.

But it beats a bathroom stall.

Yasmin slunk across the field and slipped through the unlocked doors of the gymnasium.

Part of the roof had collapsed into a pile of wooden slats near the far corner. Sunlight streamed through, highlighting the thick layer of dust particles floating in the air. Half of the bleachers were gone, knocked over by a demolition team before the school's administration saw how much destroying the gymnasium would cost.

Deflated balls and torn floor mats lay in a pile beneath a fallen basketball hoop near the door. It blended with the rest of the rubble.

The scent of death filled Yasmin's nostrils. She kicked one of the balls, revealing the flattened lower half of a dead rat. Yasmin covered her mouth with her notebook, gagging as she hurried away.

Maybe this should be my story.

The gym had to be breaking dozens of health code violations.

Yasmin swept aside cobwebs with her bag, carving a space beneath what remained of the bleachers. It was as far away as she could get from the dead rat.

She unwrapped her sandwich, holding it one hand and clicking her pen in the other. Her next story had to be big.

A loud sneeze echoed through the gym.

Yasmin's back snapped straight. It was lucky she was short, or her head would have clonked against the seat of the bleachers.

Who else would come in here?

Yasmin rose onto her knees and peeped through the slats.

Mason Wick covered his mouth, eyes squinting as he stepped away from the dead rat. His sneakers kicked at the dust causing it to rise and around his feet in a white swirl.

His usual pair of lackeys were nowhere to be found.

Lunch had to be almost over. Was Mason skipping class? Alone? In the gym?

That made no sense. Yasmin drew closer to the bleacher.

Mason stopped beneath the hole in the roof, standing in center of the sunlight. He glanced over his shoulder, nose twitching as he scanned the gym, before turning his face toward the sky.

Something golden and yellow stretched from his back.

A trick of the sunlight?

Yasmin's book trembled in her arms as she hugged it to her chest. She blinked, trying to clear her eyes.

The sunlight turned into scales—a glittering golden yellow. They stretched into a pair of wings the most beautiful color Yasmin had ever seen.

Mason Wick has wings.

Her pen scribbled the words even as her mind struggled to believe her own thought. He couldn't. That was impossible.

With a single flap, Mason rose into the air, disappearing through the hole in the roof.

Yasmin's head spun. She stared at the empty space he'd occupied a second before, unable to move.

It couldn't be real. It must have been at trick.

But how? He didn't know she was there. And the wings had been attached to him.

And he flew.

It was too much.

Yasmin's stomach turned. The contents of her lunch rushed in the wrong direction through her esophagus. Dark spots danced before her vision, and she collapsed forward, head bumping against the bleachers.

PLOTWORKS PUBLISHING

Visit Plotworks Publishing to continue exploring the Castor's Grove universe—and to find many other titles as well!

ABOUT THE AUTHOR

A.J. Renwick is a lover of all things fantasy, from mermaids and unicorns to vampires and dragons. She writes young adult paranormal romance with strong plots, dual points of view, and happily ever afters.

When she's not writing, A.J. Renwick enjoys reading (duh!), baking (some things more successfully than others), and spending time with her three dogs (the Dragon Squad).

www.ingramcontent.com/pod-product-compliance
Lightning Source LLC
Chambersburg PA
CBHW020636020726
47494CB00001B/223